THE SEA of TROLLS

Also by the Author

The House of the Scorpion
A Girl Named Disaster
The Warm Place
The Ear, the Eye, and the Arm
Do You Know Me

THE SEA TROLLS of

NANCY FARMER

SCHOLASTIC INC.

New York Toronto London Auckland Sydney
Mexico City New Delhi Hong Kong Buenos Aires

No part of this publication may be reproduced, stored in a retrieval system, or transmitted in any form or by any means, electronic, mechanical, photocopying, recording, or otherwise, without written permission of the publisher. For information regarding permission, write to Atheneum Books for Young Readers, Simon & Schuster Children's Publishing Division, 1230 Avenue of the Americas, New York, NY 10020.

ISBN 0-439-79799-3

12 11 10 9 8 7 6 5 4 3 2   5 6 7 8 9 10/0

Printed in the U.S.A.   23

First Scholastic printing, September 2005

Book design by Ann Sullivan
The text for this book is set in Edlund.

To Harold, as always,
for finding Mimir's Well

ACKNOWLEDGMENTS

Many heartfelt thanks to Kristin Johannsdottir, Icelandic scholar, for reading my manuscript and providing the Icelandic dialogue.

Thank you to Dr. William Ratliff for getting me access to the Stanford University Library.

Warmest appreciations to my son, Daniel, and my nephew, Nathan Stout, for providing me with the inspiration for Olaf One-Brow.

Thanks, as always, to Richard Jackson for taking chances.

CONTENTS

CAST OF CHARACTERS

HUMANS (SAXONS)

Jack: Age eleven at the beginning of the book

Lucy: Jack's sister; age five at the beginning of the book

Mother: Jack and Lucy's mother; a wise woman

Father: Giles Crookleg; Jack and Lucy's father

The Bard: A druid from Ireland; also known as Dragon Tongue

Allyson: Thorgil's mother

Colin: The blacksmith's son

Brother Aiden: A monk from the Holy Isle

HUMANS (NORTHMEN)

Olaf One-Brow: Leader of the Queen's Berserkers

Sven the Vengeful: Member of Olaf's crew

Eric Pretty-Face: Member of Olaf's crew

Eric the Rash: Member of Olaf's crew; afraid of the dark

Eric Broad-Shoulders: Member of Olaf's crew; afraid of the dark

Rune: A skald who can no longer sing

Thorgil: A berserker wannabe; age twelve

Thorgrim: Thorgil's father; a famous berserker

Egil Long-Spear: Captain of a ship, not a berserker

Gizur Thumb-Crusher: Village headman; an oath-breaker

Magnus the Mauler: Village headman

Einar the Ear-Hoarder: Village headman; likes to collect ears

Heide: Olaf's chief wife; a wise woman from Finnmark

Dotti and Lotti: Olaf's junior wives

Skakki: Heide and Olaf's son; age sixteen

Thorir: Thorgil's brother

Hrothgar: King of the Golden Hall

Beowulf: A famous warrior

Ivar the Boneless: Olaf's king; married to Frith Half-Troll

Tree Foot: Friend of Eric Pretty-Face; leg bitten off by a troll

Pig Face, Dirty Pants, Thick Legs, Lump, and She-Lump: Thralls

Hilda: Olaf and Lotti's daughter

ANIMALS

Bold Heart: A noble crow

Cloud Mane: A horse whose sire came from Elfland

Maeve: An Irish wolfhound

Slasher, Wolf Bane, Hel Hag, and Shreddie: Maeve's puppies

Golden Bristles: A troll-boar with a filthy disposition

Freya's Cats: Nine enormous troll-cats with beautiful red-gold fur

The Snowy Owls: A family of four Jotunheim owls

The Dragon: A mother with a nest of dragonlets

The Capercaillie: A turkey-size grouse with ten speckled chicks

Ratatosk: Gossip-bearing squirrel that runs up and down
  Yggdrassil

JOTUNS (TROLLS)

The Mountain Queen: Glamdis; ruler of Jotunheim

Fonn: The Mountain Queen's daughter; speaks to humans

Forath: The Mountain Queen's daughter; speaks to whales

Bolthorn: Fonn and Forath's father; the Mountain Queen's chief
  consort

UNCLASSIFIABLE

Frith Half-Troll: A shape-shifter; daughter of the Mountain Queen and an unknown human; wife of Ivar the Boneless

Frothi: Frith's sister; a shape-shifter; mother of Grendel

Grendel: A monster; his father was an ogre

The Norns: Nobody knows exactly what Norns are, but they're very powerful

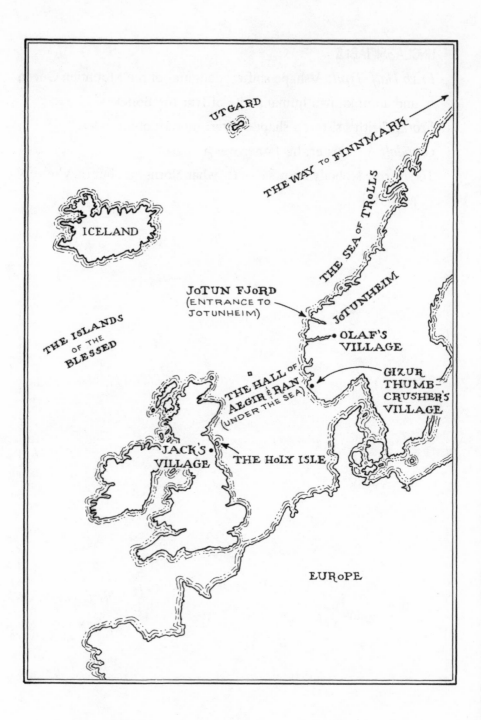

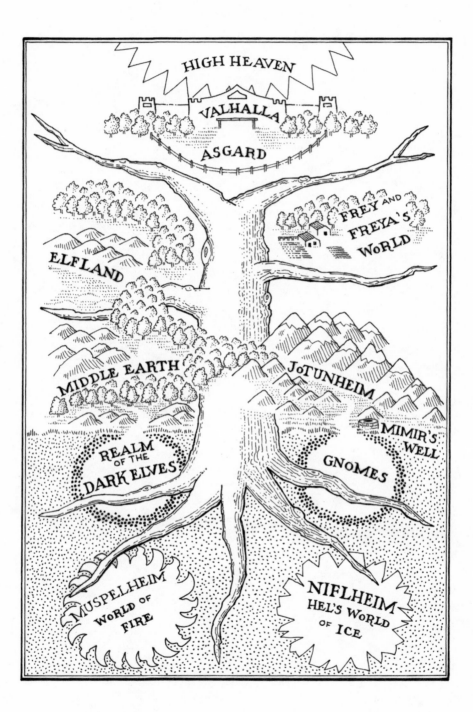

THE SEA of TROLLS

Chapter One

———⟨⟩———

GATHERING THE LAMBS

Jack woke before dawn and listened to the cold February wind lash the walls of the house. He sighed. It was going to be another rotten day. He stared up at the rafters, savoring the last minutes of warmth. He was bundled in a cocoon of wool blankets over a bed of dried heather. The floor was deep, below the level of the ground. The wind that found its way under the door passed over his head.

It was a good house, with oak pillars planted the root end up to keep damp from rising from the ground. Jack had watched Father build it when he was seven. Father had thought a child couldn't understand such a complicated task, but Jack had. He'd paid close attention and thought he could build a house even now, four years later. Jack forgot very little of what he saw.

At the far end of the long room Jack could see Mother stir up the cooking fire. The light danced on the loft. It was warmer up there, but smoky. His parents and sister slept up there. Jack preferred the fresh air near the door.

Mother scattered oats into boiling water and stirred the porridge vigorously. She added honey—Jack could smell it. A poker glowed in the coals to heat the cups of cider Mother lined up on a shelf.

"It's so *cold*," complained Lucy from the loft. "Can't I have breakfast in bed?"

"A princess isn't afraid of a little thing like cold," said Father.

"Princesses live in castles," Lucy pointed out.

"Ah, but that isn't true of *lost* princesses."

"Don't encourage her," said Mother.

"Am I really lost, Father?" said Lucy. Jack knew she loved this story.

"Not for long. You were found by us," Father said fondly.

"I was lying under a rose tree with a gold coin in my hand."

"You were born in this house, not in some airy-fairy castle," Mother snapped. She plunged the hot poker into the first mug of cider. Jack could smell the rich tang of apples. He knew Lucy wouldn't listen to Mother. It was far more interesting to be a lost princess than a farmer's brat. The gold coin was real, though. Father had found it while digging in the garden. It showed the head of a man, who Father said was a Roman king.

"Someday a troop of knights will come riding by," Lucy said.

"They've been searching for you ever since the trolls carried you off," said Father. "The trolls were going to eat you, dearest—but being trolls, they started fighting among themselves."

"'Shall we roast her with an apple in her mouth?'" said Lucy, repeating the often-told tale. "'Or shall we make her into a pie?'"

"'Pie! Pie!' roared half the trolls," said Father. "The other half shouted for roast baby. They began to fight, and soon they had knocked each other senseless. That's when I came by and found you."

"Someday the knights will knock at our door," said Lucy. "They'll bow to me and say, 'Come and be our queen.'"

"Why do you fill her up with this nonsense?" Mother said.

"What's the harm in it?" said Father.

Jack knew Mother had lost two babies before he was born and two afterward. She thought she would never have another, but to everyone's surprise, she produced this last, perfect child.

Lucy had golden hair that made you think of sunlight. She had eyes the color of violets that grew in the deep forest. She was light as thistledown, merry as a lark. And because, at age five, she had always been loved, she loved everyone back. In spite of everything, Jack couldn't dislike her.

Right now she was being carried down the ladder by Father. She was too big for it. Jack could see pain flit across his father's face as he stepped clumsily from one rung to the next. But he also saw joy—joy that was rarely present when Giles Crookleg looked at his son Jack.

Jack threw back the covers and stood up, stretching to let the new day flow into his body. Like everyone else, he slept in his clothes so there was no problem getting dressed.

He pulled away the wool plugging the door crack and climbed outside. A gray light was creeping over the eastern sea. It seeped into the moors and died abruptly in the dark forest to the west. The sky was the color of black ice. It was going to be a miserable day.

Jack ran to the privy. He bounced up and down to keep the frozen ground from sticking to his shoes. The Bard said the frost giants lie in wait for unwary humans, stunning them with their misty breath. You could never lie down outside in the dark of winter, no matter how tempting it was. That was how the frost giants got you, whispering of warmth to be found in sleep.

Jack ran back to the house, sliding on a patch of ice he hadn't seen. He banged through the door and stood, steaming and stamping, to get the feeling back into his feet.

"Cold, eh?" said Father. He was sitting next to the fire with Lucy on his lap.

"Cold as a troll's—"

"We'll have none of that language," Mother said sharply.

Jack grinned and flopped down next to the fire. Mother gave him a mug of cider, and he warmed his hands on that.

"The ewes will be lambing," Father observed.

"Oh, aye," agreed Mother.

"I *love* little lambs," Lucy burbled, cradling her cup of cider.

"You don't have to go out and find the little beasts," said Jack.

"It's God's way," Father said. "Adam sinned, and so the rest of us must earn our bread by the sweat of our brows."

"Amen," said Mother.

Jack wondered why something that had happened at the beginning of the world still plagued them. How long did it take for the punishment to run out? Wouldn't it make sense, after a thousand years or so, for God to say, *All right, that's enough. You can come back to Eden?* But Jack didn't say that aloud. Father had a very short temper where religion was concerned.

Father had wanted to be a priest, but his family had not been rich enough to pay the entrance fee to the abbey. It was a constant sorrow to the man, for his deformed leg made it hard to do the chores of a farmer.

Father's finest memory was of having visited the Holy Isle as a youth. He'd been taken there in hopes of a cure, and the sight of the monks going about their peaceful lives had filled him with awe. They didn't have to drag a plow through a stony field. They didn't have to cut wood in a terrifying forest, listening for wolves or—worse—the goblins that devoured boys.

Alas, not even the kindly monks could heal Giles Crookleg's injury. The best they could do was feed him soft, white bread and roast lamb flavored with rosemary. They prayed over him in a chapel with a stained-glass window that shone with the colors of the rainbow when the sun was behind it.

"I thought I'd mend the barn roof today," Father said.

Jack frowned. That meant the nasty chore of hunting for lambs fell on him. He shoved last night's bread into his porridge. If it wasn't soaked, it was too hard to eat. Jack's teeth grated on the sand that was always a part of the dark, dense loaves Mother baked.

"Can I watch, Father?" asked Lucy.

"Of course, darling. Just don't sit under the ladder. It's bad luck."

It's bad luck because Father might drop a hammer on her head, Jack thought. He didn't say this aloud either.

"It's our turn to feed the Bard this week," Mother said.

"I'll do it," Jack said quickly.

"Of course you will," said Father. "Don't think you're going to weasel out because of lambing."

Isn't that just typical? Jack thought. Here he was, offering to help, and Father had to put the worst face on it. But Jack was too pleased by his new task to stay irritated.

Very soon he finished his bread and porridge, swigged the hot cider, and prepared himself for the long day. He stuffed wool into his thin shoes to keep his toes from freezing. He wrapped an extra layer of cloth around his legs, put on an extra shirt, and covered it with a cloak. The cloak was oiled with tallow to keep out rain. It was heavy, but the warmth was worth it. Last of all, Jack shouldered a pack of food.

"Mind, you're not to hang around the Bard making a nuisance of yourself," Father said as Jack went out the door.

The wind whipped the cloak over Jack's head. He pulled it back down and wrapped it close. Frost crackled under his feet as he walked. Everything was crystal bright, and Jack could see mountains to the west beyond the forest and the cold sea to the east. On a cliff overlooking the shore was the old Roman house where the Bard lived. Jack saw a tendril of smoke being shredded by the wind.

He wondered why the old man chose to live there. The house was in such bad repair, no amount of wood could quell its chilly dampness. Perhaps the Bard liked being near the sea. He had come to them from there, in a little coracle bobbing up and down like a child's toy. It was a wonder he'd survived, but perhaps the Bard had kept his boat safe with magic.

Jack's heart beat faster. He knew, of course, about the small magic his mother practiced. He had learned from her how to talk to bees and how to soothe frightened animals with song. But the Bard knew important things. It was rumored he could drive enemies mad by blowing on a wisp of straw. And he could call up the north wind and talk to crows.

The old man had come to the village two years ago and had immediately set about giving orders. In no time, he was settled in the Roman house with a bed, a table, a pile of blankets, and a store of food. No one questioned his right to these things.

"Sir, I've brought supplies," Jack called at the door of the ancient house. He listened for the old man's step. Presently, he heard a sigh and the thump of a staff. The Bard pulled the door open, and his face lit with pleasure.

"Jack! What a treat!"

That was one of the reasons Jack liked him. He didn't say, *What, you again?* He actually seemed pleased.

"Do you want me to heat the cider?" Jack said.

"Ah! Your mother's wonderful work," said the Bard. "She has wisdom in her fingers, boy. Mark my words."

Jack placed a poker in the fire and poured out a cup.

"I suppose you'll be hunting lambs this morning," said the Bard, sitting and stretching his bony feet to the fire. "If you want to know, six ewes have dropped their young. They're in the westfold."

Jack didn't question it. Everyone knew the Bard had far sight. Whether the old man changed his shape into that of a bird and soared over the fields or whether he talked to passing foxes, no one was sure. But the Bard knew what was going on around him and a good deal else as well.

Jack watched the poker until it glowed and plunged it into the cup with a hissing sound. "Shall I gather driftwood, sir?" he asked. He wanted to stay as long as possible.

"It will take you half a day to round up those lambs," the Bard said as he savored the steam from the hot cider. "You can come here when you're finished."

Jack wasn't sure he'd heard correctly. No one wanted him around unless they had a job for him. "Do you need help, sir?" he inquired politely.

"Help? *Help,* you unsprouted acorn? By Odin's eyebrows,

I'm asking you to lunch. Do I have to write out an invitation? No, no," the old man said with a sigh. "You couldn't read it if I did. No one's taken the trouble to teach you. I excuse your mother. She's done the best she could, with that monk-struck husband of hers. . . ."

The Bard went on arguing with himself as he warmed his hands on the cider cup. He seemed to have forgotten Jack's presence.

"I'd like to come," the boy said.

"What? Oh, very good," said the Bard as he waved him out the door.

Jack was so amazed, he found himself climbing the hills to the westfold without remembering how he got there. The wind tore at his cloak and the ice dug into his shoes. What could the Bard possibly want with *him*? A dozen boys carried driftwood and buckets of water to the Roman house, but none of them, as far as Jack knew, had been invited to lunch.

Why had he been singled out? The chief's son was taller and better educated. The blacksmith's son was stronger. The miller's son provided fine white loaves for the Bard. Jack—to be honest—had nothing special to recommend him.

He found the first of the lambs huddled by a hedge. The mother attacked him, but Jack kicked her away. The black-faced sheep were as wild as mountain goats. He cradled the shivering newborn under his cloak as he hurried down the hill, all the while fending off its mother. He thrust the lamb into a heap of straw in the barn and dodged the ewe's horns on the way out.

Back and forth he went until he'd found all six. By then he was muddy and sore from head-butts. *I hate sheep,* he thought as he slammed the barn door.

"Don't forget to feed them," called Father from the roof.

"I've already done it," said Jack. Why couldn't Father say, *Six lambs? Well done!* Why wasn't he ever pleased?

Lucy sat under the ladder in spite of Father's warnings. She was nestled in a sheepskin and looked, more than anything, like a fat bunny. She waved cheerfully, and Jack, in spite of his irritation, waved back. It was hard to get mad at Lucy.

Chapter Two

THE APPRENTICE

"Come in!" cried the Bard as Jack stood nervously in the doorway. The boy looked around for an empty bucket or depleted woodpile to justify his presence. Everything seemed in order.

"I didn't ask you here to work," said the Bard, making Jack flinch. Could the old man read minds, too?

Between the mouthfuls of cheese, bread, and cider that made up their lunch, the Bard quizzed Jack about things so ordinary, they hardly seemed worth mentioning. How did water sound when it rushed over grass? How did it sound oozing through a bog? How did the wind change its music as it passed from the river reeds to the foxtail grasses of the meadow? Could Jack tell the difference between a lark and a swallow high in the clouds?

Of course he could, Jack said. Everyone could, by the way the birds dipped their wings.

"Not so," said the Bard. "Very few people see beyond the ends of their noses. Another piece of cheese?"

Jack ate more than his share and felt rather guilty about it. He rarely got enough to feel satisfied.

"In my opinion, you aren't a total waste of time," said the Bard. "Don't let that go to your head, boy. You could easily be a *partial* waste of time. How'd you like to be my apprentice?"

Jack gaped at him. His brain couldn't grasp the meaning of it. He'd never heard of a bard's apprentice.

"That's the first habit we'll have to get rid of," said the old man, sighing. "You should look intelligent, even when you aren't. Get along with you now. I'll talk to your father later."

That night Jack huddled in his blankets, listening to Father and the Bard discuss his future. He hadn't really expected the old man to come, but at nightfall the Bard had shown up, dressed in a thick, white cloak and leaning on a blackened ash wood staff. He looked extremely impressive with his white beard blowing in the wind. Father invited him in and turned Jack out of his seat by the fire.

But Giles Crookleg wasn't pleased when he learned what the old man wanted. "I can't let Jack go," Father cried. "If I had more sons or if my leg were straight—you couldn't fix it, by the way?"

"I'm afraid not," said the Bard.

"No harm in asking. It's the penance I bear for Adam's sin."

"Amen," said Mother.

Father, Jack, and Lucy muttered "Amen" as well. Jack noticed the Bard said nothing.

"At any rate, I need help with the repairs and plowing. I need someone to herd sheep and gather wood in the forest," said Father. "I'm honored you should consider my son, but there's no proof he's bright."

"I have faith in him," said the Bard.

Jack felt a rush of gratitude for the old man and an equal rush of annoyance at his father.

"Jack's ability isn't the question here," argued Father. "I need him and that's that."

"It would be nice if he got an education," Mother said hesitantly. "You always wanted to study with the monks—"

"Be still," said Father in a voice that allowed no argument. "I wanted to devote myself to religion on the Holy Isle," he told the Bard. "I wasn't given the opportunity. Not that I fault my father for it. I honor him and would not commit the sin of anger against him. I offer up my pain to God every day."

"Amen," said Mother.

"Amen," murmured Father, Jack, and Lucy.

Just what did God do with all the pain Father offered up to Him? Jack wondered. Did He put it in a box with the toothaches and headaches people sent Him?

"My son shouldn't try to rise above his station," finished Father. "In fact, it's good for him to learn that life is full of disappointments. Pain, cheerfully endured, is the surest way to salvation."

"Oh, Jack won't have fun being my apprentice," said the Bard, his eyes twinkling. Jack wondered what he found so amusing. "I assure you I'll make him work like a donkey in a lead mine. He'll suffer with the best of us. As for your farm, Giles, I've discussed that with the chief. I won't be needing the other boys if I have Jack, and so the chief is sending them to you. I think you'll have more help than you know what to do with."

Jack saw how clever the Bard had been. He'd waited until Father presented his objections and then closed the deal like a trap closing on a fox.

"Oh! Very well. In that case," sputtered Giles Crookleg. He cast a look of irritation at the Bard. "I *suppose* the other boys *might* do—though they're a villainously lazy lot."

And that, Jack realized, was as close as Father had ever got to saying he, Jack, was industrious.

"He'll work hard, won't he?" Giles Crookleg said.

"I guarantee he'll fall into bed with exhaustion," said the Bard.

"But he'll come home sometimes?" Mother said softly.

The old man smiled at her. "He can come to you on Sundays and when I go to the forest. He can help you work the bees."

Something seemed to pass between Mother and the Bard then, although Jack couldn't tell what it was.

"That would be nice," Mother said.

"Women's work," grunted Father, tossing a chunk of peat into the fire.

❖❖❖

The next morning Jack packed up his possessions. He put his extra shirt and leg wrappings into a bag, along with a cup and a trencher. He added his collection of treasures— shells, feathers, a knot of wood that reminded him of a squirrel, a stone you could see through. He wore everything else, including a knife Father had given him at Yuletide.

Jack felt strange taking everything that belonged to him. It was as though, without evidence of his presence, his family might forget about him. He might be like one of those poor souls who were carried off to Elfland. They returned after what seemed a week, only to find they'd been gone a hundred years. Lucy clung to Jack, weeping, "Don't go! Don't go!"

"I'll be back Sunday," Jack said.

"Come, now. Princesses don't cry," said Father.

"I don't want to be a princess if it means losing Jack," wailed Lucy.

"What? You don't want to live in a palace? Or eat sweetmeats from a golden plate?"

Lucy looked up. "What kind of sweetmeats?" she said.

"Rowanberry pudding and greengage tart," Father said. "Apple dumplings and flummery."

"Flummery?" Lucy let go of Jack's cloak.

"The best kind, with nutmeg and cream."

Jack knew Father was describing food he'd eaten on the Holy Isle. Neither Lucy nor Jack had ever tasted flummery, but Jack's mouth watered all the same. It sounded so good.

Lucy ran to Father and he scooped her up. "Bannock cakes and strawberry jam, cherry pies and custard," he crooned.

"And flummery," said Lucy, now entirely distracted from Jack's departure.

Jack sighed inwardly. It had been rather nice to be mourned, but Lucy never kept her mind on things long. Well, she was hardly more than a baby.

The Bard strode ahead with Jack trying to keep up. The boy was weighted down by sacks of provisions as well as his own stuff. On the way they met the blacksmith's son. Obviously, he was the first boy sent to take over Giles Crookleg's chores. When the Bard's back was turned, the blacksmith's son aimed a punch at Jack's arm, and Jack neatly sidestepped it. "Enjoy the sheep," he called, hurrying to catch up with the old man.

Jack toiled from dawn to dusk, but he found it interesting. Some nights he carried the Bard's harp when the old man went visiting. This task was altogether delightful. Jack sat in a place of honor by the fire—a place that had been forbidden when he was merely Giles Crookleg's brat. He was given a hot drink, and then he had nothing to do except bask in warmth and listen to the Bard's stories.

On an average day Jack rose before dawn, built up the fire, and cooked porridge. He carried water and hauled driftwood. Then he was sent out into the wilds. "Look around you," said the Bard. "Feel the wind, smell the air. Listen to the birds and watch the sky. Tell me what's happening in the wide world."

And Jack, without knowing exactly what he was supposed to see, climbed the long hills to their summits. He crouched in old sheep byres when the weather was foul. He stretched out in meadows when the weather was fair. He watched puffy white clouds hurry across the sky and hawks drop like arrows to catch unlucky mice.

Jack quickly learned that a simple answer wouldn't do. If he was lazy or unobservant or—worst of all—*made things up*, the Bard rapped him on the head with his knuckles. He knew exactly when Jack was lying. "Open your eyes!" he would shout. "If this is the best you can do, I might as well throw you back like an undersized minnow!"

Jack found he saw more and more as the weeks went by, as though the wide world had opened up still wider. He learned that a hawk didn't wander aimlessly in the air. It followed paths. It took its rest on certain crags and had its courtesies to other hawks. He saw that the creatures of the wild dealt with one another like the people in his village. There were timid ones and bullies, boastful ones and humble creatures who only wanted to get on with things and avoid trouble.

When Jack returned from his journeys, he went straight to the cauldron of soup over the fire. It hung there day and night, a rich pottage of peas, barley, parsnips, and onions. Now and then the Bard threw in a handful of herbs, so the character of the soup changed, but it was always good.

Jack let the heat of the fire soak into his bones as he munched a slab of bread. This, too, changed, depending on who was providing food that week. Most people made bread with a mixture of oats, wheat, barley, or beans—whatever they had on hand. The poorer families mixed acorns with their flour and produced loaves so tough, they had to be shredded and soaked before you could choke them down. But the baker used pure wheat. His bread was wonderfully soft and arrived wrapped in a blanket to keep it warm.

After lunch Jack tended the garden in the lea of the house. He gathered fleabane to smoke vermin from his and the Bard's clothes. He peeled rushes and dipped the white centers into beeswax for candles on the long, dark evenings. He plaited marram grass from the dunes into waterproof mats. Finally, during the evening meal, Jack reported what he'd seen during the day.

"Good, good," the old man would say. "You've seen something of how it works together. Not all, of course. That would take many lifetimes. But you are not *entirely* ignorant." Then he would teach Jack a song and listen intently as the boy repeated it. "You have a good ear for music. Quite a remarkable ear," he would murmur, and Jack would feel happy all the way down to his toes.

Last of all, Jack banked the fire and laid out the dried heather and sheepskins they used for beds. The Bard slept at the far end of the house in a truckle bed made of coiled straw. It reminded Jack of a large basket. Jack slept in a corner to one side of the door.

The last thing he saw at night was the glow of the hearth on the walls of the house. The old Romans had painted them with trees unlike any Jack had seen. They were hung with golden fruit, and strange birds roosted among the branches. Jack found them disturbing. Sometimes, when the light of the coals wavered, the birds seemed to move. Or the branches did, which was just as bad.

Chapter Three

———⟨⟩———

THE SHADOW ACROSS
THE WATER

"No . . . no . . ."

Jack sat up abruptly. The wind was howling outside. The house held the deep chill that seeped into it before dawn.

"No . . . I won't do it . . . it's evil . . ."

Jack threw back the covers and stumbled to the other end of the house. The Bard's bed was shaking. He saw the old man thrust up his hand as though warding something off. "Sir! Sir! Wake up! Everything's all right." He caught the Bard's hand.

"You won't bend me to your will! I defy you, foul troll!"

Something—some terrible force—flung the boy back. His head banged against the stone, and his ears rang as though a blacksmith were pounding on an anvil. He tasted blood.

"Oh, my stars, child! I didn't know it was you."

Jack tried to speak, choked on blood, and coughed instead.

"You're alive, thank Freya! Stay here. I'll build up the fire and make you a healing drink."

The ringing in Jack's ears died down, but he felt violently sick to his stomach. He heard the Bard move around, and presently, the hearth burst into light. In a very short time he was handed a cup of hot liquid. It hurt his mouth and he recoiled.

"You bit through your lip, child. It isn't as bad as it looks. The drink will make it better."

Jack managed to swallow, and the sickness went away. He found himself trembling. Perhaps he'd been trembling all along. He couldn't remember. "Is that—is that how—you destroy your enemies?" he stammered.

The Bard sat back. "One of the ways," he said.

"So that was . . . magic."

"Some call it so," said the Bard.

"Will you teach me how to do it?"

"By Thor's bushy beard! I almost killed you, and the first thing you want to know is how to do it."

"W-Well, sir, I am your a-apprentice."

"And a right cheeky one too. Most boys would have run home to their mothers after what you just experienced. Still, curiosity is a great thing. We two might just get along."

Jack felt a kind of warm sleepiness pass over him. The pain was still there, but it seemed unimportant. "What happened to you, sir?"

"That was a Nightmare, lad. Pray you never meet one."

"You mean, a bad dream?"

"I mean a Nightmare. It's far worse."

Jack wanted to ask more, but he was too comfortable. He yawned broadly, stretched out on the floor, and fell asleep.

When he awoke, he was lying outside on a bed of heather. He struggled to get up. "Rest a while, lad," said the Bard. He was sitting on a stool next to the door. His white beard and cloak shone against the weathered house. "Ah, sunlight," the old man said with a contented sigh. "It heals the terrors of the night."

"The Nightmare?" Jack said. His mouth hurt, and his speech was oddly slurred.

"Among other things," said the Bard. Jack felt his lip and found, to his horror, that it was as swollen as a mushroom after rain. "You wouldn't make a bad-looking troll at the moment," the old man remarked.

Jack remembered the words the Bard had cried out in his sleep. "Have you truly seen one, sir?"

"Oh, yes. Dozens. Most are quite pleasant, although they take getting used to. The ones you have to watch out for are the half-trolls. There's no describing how nasty they can be. Or deceitful. They're shape-shifters, and when they appear human, they're so beautiful that you can't think of a single sensible thing around them."

"Did one of them send the Nightmare?" said Jack.

"One of them *rode* it. Look, my boy, I was trying to protect you from certain things until you were older. But I may not have the time. Lately, I've felt a darkness over the sea. *She's* searching for me, you see. I can hide from her in the daytime. At night my guard is down, and she knows it."

"You could move in with the chief, sir. He could protect you," said Jack. He was beginning to get alarmed. This wasn't a saga or an amusing song. This was real.

The old man shook his head. "Your chief is a brave man, but he isn't up to handling trolls. *She* is hunting for me, and if she has found out where I am, her servants may already be on the way. I've been careless. I should have remembered that nowhere in the nine worlds is safe for me as long as she is abroad. I may even have to let her take me. Better that than let her destroy your village."

"But can't you flee?"

"Jotuns follow a trail like a hound. Her servants will come here first. If they don't find me, they'll kill all of you."

"Jotuns?" Jack said faintly.

"It's what the trolls call themselves. They can creep inside your mind and know what you're thinking. They know when and where you're going to strike before you do it. Only a very special kind of warrior can overcome them."

"We have to do *something*." Jack knew his voice sounded shrill, but he couldn't help it.

"We will," the Bard said firmly. "I'm on the alert now. I won't let her catch me off guard again. I should have been teaching you all these weeks, but the peacefulness of this place lulled me. . . ."

The Bard fell silent, and Jack saw him looking out to sea. He looked too, but he saw only cloudless sky and gray-green waves bending toward shore. If there was darkness out there, he couldn't see it.

"You can go home for the next three days," said the Bard. "I'll be walking in the forest. Oh, and I wouldn't mention any of this to your family." He reached for his black staff. "We don't want to alarm them until it's necessary. Jotuns can follow a trail of fear as easily as foxes sniff out a henhouse."

"I spend half my time chasing those scurvy boys," said Father, slurping a bowl of Mother's rich cockle soup. Jack had provided the cockles from sea cliffs near the Bard's house. "They slide away like eels when there's real work to be done."

"Oh, aye. They're a useless lot," agreed Mother. She steadied Lucy's hands on her mug.

Jack didn't think the farm was suffering. The fences looked sturdy; the field was covered with oats and barley. Mustard, lavender, and coriander bloomed in the kitchen garden, and the apple trees were covered with tiny green fruit.

It was so beautiful, it made his throat ache. He'd never appreciated the little farm until now. And he saw his father in a new light. He realized that Giles Crookleg's complaints meant no more than the muttering of crows in a tree. It was a habit crows fell into when things weren't going their way. Father, too, grumbled by way of easing the disappointments in his life. What mattered was how Father went on in spite of his unhappiness, to create this beautiful place. Jack saw how lovingly the house was made, how carefully provisions were laid up so that Mother, Lucy, and he could survive.

It could all be swept away in an instant. No one had any idea of the menace lurking over the sea.

"Jack's crying," said Lucy.

"I am not," Jack said indignantly. He turned his head away to hide the tears that had wandered down his cheek. He'd felt oddly shaken since the Bard had thrown him down. He seemed to cry more easily.

"Leave him alone, dearest," came Mother's soft voice. "His mouth is very sore."

"The Bard thrashed him," said Father.

"It was an accident," Jack said.

"Oh, aye. You may tell us that, but I know a thrashing when I see one."

Jack didn't say anything. If it pleased Father to think he'd been punished, why spoil things? And this, too, was new. Before, Jack would have argued passionately. Now he saw the lines of pain in his father's face, his hunched shoulders and scarred hands. The boy had a glimmer of another image, of his father as a child before the accident.

Jack felt like crying again. These new feelings were very odd and worrying.

Mother bent over Lucy's fair head. "You must finish your soup," she whispered.

"I don't like the bottom part. It's sandy," said Lucy.

"Washing cockles takes away the taste," said Mother, but she finished the dregs herself and gave Lucy an oatcake.

"Thrashing is good for boys," Giles Crookleg said. "Why, I was smacked six ways to Sunday by my father, and it made me the man I am today."

Then, because it *was* Sunday, Father told them a story

about the holy saints. Father couldn't read, nor could anyone in the village except the Bard. To Giles Crookleg, writing was a kind of magic. When the Bard marked letters on a scrap of parchment, Father always crossed himself to avert a spell.

But he had memorized dozens of stories from the monks of the Holy Isle. Tonight's tale was of Saint Lawrence, martyred by pagans. "He was roasted over a slow fire," said Father to Lucy's horrified gasp. "They stuck garlic cloves between his toes and basted him all over like a chicken. When he was about to die and be taken into Heaven, Saint Lawrence said, 'I think I'm done. You may eat me when you will.' The pagans were so impressed, they fell on their knees and begged to become Christians."

Trolls eat people, thought Jack. They would come over the sea and stick garlic cloves between everyone's toes. He put his head down and thought about green hills and puffy clouds instead. He must not be afraid. Jotuns followed fear like a trail.

Later Lucy wanted to hear her own story of how she had lived in a palace.

"This will come to grief," said Mother. "She can't tell the difference between fact and fancy."

Father ignored her. Jack knew he looked forward to the tales as much as Lucy did. The boy understood—how had he changed so much in a few weeks?—that these, too, were a comfort to his father. Giles Crookleg might grumble like a crow, but he lost himself like a bird in the clouds of his own imaginings. He no longer had to set foot on the earth or know that he was doomed to creep upon it.

"Once upon a time," said Father, "the queen dropped a honey cake on the ground."

"My other mother," prompted Lucy.

Mother sniffed. She had long since stopped explaining that Lucy couldn't have two sets of parents.

"It put down roots and grew," said Father.

"Until it was as tall as the oak by the blacksmith's shed," Lucy said.

"Every branch was covered with honey cakes. Invisible servants flew through the air to fetch them."

"Invisible servants! I'd like that," said Mother.

"You had a little dog with a green collar with silver bells sewn on it. You could hear it running through the house."

"Castle," Lucy corrected.

"Yes, of course. Castle. And it could talk. It told you everything that went on in the kingdom, but alas, it was very naughty. The dog ran away, and the nurse ran after it."

"With me in her arms," said Lucy.

"Yes. She got lost in the woods. She sat down to weep and tear her hair."

"She laid me under a rosebush first," said Lucy.

"A bear came out of the woods and gobbled her up, but he didn't find you, dearest."

"And that was how I got lost," crowed Lucy, not at all concerned about the fate of the nurse.

Jack fell asleep listening to the north wind fussing with the thatch over his head.

Chapter Four

THE VALLEY OF LUNATICS

The Bard's face was tanned, as though he'd been out in the sun a long time. Jack wondered about it, but he hesitated to ask.

"You look well enough," the old man said. "Everyone in the family is fine?"

"Yes, sir," said Jack.

"I've been casting about for information. It seems that things are stirring across the water. Ships are being built, swords are being forged."

"Is that bad?"

"Of course. People don't make ships and swords unless they intend to use them." The Bard strode ahead, leading Jack along a path above the sea. The green cliffs broke off to their right, and Jack could hear waves foaming at the rocks far below. Seagulls coasted the breeze, sliding back and forth in the updraft with a lazy flap of their wings.

"You see, the land across the water isn't as rich as it is here. Farms are carved out of the mountains. Snow and ice cover them most of the year. Only a few people can survive there, and the rest have to go somewhere else." The Bard climbed the steep path without slowing or even getting out of breath. Jack had to struggle to keep up with him. "The Northmen who live there are looking east to the land of the Rus and south to the land of the Franks. They don't look north because that's where the Jotuns live."

Jotuns. Jack shivered.

"I'm afraid some of them are looking west. Toward us."

"Is that the shadow you felt, sir?"

"That . . . and something else." The Bard halted and looked out toward the sea and the gulls sliding back and forth on the air. "These particular Northmen—the ones who are looking west—are led by a king called Ivar the Boneless."

Ivar the Boneless! Jack felt as though a cloud had come between himself and the sun. The sound of the waves was muted, and the cries of the gulls came to him from a great distance.

"Jack, are you all right?" said the Bard.

"What a terrible name," murmured the boy.

"No more terrible than he is. His eyes are pale blue, like sea ice. His skin is as white as the belly of a fish. He can break a man's leg with his bare hands, and he wears a cloak made from the beards of his defeated enemies."

Jack felt almost dizzy with terror. What was happening to him? He'd heard plenty of frightening tales from both the Bard and Father. He liked them—the scarier the better. Now he felt as weak as a newborn lamb.

"But Ivar the Boneless is nothing compared to his wife." The Bard continued to peer out over the sea. He seemed to be searching for something. After a moment he shook his head and went on. "Queen Frith is a half-troll," he said in a lower tone.

"Did she send the Nightmare?" Jack's chest felt as though it was being squeezed in a giant hand.

"Aye, lad. Her spirit rode it like the venomous monster she is behind her lying, beautiful face. Did you know Nightmares have *eight legs*?"

But Jack heard no more. He'd fainted dead away on the grassy cliff above the foaming waters of the North Sea.

When he awoke, he saw the old man sitting on a gray stone next to the path. A crow left the Bard's shoulder and flapped off over the dense stands of gorse and heather that lay between them and the western hills. Jack rubbed his forehead. He felt as if he'd been trampled by a dozen black-faced ewes.

"Tell me," said the Bard, turning his attention from the crow. "Have you felt anything unusual since I knocked you down?"

Jack told him about wanting to cry all the time. He said he'd noticed a lot more things—colors and smells, for example. He said his father seemed like a child one moment but turned back into an adult the next. "I'm putting it badly," he said.

"You're putting it very well," said the Bard. "I must say this is an unexpected development."

"Am I going mad?"

The Bard chuckled. "Oh, no. You've merely spread your wings." The old man felt around in the bag he carried on hikes and fished out a pair of biffins—whole, dried apples. He tossed one to Jack. "You see, lad, most people live like birds inside a cage. It makes them feel safe. The world's a frightening place, full of glory and wonder and danger. It's better—so most people think—to pretend it isn't there. Ow!"

The Bard ran his finger around his mouth and extracted a seed. "I *wish* the baker would take out the cores before he dries apples." Jack was struggling to understand what the old man was saying.

"A few people realize the door isn't locked," the Bard continued. "They keep pushing and pushing until—presto!—the door swings open and they fly away. The world looks completely different outside. Suddenly, there's hawks and crows and snakes and rats—"

"Stop," cried Jack, flinging up his hands.

The Bard looked at him sharply but said nothing. He fished in his bag and found a scrap of oatcake, which he held up. Presently, a seagull swooped down and took it. "Is that magic?" said Jack, greatly impressed.

"It's patience. If you sit quietly, most things will come to you. That's what I've been trying to teach you these past few weeks. Sit quietly. Look at things. It's how I was trained. It's a long, slow process because real magic is dangerous. Now you've opened the door too soon. When you touched me, while I was battling the Nightmare, the life force I was gathering flowed out of my hand and into you. It cast you down. It very nearly killed you."

Jack climbed to his feet. His legs felt suspiciously wobbly.

"Your defenses have been torn away," said the Bard. "Everything, from the plight of a chick fallen from its nest to the terrible beauty of the hawk swooping down to kill it, will shake your very soul. It's a pity. You aren't ready to face so much reality, but there it is. Can you walk?"

"I'll try, sir."

"Good lad." The Bard led the way, going more slowly now. The path moved away from the cliff and into a small valley with a rowan tree at the bottom. The tree shadowed a pool fed by a spring. Its smooth gray branches were dotted with clusters of creamy flowers, over which hovered a cloud of bees. Their hum was so intense, it swamped the noise of the spring. Jack wondered if they came from his mother's hives, and presently, as one of the insects landed on his sleeve, he knew they did. He recognized the bee. He could feel its tiny mind at work, excitement at finding the honey-rich tree, eagerness to get back to the nest Mother had provided. Jack stumbled.

"We're almost there," said the Bard. He led the boy to a shelf of rock on which they sat to rest. The valley seemed to tremble, like heather on a hot day.

"We've been following one of the courses of the life force. That's why you feel strange," said the Bard.

It seemed hot. Jack's skin prickled as though ants were crawling on him. He slapped himself to get rid of them.

The old man spoke, but Jack found it hard to concentrate. Sometimes the words seemed to come from nearby, and sometimes they floated to him from a great distance. They were important. Jack knew they were. The sound of the bees was important too, and the bubbling spring and the stealthy rustle of the tree.

"Wake up!" Jack felt himself shaken and gaped at the Bard's worried face. "You *must* pay attention. I was telling you about how the life force flows in streams deep in the earth. It is this that feeds the great forests and meadows sweet with grass. It is this that calls forth the flowers and the butterflies that are so like flowers. The deer follow its courses as they browse. The badgers and moles build their homes over it. It even draws the swallows in the midst of the sea. All things are subject to it—except people."

The Bard got up and paced around the small meadow beside the pool. Jack got up too, just to be moving. He felt he might fall asleep if he didn't.

"Long ago, people decided they didn't want to be like animals. They wanted to choose their own destinies, and so they did a very dangerous thing. *They walled themselves off from the life force.*" The Bard spread his arms wide to the sky. He looked, Jack thought, like a great bird about to fly. The light of the little valley seemed to gather around him. Then he lowered his arms and the light faded.

"In doing so, they lost the ability to understand it. They could no longer merge themselves thoughtlessly like the animals. And this cut them off from a great joy. They felt as if their lives were dull and meaningless. A few people tried to tear down the wall, but they were no longer able to endure such reality. Did you ever hear of the Valley of Lunatics?"

Jack pushed himself away from the rowan tree. Without quite realizing how he'd got there, he had found himself leaning against it in a quiet daze.

"Come on, get moving," cried the Bard. "Things are worse than I thought." He pulled Jack into the meadow and whirled him around. "Jump! Run! Do handstands!" he ordered. And so Jack danced and cavorted around the meadow, feeling silly and exhilarated at the same time. His mind seemed to clear. The heavy air of the valley freshened. Finally, he threw himself to the grass, laughing and panting.

"That's more like it," said the Bard with his hands on his bony hips.

"Where's this Valley of Lunatics?" Jack asked.

"In Ireland." The Bard lowered himself carefully to the grass. The boy could almost hear his bones creak.

"That's on the other side of the world," said Jack.

"Not really. You could reach it in a few weeks."

"Father says the Irish walk upside down and have eyes in their feet," said Jack.

"Your father—don't get me distracted, lad. The monks told him that as a joke. Half of *them* are Irish. The Valley of

Lunatics is real, though." The old man flexed his fingers, and Jack heard his joints pop. "My best friend and I trained as bards in Ireland. We studied for many years before we were trusted with the secret knowledge of the life force. We were taken to a place where it pooled under the earth. That's where its strength is greatest. Day after day we sat, struggling to open our minds to its power. And just as quickly retreating when it got too close. The minute we felt it taking over, we had to get up and run around."

"Is that why you had me do handstands?" said Jack.

"Exactly. It puts you back in your body, keeps you from being overwhelmed. But my friend liked the feeling of power." The Bard sighed and fell silent for several minutes. Jack found himself growing drowsy again.

"Move around if you have to," said the Bard. So Jack did a few somersaults and finished up by walking on his hands, as he'd seen a jester do at a village fair.

"You see, whatever power a bard has," the old man continued, "comes from the life force: his music, his ability to hold an audience, his skill in calling up storms."

Jack straightened up. That last one sounded interesting.

"It takes years to control it, and my friend didn't want to wait. He refused to stop while it was still safe. At first he was successful. He could cause a fire to hang in midair or birds to fly upside down. But one day—while he was trying to make a forest pull up its roots and walk—something went *snap*. I could actually hear it. He fell over. A second later he sprang up and his body shook as though a giant dog had him in its jaws. Then he gave a mighty howl and ran off as fast as he could go."

Jack was horrified. The Bard had said *his* defenses were gone. Was it his fate to go mad as well?

"I followed him," said the old man. "It wasn't easy, for I had to stop at nightfall and go around bramble bushes and streams. My poor friend went straight ahead no matter what was in his way. I found pieces of his clothing on thorns. At last I came to the Valley of Lunatics."

A mist had blown up from the sea, and the air was beginning to chill. The bees had left their feeding. Each moment there were fewer of them as they sped off to their warm hives.

"I could hear them cackling before I could see them," said the Bard. "It was a terrible sound, so like laughter and yet so completely joyless. All the failed bards in Ireland had found their way to this one place where the life force was stronger than anywhere else. And there they stayed. I saw my friend, but he was nothing like the man I'd known. His eyes and hair were wild. He was in the grip of a power far beyond him, and I, poor apprentice that I was, had no way to free him."

The old man climbed to his feet and held out his hand. "Let us not dwell on the unhappy past. I may have done you harm, but I'm no longer a raw apprentice. I can help you. And perhaps it was all for the best. Dangers sweep upon us. Storm clouds are gathering. Swords are being forged. . . ." Muttering to himself, the Bard made his way up the path.

Jack followed him. He felt somewhat dazed. The sleepiness that had come upon him earlier was creeping back, but the farther they got from the little valley, the better he felt. And by the time they reached the Roman house on its windswept cliff, he was fine.

Chapter Five

———⟨⟩———

HROTHGAR'S GOLDEN HALL

Moons waxed and waned over the little village. The apples on Father's trees turned golden. Grain bent in waves before the west wind, and presently, harvest time arrived. Sheep were shorn, honey was taken from the hives, pigs were slaughtered in preparation for winter. Jack stayed in the Roman house. He couldn't hear the killing of the pigs, but he could feel it. The air trembled with their deaths.

All the while he practiced magic with the Bard. He learned to call up mist, make apples drop from a high branch, and call birds down from the sky. It was small stuff, but it delighted him.

Then it was winter. Snow settled over the high hills. The sea turned dark and the sun fled. Jack stayed indoors and memorized poems. The Bard had made him a small harp, but the cold was so intense, Jack's fingers were clumsy on the strings. The old man decided it was time to teach the making of fires. "Concentrate on heat," he said, sitting across from a jumble of sticks and straw.

"I'm freezing," said Jack. The Bard had put out the fire at dawn, and the air was so cold, it was frightening. Ice rimed the paintings on the walls.

"It's only freezing if you think it is," the Bard said.

That's all right for you, Jack thought resentfully. *You've got a thick woolen cloak and fur-lined boots. I've only got this miserable tunic.*

"If I've told you once, I've told you a hundred times." The old man sighed. "Don't use anger to reach the life force."

How does he know what I'm thinking? thought Jack. *Anyhow, it's true. I've outgrown my tunic, and my shoes have been through so much mud, you could bake them like pots.*

"Anger belongs to death," said the Bard. "It turns on you when you least expect it."

Jack, with an inward sigh, thought about the hot sun pouring down last summer. Rain fell on the earth and flowed out of hillsides months later. Surely light remained trapped as well. He searched for it, going deep into the soil, beyond the nests of mice and voles, beyond even the gnarled roots of the forest, until he came to rock. And beyond the rock he found heat. He saw a faint glow in his mind and drew it forth. He called to it, mentally held out his hands to it.

Jack felt sick. Magic sometimes did that to him. The power roiled in the pit of his stomach, and he thought he was going to throw up. He opened his eyes to see a thread of smoke curling up from the straw.

"Don't give up now," said the Bard. "Keep calling it. *Keep calling.*" But the nausea won out. Jack stumbled to the door, and when he returned, the spark had died.

"Don't worry," the Bard said cheerfully. "What's done once can be done again. We have all day."

So we do, thought Jack as the north wind buffeted the walls of the house.

"If you feel sleepy, walk around," said the Bard.

I'm not sleepy, I'm cold, thought Jack. But he found he was sleepy after all. It would feel so nice to give himself up to the sensation. He could almost see the frost giants calling to him. *Lie down, boy,* they said. *It's a fine old bed, ice is. Nothing like snow for a cover either.*

He felt himself being shaken. "I said, walk around!" the Bard shouted. "You've got to recognize the danger." He forced the boy to put first one foot, then the other before him. Jack almost fell over before he got the hang of walking again.

"Life and death are in constant battle," said the Bard. "In winter death is strongest. The frost giants lie in wait for the careless. When you work magic in winter, you have to be especially careful."

"Y-Y-You d-don't stare out o-over the sea any-ah-anymore," stammered Jack, his teeth chattering. "A-Aren't you w-worried about Q-Queen Frith?"

"Very observant of you." The Bard briskly marched Jack up and down the house. "I'm not worried because the servants of Queen Frith can't travel now. No Northman would take his beloved boat out in winter. And those ox-brained oafs do love their boats. They sing to them and buy them jewels as though they were women. When a chieftain dies, he is sent out with all his worldly goods in a blazing ship. He even has a slave woman to wait on him."

"A woman?" Jack gasped. "Is she—? Do they—?"

"Do they kill her? Yes. An old hag called the Angel of Death strangles her. Then she is laid next to her lord and they are both burned."

Jack shivered again, this time not entirely from cold. The more he heard about these Northmen, the worse they sounded.

"Try the fire-making again," said the Bard. "I'll watch to make sure you don't go too far."

Jack's second attempt went more smoothly, and the third, fourth, and fifth almost succeeded. Finally, on the sixth try, hours later, he got the plume of smoke to burst into flame.

"I did it!" he cried. He danced around the room, feelings of cold and defeat gone. "I'm a bard! I'm a wonder! I'm the cleverest boy in the world!" The heat was pouring out of the earth now. The rime on the walls melted. The frozen thatch softened and dripped. It began to smolder.

"Begone!"

The room suddenly darkened and the air filled with ashes and smoke. Jack stopped and stared.

In the dim light of the doorway the Bard stood with folded arms. "I've told you before. Know when to quit."

Jack felt as though he'd been struck. "How dare you put out my fire!" he screamed. "How dare you spoil my work!" Jack felt the power rise through his feet and heat his whole body. He was filled with a savage joy. He could do anything—*anything*—better than this old fool who didn't appreciate what a great magician Jack was.

The Bard raised his staff. "Stop now," he said quietly. "If I can repel a Nightmare from across the sea, you don't want to know what I can do to a fledgling apprentice."

The power vanished. Jack sank to the floor. He felt like he was alone on a dark sea with devouring waves all around. He was a mere insect crawling on a fragment of driftwood. How could he have imagined hurting the one person who had tried to help him? How could he have been so stupid? He began to cry.

"Oh, my, my, my," said the Bard. "You really are a child. I've pushed you too hard." He knelt down and put his hands on Jack's head. Presently, the boy felt something drop over him like a soft blanket. It felt safe and warm. He wanted to wrap himself up and never come out.

"Listen, child," came the old man's soft voice. "You must respect the limits of your power. You can cause a great deal of harm if you don't. I've cast a spell of protection over you. Let all wandering spirits see my mark and keep away."

Jack heard no more words, though he did register the sound of the wind. It was like many voices calling to one another. And he heard the crackling of fire and felt its warmth—true warmth and not the false heat of anger.

❖❖❖

On the long evenings Jack went back and forth to the heap of driftwood he had gathered during summer. It was then that the Bard told stories, and he wanted a cheerful fire in the background. "They are cruel tales," he said. "They should be told in the light, with good friends and a merry heart."

How you could tell a cruel tale with a merry heart was a mystery to Jack, but it wasn't his place to argue. "If you were trained in Ireland, sir," he dared to ask one night, "how did you meet up with . . . um . . . that northern king?"

"Ivar the Boneless?"

"Yes." Jack hated to say the name. It sounded so horrible. It was like a long, green worm slithering through a swamp.

"I was young and foolish, like you," said the Bard. "I had earned my harp from the College of Bards and had been awarded the Golden Mistletoe for outstanding spell-casting. Have I told you about that?"

"Yes, sir."

"I was ready for adventure, and thus it came to me, as adventure always does to the foolish. A northern warrior arrived at the college. He asked for a bard to accompany him to his lord's castle. It sounded wonderful! Hrothgar was a mighty lord who lived in a golden hall. There was none like it in the world.

"It was as large as a hundred houses and filled with brave warriors and shield women. The fire pit alone could hold an entire oak tree. Hrothgar was generous as well. He gave gold rings to his followers and lavish feasts to all who sought shelter under his roof. But the one thing Hrothgar didn't have was a first-rate bard. Have I told you I was awarded the Golden Mistletoe for outstanding spell-casting?"

"Yes, sir," said Jack.

"So you see I was the natural choice for this honor. And the thought of traveling didn't bother me. It's what we bards do. I sailed to Hrothgar's kingdom, and it was even better than described. His hall was like a great light in the midst of a wilderness."

Jack listened breathlessly. The walls of the Roman house trembled in a winter storm, and the stones on the beach far below rattled like an army clashing its shields. No matter how carefully Jack stuffed heather and wool into crevices, the wind still found its way inside. The coals of the fire brightened and light danced on the walls.

But Hrothgar's hall had allowed no winter. It was as sound as a nut and as warm and friendly as a summer afternoon. Its walls rang with laughter, even more so after the arrival of the Bard.

"I should have known," mourned the Bard. "I should have *guessed.*"

"Guessed what?" said Jack, unable to contain himself.

"It's as I have told you. Life and death are in constant battle. There's no way in this world for happiness to exist alone. The golden hall was too beautiful, and so, like all bright things, it attracted destruction. In the deeps, in the depths of a murky swamp, lived Grendel, who was a monster."

"Was he a *troll*?" gasped Jack.

"Partly," said the Bard. "His father was an ogre. Anyhow, monsters hate light," said the Bard. "They cannot bear laughter, and the smell of feasting enrages them. Grendel waited until everyone was asleep. Then he crept into the hall and bit off the heads of ten warriors sleeping near the door. Don't wince like that, Jack," said the Bard. "When you retell this story, you'll have to look confident."

"I'm sorry," said Jack.

"Grendel took home the bodies for dinner. I can tell you, *that* cast a shadow over the fun and games at the hall. The warriors all swore they would avenge their comrades. But that night they discovered a terrible thing. *Grendel could not be harmed by weapons.* He was protected by a charm. The warriors slashed at him until their swords broke, but they couldn't make a dent in his scaly hide.

"It went on for weeks," said the Bard. "Whenever the monster got hungry, he dropped off at Hrothgar's for a snack. No one asked for songs from me anymore. They were too depressed."

Jack might have been mistaken, but it seemed the Bard felt insulted. "Weren't you scared, sir?"

"Of course! But there's no point giving in to fear. That's like opening the door and saying, 'Come right in, Master Grendel, sir. Wouldn't you like to bite an arm or a leg off me?' No! Death must be fought with life, and that means courage and that means joy. I can tell you, I was disgusted by the way Hrothgar and his crowd were handling their problem. They hid under the stairs like rabbits. Until Beowulf showed up."

"Beowulf?" said Jack. The fire had died down. The flaring coals cast weird shadows. As often happened when the light was dim, the painted birds on the walls seemed to open their wings. Their feathers stirred in a breeze that was nothing like the fierce storm outside. Jack hastily got up and put more driftwood on the fire.

"Beowulf. Ah, there was a warrior!" said the Bard, his eyes gleaming. "No hiding under the stairs for *him*. Hrothgar embraced him. The queen offered him a cup of foaming mead. When midnight came, all had fallen into a weary sleep brought on by fear. All but Beowulf . . . and me.

"Beowulf sat by the door. When Grendel arrived, the warrior grasped him by the arm. No weapon wrought of steel could harm the monster, but honest human hands could destroy him. Grendel took fright and ran. Beowulf held on so tightly, *he tore Grendel's arm right off.*"

This time Jack managed to keep from wincing.

"Shrieking, the monster staggered back to the swamp and plunged into its depths. But before he reached the bottom, he was dead."

"Hurrah!" cried Jack.

"Wait. There's more."

"More?" said Jack. "You mean, where everyone celebrated the victory?"

"Of course they celebrated," the Bard said. "What they didn't know, however, was that Grendel had a *mother*. This is where it gets interesting."

How can it possibly get more interesting? Jack thought. The earlier story had been so thrilling, Jack's heart was still pounding.

"Grendel's mother clawed her way out of the swamp, howling for revenge. She broke down the door, bursting the bars asunder. The warriors felt for their spears, but in a trice she was across the hall. She tore Grendel's arm off the wall. Hrothgar had nailed it there as a kind of trophy. I *did* warn him it was a bad idea."

"Please go on, sir," said Jack, wriggling in his seat.

"Then the she-monster killed the king's best friend and went back to the swamp. Beowulf had been sleeping in a back room and had heard nothing.

"In the morning the warriors rode to the lonely mountains where the creatures of the night lived. Toads bleated melancholy cries from slime pits. Trees trailed twisted roots into swamp. Frozen water hung like fallen daggers over the gloomy cliffs. Beowulf blew his battle horn, and all manner of snakes and scaly beings came hissing out. Hrothgar and his warriors fought them with axe and arrow until they were all dead. But one creature remained."

"Grendel's mother," whispered Jack.

"Did I tell you her name was Frothi? Or that she was a half-troll?"

Chapter Six

THE WOLF-HEADED MEN

Jack crept closer to the fire. The driftwood burned green and blue, as driftwood did when it had been at sea a long time. The Bard pulled a goatskin bag from a peg. He took a hearty drink and offered it to Jack. The apple cider was warm from being close to the fire. It reminded Jack of the sunlight that had ripened the apples.

"I didn't know who Frothi was until later," the Bard said. "I only knew that a foul monster lived at the bottom of the swamp. Beowulf blew his horn to call her forth to battle. 'Coward!' he shouted. But the water only quivered. Nothing stirred, not in the swamp, the trees, or the mountains. 'If she will not come to me, I shall go to *her*,' he announced.

"Beowulf was a fine man," said the Bard, "but he wasn't overly furnished with brains. That's the way it is with great warriors. They'll rush out to fight a dragon ten times their size. Sometimes they'll even win, but most of the time the dragon winds up picking its teeth with the sword.

"'Beowulf,' I said, 'you're going to sink like a stone with all that armor. And what are you planning to use for air down there?'

"'I care not! This battle will win me fame or death,' he bellowed.

"'Old friend,' I said, 'let's not start thinking about death. I think I can help you.' I sang him a charm for the swiftness of a trout, the suppleness of an eel. I made his sword shine, to light his way in the dark swamp. I gave him the ability to breathe under water."

"You can do all that?" Jack cried.

"For a short while. I can only bend the laws of the world, not change them."

Jack was wildly excited. Up till now the Bard had only hinted at the magic he could accomplish. If the old man could do such wonderful things, couldn't he—*wouldn't* he—teach his apprentice how?

"Beowulf plunged into the swamp. The darkness swallowed him, and with it came silence. The toads stopped croaking. The wind died. All seemed to be watching and waiting. 'Hurry,' I thought. Beowulf had only a short time to carry out his mission. If he took too long, the charm would wear off and he would drown.

"But the silence went on and on, broken only by small wavelets breaking on the shore of the swamp. Hrothgar and his men began to lament. 'Poor Beowulf! He was like a son to me,' wailed the king. 'We shall honor his memory and sing his praises around the fire.' Then they gathered their weapons, climbed onto their horses, and rode home.

"I couldn't believe it. They were slinking off like hounds with their tails between their legs. I'd never seen such a pack of quitters. I vowed I would sing no more praise-songs about Hrothgar."

"What happened to Beowulf, sir?" Jack said.

"Ah! I was forgetting. 'What to do, what to do?' I thought. I had no sword. I had nothing but my brain—no small weapon, I might add. I had to get down to the bottom of the swamp and find out what was keeping our hero. So I cast my spirit into the body of a pike."

"You turned into a *fish*?" Jack said.

"No, no. I merely borrowed one. My spirit found a bad-tempered old pike and traded places with him. That's a dangerous trick, lad. The longer you're in an animal's body, the more you forget about being human. Some apprentice bards never made it out of their animals during exam week."

"What about Beowulf?" Jack asked patiently.

"I dived to the bottom of the swamp, and there I found a lofty hall with pillars and a roof so strong that it held up the water. Some magic kept the air inside. By then Beowulf's charm had worn off, but he no longer needed to breathe under water. I, however, was stuck in the body of a fish.

"A fire blazed in a hearth. By its light I could see Beowulf standing as though he'd been turned to stone. His sword had fallen out of his hand. His mouth gaped open. Before him was the most beautiful woman I had even seen."

"Frothi," whispered Jack.

"She was watching him like a cat watching a tasty pigeon. Beowulf was enchanted by her beauty. It never occurred to him that finding a lady at the bottom of a swamp was, well, somewhat odd."

"Couldn't you warn him?" cried Jack.

"I was a pike, remember? I was in the water. Frothi stroked Beowulf's face, as a cat might play with a helpless mouse. And then I knew what I was seeing. This was no woman. No human could have torn down Hrothgar's door and burst the iron bars asunder. I was looking at a half-troll.

"Such creatures have a foot in each world. They can shift from one form to the other. At the moment Frothi was human. Soon she would change to her troll form and crush the life out of Beowulf.

"She reached toward him, and I knew what I had to do. I threw myself into the hall, wriggled across the floor to Frothi's feet, and sank my teeth into her ankle.

"She screamed. Her concentration was broken. She turned into a giant troll with arms and legs like tree trunks. Beowulf sprang back with a shout. He grabbed his sword, and the battle began. I won't bore you with the details. It went on as such battles do, with slashes and curses and bones crunching and blood everywhere. Beowulf eventually landed the fatal blow, but I was too busy wriggling back to the water before my host died.

"Up to the surface I sped and regained my body. Not long after, Beowulf climbed out, pleased as punch. I, of course, told him about my clever trick, and he, of course, thanked me. He had excellent manners. But I should have kept my mouth shut." The Bard sighed.

The fire had burned down. Jack dragged over a log and settled it carefully so the sparks wouldn't fly up and set the thatch on fire. He was so excited, he wanted to run around the house five times. The Bard really could do magic! In time Jack would do it too. *What animal shall I be?* he thought. *A hawk so I can see the whole village? Or a seal so I can catch fish? Wait! Wouldn't it be great to be a bear and scare the stuffing out of the blacksmith's son?*

"If you're quite finished wool-gathering, I'll finish the story," said the Bard.

"Sorry, sir." Jack sat down.

"The tale of Beowulf's victory went everywhere—helped, I might add, by the excellent poem I wrote about it. Eventually, it got to Jotunheim, the kingdom of the trolls."

"Uh-oh," said Jack.

"Frothi had a sister."

"Frith?" Jack guessed.

"I'm afraid so. Many years had passed, but Frith had never given up her thirst for revenge for her sister's death. She sent a fire-breathing dragon to destroy Beowulf's land. Jotuns are long-lived, and Frith was hardly past her youth, but Beowulf was an old man. The battle was too much for him and he died."

That's the problem with stories going on too long, Jack

thought. *Sooner or later you get to a bad part.* When he, Jack, became a bard, he'd stop talking while everyone was still happy.

"By then I was working at the court of Ivar the Boneless. Don't scowl, lad," said the old man. "Bards have to work like everyone else. Ivar wasn't so bad in those days. He was your usual pea-brained bully, but he had a sense of honor. Not after Frith got hold of him, though. She was as beautiful as a ship under full sail. An illusion, of course. She got hold of him, sucked the marrow out of him, and turned him into the half-mad tyrant he is today. Probably the last decent thing he did was save my life."

"That's when you came to us," Jack said.

"Indeed it was. Ivar took me out in his ship and put me adrift in a flimsy coracle. Perhaps he thought I would drown. I'm sure he told Frith that. But I like to think he gave me a chance to survive."

"I'm so glad you came here," Jack said in a burst of gratitude.

"I am too." The Bard took down his harp and played a tune the villagers danced to at summer fairs. It made the firelight flicker on the walls of the Roman house. The painted birds spread their wings and swayed from side to side.

The harp was carved from the breastbone of a whale. After a while the old man played something grander and more sad. Jack wondered if the long-dead whale was remembering its life and whether the music came from the Bard or from the sea.

❖❖❖

Jack ran along the shore, stopping once as a wave washed over his feet. The March sky was blue, the air filled with the cries of migrating birds. He was headed toward a line of rocks. With the tide out, he had an excellent chance to gather whelks. His collecting bag was slung over his shoulder. He had spent over a year as the Bard's apprentice and now felt he had earned this chance to play.

He reached the rocks and flopped down to catch his breath. "What a beautiful day," he said to no one in particular. The air was soft with spring, and sunlight polished the seaweed tossing at the edge of the waves. Jack lay back against a sand dune and watched a line of geese pass overhead. He could call them down. He could even—but wouldn't dare—kill one for dinner. The Bard said using the life force in that way was evil.

The winter had been so cold, and the Bard had driven him for such long hours, even Father had been pleased. Today was the first time Jack had managed to get away. He was supposed to gather whelks and sea tangle. If there was time, he was to practice calling up fog.

"I . . . *really* . . . hate fog," Jack said as he gazed up at the sky. After a while he felt guilty and got up. He shaded his eyes. There was something out at sea. It was small, almost hidden in the vastness. At first Jack thought it was a bird, but as the waves brought it closer he saw it was a box.

Perhaps it contained treasure. Perhaps it carried a ring that could grant three wishes or a cap that made you invisible.

Jack tore off his clothes and plunged into the water. He was a good swimmer. He raised his head between strokes to keep track of the box's location, and soon he had it.

Back on shore he eagerly studied it. It was locked, although water sloshed when it was shaken. On five sides it was plain. On the sixth was a carving of a man.

Or at least Jack thought it was a man. The stocky creature had legs and shoes. It carried a sword. But its body was covered with hair and the head was that of a wolf.

The boy shivered. The box smelled—not rotten, exactly, but *strange*. Sweet and bitter at the same time. He had intended to bash it open with a rock. Now he thought it wiser to consult the Bard. Jack quickly gathered the whelks and hurried home.

The old man took one look at the box and rushed outside to the edge of the cliff. He gazed at the sea. "It has come," he murmured.

"What has come? What's the matter?" cried Jack.

"I can't see them, but I know they're out there. They're smashing . . . and burning . . . and spreading death like a red tide."

"Please, sir! Tell me what's happening."

The Bard turned over the box. Water dripped out of a small crack. "I hoped never to smell this again," he said. He pressed the wood in various places until it made a small *snap*. The carving of the wolf/man slid out. Beneath was a mat of dark green leaves. The Bard drained off the seawater. "That, my lad, is bog myrtle."

Jack was deeply disappointed. He had hoped for magic.

"And that"—the Bard tapped the lid—"is the fellow who owns it."

"Is he a Jotun?" asked Jack.

"Jotuns aren't our immediate problem. This fellow is a berserker, and from the condition of the box, I'd say he's not far away."

Jack followed the Bard into the house, wishing the old man would explain things more clearly. "Is a berserker a man or a wolf?"

"A very good question," said the Bard. "Most of the time they're men, but when they make a drink of this plant, they become as frenzied as mad dogs. They bite holes in their shields. They run barefooted over jagged rocks without feeling it. Neither fire nor steel can stop them. They believe themselves to be wolves or bears then. My observation is that they're merely nasty, dim-witted thugs. They're just as dangerous, though.

"Somewhere, not far from here, a pack of them has landed. Run and warn the village, lad. Tell the men I'm coming. Tell them to send their loved ones into the forest and to gather axes, hoes, whatever can be used for weapons. They will need them soon."

Chapter Seven

‑‑‑‑ᴖ‑‑‑‑

THE END OF DAYS

But Jack didn't have to tell the villagers anything. He met the blacksmith's son, Colin, running up the path. "Jack! Jack! Call the Bard. Something awful has happened!" Colin stopped to catch his breath.

"He's on his way," said Jack.

"Good old Bard," said the blacksmith's son. "Dad said he'd know what to do. He'll throw those pirates back in the sea and let the fishies eat them."

"Pirates? *Already?*" cried Jack.

Colin wiped his nose on his sleeve and then put the same arm around Jack's shoulder. "You knew about them? Oh, of course. You're an apprentice bard."

Colin didn't seem worried by the appearance of pirates. Jack noted his new friendliness and warmed to it. Jack was no longer a farmer's brat to be bullied. He was an apprentice bard, soon to be a real one with powers to drive people mad or make them come up in boils if they displeased him.

"They haven't arrived yet," said the blacksmith's son, removing his arm and wiping his nose again. Jack moved out of reach. "Dad says there's going to be an awful fight. Aren't we lucky? Years go by without the least excitement, and now we'll go to war like heroes of old. Maybe the king will knight us."

Jack knew there was a king far to the north. No one had ever seen him. There was also rumored to be a king to the south. Which one might show up and knight them was unclear, but Jack was just as thrilled as Colin by the possibility.

The two boys ran down to the village, where they found everyone gathered outside the chief's house. The men had clubs and hoes. A few carried the bows they used to hunt deer, and all were armed with knives. Even Father carried a scythe. He swished it through the air to demonstrate what a fine weapon it was. Lucy cheered.

Jack suddenly felt cold. That scythe wasn't going to cut down harmless grain. It was going to slash arms and legs. The same dizziness that came over him when the pigs were slaughtered made Jack's senses reel. The air was full of cries. Horses whinnied. Crows croaked as they gathered over a battlefield.

"Jack, are you all right?" came Mother's voice.

He looked up to find everyone staring at him. He was kneeling on the ground—how had he got there?—with his hands out to push away the evil vision. He scrambled to his feet. "I was looking for the pirates. It's a bard thing."

He was gratified to see everyone smile. "Are they coming soon?" cried Lucy, clapping her hands. "Oh, I do want to see one!"

"Tell us the direction, lad," said the chief with more respect than even Father got. Jack was ashamed. He had no idea where the pirates were. He'd simply said the first thing that came into his head.

"We have to form a battle plan," the chief said. "Are they on the old Roman road? Or in the marshes?"

Jack tried to sense where the pirates were and failed. He had a one-in-two chance of getting it right. If he guessed right, he would be a hero. If he got it wrong, the villagers might find the wolf-headed men waiting for them when they came home.

"How did you hear about them?" he said, to stall for time.

"John the Fletcher was searching for wood to make arrows," said the chief. "He saw a ship just as darkness was falling. It was long with many oars. It ran before the wind like a bird flying to its nest, and it was coming our way. I haven't seen a pirate ship, but I've heard descriptions."

"It wasn't a fishing vessel, that's for sure," said John the Fletcher, who was one of the men carrying a bow.

"Well? Where are they?" said the chief.

Jack knew then he would have to admit his ignorance. It would be too dangerous to make a mistake. He opened his mouth to speak.

"I've *told* you not to do magic without my permission,"

said the Bard. Jack spun around. He felt limp with relief and gratitude. The old man wasn't going to expose his foolishness. "The enemy is on the Roman road, O Chief. You won't fight them, however. Your weapons are to be used only in direst need. Gather your families and whatever goods you can carry, and hide in the deep forest."

"I do not like to hide," said the chief.

"Me neither!" shouted the blacksmith.

"Nor I!" cried several other men.

"We Saxons don't slink away like dogs," the chief said. "We are the proud masters of this coast."

"Once you were," said the Bard. "*Once.* But you've forgotten your war skills. You've let your swords grow rusty and your spears fall into decay. You've grown fat along with the sheep."

"If you weren't our bard, I'd have your tongue for saying such vile things!" cried the chief.

"But I *am* your bard," the old man said calmly. "The men you want to battle are not such as you and I. They are berserkers." A murmur went through the gathering. Apparently, berserkers weren't unheard of. The Bard held out the box Jack had found. The chief passed it around, and each man smelled it. The odor clearly did not cheer their hearts.

"Do they . . . really . . . have the heads of wolves?" said the chief. Jack could see he was trying to look bold, but the confidence had drained out of him.

"No one knows," said the Bard. And Jack saw that uncertainty was worse than actually knowing your enemy was half beast. "What I understand is this: The berserkers feel neither fire nor blade. They live only to fall in battle. Any other death is shameful to them, and so they fight on and on, no matter how terrible their wounds are. They say you can cut off their heads and the heads still try to sink their teeth into your ankles. I don't know if that's true, but it gives you an idea of what they're like."

"Indeed," said the chief, turning pale. "Indeed."

"There's no shame in retreating from such a foe," the Bard said. "Your aim is to protect these women and children. A wise leader relies on strategy and leaves the empty heroics to the yokels in the next village."

"They *are* yokels over there, aren't they?" said the chief.

"Their chief is probably leading them into battle now—the idiots!" said the Bard.

"Well, I'm not going to be stupid," declared the chief. "You, Blacksmith! Organize the women to clear the houses. We'll drive the sheep into the hills."

"Speed might be advisable," said the Bard.

"Right! Everyone move on the double. We'll show those pirates. They won't take *us* by surprise!"

The Bard signaled Jack to stay with him. "Our work begins when theirs is over," he said in a low voice. Jack watched as women carted out furniture and hid it in the hedges dividing the fields. Girls ran down to the beach to bury pots and utensils. Boys thrust squawking hens into baskets. Grain was poured into carrying bags, fruit piled into packs. The blacksmith strode around bellowing directions, although it seemed the women and children were doing fine on their own.

In the midst of this bustle Jack saw a distant figure stumbling along the road. It came over a rise and almost fell. The person managed to right himself by leaning on a staff and dragged himself on. "Look, sir," whispered Jack, pointing at the road.

"Oh, my stars, it's a monk," said the Bard. He made his way through the villagers with Jack following behind. No one else had noticed the man.

As they drew near, Jack saw that the monk's robes weren't black as he had thought, but smeared with soot. A reek of smoke blew toward them. The monk stumbled again, and this time he didn't rise.

The Bard hurried to him. "It's all right. You're among friends," he said.

"Gone, all gone," moaned the monk. "Dead. Burned to ashes."

"Fetch help, Jack. This man is no longer able to walk."

Soon the monk was lying on a makeshift bed of dry grass. Jack's mother was feeding him lettuce juice to ease his pain, and the blacksmith's wife was rubbing goose fat over his burns. Jack's father and the chief knelt by his side.

"I think it's Brother Aiden from the Holy Isle," whispered the chief.

"Yes! Yes!" cried the monk. "That was my name." He thrashed his legs, knocking over the pot of goose grease. "Flee, all of you. The End of Days has come."

"We were about to do so when you showed up," said the Bard, who was sitting on a stone nearby.

"What about the Holy Isle?" said the chief.

"Gone," Brother Aiden moaned.

"How can it be gone?" said Father, his eyes widening.

"Dead. Burned to ashes."

"That's not possible!" Father lurched to his feet. He looked ready to faint. "No one attacks the Holy Isle. It's the one safe place on earth. God protects it. God would not allow such a thing!"

"Be quiet, Giles. The man doesn't have the strength to out-shout you," said the Bard.

Little by little the terrible story came out. It had been a wonderfully warm day, and the monks were in the fields cutting hay. The nuns were churning butter and sewing a new altar cloth. Servants were piling stones to make a new cattle barn.

Around midday someone spotted the ships. Four of them, or perhaps five. They were speeding for shore. *Visitors,* someone said. *What a nice surprise.*

Brother Aiden ran to tell the cook. They would prepare a meal for the unexpected guests. But when the ships reached the shallows, men streamed ashore, swinging axes and screaming curses. "They chopped the first ones into mincemeat," wept Brother Aiden.

Grim warriors tied stones around others and threw them into the sea. They killed everything in their path: men, women, servants, cattle, and sheep. Then they destroyed the buildings. They tore down the silk tapestries and trampled them. They smashed the stained-glass window.

"Not the window," groaned Father.

"Yes, that and more," said Brother Aiden. "They over-turned the altar and urinated on the books. They ran through the library and ripped manuscripts that had taken the monks fifty years to copy.

"That's where I was," said Brother Aiden. "I was hiding in a loft just under the roof. They tore up the manuscripts and then they set fire to them. I dared not leave. I stayed curled up under the roof while the smoke came on thickly and the heat almost set my robe on fire. When I couldn't stand it any-more, I dropped down into the flames and ran."

By then the whole island was afire, the monastery and nunnery, the church, the granary, the barns and fields. Brother Aiden had stumbled around, looking for anyone who might have survived, but there was no one. The longships had gone with their cargo of treasure and slaughtered animals. There was nothing left but smoking ruins and corpses.

"Oh, horror, horror!" cried Father, falling to his knees. Mother burst into tears. The blacksmith's wife ran to the other villagers, who were still packing, and gave them the news. Cries of disbelief and stormy weeping spread outward like a wildfire. Jack was crying too. He had never seen the Holy Isle—few of the villagers had—but it had always been there like a kindly light on the edge of an uncertain world.

Suddenly, Jack remembered the Bard's words: *There's no way in this world for happiness to exist alone. The golden hall was too beautiful, and so, like all bright things, it attracted destruction.* "It's like Hrothgar's hall," he said aloud.

"Very good," said the Bard, and Jack saw that he alone was not weeping. "Sometimes you quite surprise me with your intelligence."

"I should have been there," groaned Father. "I should have been a monk and fallen like a true martyr. Oh, horror!"

"Giles, you idiot. If you'd been a monk, you would never have had this good woman for a wife or these fine children. You'd be lying there in the ashes." The Bard stood up and spread his arms to the sky. From the distance came the harsh cry of a crow. Presently, it appeared, circled overhead, and came down to rest in a tree.

"It's probably been feasting on the dead," said Father.

"We should be going," the Bard said to the chief, ignoring Father. The chief shook himself.

"Of course," he said in a distant voice.

"I'll organize the boys to make a litter so you can take Brother Aiden along."

Soon a line of villagers, many still crying, made its way west to the forest. The squawking, clucking, hissing, and bleating of the livestock faded away. Silence settled over the fields.

Jack felt sore inside. Every time he thought of the Holy Isle, tears came to his eyes. It had been an enchanted place where they ate roast lamb flavored with rosemary and rowanberry pudding and flummery—the best kind, with nutmeg and cream. Gentle monks prayed over the sick beneath a stained-glass window that shone with the colors of the rainbow when the sun was behind it.

"The women did a good job," remarked the Bard, breaking into Jack's thoughts. "Of course, I trained them. They've been practicing for months."

"You knew this would happen?" said Jack.

"Not exactly. I knew some kind of trouble would arrive when the winter storms were over. I sent directions to the other villages as well. I hope they listened."

"Now what?" said Jack, talking to keep the silence of the village from depressing him.

"Now we make the biggest and wettest fog you've ever seen."

Chapter Eight

THE RUNE OF PROTECTION

They sat outside the old Roman house, calling to the life force. Rivers in the earth quickened their flow. Rivers of the air began to churn. Never had Jack felt them so strongly. Tears flowed down his cheeks at the wonder and beauty of it, and just as quickly the tears curled off his face as mist.

A flock of crows dropped out of the sky as though felled by arrows. They landed clumsily on the roof and clung to the thatch. Their beaks opened and shut. They were too dazed to even squawk.

The sea rolled far below, a dim white ribbon in the fog, glimmering and then gone. Cold wetness sank into Jack's shirt, but it was a *good* wetness. He felt like laughing. He did laugh, and the crows answered with a muted grumble.

"We should rest," said the Bard.

Jack woke up to find the light fading. The sun had set! The whole day had passed! He stood up, feeling as exhausted as though he'd wrestled a hundred black-faced ewes. His arms and legs ached, his head throbbed, and even his skin hurt.

The Bard hunched over, and Jack realized the old man was at the end of his strength. "I'll build a fire, sir," the boy said. "I'll get you food." He took flint and iron—he had no energy left to call up fire—and soon he had a fine blaze going and a cauldron of porridge bubbling. He led the Bard to the fire pit and folded his hands around a steaming cup of cider. As hungry as Jack was, he was even more concerned about reviving the Bard.

"Ahhh, the blessings of Frey and Freya upon you," the old man said with a sigh. He drank the hot liquid and allowed Jack to spoon porridge into his mouth. "It takes it out of you," he said at last.

"Do we need to make more fog tonight?" Jack said.

"I'm not up to it. I'm counting on darkness to protect us." The old man shuffled outside to the privy. Jack came along with a torch to be sure the Bard didn't fall over the cliff. The night was as black as the inside of a lead mine.

When they returned, the Bard fell into his truckle bed and was asleep between one breath and the next. Jack banked the fire and pulled the remaining porridge to one side for breakfast. There would be no more deliveries of food from the village.

Where were the villagers sleeping? Jack wondered as he watched the painted birds shift on their painted trees. Were they outdoors in the wet? Lucy wouldn't like that. She insisted on a soft bed and warmth. *I'm a lost princess,* she would say. *Lost princesses need their beds.* Lucy's complaints were endearing at the house because she was so small and beautiful. Father and Mother might not find them so endearing in the woods.

Jack fell asleep to the sound of crows' feet scraping on the roof.

"Wake up!" called the Bard. Jack sat up. Sunlight was streaming in the door, and for a moment he was pleased. Then he remembered the need for bad weather.

"Shall I heat the porridge, sir?"

"No time. We'll eat it cold."

Jack pried the gummy, lumpy porridge from the pot. It tasted smoky from the fire—not a bad thing, the boy decided. At least it filled the yawning pit in his stomach. He soaked a chunk of hard bread in cider.

"Come on!" said the Bard. "The berserkers won't be dawdling over *their* breakfasts."

I'm not dawdling, Jack thought bitterly. *I'm tired and hungry, and I have to work while the villagers get to relax in the forest.* But he knew that was unfair. The villagers would be huddled together like a flock of stunned sheep. He'd seen it happen when a flock lost its lead ewe far from home.

Sighing, he settled outside with the Bard and began to call to the life force. This time it was much easier. The earth and air responded as though they had only been waiting. Fog rolled in with a speed that was almost frightening. *What if we can't make it go away?* Jack thought. *What if the sun never shines again and the land is covered with eternal darkness?*

"What's wrong?" the Bard said.

Jack opened his eyes. The fog was shredding before a sudden sea wind. Rifts of blue appeared overhead.

"What were you thinking?" the old man said.

"Why—why, only that the fog was so thick," stammered Jack. "And that it might not go away."

"Lad, listen to me. The life force is ever moving, altering its appearance. Only death is unchanging."

"B-But if it *didn't* move"—Jack felt a bleak terror from somewhere he couldn't identify—"It w-would get dark forever. Like Father says happens when sinners are cast into outer darkness."

"Thor's hammer and anvil! Preserve me from Giles's ravings!" The Bard raised his arms as though asking the thunder god to witness such idiocy. The crows on the roof—how long had they been there?—cawed loudly. It sounded almost like laughter.

"But it's possible—it's just barely possible . . . ," the Bard said.

"What?" cried Jack.

"Keep your voice down. *She* may be working against us. *She* may be sending her thoughts across the sea. Her influence is lessened by passage over water. I didn't notice her spell because it was too feeble to affect me. At this distance she can only work on a weak mind."

"Hey," said Jack.

"But I'll fix her. I'll throw up a barrier to chip her rotten fangs if she tries it again. Here." The Bard felt inside his shirt and drew out a pendant on a chain. He settled it around Jack's neck.

The boy had never seen it before, though he'd been with the old man for months and months. He held it up, his mouth in an O at the wonder of it. It was a square of heavy gold. On it was a pattern that might have been a sunburst, except that each ray had branches like a budding tree. As Jack looked the pendant vanished. He gasped. This was real magic. He could still feel the heaviness of the gold on his neck.

"That's a rune for protection," said the Bard. "I wore it when I walked through the Valley of Lunatics in Ireland. It kept my wits about me when others were losing theirs. You may keep it."

"But, sir." Jack felt close to tears again. No one had ever thought him worthy of such a gift. The Roman coin Father had found was destined for Lucy. "What if Frith attacks you?"

"*Do not name her!* She flies to the mention of her name. Don't you worry about me," the old man said gruffly. "I've peeled the hide off more than one monster in my life. Now let's go make some fog."

Jack didn't know whether it was the rune or simply the joy of being cared for, but he felt strong and happy. He called up the waters of the earth. He pulled down clouds from the sky. He felt the wet smack of mist on his face and the soak of it in his clothes. His hair was plastered down, his chin dripped, and water trickled into his shoes. But he was as happy as a frog in a sunny pond.

He heard a rasping cough. His eyes flew open and saw nothing. The world had gone black. For an instant he was swept with panic. Then he heard the cough again. It was the Bard.

Night had fallen while Jack had been absorbed in his magic—pure, simple, innocent night. The fog he had called was so thick, every scrap of starlight was hidden from the earth. Jack felt for the door of the house. The cough came from there.

Inside, only a tiny coal shone in the fire pit. "Sir? Are you all right?" he whispered. It seemed right to whisper.

"In bed," the old man said.

The boy felt his way to the truckle bed. He touched the Bard's face and found, to his shock, that it was burning with fever. "I'll build up the fire, sir, and make you a healing drink."

"You're a good boy," the Bard said faintly.

Working quickly, Jack blew the coal into flame. He heated water mixed with willow bark. He added coriander to take the curse off the bitterness. This was a remedy he'd learned from Mother. Father wasn't pleased when Mother taught him such things. They were women's secrets, Father said, not fit for men, perhaps not safe for good Christians. Mother had smiled and gone on teaching.

"Foo," said the Bard when he tasted it.

"Mother swears it brings down fever."

"I'm sure it does. That doesn't mean I have to like it." The old man finished the drink. Presently, he doubled up with long, rattling coughs that frightened Jack.

"Take the pendant," the boy cried. "You need protection worse than I."

"Can't," said the Bard, struggling to talk. "Once given, can't be returned. Anyhow, wanted you to have it." He lay back, and Jack covered him with a sheepskin.

The boy rummaged through the stores at the far end of the house. He would have to set beans to soak. He would have to gather shellfish in the morning. How long could they go on like this without food from the village? How would they know when the wolf-headed men had gone?

Jack set the cauldron simmering with dried peas, onions, and turnips. He added a chunk of bacon that was only slightly green with age. The smell of food drove him mad with hunger, but it wouldn't be ready for hours. Jack found a rock-hard chunk of bread and soaked it in cider. When he had a soft mush, he fed it to the Bard.

Jack was so tired, he kept tripping over things. His eyes blurred. His hands fumbled as he went about his chores. Yet he found time to light a bundle of coltsfoot and leave it smoldering on a stone shelf near the Bard's bed. The smoke would ease the old man's lungs.

Jack had no memory of lying down. He hadn't meant to until he'd fetched more wood. But somehow his body sat down, and then it was only a short distance to the floor. At any rate, Jack was sound asleep with a sack of beans for a pillow when the Nightmare arrived.

Chapter Nine

THE RIDER ON
THE NIGHTMARE

The first thing Jack heard was the wind. It drove out of the sea and howled past the house, making the roof shake. It burrowed under the door. Cold air spread along the floor, and the fire sprang to life. Behind this was a rattling like pebbles rolling on a beach, except that it grew louder and louder until it burst upon Jack's sleep like thunder.

He jumped up. Coals were being blown out of the fire pit by the wind gusting under the door. He ran to sweep them back. The roof groaned, and a huge chunk of thatch lifted up and was torn away. Four or five crows that had been sheltering there tumbled into the room and fluttered to the safety of the Bard's bed. From a distance came the hideous pounding of hooves coming closer until the whole sky rang with it.

Jack could see the sky. It stretched over the gaping

roof, cold and black and filled with heartless winking stars where there had been protecting fog before. He had to do something, but what? He couldn't think. The pounding drove everything out of his brain. He wanted only to flee. He stepped back, and his foot came down on a live coal. The pain cleared his wits enough for him to realize what was happening.

It was the Nightmare. She'd returned under cover of darkness. She'd discovered the Bard's weakness and had come to destroy him. Jack grasped the rune of protection around his neck. It was strangely warm—no, *hot*. It poured its heat into his body like a noonday sun.

Jack heard the Bard give a long, terrified wail. It was a dreadful sound, like a rabbit caught in the talons of a hawk. The old man thrashed, and the crows clung to the sheepskin over him. "Move! You're scaring him!" shouted the boy, but the crows only clacked their beaks and held on grimly.

The thundering was almost overhead. It was worse than the worst winter storm. It was more violent than the sea dashing against a cliff. Jack had never heard such a loud noise before, and it dazed him. He clung to the bed and stared up at the hole in the roof. He was no more capable of moving than the crows.

Suddenly, out of the deep sky came a figure so large and so terrifying that Jack shouted and the birds shrieked in fear. It was a horse draped in shrouds of icicles that broke off and clattered into the room. Its body was gray, its mane was ragged and cobwebby, *and it had too many legs*! Jack didn't count them, but he knew there were far more than there should have been.

On the horse's back was a rider even darker than the sky, so black that it sucked the light out of the stars. Its thorny legs clasped the belly of the horse, drawing blood—white, oozing blood that was more like pus than anything. The horse screamed. Jack fell to the floor, all thought gone, all consciousness of anything gone but the pulsing warmth of the pendant nestled over his heart.

He woke in darkness. The fire was out. The hole in the roof showed stars but no Nightmare, thank goodness. The air was still, as though the storm had never happened.

Jack felt his way to the truckle bed. The Bard was breathing peacefully, and he appeared to be asleep. Jack's heart turned over with relief. He reached for the sheepskin cover, touched one of the crows, and got a nip.

"Go away!" he yelled, slapping at the bird. He heard several low grumbles in the dark. "Nobody asked you to come," Jack cried. He thought about sweeping the creatures out with a broom, but it occurred to him that it was nice to have company, even bad-tempered crows. He wasn't sure he could have stood solitude after seeing whatever that was on the Nightmare's back.

I mustn't dwell on it, he told himself. The Bard said it was wrong to brood about evil. It was better to think of good things like sunlight and green trees. There was no telling what drove the Nightmare off, but at least she was gone and the old man had come to no harm. Tomorrow they would make a plan to defeat her.

Jack searched until he found flint and iron. He gathered the dead coals and relit them. The pot of soup was ice-cold. Either he'd been out longer than he thought or the Nightmare's rider had sucked the warmth out of it.

Mustn't think of that. Mustn't think of that, Jack told himself.

He lit as many rushlights as he could find. They made a huge difference. They even cheered up the crows, who hopped out of the truckle bed and approached the fire pit. The birds eyed the cauldron thoughtfully. "Don't even think of eating that," Jack said. The crows clacked their beaks as if to say, *We'll see.*

Jack stayed awake until the hole in the roof turned gray. *Must gather thatching grass,* he thought, adding the chore to an already overwhelming list. When he looked again, the sky was bright blue and it was clear he'd taken a nap.

"I know we should make fog, sir," Jack said in the Bard's direction as he rubbed the stiffness out of his arms and legs. "But you need to rest, and I need to find food. I'll go down to the beach after breakfast." He stirred the cauldron. The peas had melted into a satisfying mush. The smell of onions and bacon made his stomach rumble. One crow, bolder than the rest, hopped closer.

"Go away," Jack said, waving the spoon. A dollop of stew flew off and was pounced on. "Shoo! This food's for people, not you. You can gather whelks if you're hungry." Jack filled a bowl and placed a heavy iron lid on the cauldron. He kicked at the birds as he walked to the truckle bed. He'd never seen such bold creatures.

The Bard lay with his eyes open. "Would you mind sitting up?" the boy said politely. "It'll make it a lot easier to feed you." The Bard blinked and sniffed. A line of drool appeared at the edge of his beard.

"Let me help you," Jack said. He wedged the bowl between his knees to keep the birds away from it. He reached for the Bard's arms.

"Wud-*duh,*" said the old man.

"What did you say? Water?" said Jack. "Do you want water?"

"Wud-*duh.*"

"I don't understand," the boy said, suddenly frightened.

"Gaaw," said the Bard. Only the line of drool on his beard showed his interest in the stew.

"Are you sick? If you're too sick to talk, nod your head."

"Wud-*duh!*" The Bard appeared to be getting angry. His eyes flashed and his mouth puckered. Jack was thunderstruck. What had happened to the man? This was an illness far beyond Jack's ability to understand. Had the Nightmare stolen the Bard's wits? Or his *soul?*

"Please, sir, you're frightening me. If you'd only try to sit up, I could help you." But the old man continued to make strange noises, and presently, he grew so enraged that his face turned red and he roared like a baby having a temper tantrum.

Jack tried to spoon food into the Bard's mouth. The old man turned his head and sprayed stew all over the truckle bed. "Gaaw!" he screamed.

"It's good, it's really good. See, I'll taste it first," said Jack frantically. The stew *was* good. Jack's stomach clamored for more, and he had to be strict with himself not to empty the bowl. He tried to feed the Bard again and was rewarded with a gobbet of food spat in his face. The crows exploded with caws.

"Laugh at me, will you?" Jack shouted, beside himself with frustration. He hurled the bowl at the birds, which of course gave them the opportunity they were waiting for. They landed on the spilled stew and gobbled it up in a trice.

"How could I be so dumb?" Jack felt close to tears. The food was almost gone, and he'd thrown part of it away in a fit of rage. He was no closer to rousing the Bard from his strange enchantment. "At least drink something," Jack said. He soaked a scrap of woolen cloth in water and dribbled it into the old man's mouth, the way Mother had fed Lucy when she was a baby. The Bard fastened on to the wool and began sucking for all he was worth.

"At last we're getting somewhere," muttered Jack. He continued pouring water on the cloth until the Bard had had enough. Then the boy refilled the bowl and this time dipped the wool in the stew and gave it to the old man to chew.

It seemed to take hours, dipping and feeding, each time prying the Bard's jaws apart. Finally, the man spat out the wool and belched. A sleepy, contented look came into his eyes. Jack sat down by the cauldron and—at long last—satisfied the hunger that had been gnawing at him.

What was he to do now? Call up fog by himself? Go to the

forest to seek help? He wasn't sure it was safe to leave the Bard alone.

All but one of the crows had departed through the hole in the roof. This one waited just out of reach of Jack's foot and watched him with sharp eyes. It was a fine creature with black feathers groomed to perfection. Its only defect was a missing claw on its left foot. Jack thought it must have come too close to a fox.

"All right. You can have a spoonful. *One* spoonful," said Jack. He held it out, and the bird fed delicately, like a cat. "Who taught you that?" the boy cried with delight. He gave the crow another spoonful. "Maybe the Bard did. People say he talks to birds, though he's never shown me how.

"I wish you could tell me what to do," the boy went on. "I've got to protect the village, but I also have to protect the Bard. And I can't go long without food. Magic makes you really hungry." The crow bobbed up and down as though to say, *You got that right.* Jack laughed and gave it another dollop of stew.

"I ought to take the Bard to the forest," Jack mused aloud. "That way he'll be safe and I can protect the villagers." Something stirred deep inside the boy's heart, like hearing a hawk scream on a frosty morning or seeing a dolphin leap out of a wave. It was unexpected—and scary—and yet wonderfully exciting. *I can do the job by myself,* he thought. *I won't be an apprentice anymore. I'll be a real bard.*

The crow hopped to the door and tapped on the wood with its beak. "You're right," Jack said. "The sooner we get going, the better." He threw open the door. The sky was clear, and the sun had risen almost to noon.

Jack tugged at the Bard until he had the old man standing. Then it was merely a matter of keeping him going. To do this, Jack tied a rope around the Bard's waist and pulled. Slowly, steadily, the old man put one foot in front of the other, apparently quite willing to go for a walk. "Wud-*duh*," he said with great authority.

"I couldn't agree more," said Jack as he led the Bard down the path to the village.

Jack's original plan was to go through the village to the forest. But the Bard moved so slowly, he began to despair of getting there before dark. They passed below Jack's farm. The boy looked up with longing. What a fine, well-built place it was! Every building, every fence and field of it had been shaped by Father's hands. It looked so terribly deserted now. Jack wiped his eyes with a sleeve and grimly yanked on the rope tied around the Bard's waist.

No response. Jack turned and saw that the old man had taken it into his head to sit down. "Not now," the boy said. "I know you're tired, sir, but we simply can't stop until we've reached shelter."

"Gaaw," said the Bard, staring up at the house.

Jack followed his gaze. There was a wisp of white coming out of the smoke hole. Was the place on fire? Jack dropped the rope and sprinted up the hill. It was definitely fire. He could smell it. He threw himself at the door, found it bolted, and pounded on it with his fists.

"Don't move, Lucy," whispered a voice Jack recognized.

"It's me, Mother! It's Jack! What's wrong? Why are you here?"

There was a pause and then the sound of an iron latch being drawn back. Father peered out. Jack saw he had a pitchfork ready to jab whoever stood outside. Behind him Mother held a pot of boiling water.

Lucy shrieked and pushed by her father. "Oh, darling," said Mother, putting down the pot.

"Welcome home," said Father mildly, as though it were perfectly normal to aim a pitchfork at a visitor.

"Now everything's perfect," Lucy cried, dancing around. She pulled Jack inside. The house was bare, with most of the belongings buried or hidden in the forest, but beds of heather lay close to the hearth and a bag of provisions leaned against a wall.

Jack felt dazed. "Has everyone moved back to the village?" he asked.

"Only us," said Father.

"We're the smart ones," said Lucy.

Jack looked at Mother, who was the only one who seemed uneasy. "It was Lucy," she began.

"The forest was nasty! It was all wet and cold," Lucy cried. "The ground was covered with rocks. It was no place for a lost princess."

"It was a *safe* place for a lost princess," said Jack. He knew at once what had happened. Lucy, faced for the first time with discomfort, had demanded to return. He knew how persistent she could be. She would go on and on until you wanted to slap her, only you didn't, of course, because she was so small and beautiful. "I think it's a really bad idea to stay here," Jack said.

"I know, but—" Mother gestured at Father. Giles Crookleg had clearly caved in to Lucy's pleas. He had never denied her anything.

"I'm *not* going back!" yelled Lucy. "Not after last night!"

"Well, there was something awful," Mother said.

"It was like the End of Days," said Father in a hollow voice. "It came screaming out of the sky. Ice fell like daggers. The stars were blotted out. People ran around, banging into trees. The blacksmith's son knocked himself out, and the horses broke their tethers and ran off. They were still looking for them this morning."

"The Nightmare," murmured Jack. And then he remembered. "Oh, my stars, I forgot. The Bard was attacked last night—something magic, I don't really understand it—but his wits have fled. I was taking him to the forest."

They went down to the road. The old man had planted himself in the middle like a tree stump. "The wolf-headed men will get you if you don't move," said Jack. He grabbed the Bard's arms and pulled.

"Wow-wow-wow-*wow*!" the man screamed.

"Shush. Don't make a noise." Jack tried to cover the Bard's mouth, and the man's teeth came down hard.

"Wud-*duh*!"

"I'll wudduh you right back," Jack shouted, nursing his hand. "No, I won't. I didn't mean that. But you're driving me crazy. I know you're under a spell, sir, so I won't take offense. *But couldn't you help out just a bit?*"

"No point reasoning with him. He's like a sheep." Giles Crookleg lifted the old man right off the ground. He staggered back to the house as the Bard bellowed and tried to kick him. Father might have been lame, but years of hard work had toughened his muscles. "Whew!" he said, dumping the old man, none too gently, on the floor. "You're right about his wits, son. They're clean gone. Did you say the Nightmare got them?"

"I don't know. Maybe it's a spell."

"Or maybe it's just age," Mother said gently. She wiped the Bard's face with a damp cloth and put a rolled-up cloak under his head for a pillow. "With rest and care, it may come right."

Jack sat on the floor, trying to think. It wasn't easy with Lucy climbing over him and telling him of her woes in the forest. "The fog was awful! It got into everything, and the chief wouldn't let us light a fire. He's so mean!"

"The Bard called up fog to protect you," Jack said.

"Pooh!" Lucy sneered. "Anything can walk through that. Monsters! Trolls!"

"Don't talk about trolls."

"I will if I want. Trolls and trolls and trolls and trolls!"

Jack's hand itched to slap her.

"Leave him alone, dearest," said Mother. She distracted Lucy with a handful of hazelnuts. The little girl applied herself to smashing them with a rock and picking out the kernels.

"You mean the *Bard* called up the fog?" said Father. "That's not the act of a God-fearing man. That's wizardry."

Why didn't I keep my mouth shut? Jack thought. Anything to do with magic set Giles Crookleg off. It was evil. It reeked of fire and brimstone. Demons with long claws would drag you off.

"I hope he hasn't been leading you down the paths of wickedness," Father said. "Hellfire awaits those who transgress the laws of God."

"It was a normal fog," Jack said wearily. "I was only trying to explain things to Lucy." He felt overwhelmed by the situation. His family had walked back into danger. The Bard was out of his head. And the wolf-headed men might be moving along the Roman road at this very moment. He felt very, very tired.

"Perhaps you'd like to sit in the garden and eat something," Mother said. Jack realized she knew far more than she was letting on. He suddenly understood the unspoken sympathy that existed between the Bard and his mother. She was a wise woman herself with magic to charm bees and wild beasts. Why had he never understood this before? But perhaps working with the life force had sharpened his wits. Now he recognized the gentle spells that had been woven around his childhood, the songs that cooled fevers, the touch that made even the plainest food taste good.

"Thank you, Mother," Jack said. Soon he was in the herb garden with a cup of hot cider and bread spread with honey. Mother looked north to the Roman road. She said nothing, but she knew. It was from there the danger would come.

As soon as Mother left, Jack got to his feet. He was tired and achy. More than anything he wanted to be a small child again, with no worries and no responsibilities. But it was not to be. That time was gone. Only he stood between the village and the wolf-headed men, and it was his duty to see the job through.

Chapter Ten

—◦◦◦—

OLAF ONE-BROW

Jack sat in a hollow near the Roman road. He was surrounded by bracken like a rabbit hiding from a fox. No one would be able to see him, but Jack intended to be even more invisible. He breathed in the green odors of earth and fern. He felt with his mind the damp roots of trees. *Come forth,* he called. *Come forth to me. Cloak the air with your gray presences. Bring sea and sky together.*

He felt, rather than saw, the curling mist. Sunlight muted to pearl white, to dove feather and dusk. Dampness flowed into his lungs. Water gathered on ferns. Round drops paused on the tips of leaves and fell, sending pale threads over moss. The air sighed and rustled with it.

He had never been so deep in the life force. He swam through it like a minnow, like a woodland creature with no more thought than to *be*. It was enough. It was more than enough. The glory and wonder of it swept him on.

"Jack . . . Jack . . ."

The voice reached him from a great distance. He turned from it, unwilling to become human again.

"Jack . . . oh, please! I'm so cold and scared!"

He came to his senses. For a moment he was filled with unreasoning anger. How dare anyone disturb him!

He heard gulping, hiccuping cries that cut him to the heart. It was Lucy! She was nearby but hidden by a fog so thick and heavy, it frightened even Jack. He'd really outdone himself this time. "Lucy, I'm here," he called.

"Where's 'here'? It's so dark and awful. I know there's monsters." She began to sob.

"Don't move, Lucy. Just keep talking so I can find you."

"When I went outside, it was sunny. You were *supposed* to be in the garden. Father said you were in the garden, but you *weren't*." Some of Lucy's fear was replaced by indignation.

Jack tripped over a rock and scratched himself on a branch.

"I saw you from far away," said Lucy. "You were walking fast. I wanted to call, but I didn't want Mother to know I was outside. She's been so mean to me today. She wouldn't let me play outside or anything."

Jack thought Mother was out of her mind with worry. She knew the danger they were in. So did Father, but he chose to ignore it.

"I walked to the Roman road, but you were gone. You

went off and left me. Bad Jack! Then the fog came in really fast. It got dark and I got scared. Have you been doing magic? Father says wizards do magic and then they go to Hell. Are you going to Hell?"

"I couldn't even find it in this fog," muttered Jack. He felt the edge of the road with his feet. A moment later he saw Lucy crouched on the stones. He touched her arm, and she screamed. "It's me," he said, fending off her blows.

"Why did you sneak up on me like that?" she wailed.

"I wasn't sneaking—oh, never mind. Listen, I've got a very important job to do, and I need you to be quiet."

"I'm always quiet. I can keep my mouth shut for hours. Father says I'm like a dear little mouse. He said I was changed into a mouse by a bad fairy when I lived in the palace, but a good fairy changed me back."

"How about being quiet now?" Jack said. It seemed to him the air was beginning to move. Perhaps a sea wind had sprung up.

"It's a good story. I can tell it really well. Father says I know as many words as a ten-year-old."

"Shh!" Jack pulled her down into the bracken.

"I'm getting wet," cried Lucy.

"Be quiet. Someone's coming along the road," Jack whispered. "Maybe a monster," he added. Lucy clung to him and made no more complaints about wetness. In the distance they heard voices. They were too far to distinguish words, but something about the sound made Jack's hair prickle on the back of his neck. Then, shockingly, someone blew a hunting horn nearby.

Lucy tried to dive under Jack's shirt. He held her close, feeling her tremble and himself tremble. Far away another horn answered.

"*Hvað er þetta?*" someone said so close that Jack almost yelled. He heard more voices—four or five. The fog was definitely thinning. He could see shapes on the road, shaggy beings who walked with a heavy tread. He heard the clank of swords.

Come forth. Come forth to me. Cloak the air with your gray presences, he called to the life force, but his concentration was broken. Terror threatened to overwhelm him. These were the wolf-headed men. They were real. They were on the way to the village.

"Are those knights?" whispered Lucy.

"No. Be quiet." Even without fog, Jack thought they would be well hidden in the bracken. They could escape. But what of Father and Mother? Or the Bard?

"I think they're knights," Lucy said.

"They're monsters. Be quiet."

"*Hvað?*" said one of the men on the road. He strode to the edge and peered out over the bracken.

"*Ekkert. þetta er bara kanína,*" said another.

The words were almost like Saxon, Jack's own tongue. He'd heard a few other languages in his life, from people who passed through at village fairs. He'd heard Welsh, Erse, Pictish, and of course Latin, but he could speak none of them. They were nothing like his own speech. This was. He was almost certain the first man had said *What?* and the second had replied *Nothing. It's only a rabbit.*

Lucy wriggled beside him, and he tightened his hold on her. The warriors above were growing ever more clear. They were cloaked in sheepskins and wore leather caps over their long, pale hair. Swords and axes hung from their belts. One was only a boy.

For a long moment the men conferred, and then, miraculously, they turned back the way they had come. They would miss the village! Jack hugged Lucy. "They're going," she whispered.

"Shh," said Jack. The boy had turned and was once again scanning the bracken.

"*Komdu,* Thorgil," called one of the men.

"They're the knights come to take me to my castle," Lucy cried out suddenly. "Here I am! Here!"

The boy on the road shouted, "*Parna er kanínan!*" He leaped into the bracken, knife in hand, and grabbed Lucy. Jack tried to knock him down, but the boy yanked her up by the hair and held the knife to her throat. By now the men were running back.

Jack had one instant—only one—in which he could have fled, leaving Lucy behind in the clutches of the berserkers. He couldn't do it. She was so little and helpless. He was her brother. He had no hope of defeating such a band of warriors, but he could stay with her, little though that might accomplish. At least they would die together.

In the next instant a huge man with one bushy eyebrow extending across his forehead fell on Jack like a tree and knocked him senseless.

❖ ❖ ❖

The ground was moving. It tossed him up first and then slid him down in a nauseating roll. Jack gulped for air, got foul-tasting water instead, and then he did vomit. He crouched on hands and knees. He had been lying facedown in a filthy pool, and his whole body was wet and cold. The ground heaved again.

"*Þrællinn er vaknaður,*" someone said.

Jack's head throbbed. He looked down to see a drop of blood plop into the disgusting pool. He felt his hair. It was matted and sticky. How had that happened?

"*Hei þræll! Þú hefur svolitið kettlingaklór þarna.*" There was crude laughter, and several other voices joined in.

Jack struggled to understand. They were speaking something like Saxon, but the accent was so barbaric, he could make out only one word in three. Was *þræll* their word for *thrall*? If so—Jack had to think hard—it meant "servant" or possibly "slave." That didn't sound good. *Kettlingur*, which was close to *kettlingaklór*, meant "kitten." What did kittens have to do with him?

Jack looked up—his head hurt so much, he was afraid to move quickly. The ground pitched again, and he saw, beyond a wooden railing, a vast expanse of gray water. He looked to the other side. More water.

He was on a ship! Jack had been in little coracles close to shore. He used them to reach small islands at low tide, to gather seagull eggs and whelks. He never went far. Now he saw no islands, only a heaving gray sea with a pitiless gray sky above. He moaned and ducked his head to shut out the terrible sight.

"*Skræfan þín.*"

Skrafan thin. Jack easily translated that into his own language. It was a favorite insult thrown back and forth between the village boys: "scaredy-pants." Well, he *was* scared. Who wouldn't be? He was adrift on the open sea with no memory of how he got there.

He turned to get a look at who was talking and flinched. It was a *giant.* Maybe not a true giant—they were supposed to have hands big enough to pick up an ox. But this creature was certainly taller than any man Jack had seen. He had blond braids hanging past his shoulders, a massive beard covering his chest, and one bushy eyebrow extending all the way across his face.

Now the boy remembered. In that fragment of time between seeing Lucy with a knife at her throat and the utter darkness that followed, there was an instant where a huge one-browed man had hurled himself at Jack. This was he! This was a berserker in the flesh, every bit as dreadful as the stories said. Beyond him Jack saw other men pulling on oars. They were smaller than the giant but just as evil-looking.

Lucy! What had happened to her? Had they—? It was unthinkable! But men who could slaughter the gentle monks would think nothing of killing a girl. Jack closed his eyes. He had failed to save the one person he was bound to protect. His fragile little sister had been tossed aside as if she were of no more importance than a mouse.

He found that having his eyes closed made him even more seasick.

Jack pulled himself up and staggered to the rail. It would take only a small effort to throw himself over the side. Why not? What did he have to live for? Lucy was dead, perhaps even his parents. He didn't know what had happened while he was unconscious. His future was bleak. The berserkers would probably kill him in some entertaining way. They might even *eat* him.

Jack felt dizzy with pain and despair. He'd failed everyone, even the Bard. If the old man hadn't given him the rune of protection, he might have withstood the Nightmare.

Jack felt at his neck. There it was, invisible but still warm to the touch. What a laugh! It saved his life for what? He was a miserable failure who let berserkers kill his sister. He let the Nightmare steal the Bard's wits. The poor old man would wander until he found the Valley of Lunatics. At least there he'd make friends.

Jack's mouth quirked. What was *wrong* with him? He had nothing to smile about. Yet the thought of the Bard having a party in the Valley of Lunatics—all of them saying "wudduh" and "gaaw" and nodding wisely—well, it was *kind* of funny. *No, it's not,* Jack told himself sternly.

Yes, it is, said his mouth, insisting on quirking up.

He felt warmth spreading from the hidden rune. It filled him with a distant hope. After all, he didn't know that his parents were dead. The Bard might recover. Life was precious and not to be thrown away heedlessly.

At that moment Jack looked down the length of the boat and saw the boy who'd killed Lucy. Jack lurched forward, but he saw he wouldn't get past the men. They sat squarely in the middle, each one hauling on a pair of oars. The giant sat in front on a wooden chest.

"*Hvert ertu að fara?*" said the giant.

Where are you going? Jack translated.

"To kill that boy," he said, pointing.

For a moment the giant appeared to be working it out. Then his eyes opened wide. "*Að drepa þetta brjóstabarn. Ha! Ha! Ha! Ha!*"

"*Ég er ekki brjóstabarn!*" came the outraged voice of the boy.

"*Jú, það ertu!*"

The men all seemed to find this extremely funny. They roared and hooted. The boy protested in his higher, shriller voice.

"*Það er gott,*" said the giant, wiping tears from his eyes. He moved his tree-trunk-size legs to one side and signaled the other men to do likewise. "*Að drepa þetta brjóstabarn. Ha! Ha! Ha! Ha!*"

What kind of people were these? thought Jack. They knew he wanted to commit murder, and they liked it! He didn't understand the word *brjóstabarn,* but *drepa* most definitely meant "kill." He pushed his way past the berserkers, stepping over legs and under elbows. He didn't know what he was going to do when he got back there.

He came out from under the last smelly, sheepskin-clad

arm and tripped over Lucy. She was crouched in the dirty water at the bottom of the boat. "It's about time," she sniffled. "I've been suffering most horribly, and all you did was sleep."

"You're alive! Oh, thank Heaven!" He hugged his little sister, who at once burst into tears.

"I've been trying to tell these knights to take me to the castle," she sobbed.

"They aren't knights," Jack said, unsure of how much to tell Lucy.

"You can say that again! They smell like hogs and bark like dogs. And they laugh at me. Tell them to take us home right now."

"I don't think they'll obey me," said Jack.

"*Hei þræll! Því drepurðu ekki þetta brjóstabarn?*"

"He's asking why you don't kill me," said the boy in perfect Saxon. "If you try, I'll cut your head off." He continued plying his oar, which was different from the others. It hung from a kind of hinge and went straight down into the water.

"You're the *brjóstabarn*?" Jack said.

For answer, the boy kicked Jack in the stomach and followed up with another blow to the head. "You're a dirty thrall. I can kill you whenever I want."

The blow opened up the cut on Jack's head. He wanted to fight back, but he was too weak. All he could manage was to hold his stomach and try to keep from vomiting.

"You monster!" shrieked Lucy. "You—you *brjóstabarn*!" She scrambled under the forest of arms and legs to the giant and climbed onto his lap by pulling on his braids.

"No . . . no . . . ," moaned Jack. He expected the giant to hurl Lucy into the sea.

"You've got to do something!" Lucy was screaming. "You're my knights, and you're supposed to be taking me to my castle. Get off that box and beat that *brjóstabarn*!"

Instead of getting angry, the giant gave another of his barking laughs. He put Lucy down and made his way to the stern of the boat. It swayed sickeningly under his weight. *"Hann er þrællinn minn,* Thorgil," he said, slapping the boy so hard, his head snapped back. *"Þú mátt ekki drepa hann."* Then he trudged back to his box.

Thorgil ground his teeth, but he didn't utter a sound. He glared at Jack with a hatred so intense, Jack could almost feel it. Meanwhile, Lucy had returned. She squatted in the dirty water and patted Jack's arm. "I'll protect you," she said. "After all, I'm a princess."

Gradually, the bleeding stopped, and Jack was able to recover from the vicious blow to his stomach. He couldn't think of a thing to do, other than stay alive for Lucy's sake. She had no idea of their extreme danger. To her, this was merely an uncomfortable adventure.

After a long while Thorgil turned to Jack and once again spoke in perfect Saxon. "I will not kill you because you belong to Olaf One-Brow. It is his privilege to do so. However, the girl is my thrall." He smiled coldly. "I will kill her whenever I wish, if you displease me." And he turned again to ply his single oar.

Chapter Eleven

THE SHIELD MAIDEN

They traveled all day, with breaks to let the oarsmen rest. The sky remained gray, but the clouds lifted enough for Jack to see land far to the left. At one point they passed an island that trailed plumes of smoke. Was that the Holy Isle? It was too hazy to tell.

At one point the rowers halted, and Olaf One-Brow passed out smoked fish, cheese, and a kind of flatbread Jack had never seen before. He thought it delicious until he realized it had been stolen from some poor village. Olaf found a pot of honey and smeared it on the bread for Lucy. No one else got this treat.

"*Litla valkyrja,*" the giant rumbled, tousling Lucy's hair.

"Princess," corrected Lucy. They smiled at each other.

"Pest," said the boy at the oar.

Jack studied him. Thorgil was handsome, in a sullen way. His eyes were blue, and his hair would have been as golden as Lucy's if it hadn't been so dirty. The berserkers were all filthy, Jack realized. Their boots smelled like carrion, and their sheepskins reeked of sweat. Lucy, in her sky blue dress, looked like a flower dropped into a pigsty.

What was he to do about her? Jack might try swimming to shore by himself, but he couldn't leave her behind. Olaf One-Brow might possibly be talked into setting her free, but Lucy didn't belong to him. The berserkers set great store by ownership. Once Thorgil had pinched her, to see Jack's reaction, and Olaf had done nothing about it.

They slid north on the gray ocean until the sun broke out in late afternoon. It hovered, red and swollen, over the horizon as they turned toward land. Jack saw a dense forest and fires along the shore. Two other boats had been drawn up. Shouts greeted their arrival.

Altogether the warriors numbered about forty men and seven boys. The ones on shore were showing off the booty they had taken—embroidered shawls, necklaces, even pairs of dainty ladies' shoes draped about their necks like trophies. They pranced around, guffawing and pointing at one another. Other loot was displayed on the sand: metalwork, pottery, spoons, swags of richly colored cloth, and a jeweled cross that might have come from the Holy Isle. Huddled next to the forest were the captives, with their legs hobbled.

Jack was hustled to this group, but Lucy was presented like a rare prize to the assembled warriors. Olaf lifted her over his head and boomed *"Litla valkyrja!"* before he put her down. Everyone admired her. Lucy bowed. They bowed back. She clapped her hands and they laughed. She was caught up in her princess fantasy, but Jack was desperately worried about the berserkers' true motives.

"She's a little charmer, isn't she?" a woman said. She was thin, her eyes full of grief. "I had a daughter. She wasn't as beautiful as your sister." She fell silent, and Jack thought he knew what had happened. The woman's daughter had not been pretty enough to keep.

"The girl's a slave like the rest of us," said a man in a torn monk's robe. "They'll raise her like a prize pig and then sell her."

"At least she's alive," Jack said.

"Sometimes death is better."

"No, it isn't."

The monk laughed harshly. "Hark at him! The child presumes to lecture his elders. Listen, boy. Long life is but a chance to commit more sins. The longer you live, the more Satan whispers in your ear. Your soul grows so heavy, it gets dragged down to Hell. It's better to die young, preferably right after baptism, and be taken into Heaven."

"My daughter is in Heaven," said the sad-eyed woman.

"Yes, well, you don't know that," the monk said. "Even quite small children are capable of evil."

"I *know* she is," the woman said fiercely.

"And I believe you," said Jack. "I think it depends on whether someone means to be bad. My sister Lucy can drive you crazy, but she hasn't an evil bone in her body."

"Man is born corrupt," the monk said in a hollow voice. Jack made no answer. That was the sort of thing Father said all the time.

The warriors gorged themselves on roast meat until their bellies bulged and their beards shone with grease. They drank mead until they fell over. Fights broke out. More than one man went to bed with a cut lip or a bloody nose, but it seemed to be in good fun. Jack noticed, however, that some did not take part.

Olaf One-Brow's group camped by themselves. No one playfully punched them or threw sand in their hair. No one uttered a catcall in their direction. It seemed that Olaf's men were too important to indulge in horseplay.

The exception was Thorgil. Another lad with chopped-off hair ran past the group and threw a pebble at the boy. Thorgil sprang to his feet with a shout and took off after the offender. Round and round they went until Thorgil caught up with his tormentor.

"*Hættu!*" cried the short-haired lad.

"*Aldrei! Nei!*" shouted Thorgil.

The others danced around, singing, "*Dreptu hann! Dreptu hann!*"

"They're saying, 'Kill him! Kill him!'" the monk said quietly.

"You know their language?" said Jack. Thorgil was getting the best of the fight because he was so much more frenzied.

"Oh, yes. I have had occasion to preach to these . . . animals."

By now the short-haired lad was trying to escape, but Thorgil pulled him back and proceeded to pound and kick him in a sickening way. The cries of the watchers changed to *"Nóg! Hættu!"*

"They're saying, 'Enough! Stop!' But she won't," said the monk.

"She?" Jack was startled from his fascination with the fight. It was getting nasty, with Thorgil pulling the boy's head back in an attempt to break his neck.

"Oh, yes. That's a girl."

"Nóg," growled Olaf One-Brow, plucking Thorgil from the fray as easily as picking up a kitten. The short-haired boy scuttled off on hands and knees. The others scattered.

"I'm surprised," said the monk. "Olaf usually lets a fight go through to the end." The giant lumbered back across the sand with Thorgil tucked firmly under his arm.

"How can that be a girl?" said Jack. He'd known some bad-tempered girls in the village, but none of them would have thrown themselves into such a vicious fight. None of the boys, either, for that matter.

"She's a shield maiden," said the monk. "A little abomination who will certainly toast her heels in Hell for all eternity. She's trying to make the grade with Olaf, so she's twice as likely to pick fights as his men. And they're no slouches." The monk stared long and hard at the group. By now most of the warriors had collapsed on the sand in a drunken stupor. Only Olaf's men spread cloths and lay down properly.

They formed a square as though, even in sleep, they were

in military formation. In the middle lay Thorgil. Next to her, on a blanket, was Lucy. She had a real pillow and a richly embroidered cover that might have been taken from a church altar.

"What's a *brjóstabarn*?" said Jack.

"What a strange question," said the monk.

"It's what Olaf called Thorgil."

"Ah." The monk nodded in somber understanding. "It means 'suckling baby.' He's calling Thorgil that to make her angry. Making people angry is a favorite pastime of the Northmen."

"And what is a—" Jack had to stop to recall the word."—a *kettlingaklór*?"

The monk laughed bitterly. "It means 'kitten scratch.' It's what these people call a blow that knocks you flat. I gather you had one."

"Yes," said Jack.

"You seem no worse for it. Trust me, you don't want to find out what a really big cat scratch feels like."

With that, the monk withdrew into his own thoughts and refused to talk. Jack watched the flickering fires, the sprawled warriors, and the neat square where Olaf and his people lay.

The captives were guarded by three men, who had not been allowed to drink. Escape was impossible. Besides, Jack thought as he stretched out on the cold, damp ground, he couldn't leave without Lucy. And there was no way he was going to rescue her from that ominous square of Olaf's men.

❖❖❖

They camped on the beach for several days. Boats went out and returned with booty. Finally, when the warriors had amassed as much as they could carry, the whole group sailed north.

It was extremely uncomfortable. Jack and the other captives were packed like trussed-up chickens. They lay faceup, able to see only the sky and to feel the cold water sloshing under their backs. The boats leaked continuously. Captives were freed in shifts to bail them out. When it was Jack's turn, he was horrified to see how near the sea came to spilling inside. The boat was so heavily laden, one more roll of cloth could send them to the bottom.

That's a girl, he thought, eyeing Thorgil. He now understood that her oar was a rudder used to steer the boat. Plying a real oar would have been beyond her strength. Jack tried to imagine her in a dress and couldn't. She was too brutish. When the men tossed insults back and forth, she outdid them in malice. When they spat and farted, she joined in.

Altogether she was the most disgusting creature—male or female—Jack had ever seen. He had always to come between her and Lucy, for Thorgil's greatest joy was to cause pain. She never—quite—drew blood, but Lucy's arms were covered with bruises from pinches.

Jack wondered at the little girl's ability to keep up her spirits. Surely by now she knew she wasn't headed for a castle. At the very least she must miss Mother and Father. Yet Lucy picked herself up after every pinch, wiped her eyes, and found Olaf. She ordered him around like a favorite hound, and if the giant didn't actually obey her, Lucy pretended he did. It was curious and disturbing at the same time.

Olaf wasn't a safe companion. He dealt out punishment with a quick hand, breaking teeth or cracking a rib according to his mood. Seeing Lucy with the monster made Jack sick. But there was nothing he could do about it.

On the third day a storm rose. The boat rolled frighteningly and waves splashed over the side. All the captives bailed furiously while the oarsmen struggled to reach shore. The sad-eyed woman collapsed. She hadn't been strong to begin with. Olaf dragged her up, and with a swift movement that made Jack cry out, he cut her throat and threw her over the side.

Jack and the others were frozen for one long moment. Then they redoubled their efforts before Olaf turned his attention to them. Even so, the shore remained agonizingly distant. The oarsmen were pushed back by the wind and lost two strokes of progress for every three they made. Thorgil clung grimly to her rudder. The sea attempted to snatch it out of her control, but she ground her teeth and fought back.

"May angels carry you to your daughter's side," whispered the monk as he toiled. "May your time in purgatory be short."

He was praying for the poor, murdered woman. Tears rolled down Jack's face, mixed with rain. He didn't even know her name, and already her face was blurred in his memory. *May the life force hold you in the hollow of its hand,* Jack thought, repeating words he had learned from the Bard. *May you return with the sun and be born anew into the world.*

It wasn't a prayer Father would have liked. He would have

knocked Jack six ways to Sunday for saying it. But Jack thought it right and sensible to call on two religions, in case one failed.

Lucy was packed between rolls of fur and cloth. Jack could hear her crying over the storm, which was so intense now, he couldn't see the stern of the boat. He tried not to think about the poor, dead woman. His duty was to see that Lucy didn't suffer the same fate—if they didn't both drown, that is. Jack no longer felt the sharp terror that had been with him in the first days of their captivity. The best he could manage was a dull, oxlike misery.

Olaf moved down the ship, handing out coins to the men.

"Now we're in real trouble," grunted the monk.

"Is he *paying* them?" said Jack, who was so exhausted, he no longer felt pain.

"He's giving them gold so they won't show up empty-handed in the halls of their sea god. Satan will take that gold off them and kick them straight down to Hell." The monk smiled cheerlessly.

Even a little hellfire would be welcome now, Jack thought. The cold made him clumsy, and the bailing bucket kept slipping out of hands. He was so tired, he saw spots before his eyes. He was terrified of fainting. Fainting meant death.

"*Land fyrir stafni!*" someone shouted. A gap in the driving rain showed they were, in fact, quite close to shore. A moment later Jack felt sand under the keel. The oarsmen jumped out and wrestled the boat through the waves to safety.

❖ ❖ ❖

They lay like so many drowned rats on the shore. No one, not even the berserkers, had the strength to move. They had dragged the boat as far from the waves as possible and then collapsed. Jack managed to reach Lucy and held her in his arms. The sea boomed, the wind howled, and rain poured endlessly. In the boat were oilskins to erect as shelters, but no one made a move to unpack them.

Presently, darkness fell. Sunset had not been far off when they came to shore. Jack felt Lucy shudder and tried to dig a hole for her in the sand. At least that would give her some protection from the growing cold. He sat up. A few warriors—Olaf among them—had recovered enough to rise. They bellowed orders, following them with kicks. Slowly, painfully, the captives struggled to their feet. Those who could not were dragged roughly to a field above the tide line.

By now darkness was almost complete. Jack felt a rope being tied around his ankles. He was hobbled to the others, but fortunately, Lucy was not taken from him. He held her close again and, to his relief, felt an oilskin settle over them. The berserkers were not going to lose their cargo to illness.

"There, there," murmured Jack as Lucy continued to shake. His throat felt ragged from shouting over the storm earlier.

"Why won't they take me to my castle?" she said between chattering teeth.

Jack was astounded. Surely she didn't believe that anymore. He paused, uncertain how to answer.

Lucy began to cry. "I keep telling them again and again. They don't listen."

"Dearling, they aren't knights."

"Oh yes they are! Bad ones."

Jack bit his lip and decided to go for the truth. "They're slave traders."

"Don't tell me that!" wailed Lucy. "I don't want to hear it!"

"We have to face it, dearest. We're slaves."

"I don't want to hear it!" She sobbed until her strength was used up. She clung to Jack, shivering and moaning. He couldn't think of a single way to help her. Then, amazingly, Lucy said in a voice that was almost steady, "I know those men aren't knights. I saw that—that poor woman die. I know Thorgil hates me and—and that she'll probably kill me. I'll go to Heaven then, won't I?"

"Of course." Jack's throat felt raw with the urge to cry.

"So that's all right. But until it h-happens, I don't want to think about it. Don't you see? I can't live knowing about it."

And Jack understood. Lucy was like Father. Father was so miserable about his twisted leg, he had to make up stories. Lucy was devastated at being torn from all she had ever known. So was Jack, but he was older. He could stand it. All that stood between Lucy and madness was a thin enchantment of belief. He made a quick decision.

"Most princesses have adventures before they get to their castles," Jack said.

"Sometimes awful ones," said Lucy. She yawned and snuggled close.

"They get carried off by ogres or even fed to dragons. Can

you imagine a worse thing than being tied to a tree in front of a deep dark cave?"

"With smoke coming out." Lucy's voice was getting muzzy.

"Black, ugly, foul-smelling smoke."

"But a knight always comes and rescues them."

"Yes, always," said Jack. He blinked back tears. Lucy's hand relaxed its hold on his tunic. Very soon he heard her babyish snores.

He mustn't cry. He mustn't cry. He was all Lucy had, and he mustn't fail her. Jack felt at his neck. The rune of protection spread warmth over his hand and up his arm. Taking care of Lucy wasn't a bad thing, really. It was much better than having no one at all. *How odd,* Jack thought. He had no more control over his life than a dog on a chain, but caring for Lucy made him feel . . . well . . . strong.

I wish the Bard could explain it to me, Jack thought. He sighed and prepared himself for a long night with the rain pounding on the oilskin over their heads.

Chapter Twelve

THE SLAVE MARKET

After a day's rest they went on, northward along the coast. The land became wilder. Few villages lay in these parts, and those few clung to the rocky shore as though they expected to be blown away by the wind.

The sea was still high, although the rain had stopped and the sun had come out. The captives worked in shifts to bail the ship, a never-ending chore. Now and then Jack saw round towers on the distant hills. They were solitary and somehow threatening. He never saw people around them.

"They're the strongholds of the Picts," said the gloomy monk.

Jack had seen Picts. They sometimes came along the road to his village, trading ironware for food. They were a small, secretive people, covered in blue designs that were said to be permanent. It gave them an almost ghostly appearance, for they could melt into the dappled shade of a forest as easily as an animal. He had never seen more than one or two at a time.

"Are there many of them?" Jack asked, more to pass the time than anything else.

"No one knows," said the monk. "They come out at dawn and dusk and hide from the noonday sun. Some say they are weakened by sunlight. They're fierce warriors, though."

Jack watched the towers with interest, to see a thread of smoke or some other evidence of life. But nothing moved in those hills except the hurrying shadows of the clouds.

Since the storm Jack had felt a weight lift from his shoulders. His situation was no better. He was getting farther from home, yet the sea air seemed full of promise. He understood the motion of the waves now and how the ship responded. He was no longer afraid. In fact, he was beginning to enjoy himself. It was a wonderful thing to travel so swiftly.

"Það er gott. Þú ert hrifinn af sjónum," rumbled Olaf from behind him. Jack flinched in spite of himself.

That's good. You like the sea, the giant was saying. Jack understood more and more of the Northman language. It was like looking into a rippling stream. When you got used to the distortions, the image on the bottom became clear.

"Mér líkar hann," Jack replied. I like it.

This seemed to please the giant, and he took time to teach Jack more words. "Skip," he said, waving his arm at the ship. "Vígamenn." He indicated the warriors. "Brjóstabarn. Ha! Ha!

Ha! Ha!" he said, pointing at Thorgil. Thorgil gritted her teeth.

Even she seemed different after the storm. She tormented Lucy less often and spent her time staring out at the water. She rarely joined in the belching and farting games so beloved of the berserkers. If Jack had to put a name to it, he would have said she was unhappy.

What on earth did she have to be unhappy about? Jack wondered. She was with her own kind, she was going home. It figured that a brute like Thorgil got nicer when she was depressed.

One day they rounded a cape and sailed into a wide bay. At the far end was a large town and a fine wharf. The other berserker ships, which had become separated in the storm, had already arrived. A cheer rose as Olaf stood and blew his battle horn. The ship slid to its berth as smoothly as a bird flying to its nest. Ropes were thrown. Wrestling matches broke out, with warriors being tossed overboard and clambering back for more.

It was such a cheerful gathering, Jack forgot his place in it. But then he saw a crowd of other captives hobbled on the shore. He was a slave. Lucy was a slave. There would be no merrymaking for them. This was probably the place where they would be sold. It was large enough.

Olaf's captives were hustled off to join the others. There they waited through the long day while the warriors celebrated. People came to gawk at them. Jack was prodded and made to stand and turn. His teeth were studied, his eyes pried open to check (so he guessed) for disease. If he'd been unbound, he thought the people would have thrown sticks for him to fetch.

But he wasn't unbound. This was one place where escape was possible and the prisoners were well guarded. Only Lucy was kept separate from the insulting shoppers. Finally, in late afternoon, a new group arrived at the edge of town.

It was hard to tell how many there were. Long blue shadows stretched from the houses and met the darkness under a grove of trees. In this darkness a band of people gradually appeared. Their bodies seemed to writhe with vines, and it was as though the forest itself were waking up. The hair prickled on Jack's neck.

The men approached carefully, silently, like a herd of deer. It was then that Jack saw they were naked—or nearly so. What took the place of clothes were wild, blue designs painted on their skins.

"Picts," he whispered. They were not like the furtive traders in his village, but strong in their numbers and growing stronger with the dark. All at once the Picts crowded forward to the captives, pinching them to see how fat they were.

"*Hættið!*" cried one of the berserkers. *Stop it!* For once Jack was glad of their presence. The warriors pushed the Picts to one side, and Olaf One-Brow strode out to confront them.

"*Ekki núna!*" he roared. *Not now!*

Not ever, thought Jack with his heart pounding.

"*Farið!*" *Go away!*

With a hissing sound, the Picts withdrew. One moment

they were there at the end of the lane, the next they had disappeared back into the forest.

Anything had to be better than being bought by one of them, Jack thought wildly. He would rather slave in a lead mine, lift heavy rocks, shovel manure to the end of his days than be carried off by Picts.

Olaf now set his men to tidying up the captives. They were plunged into icy water, their hair scrubbed with ill-smelling soap. The cold and dripping captives were lined up by crackling bonfires to dry. They were given slabs of bread topped with a hearty meat stew.

It was the best food Jack had eaten for weeks. He bolted it down and licked his fingers for the last savory drops. Bags of cider were passed around, as much as they could drink. Finally, bloated and woozy, Jack stretched out with the others on the ground.

I'm like a farm animal, he thought as the rich food churned in his stomach. *I didn't say grace. I didn't offer a portion to the life spirit. I just gobbled like a pig being fattened with apples.*

He rose and watched the sparks fly up from the bonfires. He tried to call to the life spirit, but his belly was too full and he was too tired. *I've turned into a real slave,* he thought miserably as he went to sleep.

It was market day in the town. Farmers brought baskets of apples and turnips. Bakers laid out trays of hot, maddeningly fragrant bread. Chickens were lined up in baskets, and horses, goats, and pigs were paraded for the inspection of buyers. But the big event, the one that probably didn't happen often, was the sale of slaves.

The captives were separated into groups—young men and women, older ones, a special category for pregnant women. *"Tveir á verði eins,"* cried Olaf. *Two for the price of one.* The actual sales were handled by a friend of Olaf's called Sven the Vengeful, who could speak several languages.

As for children, there was only Jack. Lucy was kept back, for what reason he couldn't tell. *Please don't let us be separated,* Jack prayed. A jolly-looking couple was quite taken with him and turned him around admiringly. But then the wife said something. The husband shrugged and walked on to the adults.

It seemed children weren't that useful. Jack caught snatches of conversation. He couldn't understand Erse or Latin, but some of the townspeople spoke Saxon. Children were puny and caught diseases. It was like throwing your money away to buy something that curled up and died the minute you got home.

Gradually, the captives were sold and led off by their new owners. The strongest went first, followed by the pregnant women. The older and less healthy went next. They made up for their shortcomings with experience. One was a cobbler, another knew how to train horses, and one frail old woman could cook six kinds of pudding as well as brew beer.

But there were rejects. Two men had scarred backs, a sure sign of being troublemakers. One of the women had a twisted leg, which painfully reminded Jack of Father. Another spat at anyone who came near. No one even tried to bid on the monk. Jack heard a man say monks put curses on you and turned your milk sour.

By the end of the day only these remnants were left. Thorgil at last appeared with Lucy. The shield maiden sat on the ground to trim her toenails with a wicked-looking knife, while Lucy glued herself to Jack's side. He was glad, of course, to see his sister, but he remembered the Picts. The sun was almost at the horizon, and he just *knew* they were coming back.

As the marketplace emptied and most of the townspeople went home, a few vendors remained with inferior animals. They watched the grove of trees with great attention. The shadows seemed to stir, and Jack clutched Lucy's hand. Olaf stood in front of a bonfire, waiting.

It was clear the giant didn't like the painted men, but he was there to make a profit. The Picts carried a clanking assortment of weapons and bags of ornaments as they made their stealthy approach from the forest. They spread these on the ground before the fire.

"Troll spawn," murmured Thorgil. A strange light gleamed in her eyes.

Jack had to admit the weapons were beautiful. They were decorated with fanciful designs much like the patterns on the Picts' skin. The jewelry—pins, brooches, earrings, and bracelets—was finer than anything Jack had expected from such wild creatures. Perhaps they weren't so bad. But he looked into their brooding eyes and knew that nothing good could be expected from such folk.

The Picts examined the captives. They seemed uninterested in the scars on the men's backs or the lameness of one of the women. They drew back when the other woman screamed at them but returned at once with secretive smiles. They were clearly delighted by the plump monk. They pinched him all over, exclaiming and hissing. Sven the Vengeful translated, setting a price for the lot.

Then it was Jack and Lucy's turn.

A broad-chested Pict with a shaggy beard and drooping eyebrows inspected them. He seemed to be the leader. He felt Lucy's fair hair and admired her small hands and feet.

Jack clenched his fists, longing to drive his head into the man's stomach.

The Pictish leader smiled and brought out a weapon not displayed yet. It was a magnificent sword with a dragon etched along its shining blade. The handle was of dark wood inlaid with gold. Thorgil gasped.

"It's your decision," Olaf said in a low voice.

"Yes," said Thorgil with that strange light in her eyes.

"You would please the queen if you kept the girl. You would please me, too."

"I *know*!" Thorgil scowled and reached for the magnificent sword. She turned it over in the leaping light. She ran her finger along the dragon design.

"Dainty work. Not strong, but pretty," commented Olaf.

"All right! All right! I know what you want me to do," shouted Thorgil. She threw down the weapon and grabbed Lucy by the hair, pulling her away.

The Pictish leader replaced the sword in his bag and put out a small, cheaply made dagger. He pointed at Jack. Jack was obviously not worth much.

"You're joking!" said Olaf. The Pict produced a blanket pin of some dull metal. "Better," said the giant. They bargained back and forth until the dagger, the pin, and a thin copper ring lay on the sand. Olaf raised his hand to clinch the deal. He looked at Jack as if assessing whether he could get more.

No! No! thought Jack. He was about to be taken away from Lucy. He was about to go with *them* into their dark forests and silent hill forts. All at once it came to him that he'd understood every word Olaf had said.

For weeks he'd been listening and translating. The Northman language was not that different from his own, but he'd been afraid to speak it. Afraid of being laughed at! How stupid could that be? "Don't sell me," he said.

Olaf put his hand down. "What?"

"I said, don't sell me."

Olaf One-Brow chuckled. "And why not?"

Jack cast desperately around in his mind. He knew better than to plead. Berserkers hated whiners. He had no skills to offer unless you wanted someone who could catch sheep. But wait! He did have a skill. He didn't know if it would impress a berserker, but he knew music.

Without pausing to think, he sang a charm the Bard had taught him. It was in Saxon, but that couldn't be helped. Sven the Vengeful could translate.

These chants I know. No noble lord or lady knows them.
The first is called "help." It helps me against strife.
It saves me from every sort of misery.
The second is to hold my foes in check.
I blunt the blades of enemies.
The third is this: If men put shackles on my legs,
My chant will let me walk free.
The chains fall from my arms.

Olaf looked absolutely stunned. "Is that what I think it is?"

"A magic charm," said Sven in a shocked voice.

"I've heard it before. I can't think where," said Olaf. "Is it likely to harm us?"

"I wouldn't take a chance on it," said Sven.

"Are you a bard?" Olaf asked Jack. For answer, Jack sang the first verses of "Beowulf's Saga." It was one of his best pieces, full of adventure with a rousing melody. His voice was rather fine, he thought, even better than when he last sang for the Bard.

"Here! Take back your trash!" shouted Olaf, kicking the dagger away with a tinny sound. "Be off with you before I sharpen my axe on your skulls."

The Picts carefully gathered up their goods. Olaf's threat made no impression on them even though they were half his size. The giant hoisted Jack under his arm and strode off to the berserkers' camp. The last Jack saw of the monk was his pale, unhappy face in the firelight.

Chapter Thirteen

———

OLAF EXPLAINS
THE AFTERLIFE

They sailed the next day. The wind was strong, and the great sails filled and drove them along at a breathtaking pace. Olaf's ship was by far the swiftest in a good breeze and left the others in the haze to the south. The land broke up into inlets and wide channels to their left, and the sea turned milky green. The air smelled fresh and wild. Gulls, terns, and puffins scattered before them, and even a few crows wheeled from the rocky islands as they passed.

"Odin's birds," said Olaf, pointing.

Jack nodded. The Bard had told him about that. The one-eyed god of the Northmen rarely left his fortress in the far north. Instead, his black-feathered servants flew far and wide to bring him news of war and bloodshed and other things that pleased their cruel master.

A gray bulge appeared in the water to their right. Eric Pretty-Face, a hulking monster with a scar running diagonally across his face, shouted, "Whale ho!"

"Turn! Turn!" roared Olaf. The warriors scrambled for the oars, which they had not been using because of the fine wind. They gave chase, and the gray bulge fled before them until it dived beneath the surface of the water. "We gave it good sport," said Olaf, returning to his seat by Jack. "If we weren't so laden, I'd hunt it down."

"*That* was a whale?" said Jack. He'd heard of the creature. He'd never imagined how enormous it would be close-up.

"Quite right, young skald," replied Olaf, using the Northman word for *bard*. "The trolls ride them for their horses. Fine sea ivory they contain, and lamp oil to light a village through the winter." Ever since discovering Jack's talent, Olaf had spent much time explaining things to the boy. He also taught him vocabulary and poetry. The giant had a wide repertoire of verses, though his voice was anything but sweet. "I want you to have the words when it comes time to sing my praises," he explained.

Jack wasn't sure he liked the attention, but it was better than being carried off by Picts.

He and Lucy were the only slaves left. The rest of the sad-eyed captives had been replaced by furs, pottery, metal tools, medicines, and bags of grain. This was in addition to the booty taken earlier. All the berserkers were going home rich and happy. All, that is, except Thorgil. She slumped hopelessly at her post in the stern of the ship. Sometimes she roused herself enough to pull Lucy's hair, but most of the time Jack was able to protect his little sister. Olaf was inclined to listen to his complaints now that he knew Jack was a bard.

The other berserkers, too, were careful around him, as though Jack could unleash lightning on their sorry hides. He would have loved to fry them with a thunderbolt, but he didn't know how. *I wish the Bard had taught me how to drive people crazy,* Jack mused as Olaf droned on about the uses of sea ivory. *I'd send them all over the side for the whales to gobble up.*

"I want bread and honey," said Lucy, who was curled up by Jack's knee. She had learned the berserkers' language even faster than he and used it to order them around. She sounded utterly confident, like a real princess. Only Jack knew the fragile shell that protected her sanity. Only he saw the signs that indicated her despair. Lucy's face had become pinched and somehow older. Her voice had a shrillness that bordered on hysteria. "I want bread and honey *now,*" said Lucy.

Olaf laughed and untied the lid of a food basket. "And what will you do if I don't fetch it?" he teased.

"I'll tell my brother to make your beard fall off."

"Be quiet," Jack said in a low voice. He was terrified someone would ask him to work magic.

"Oho! I'm shaking in my boots," said Olaf, handing her the desired treat.

"You'd better," the little girl said. She licked the honey off and started to work on the rock-hard bread.

"Olaf," Jack said hesitantly.

"*You're* hungry too? You kids are worse than a pack of wolves."

"I'm not hungry." Jack wasn't sure how to approach Olaf on this subject. Much of the time the man appeared friendly, but he was capable of great rages. "I was thinking. . . . You don't need Lucy. I mean, she's awfully little, and you're going to get twice as much work out of me. Singing your praises and so on. Couldn't you—couldn't you let her go? I mean, drop her off at a monastery so she'd be taken care of." Jack talked rapidly, for he could see Olaf's face turning red. "I'd pay you back somehow. I don't know how, but I'd do it. Please—"

The blow knocked him sideways into the bilge. Jack's ears rang, but he knew Olaf had pulled his punch at the last minute. He'd just got another kitten scratch. A full-grown cat mauling would have sent him into the next world.

"Stop it! Stop it!" shrilled Lucy. "I forbid you to hurt my brother! You're—you're a rotten *kindaskitur!*" The curse took Olaf completely by surprise. He bellowed with laughter and swung the little girl around in a kind of dance. The boat swayed dangerously.

"So I'm a pile of sheep droppings, little Valkyrie. You must have been taking language lessons from Thorgil." The giant plumped her down on a bundle of furs. Jack crawled to his feet. It had been worth a try, but he saw now that being a bard didn't protect him from everything.

He rubbed the blood from his nose on his sleeve. He didn't dare cry. Nothing disgusted the Northmen more than sniveling. Jack hugged himself to keep from shivering. He had to stay in control if they were ever to survive.

Presently, Olaf sat down to continue Jack's lessons as though nothing had happened. "You have to learn the ways we speak of important things," he said. "It's not enough simply to say 'ship.' That doesn't show respect, and so we call it the 'horse of the sea' or 'ocean's chariot.' In the same way, a sword is not merely a sword, but a 'serpent of battle.' That honors its ability to bite."

"What's wrong with her?" Jack said, interrupting what promised to be a long discussion. He'd been watching Thorgil. The girl had been slumped against the side of the ship for hours. She'd neither moved nor spoken.

The giant shaded his eyes as he looked toward the stern. "The *brjóstabarn*? She's unhappy because she didn't fall in battle."

"I don't understand."

"She didn't die. She wasn't killed."

"Now I'm really confused," said Jack, watching the drab, dirt-streaked face of the shield maiden.

"I told her, wait a while," said Olaf. "We can't all die the first time we go out. Sooner or later you'll make it. But she didn't listen. She's always been inclined to gloom."

"Why would anyone want to die?" cried Jack.

"It's the only way to get into Valhalla. Surely you know that? But of course you've been raised a Christian." Olaf then explained about the various heavens a Northman could try for. The best was Odin's stronghold called Valhalla. There the best and brightest spent all day in ferocious battle, killing and being killed. At evening the dead rose and spent the night feasting and drinking with their murderers. The roast boar never ran out, the mead cups were always full. It was a wonderful place, but only those who had been slain in battle were allowed in.

"Some warriors, and women who have died bravely, are chosen by the goddess Freya to live in her world," Olaf explained. "Personally, I'd find that boring. Freya is interested in love, so there's no fighting there. You get to farm and train horses. The women spin and sew. It's like ordinary life, only there's no suffering."

"Sounds all right to me," said Jack.

"If you die at sea, you are taken into the halls of the god Aegir and his wife, Ran," said Olaf. "That's a fine place. The beer is good, the feasting excellent if you like fish. You get to sail in all kinds of weather, and you never have to worry about drowning because you've done that already. To be really welcome, you bring Ran a gift."

"That's why you passed out gold when we were about to sink," said Jack.

"Very good! You were paying attention." The giant beamed.

"But the captives didn't get any."

"Of course not. They're only thralls."

"So where do thralls go?" Jack asked.

"To Hel," Olaf said simply.

Wouldn't you know it? thought Jack. It wasn't enough to

take people captive and destroy their lives. The berserkers had to mess up their afterlife as well. Not that Jack believed he would go to one of Olaf's heavens. The Bard said people wound up with the afterlife they expected, so it was important to have a good one. He said *he* intended to retire to the Islands of the Blessed with the ancient kings and queens of Ireland.

The giant had stopped speaking. He gazed out at the ocean, his blue eyes soft with admiration. It was a fine day, with waves neither too large nor too small and with a following wind. The great sail bellied out over a ship loaded to the gunwales with booty.

Jack saw that Lucy had fallen asleep with a half-gnawed crust of bread in her hand. He got up and covered her with a fur. Then he stood brooding over the deep water, wishing he'd never seen Olaf and his evil crew. At the same time the rushing waves stirred something deep in Jack's soul. His lungs filled with a cold, bracing wind. It was a great thing to be alive. The world was a beautiful place even if you were a thrall. The sun was as warm and the air as sweet to you as it was to Thorgil. Better, probably, to go by her sour face.

"Father talked a lot about Hell," Jack said after a while. "You got there by being wicked."

"Hel is a monster, not a place," corrected Olaf. "She claims cowards, oath-breakers, and people without honor. Her fortress, the World of Ice, is filled with mist and darkness. It's forever cold. The silence is broken only by the slither of snakes."

"Our Hell is hot, but I suppose it doesn't matter," said

Jack. "It's a nasty place for people you don't like. I still don't understand why Thorgil wants to die."

"You haven't been listening," said Olaf. "Warriors *have* to fall in battle. If they die of sickness or old age like any sheep-herder, they're deemed cowards and wind up in Hel's fortress with the thralls. Thorgil has set her heart on Valhalla. She will not be happy until she gets there."

Olaf sent Jack to bail out the ship. This was a constant chore and one the Northmen shared now that they had no adult slaves. Jack toiled alongside Eric Pretty-Face, whose bulging arms could lift five times as much water as he. Eric whistled a tuneless song through broken teeth. One of his legs was ravaged by what looked like an enormous bite.

Steeling his nerve—for Jack knew all the Northmen were quick to anger—he said, "How did you get that?"

"EH?" said Eric, whose ears had been dulled by years of blows and who bellowed all the time.

"How did you get that?" Jack pointed at the scar.

A ragged smile broke out on Eric's face. "TROLL BITE," he replied.

"It's—it's so big." Jack's stomach did a flip-flop as he cal-culated the size of the mouth that had caused the damage.

"NAW, IT WAS A LITTLE BUGGER. GOT HIS TOOTH HERE." Eric hauled up a lump hanging on a thong around his neck. It was a fang the size of a billy goat's horn. Eric, not much on conversation, went back to bailing.

These people are crazy, thought Jack as he bent to work. *I couldn't drive them mad even if I knew how. They're already as loony as the crowd in the Valley of Lunatics. They deserve to spend eternity in Valhalla.*

At last the three ships reached a lonely island, where a small colony existed. Low houses made of turf bulged out of the soil. They looked like small hills. *Or graves,* Jack thought with a shiver.

This was the last stop before the ships turned east. They would sail out of sight of land now. They would be alone on the gray ocean with only the whales—or troll-horses, as Olaf called them—for company.

The warriors traded for freshwater and dried fish. One last time Jack looked at the land as it fell behind them. It was barren and windswept, but to the far west lay a gentle light. It was as though something lay shining beyond the margin of the sea. It was the Islands of the Blessed, where the old gods ruled and where the ancient heroes and heroines still had their dwelling. Perhaps the Bard was there, sitting under an apple tree.

To the east, the direction they were traveling, the sky was leaden. No light there. Jack sighed and felt for the rune of protection. So far it had done its work. He and Lucy hadn't been murdered. They weren't shut up in one of those dark Pictish towers. Of course, he was miserable and Lucy wasn't far from madness, but the rune promised only life, not happiness.

Chapter Fourteen

THE LOST BIRD

The unending water filled Jack with a kind of dread. With each day his home fell farther behind on the trackless waste. Even if, by some magic, he was able to gain control of the ship, he could not ply the oars or reef the sail. He would never find his way back.

Jack felt helpless, like a bug on a floating leaf. Anything could send the leaf spiraling down. Or a sea serpent could rise and swallow the ship. Olaf swore he had seen one on the way over.

Lucy stared at the gray expanse with listless eyes. "I want trees," she said. "I want it to stop moving."

"Me too," said Jack. The seasickness he'd had in the early days came back. The ship slid up and down in a gut-wrenching way. When it didn't meet the waves directly, it tipped to one side, sloshing the bilgewater over everyone's feet. Jack understood now why the Northmen's boots smelled so vile.

At first the wind was gentle but steady enough to fill the sail. The warriors lounged around and played a board game called Wolves and Sheep with movable pegs that fit into seven rows of holes. A peg in the middle was the wolf. Around it was ranged a flock of thirteen sheep. The object was for the sheep to crowd the wolf into a trap, while the wolf tried to devour the sheep. It was an interesting game, and Jack watched it when he wasn't being sick.

But soon the wind strengthened. Foam began to form on the tops of the waves. *Oh no! Not another storm,* Jack thought. The mast creaked ominously, and Olaf gave an order to shorten the sail. The warriors bent to their oars. "Now would be a good time to use your skills," rumbled the giant from over Jack's head.

Jack knew what Olaf wanted. He was supposed to calm the waves, and he didn't know how. He wasn't really a bard, in spite of what he had allowed Olaf to believe.

The terrifying Northman loomed over the deck. Everything, from his smelly boots and tree-trunk legs to his ice blue eyes peering out from under a single, bushy brow, spelled doom. Jack knew he had to do something quickly.

"I need complete silence," he said, inwardly quaking with fear.

"You louts keep quiet!" roared Olaf at his crew. "If I hear one word, I'll send whoever it is to Aegir's halls. Anything else?" he asked Jack.

"I want Lucy at the other end of the ship. Feed her sweets or something to keep her quiet. She's too little to understand. But if I hear Thorgil hurting her, I'll stop doing magic."

"Fair enough," said Olaf, lumbering to the stern to threaten Thorgil.

The wind was stronger now. Waves were beginning to spray over the side. Two of the warriors stopped rowing and started bailing.

The only thing I know is how to make fog, Jack thought desperately. *What good is that? And how can I do it here, out of sight of the trees and land?* Then, as though a voice were speaking in his ear, he remembered something the Bard had said: *I was telling you about how the life force flows in streams deep in the earth. It is this that feeds the great forests and meadows sweet with grass. It is this that calls forth the flowers and the butterflies that are so like flowers. The deer follow its courses as they browse. The badgers and moles build their homes over it. It even draws the swallows in the midst of the sea.*

In the midst of the sea! If birds could feel the life force in the air, he could certainly call to it down here. Jack closed his eyes and felt with his mind the bowl of ocean surrounding him. He breathed in the sharp odor of the wind. He heard—yes, heard!—the moans of the whales as they followed their paths over the deeps. He cast his mind down to where the light failed and found, far below, a current of fire. *Come forth,* he called. *Come forth to me. Cloak the air with your gray presences. Bring sea and sky together.*

Sunlight muted. The wind faded—was it leaving him or he

it? Dampness flowed into his lungs. Water soaked into his clothes, but it was a clean wetness, not like the bilgewater. After a while he opened his eyes and saw Olaf looking—was it possible?—*scared.*

A heavy fog cloaked the sea, and the ship bobbed gently. Of course. Fog and wind did not happen together. Without realizing it, Jack had hit on the one thing that would calm the waves. *I did it,* he thought exultantly. *I'm a real bard.*

But he remembered what had happened when he stopped calling up fog by the Roman road. The wind had risen, blowing the clouds away and revealing him and Lucy to the Northmen.

Jack closed his eyes again. He reached out to the life force and found it everywhere. It swirled in the hidden currents far below, carrying a flurry of creatures that glowed in the dark. Jack had never seen such things before. He didn't know how he could see them now. He felt the quicksilver movement of a school of fish near the surface. He felt a crow coasting the upper air above the fog bank. Sunlight polished its black feathers.

A crow? What was a land bird doing so far from shore? As far as he knew, crows couldn't swim. They weren't like seagulls. He remembered finding one drowned in a farm dam. Its fellows filled the trees, cawing and clacking their beaks as though they were at a funeral. Their behavior had impressed him so much, Jack had waded into the water and taken the poor creature out. He laid it on a rock for the sun to dry—it seemed somehow better for it to rest under the

sky. And all the while the other crows sat in the trees, cawing and bowing as they shifted their feet on the branches.

This bird, the one above the fog, must have been blown away
by the storm. Jack felt its extreme tiredness. Its wings ached. Its
chest labored to breathe. It wouldn't be able to go much farther.
Come down, Jack thought. *Come to me.* He didn't know why he
was doing this or whether the bird could even hear him. He
couldn't protect himself or Lucy, let alone an exhausted crow.
But it seemed terrible to let the creature fall into the sea.

Come to me, come to me, thought Jack. He felt the crow fal-
ter, and then it lost its place in the sky and tumbled into the
fog. Jack felt its panic. *It's all right. I'll save you. Come to me.*
The crow circled, coming ever lower. It was moving blindly.
It opened its beak to caw—

—and blundered into the sail. It slid down the wet sheet
and landed on the deck. The warriors closest to it jumped up
as though they'd been stung. "Don't hurt it!" Jack cried. He
staggered across the swaying boat until he had the crow in his
arms. It shuddered violently, but it didn't try to get away.

Jack became aware that Olaf's eyes were almost popping
out of his head. "That's Odin's bird," he said in a voice shrill
with alarm. If the warrior hadn't been so huge and menacing,
Jack would have laughed out loud. "It came to you. Out here.
Where no crows fly."

"I called it," Jack said. He understood at once that this had
raised his status in the Northman's eyes.

"Where did you learn this art?" said Olaf. The bird clacked
its beak, and he flinched.

"From my master," Jack said grandly. "He taught me many things—the speech of animals, the calling of winds. Also how to drive men mad by blowing on a wisp of straw—ow!" The crow had dug his beak into Jack's hand. "This bird is hungry, and for that matter, so am I. We would like dried fish and bread."

If he was going to tell a lie, it might as well be a big one, Jack figured. He was gratified to see Olaf hurry to obey. Soon Jack was shredding bits of fish for the crow to devour. When it was satisfied and had finished with a draught of water, the creature crept into a hollow between sacks of grain and fell asleep.

Jack went back to check up on Lucy. "You think you're so clever," said Thorgil in Saxon. Jack had noticed she used Saxon when she wished to be particularly aggressive. She knew Olaf did not like threats to his bard.

"I *am* clever," Jack said with a cheerful smile. He was rewarded with a tightening of Thorgil's lips.

She leaned against the rudder, her skills unneeded at the moment. The Northmen had unshipped the oars and were stretching their arms and legs. The air was so still now, it barely ruffled the water. "You notice they haven't lengthened the sail," she said.

"Why would they?" said Jack. "There's no wind." Lucy climbed onto his lap and stared vacantly at the gray gloom surrounding the ship. She sucked her thumb.

"They aren't rowing, either."

Something uncurled at the back of Jack's mind, some

menace he couldn't quite see yet. "So what? Even brainless berserkers get tired."

Thorgil's face turned even more sour than usual. Jack knew he was baiting her, and he didn't care. Just let her try to hurt him!

"You think you're safe. How long do you think Olaf's good humor will last if the fog doesn't lift?"

"It'll lift when I tell it to," Jack said.

"I wonder. I wonder how many tricks a real bard would teach a servant. Or did you merely steal one or two of the simpler ones?"

"I'm not a thief!" said Jack, stung.

"You *say* you can talk to animals and drive men mad by blowing on a wisp of straw. You're awfully young for a bard, if you ask me. The only one I ever saw had a long, white beard. Even he was no match for us. Our king set him adrift in the middle of the sea."

"Wait a minute," said Jack as a horrible thought occurred to him. "How long ago was that?"

"Three years," Thorgil said. "The queen wanted him burned alive, but the king showed him mercy. *I* wouldn't have! King Ivar's gone soft in his old age."

Jack's spine turned to ice. "King Ivar . . . the *Boneless*?"

"Don't call him that to his face." Thorgil laughed, a grating sound like a nail being wrenched out of a board. "He was Ivar the Intrepid before he met the queen. She's the real warrior. When I grow up, I'm going to be one of the Queen's Berserkers and kill hundreds of enemies." For the first time

Thorgil's face glowed with something approaching happiness. It made her almost pretty.

"Ivar the Boneless," murmured Jack, stroking Lucy's hair.

"He sounds awful," said the little girl, snuggling against his chest. How thin her arms were! How stretched was the skin over her cheekbones! He realized she had eaten almost nothing since they lost sight of land.

"He *is* awful," Thorgil said, leaning forward to savor Lucy's terror. "His eyes are like peeled eggs with pale blue dots in the middle. When he gets mad—which is all the time—you can hear his teeth grind at the other end of the hall."

"I won't let him hurt you, Lucy," said Jack, trying to keep the fear out of his voice. "I was trained by the Bard. Ivar may have thrown him into the sea, but he bobbed up like a cork and came to us."

"*You?*" cried Thorgil. "*You* were trained by—Olaf! Olaf!" She sprang to her feet and shouted in Northman, "This thrall says he was trained by Dragon Tongue!"

Olaf galumphed to the rear of the ship. He pushed Lucy to one side and yanked Jack up by his tunic. Olaf's face was so close, his eyebrow was blurred and his fishy breath made Jack's eyes smart. After a moment the giant dropped him into the bilge. "That explains a lot of things," he growled.

Sven the Vengeful let go his oar and also made his way to the stern. "The queen swore the old troublemaker had cheated the fishes."

"That's why she sent the Nightmare to destroy him. When I saw it, I assumed—" Olaf shook his head.

"We all assumed," said Sven.

"We were sent to terrorize the natives. Let them know it wasn't smart to harbor enemies of the queen. I was supposed to confirm the death of Dragon Tongue. But I got lazy and didn't finish the job."

"Don't blame yourself, Olaf," Sven said. "Who could turn his back on such fine plunder? By Odin's eyebrows, we had fun!"

"Yes, but I should have searched for the body," mourned the giant.

"I saw the Nightmare," Lucy said suddenly. Jack put his hand over her mouth. He didn't want her to reveal that the Bard was still alive. "Don't shush me!" she cried, clawing at his hand. "It was screaming in the sky. Ice fell all around. I wanted to go home, but Father said no. I cried and cried!" Lucy was sobbing now, beyond speech.

"A Nightmare is no joke," said Olaf with far more gentleness than Jack thought he possessed. "Its weapon is the mind-fetter that causes the sword to fall from the strongest warrior's hand. If it—*she*—found out Dragon Tongue, his chances of survival were small indeed."

"She did find him," said Jack. *Please keep Lucy crying,* he prayed. *Please don't let her spoil my story.* "I was there. I saw him fall." Jack bowed his head, hoping to give the impression that the attack had been fatal. In a way, the Bard *was* dead. Without his brain, he was nothing.

"Well. That's all right, then," said Olaf, cheering up.

"But this thrall is his apprentice. What do we tell the queen about him?" said Sven.

"Nothing," replied Olaf. "We've done our job. We've got a shipload of booty. Why upset the applecart?"

"*I* think it's cowardly to hide the truth," said Thorgil.

"It would not be wise," Olaf said carefully, "to put the queen into a snit. This young skald could be useful to us, and by the way, little *brjóstabarn*, it is also not wise to suggest I might be a coward." There was no mistaking the menace in the giant's voice.

Thorgil turned red, but she held her tongue. She gazed long and hard at Jack, looking, he thought, as though she wouldn't mind putting the queen into a snit if it would make him suffer.

"Believe me, angering the queen would spoil your chances of joining her court," Olaf said.

Thorgil frowned. "You always get the better of me," she said.

She went back to watching the rudder, and Olaf and Sven returned to their posts toward the bow of the ship. Jack ferried Lucy between the baskets and bags to his former perch.

The fog clung to the sea. It was impossible to see in any direction. They were swallowed up by the gray wetness as thoroughly as if they had been sealed in a cave. The air grew darker—sunset was coming on, though it was impossible to tell east from west. The warriors sat idle at their oars. They spoke little, as though something was troubling them.

"Who's Dragon Tongue?" said Lucy.

"Someone you don't know," Jack said. He showed the little girl the crow huddled between the grain bags. Lucy wanted to play with it, but Jack distracted her with a shred of dried fish. She obediently sucked on it, but then she spat it onto the deck by the sleeping bird.

"I want Mother's food," she said.

"You must try to eat, dearest. It's only for a little while, until we get to land again."

"We'll never get to land," moaned Lucy. "We'll always be here in the fog with these stinky monsters. For ever and ever and ever." She pressed her thin face against Jack's chest.

"That's not the way a real princess talks," said Jack. "She'd know this was only an adventure and that magic would come to her when she needed it." *Good heavens. I sound like Father,* thought Jack.

"It had better come soon," said Lucy.

"It already has. This crow flew to us from the Islands of the Blessed. He's been sent to watch over you."

"Will he grant me three wishes?" said Lucy, pulling a cloak from a bundle of clothes the Northmen had looted from a village. Jack helped settle it around her shoulders.

"When it's the right time," Jack said. "He's very tired now. He's flown a long way."

"I'd like a warm room with a fire and a soft bed. I'd like Mother and—and—F-Father." She began to cry again.

"Remember, wishes don't always get granted right away."

The smell of fish must have penetrated the crow's dreams, for he snapped his beak and flexed his claws with his eyes tightly shut.

"Look at his foot," whispered Lucy.

Jack felt the hair stir on the back of his neck. The light was going, but he distinctly saw that the bird was missing a claw on his left foot. As though a fox had nipped it off. He knew this creature. It was the crow who had stayed behind when the Bard lost his wits. It was the one who had tricked him out of food and listened intently to Jack's worries.

People said the Bard got his messages from birds, though he'd never shown Jack how. "I wish I could understand you," said Jack, reaching out to smooth the creature's bedraggled feathers. "I wish I knew why you followed me to the middle of the sea. But I'm glad you did." And the crow, as though he could hear in his sleep, fluffed his feathers and settled down more snugly between the grain bags.

Chapter Fifteen

BOLD HEART

Jack slept soundly. By now he was used to curling up in whatever corner he could find, and the movement of the sea was so gentle, he barely noticed it at all. He woke up when the first light crept over the ship.

But it was not a clear light. Fog pressed in all around, coating everything with its dank presence. Water dripped off the ropes. It sank into Jack's clothes and glued down his hair. When he looked over the side, sea and sky melted together into a blue-gray mass so thick, he could see only a few feet in any direction. The ship might have been floating in the middle of a cloud for all he could tell.

He could hear the warriors come awake—stretching, groaning, belching, and (the air was very still) pissing over the side. They didn't talk, which was unusual. On other days they woke with casual insults and rough jokes.

Lucy stirred under her cloak. Jack didn't disturb her. The longer she was asleep, the longer she could escape into dreams. The crow hopped onto the railing. He crouched there, clacking his beak irritably. Jack was certain it was a "he," though he couldn't say why.

"You don't want to fly out there," Jack said. The bird gave a low grumble so like human speech that the boy laughed. The months of watching wild creatures for the Bard gave him a fair sense of the crow's mood. "It *does* look as nasty as troll spit. Yesterday I couldn't wait for the wind to die down. Now I can't wait for it to start up again."

"Calling the wind is your job," rumbled Olaf's voice from behind him. Jack gripped the railing to keep from cowering. For such a large man, the warrior was amazingly soft-footed.

"I thought you wanted calm." Jack braced for a blow. Olaf did not like arguments.

"I did. Now I want sunlight."

"Fog never sticks around long," Jack said cautiously. He didn't know how to call the wind, and he wanted to buy time. "I'm sure it'll go away by afternoon."

The blow didn't fall, but Olaf's giant hand gripping his shoulder was almost as bad. "Listen well, little skald. We're stuck out here not knowing north from south. If we row in the wrong direction, we'll find ourselves on an endless sea. After a while the freshwater will run out, and the only liquid we will have to drink is your blood." Olaf spoke in a low, calm voice that was more terrifying than a shout.

"Oh. Since you put it that way," said Jack. The heavy hand went away. Jack sat down on a grain bag, his heart pounding. The crow threw back his head and made a gargling sound.

"If you think you can do things better, you have my permission to try," Jack said.

The crow bobbed his body up and down as if to say, *Not me, sonny. It's your job.*

"That's right. It's my job. I'm the bard around here." Jack was talking to calm his growing sense of panic. He hadn't the slightest idea what to do. "As long as you're going to stay, I might as well give you a name. How about . . . Lopsided."

The bird delivered a series of loud croaks that made the Northmen clutch the amulets they wore around their necks. They could joke about getting chewed on by trolls, but a simple crow filled them with dismay. "You *are* lopsided. A fox bit off your toe, and you can't walk straight."

The crow snapped at Jack's face.

"Oh, very well. I suppose you were courageous and fought back. I'll call you Bold Heart."

At this the crow did a flip-flop and landed on the railing with his feathers puffed out. He looked exceedingly pleased with his new name.

"Now, if you don't mind, I've got work to do," said Jack.

He composed himself on the grain bag. *What to do, what to do?* he thought. Bold Heart hopped along the railing until he was in Jack's view again. The bird lifted his wings to the sky and keened as though he saw a hawk. It was extraordinary how many sounds the bird could make.

"What does that mean?" Jack said. "I don't have time to play. If you're begging for food, you'll have to wait until I'm finished." Jack closed his eyes and prepared to cast his mind down to the life force. To his surprise, he found it easy. It was as though, once learned, the path became clearer.

He felt the fire deep below, but not only there. The life force radiated all around, in the sea and in the air. It moved together like a kind of music. It filled all with its joyful presence. Jack found himself in a dozen places at once, following a flock of geese forming a V in the upper sky, swimming with a school of herring that flowed in one direction until, startled, they all turned and flowed in another. It was wonderful! It was like being alive a hundred times over.

Finally he remembered his mission. Jack cast his mind down to the deeps again. *Return to me,* Jack thought. *Break apart sea and sky. Call down your clouds and mists.* Jack didn't know where the words came from, only that they seemed right. He felt a finger of warmth lift from the fire far below. He felt it rise through the chill dark. It pushed aside the cold currents of the ocean and rose toward him. The herring scattered as it passed. It spread out like a giant net—here, there, everywhere, catching the fog. The water dimpled in a thousand places. From far away he heard the shouts of men.

"Jack! Jack!" cried Lucy, shaking him.

He opened his eyes. Water was streaming down so hard, he could hardly see. The Northmen were cursing as they tried to protect the perishable goods. Rain roared like a waterfall. Olaf ordered everyone to start bailing.

"Make it stop," cried Lucy, her eyes wide with fright.

Jack held her tight. His mind refused to function. He could only stare at the devastation around them. Bold Heart flopped onto his lap and pushed his beak under Lucy's arm. "He likes me," said the little girl, momentarily distracted.

Jack thought it more likely that the crow was trying to stay dry, but he said, "Of course he does. He's here to protect you." Lucy gave Jack a wan smile. The water in the ship came almost to her knees. If it got much deeper, they'd sink.

"You! Bard! Do something!" Olaf bellowed. Jack closed his eyes and desperately tried to reach the life force. But the powers that ran through the earth were not to be approached by force. Jack tried and tried, but all he could do was hear the pounding rain and feel the water creep slowly up his legs. No matter how fast the warriors bailed, the rain came down faster. The ship was now so full, it barely crested the sea. Each water droplet sent it closer to destruction.

Then, just as it seemed they could take no more, the rain stopped. The Northmen continued to bail furiously. Soon they had the water level down to a dirty inch sloshing around their soaked boots. They were still surrounded by clouds, but a rift had appeared overhead. One small patch of blue showed they were not entirely cut off from the sun.

"You almost drowned us!" roared Olaf, kicking a sodden heap of clothes. "You've ruined half our booty!" He stormed around, making the ship sway.

"Temper tantrum," whispered Lucy.

Her comment was so unexpected and accurate, Jack laughed out loud. He couldn't help himself. He'd been afraid so long, he'd worn out his ability to feel terror. Olaf looked like a huge toddler, ranting and swearing with his wet beard hanging down in rat tails. In a minute the giant would hurl himself onto the deck and start kicking. Jack laughed until he could hardly breathe. When he came to his senses, he saw the other Northmen guffawing and slapping one another on the back. Olaf looked stunned.

"You—you—," he gasped. Then his face twisted and he laughed too. He threw back his head and trumpeted like a wild goose: *honk . . . honk . . . hoooonk.* The tears ran down his face into his soggy mustache. Lucy joined in with childish peals, and even Bold Heart bobbed up and down in a kind of mad ecstasy.

It went on for several minutes. Jack felt the life force shimmering around them. Everyone was gripped by joy. They were alive! They were breathing the sweet air. The sea lay before them like a path with endless possibilities. Then the fit passed, and the warriors leaned against the sides of the ship, panting.

"Hoo! You play a dangerous game, young skald," said Olaf at last. "You did stop the rain, though, and for that I shall not kill you."

Jack knew he hadn't done anything. The sky had simply emptied itself out, but he wasn't going to tell Olaf.

Gray clouds still hugged the horizon, making it impossible to tell the direction of the sun. Olaf fumbled in a pouch he wore around his neck. Jack moved closer, and the giant, noticing his interest, held out his hand. Jack saw a clear, rectangular stone that reflected the light like a small chunk of ice. It was transparent but not colorless.

"Oh, no," said Olaf, snatching it away as Jack tried to touch it. "I'm not letting you leech out the magic. This is *my* sun stone." He held it up at arm's length to the blue rift in the clouds. The light shone through, yellow like a cat's eye. Olaf turned around slowly. At a certain point the light in the stone changed to blue. Jack gasped.

"You're not the only one with powers," rumbled the giant. He turned again, and the stone changed back to its original color. Round and round Olaf went until he was satisfied. "It tells you the direction of the sun," he explained. "That way"—he pointed—"is east, where the sun lies. See, the blue is strong." He turned, and Jack saw the color shift from blue to yellow to bluish gray. "That's west, where we've come from. All right, you lazy dogs! Put your backs into it!" The Northmen immediately shipped the oars and began rowing.

They set off east with Olaf checking the direction from time to time. After a while the clouds broke up, and he was able to put the stone away. The sunlight raised everyone's spirits. The warriors sang as they worked:

Sometimes I visit too early.
Sometimes I visit too late.
Either the beer is finished,

Or it hasn't been brewed as yet.
Life's a pain in the butt, friends.
Life's a pain in the butt.

Sometimes I'm asked to dine
When I've stuffed myself at home.
What good is a ham on the table
When you've already got one inside?
Life's a pain in the butt, friends.
Life's a pain in the butt.

When they finished this song (and it had many verses), they switched to another. Their loud, clear voices rang over the sea:

Cattle die and kin die.
Houses burn to the ground.
But one thing never perishes:
The fame of a brave warrior.

Ships go down in the sea.
Kingdoms turn into dust.
One thing outlasts them all:
The fame of a brave warrior.

Fame never dies!
Fame never dies!
Fame never dies!

The last words were hurled at the bright blue sky. Jack shivered. For the first time he understood what drove these violent men. Their lives were short, but every moment burned with intensity. These men knew they were doomed. Someday Odin, who smiled on them now, would cast upon them the mind-fetter. Olaf had said as much. Odin was a tricky god. He supported his champions, but his real aim was to choose the best for his hall. One day the swords would drop from their hands. They would be helpless before their enemies, and then they would be called to Valhalla to fight and die in an endless round.

Knowing this, the Northmen still fought. It was brave and crazy and supremely stupid. But it was noble, too.

As if in response to the rousing song, the wind filled the red-and-cream-striped sail. The Northmen cheered. Aegir and his wife, Ran, had answered them. They thanked the gods loudly and rested on their oars.

Fame never dies! Jack found himself moved. It was infuriating! How could he sympathize with such murderous scum? He was supposed to hate them. But he couldn't.

Your defenses have been torn away, the Bard had told Jack long ago. *Everything, from the plight of a chick fallen from its nest to the terrible beauty of the hawk swooping down to kill it, will shake your very soul. It's a pity. You aren't ready to face so much reality, but there it is.*

"If this is reality, I don't think much of it," Jack said to the crow. Bold Heart cocked his head. "You can stretch your wings now," Jack told him. "I wish the rest of this stuff was as easy to dry."

His heart sank as he saw how wet the grain bags were. They'd been protected from above by oiled cloth, but water from below had ruined them. Stacks of bread had disintegrated. Dried fish was limp and soggy. Beans were already beginning to swell. When Jack thought of how hard the villagers had worked to make this food—and how the Northmen had killed them to get it—he wanted to break an oar over Olaf One-Brow's head.

It was all gone. All that cruelty had been for nothing.

Jack found a slab of cheese to tempt Lucy. The Northmen gnawed on limp fish, no doubt trying to use it up before it turned rotten. In late afternoon Eric Pretty-Face, on watch at the prow, bellowed that he saw land. Jack squinted at the watery east. He saw a hump of white cloud rising from the sea. As they drew nearer it appeared to flow upward like a slow, milky river. Jack was entranced. It was fog moving up over a tree-covered mountain. He heard surf breaking in the distance.

"Where are we?" said Olaf.

"I'd say, by the shape of that mountain, we're in Magnus the Mauler's territory," said a warrior.

"No, no. The currents are forming an S-pattern from that fjord," argued another. "We're in Gizur Thumb-Crusher's land."

"*That* oath-breaker!" snarled Olaf.

Aren't these people ever called Gizur the Good or Magnus the Merry? thought Jack.

"Let's send out the expert," said Sven the Vengeful. From the end of the oars rose a man Jack had scarcely noticed, except to wonder what he was doing on the ship. He was so old, he seemed hardly capable of rowing, let alone swinging a sword in battle. His hair hung in untidy wisps from under a leather cap. His hands were mottled with age spots, and his body had no more fat on it than a dry twig. He crept from his place with difficulty, having frozen into position at the oar.

"Will you help us, Rune?" said Olaf politely. Jack was surprised. The giant never asked anyone's cooperation. He gave orders, usually along with threats.

"I will," said Rune in such a whispery voice that Jack had to strain his ears to hear. Then he saw that the old man had a terrible scar on one side of his neck. It was amazing Rune could breathe, let alone speak.

The warriors helped the old man out of his clothes. If he was pitiful dressed, he was worse naked. His whole body was seamed with old cuts and gouges. He was as wrinkled as a dried apple, and his knees and elbows were swollen with the bone-ache that afflicted the old.

The men tied a rope under his arms and lowered him over the side. Jack heard a splash as he hit the water. "Slowly," roared Olaf. "We're not fishing for whales here." Jack heard Rune's arms swishing. He heard him splutter as he got a mouthful of water. Everyone stood perfectly still, waiting. A few curious gulls soared over the ship. It was late, and they circled briefly and went back to land.

"Are you finished, old friend?" called Olaf.

Rune must have said no because the Northmen didn't react. Finally, the old man was pulled, dripping and shivering, over the side. Olaf quickly wrapped him in furs and gave him a skin of wine. "The sea isn't as warm as it was in our youth, eh?" he said.

"It was always as cold as a troll's buttocks," said Rune in his whispery voice.

Olaf laughed. "What can you tell us?"

"The sea tastes of pine and spruce. It is fed by a swift-flowing river from high in the mountains. The current curves like an adder crossing the sand. It is black while the sea is green, and it sinks because it comes from the snow. The air smells of smoked venison and fresh-cut peat. A breeze comes from a valley not far to the north and swings up the river." On and on Rune went, recording amazing detail. He finished with, "We're in Gizur Thumb-Crusher's land. His village lies an hour's sailing to the north."

The warriors huddled around the old man. The sun had set, and gray evening stretched across the sea to the fog still flowing up the darkly wooded mountain. Here and there the first stars appeared.

"Who wants to go berserk?" said Olaf softly.

Chapter Sixteen

—◦◦◦—

GIZUR THUMB-CRUSHER

"I want to go! I have the right!" said Thorgil. The ship had been driven onto a beach. The warriors were unwrapping weapons and examining them by the light of a small fire.

"You have the right to obey my orders," Olaf said. "I want you to guard the ship."

"Why me?"

"Who else is going to watch your thrall?"

"I don't want her!" ranted Thorgil. "She's weak, she's useless. I wanted to trade her for a sword, but you wouldn't let me!"

"You presume too much from my friendship with your father," said Olaf. His voice was quiet and even. It was how he sounded, Jack had discovered, before he fell into a rage.

Thorgil must have realized this because she backed down: "I only wanted to make you proud."

"I am proud of you," the giant said. "But you must learn discipline. Eric Broad-Shoulders and Eric the Rash will stay with you. They're afraid of the dark and wouldn't be of much use anyhow. Rune will stay to make sure you treat Lucy well."

"Rune," muttered Thorgil.

"I can watch my sister if you need another warrior," Jack said hopefully. With any luck, the shield maiden would fall in battle.

"Oh, no. You're coming along," said Olaf.

"Me?" cried Jack.

"Him?" shrieked Thorgil at the same time.

Olaf upended Thorgil by the ankles and shook her until she was too breathless to curse. "Discipline," he grunted, dropping her onto the sand.

He dragged Jack to the campfire and selected a knife for him to carry. "This is for your protection. You're not to join in the fight," Olaf said.

"Don't worry," said Jack.

"I know how exciting pillaging is," the giant said fondly, ruffling Jack's hair. It felt like a blow. "No matter how much you're tempted, just say no."

"Just say no to pillaging. You got it."

Olaf hunkered down until he was on a level with Jack's face. His eyes gleamed in the firelight. "I want you to make a song about me. You're a young skald, but you're all we've got since Rune got his throat slashed."

"Was he"—Jack swallowed—"watching a fight?"

"Yes. He was supposed to be doing poetry, but he forgot and ran straight into battle. I couldn't blame him. Once he was one of the best warriors, but the bone-ache conquered him. Someday I'll take him on a raid and let him die with a sword in his hand."

"Kind of you," said Jack.

"It is, isn't it?" said Olaf, beaming. "Be sure and put that into the song."

Jack watched the warriors arm themselves. Most had swords, but a few were limited to short stabbing spears. All of them carried axes. One man had a bundle of torches and a pot of live coals. Each Northman carried two shields, one in front and the other slung on his back. They were made of wood and didn't seem that sturdy.

The most resplendent of all was Olaf One-Brow. While his men wore leather caps to protect their heads, he had a metal helmet. It had a ridge across the top like a cock's comb and two panels at the sides to protect his cheeks. But the most unnerving feature was a metal mask like a hawk's face attached to the front. The beak came down over Olaf's nose, and his eyes peered out of holes. It made him seem weird and otherworldly.

Unlike the others, he had a chain mail shirt. His great sword hung from his belt along with two throwing axes. Altogether he was a terrifying being. Jack thought anyone would faint dead away if he met the giant berserker in the middle of the night.

And it was the middle of the night. A quarter moon hung in the west. Olaf explained that Gizur's sentries would be asleep. If the watchdogs could be lured by the bag of half-rotten fish Sven the Vengeful carried, the warriors could move about at will.

"So you can take what you want without fighting," said Jack.

Olaf's blow sent him sprawling. "What kind of honorless brute do you think I am? If I took Gizur's wealth without engaging in battle, I would be no better than a thief. It would show him no respect—oath-breaker though he is."

Jack sat up, trying to clear his head. He would never understand these monsters.

"There's one more thing you must understand," came Olaf's voice through Jack's spinning senses. "We're about to drink the wolf-brew."

The boy looked up to see a warrior remove a metal pot from the fire. Steam rose around the man's face as the air brought a bittersweet odor to Jack's nose. The hair stood up on his neck. He knew that smell! It had come from the box he'd found in the sea.

Is a berserker a man or a wolf? Jack had asked the Bard.

Most of the time they're men, the old man had replied, *but when they make a drink of this plant, they become as frenzied as mad dogs. They bite holes in their shields. They run barefooted over jagged rocks without feeling it. Neither fire nor steel can stop them.*

"When we drink," said Olaf, "we become . . . other . . . than what we are."

"You become berserkers," Jack said.

"We're always berserkers," Olaf explained. "We're born that way. It runs in families, but we can choose the time of our madness . . . or most of us can." The giant grimaced—almost, Jack thought, as though he were in pain. "Thorgil's father was one of the finest, but madness fell upon him without his will. Before Thorgil was born, her brother Thorir was playing outside her parents' house. He was only three years old. Her father went into a berserker rage and killed him."

Jack was so shocked, he couldn't speak.

"It wasn't the man's fault. The fit was on him, and the child strayed into his path. Anyhow, the lesson here is to stay out of our way." Olaf shook his head. "When we've drunk the wolf-brew, I want you to rub yourself with the leaves. They'll make you smell like us. When we turn into wolves, our sense of smell becomes very sharp. Anyone who is not like us is an enemy."

The warriors squatted around the fire. As they passed the metal pot each man drank deeply. When it got to Jack, Olaf scooped out the leaves and squashed them over Jack's arms, legs, and face. He poured the dregs over the boy's tunic. The liquid was warm, but it rapidly turned cold in the sea breeze. The odor sent a thrill along Jack's nerves. His heart beat heavily. He became aware of a dozen things at once: the rustle of a hare easing its way through a bush, the fussing of the waves along the shore, the smell—*the smell*—of dead fish, forest leaves, pine, and fire. Especially dead fish.

Jack wanted to roll in the rotten stuff.

He heard a strange noise and saw that the warriors had begun to pant. Their eyes gleamed yellow in the firelight and their tongues protruded from their mouths. Olaf gave a low moan that made Jack's blood run cold—and excited him at the same time. He wanted to run and run and run. His hands and feet itched with the desire.

Olaf bounded from his place, and the others followed. Jack hadn't a hope of keeping up, but he heard them coursing ahead, their heavy feet thudding on the sand. They veered from the beach and went over a grassy hill, splashed through a brook, and crunched over a field of bracken and sedge. Green odors rose from the ground. They arrived at the edge of a bluff and stopped abruptly.

Jack caught up, gasping for air. It had been a very long run. The berserkers were still panting. They jostled one another nervously, like hounds waiting for a signal to bring down a deer.

Below, scarcely visible in the moonlight, was a cluster of houses. The valley was full of the smell of cattle, horses, dogs, and people. It was a rich porridge after the clean odors of forest and sea. Jack found it delightful, although he couldn't say why. Normally, the smell of barnyards repelled him.

Sven the Vengeful slipped down the bluff with the bag of rotten fish. After a few moments Jack saw his dark shape moving along the beach below the houses. Smaller shadows danced behind him, whining and begging for a share of the treat.

Olaf lit torches and passed them out to his men. His helmet gleamed red in the firelight. Its eyeholes were black and seemingly empty.

"Now!" he roared.

The berserkers shrieked. They charged down the bluff, slipping and sliding on the stones. They raced for the houses, still screaming, and hurled the torches onto the roofs. The thatch went up in flames in a dozen places. A door opened, and a villager rushed out, trying to draw his sword. He was felled by rocks. The berserkers had helped themselves to free ammunition on the bluff. More villagers staggered out. They were clubbed or speared or run through or brained with axes. It happened so fast, Jack couldn't think straight.

Nor could the villagers. They were bewildered by the sudden attack. They reeled about, calling for help. Instead, the berserkers threw them to the ground and chopped them up. Blood poured everywhere—black in the dancing firelight.

Now the houses burned fiercely. Cries came from within, from women and children. Some attempted to escape, but they were treated with the same ferocity. Jack stood on the bluff, unable to move, unable to look away. He saw Olaf behead a young woman and throw her child back into the flames. He saw the roofs cave in with fountains of sparks. He saw the berserkers drive forth cattle. Their rage unquenched, they fell upon the animals and slew them as well.

He didn't know how long he stood there. When he came to his senses, he saw that the sky had turned pink with dawn. The houses had collapsed into smoldering heaps. Berserkers poked around the ashes, digging for buried silver. They had salvaged bags of grain and dried fish from the storehouses that had not been burned. Three cows were tied to a tree. One magnificent horse, white with a black stripe along its backbone, still lived.

And that was all.

Jack had listened to the monk from the Holy Isle. He'd heard the dreadful tale of its destruction, but it hadn't sunk in. It was merely a story, like the gruesome stories of saints Father liked to recall. Or Beowulf's battle with Grendel. This was real.

He climbed down to the beach and walked into the water. He could swim out to where the sky met the sea, going farther and farther until he got too tired to stay afloat. And then, going by paths known only to departed souls, he might find his way to the Islands of the Blessed. The Bard would be sitting there with his harp. *Hello, lad,* he'd say. *It's a beautiful day.* Only, the Bard would be more likely to say, *What's the matter with you, leaving your sister in a fix?*

"She'll be all right," Jack told the old man as the cold water foamed around his legs. "She's so pretty, even the Northmen like her. Thorgil's going to give her to the queen."

Did I hear you right? said the Bard. *Are we speaking of Grendel's Aunt Frith?*

Jack walked farther into the sea. A wave knocked him over, and he went down with the bitter salt filling his nostrils. The rune of protection swung up and hit him on the mouth. Its heat was as shocking as the cold. He fought to the surface, coughing and spluttering, and treaded water as the heat spread throughout his body.

A flock of swallows circled in the early-morning clouds overhead. One of them swooped down, swift as an arrow, and came close enough to turn its head and look straight into Jack's eyes. Then it beat the air with its sharp wings and returned to its companions in the sky.

Death must be fought with life, and that means courage and that means joy, said the Bard from his place beneath the apple trees.

"Nobody told me life would be harder than death," muttered Jack as he fought his way out of the sea. He sat on the beach and let the warm sunlight dry his clothes.

"I hope you're thinking of nice things to say about me," said Olaf One-Brow, flopping down to clean the blood from his sword with sand.

Chapter Seventeen

RUNE

Jack watched the Northmen celebrate on the shore from the relative safety of the ship. First they laid out the new booty to admire. A considerable hoard of silver had been unearthed. Bags of dried beans and barley were lined up on the sand. Sven the Vengeful moved them into different patterns, stepping back to judge the effect. He settled on a wide arc of grain bags framing the silver hoard. A row of wineskins decorated the front. Eric Broad-Shoulders, who was afraid of the dark, was not at all afraid to slay the three surviving cows. Eric the Rash dug a deep pit in which to roast them.

The most interesting find had been a cache of dirty white loaves under the roof of a storehouse. At first Jack thought they were a strange kind of bread, but the warriors' excitement showed they were something quite different.

"Salt!" cried Olaf, dancing around with one in each huge hand.

"Salt! Salt! Salt!" screamed the others. They tossed them back and forth, pausing to take licks.

"Salt!" shrilled Thorgil as she balanced one on her head.

"What's so special about that?" whispered Lucy. She was pressed up against Jack. He put his arm around her.

"They're just crazy," he said.

The Northmen nibbled at the salt cakes until their mustaches were powdered white. So much would have made a normal man sick, and Jack hoped to see them vomit, but they didn't. After a while the salt madness left them and they reverently packed the loaves away.

The rotten food from the ship was dumped. A cloud of seagulls descended on it, along with crows. Bold Heart competed with the best of them. It was strange how Jack could pick him out from the mob of jostling black birds, but Bold Heart was faster, smarter, and, well, *bolder* than the others. "I suppose he'll leave now," said Jack.

"No, he won't," declared Lucy. "He's been sent to us from the Islands of the Blessed."

Jack didn't say the bird had landed on the ship out of exhaustion, but he thought it.

All day the warriors partied. They devoured roast cow and drank sweet red wine from a place called Iberia. They bellowed songs about the gods, who seemed to be as fond of debauchery as their worshippers. One long poem was about a party much like the one Jack and Lucy were observing. Aegir, the sea god, had brewed a cauldron of beer. Not only did everyone get drunk, they got into an insult competition with Loki, the god of dirty tricks. Loki called Odin a liar, and Odin called him a pervert. Then Loki said Freya, the goddess of love, farted when she got scared and that Njord, the god of ships, had been captured by trolls who used his mouth as a chamber pot. Each new verse was greeted with howls of laughter. The Northmen pounded one another on the back for joy.

"What kind of people need a god of dirty tricks?" said Jack, watching from the ship as night fell.

"That kind," yawned Lucy. For the first time in weeks she had eaten a full meal, and her head kept drooping. Bold Heart had fed well too, and he was perched on the rail with his eyes closed. "Should we escape now?" said Lucy.

"Where would we go?" Jack said bitterly.

"I don't know. Ooh." Lucy yawned again. "Maybe to that village they raided."

"The villagers ran away." Jack had not told his sister what really happened to Gizur Thumb-Crusher's people.

"They'd help us if we could find them."

"We'll never find them. Just go to sleep, dearest." And Lucy obediently curled up on a heap of furs.

Night was falling, but the revelry showed no sign of ending. The poetry was so disgusting now, Jack was glad his little sister was asleep. The crudest of all was Thorgil, who pretended to be Freya by yelling, "Oh! Oh! I'm so scared!" and farting.

"Olaf will want his song soon," came a whispery voice behind Jack. He whirled and saw Rune standing by the mast. The light was so dim and the man so skinny, he almost seemed part of the mast. Bold Heart opened his eyes and clacked his beak.

"Why aren't you out there with the rest?" said Jack.

"The bone-ache," said Rune simply. "And I no longer enjoy the pleasures of pillaging." He stopped to breathe hoarsely. It was obviously an effort to speak. "Maybe it was Dragon Tongue's fault. He was always one for enjoying life. I guess he corrupted me."

Jack turned back to the revels on the beach. Olaf One-Brow was pretending to be a lovesick troll-maiden. Bold Heart sidled along the railing until he was next to Jack. He pulled at the boy's sleeve and bobbed in the direction of Rune.

"That's quite a pet you have," whispered the aged warrior. "Dragon Tongue used to talk to crows."

"He taught me the art," Jack said. No point wasting a chance to look important.

"He was a good man," Rune said suddenly. "He was completely unlike us but a true warrior."

Jack said nothing. His eyes filled with tears.

"I know you can't write a song for Olaf," said the old Northman. Jack turned and looked at him—or as much as he could see of the man's figure in the dim light. "Dragon Tongue could never praise people he hated. He was too honest."

"What will Olaf do to me?" Jack didn't argue with Rune's

conclusion. He felt sick every time he thought of the blood-
bath in Gizur's village.

"Feed you to the fish," Rune replied. "Also, you don't
know our language well enough. You're good, but you make
mistakes."

"Are you telling me to run away?" Jack didn't know why
he trusted the old warrior, but he instinctively did. There was
something deep about him, something almost as compelling as
the Bard.

"You'd never survive. To the south lies Magnus the
Mauler's country. To the north is Einar the Ear-Hoarder.
Einar has a collection of dried ears he wants to enlarge."

"I see," said Jack.

"I will give you songs," said Rune. "I was a skald once. I
wasn't as great as Dragon Tongue, but I was still good. Day
after day the poems bubble up in me, and I have no voice to
give them. You will be my voice."

The shouts of the feasting warriors seemed far away. The
world shrank until it contained only three people: Jack, his
little sister, and this amazing new ally. "I guess Olaf won't
mind," Jack said.

"Don't tell him!" This outburst caused a fit of coughing
that went on for a long time. Jack shifted from one foot to the
other, not knowing what to do. Finally, Rune recovered and
drew several shuddering breaths. "Olaf wants his own personal
skald. He wants you all to himself, as he wants that horse of
Gizur's. It adds to his fame. If he thinks you can't perform,
he'll kill you."

The steed the old warrior was speaking of was tethered next to the silver hoard. It was a beautiful creature, white like the salt cakes, with a strange black stripe along its backbone. It gazed at the reeling Northmen with dark, intelligent eyes.

"Then . . . I thank you." Jack was grateful, but at the same time he hated the idea of being property.

"Let's begin," whispered Rune.

The lesson lasted for hours. Bold Heart went back to sleep, and Jack wished he could join him. He'd had no rest the night before, and the whole day had been spent working. Eventually, the fire on the beach sank down to coals. The Northmen went to bed. It gave Jack a chill to see them lay out cloths and lie down in orderly rows. It meant that they could appear thoroughly stupefied and still behave like warriors.

Finally, Rune pronounced himself satisfied with Jack's progress. The boy fell onto a heap of clothes and was asleep almost before he landed.

They sailed north along the coastline. After they passed Einar the Ear-Hoarder's lands, they camped on shore. From here on, they would meet no one who would dare attack.

Olaf and his crew were in no hurry. They felt they had earned a vacation. The noble horse, which Olaf named Cloud Mane, was balanced in the middle of the ship. He was led ashore each day to feed on fresh grass.

The warriors hunted in the dark forests that lined the shore, bringing back deer and wild boar. They netted trout in the streams. Eric the Rash ground up one of the salt loaves for seasoning. Jack noticed again how eager the Northmen were for salt. They craved it more than wine, and that was saying a good deal.

"We don't have it at home," Rune explained.

"We dry our salt from seawater," said Jack. "Why can't you?"

"Not enough sunlight," said the old warrior, turning away. He refused to waste his breath on such idle talk and saved his voice for poetry. Every night he drilled the boy out of Olaf's sight. Jack was amazed at how complicated the verses were. Nothing was called by its true name, and the more variations you could work in, the better. A ship was called *prow-beast*, *ocean's steed*, and *Njord's swan* in the same verse. Instead of saying *battle*, you said *a meeting of mail-coats and sword-tips*. It was very confusing and, to Jack's mind, pointless.

"No!" Rune wheezed when Jack said *The king sailed over the sea to battle* instead of *The giver of gold rings drove Njord's swan upon the whale-road to a meeting of mail-coats and sword-tips*. "No! No! No!" Rune doubled over in a coughing fit, and Jack felt ashamed of teasing the old man.

"No," said Rune when he had recovered. "You're not merely singing here. You're working magic."

"Magic?" Jack immediately woke up.

"Surely Dragon Tongue told you. Each song draws its power from Yggdrassil, the great Tree that rises through the nine worlds."

"I never heard of Yggdrassil."

"Dragon Tongue would have called it the life force. It

gives you the power to create. Now you've worn me out and wasted my time." Rune stopped speaking and gave his attention to breathing. It was a terrible sound, harsh and painful. Each time, the old warrior paused as if to gather strength for the next breath.

"I'm sorry, sir," said Jack.

Rune waved him away.

Jack returned to the campsite with a hundred questions buzzing in his mind. The Northmen weren't all consumed with slaughter and pillage. They believed in this thing called Yggdrassil, which was another name for the life force. Did the Tree really exist? And if it did, what a wonderful thing to see! Who could he ask about it?

Jack watched Sven the Vengeful and Eric Pretty-Face demonstrate the best way to crack a skull. Thorgil was so inspired, she lined up a row of deer heads and smashed them with a club. There was no point asking *them* about the life force. Sighing, he found Lucy playing with little wooden figures whittled by Olaf for her entertainment.

There was a cow, a horse, a man, and a woman. Lucy had made a fence out of sticks and had drawn the outline of a house in the sand. Bold Heart watched her intently. He picked up the cow and dropped it. Lucy squealed, and the crow bobbed up and down in apparent glee. He picked up the horse.

"Make him stop!" said Lucy, smacking at the bird. He jumped easily out of her reach. Jack grabbed the horse from Bold Heart's beak and planted it back in front of the little girl.

Bold Heart preened his feathers, looking completely uninterested. A second later he scooped up the man and flew to a nearby rock.

Lucy screamed. Sven the Vengeful dropped his axe on Eric Pretty-Face's foot, starting a vigorous argument.

"Stop that! Can't you see you're upsetting her?" Jack cried. *Why am I talking to a stupid bird?* he thought. But Bold Heart understood! He flew back and laid the toy in front of Lucy.

"About time," she grumbled.

Sven the Vengeful and Eric Pretty-Face stopped quarreling and grabbed the charms they wore about their necks. "*Seiðer*," muttered Sven. They walked away, casting nervous glances over their shoulders.

"Say-thur," repeated Jack. "What's that?"

"It means 'witchcraft,'" said Thorgil, looking up from her skull-smashing game. "We don't like witches. Sometimes"— she smiled—"we throw them into bogs to drown."

Bold Heart made a pass just over her head. Thorgil yelled and ducked. "See? That's what I mean! You're a witch and that bird is your familiar! It's not natural for crows to stay up after dark. It's not natural to talk to them. *Both* of you should be drowned in a bog." Bold Heart made another pass—claws out this time—and Thorgil ran off with her hands protecting her scalp.

Jack stood frozen, watching her grab Olaf's arm. She started arguing, but unfortunately for her, she'd interrupted the giant in the middle of something important. Olaf sent her sprawling to the ground. "Hold your noise with that witch nonsense!" he shouted. The shield maiden, spitting curses, picked herself up and staggered off.

Jack sat down to think. Thorgil wouldn't give up that easily. She'd wait for an opportunity and attack again. He had to think of a way to protect himself.

He saw nothing wrong with talking to animals. Mother did it all the time, singing to calm the bees or to gentle a frightened ewe. She'd taught him her small magic, and Jack had never thought twice about it. Did that make him a witch? And what about Bold Heart? He did fly around after dark like an owl.

Right now Bold Heart was sitting in front of Lucy. He made little chuckling noises. "I know I should have chickens on a farm," she replied. "Olaf didn't make any."

More chuckling.

"I *could* use these seashells for them. That's a good idea."

Jack's head began to ache. Now Lucy was talking to the crow, and the warriors would think *she* was a witch. "Bedtime," he ordered, sweeping up the toys. Lucy complained loudly. Jack dragged her to a heap of furs and tucked her in. "I'll tell you a story," he said.

"It better be a good one," she said.

Bold Heart flew to a nearby tree and perched on a branch over Cloud Mane's head. The horse shifted his feet nervously. Bold Heart made purring noises, and Cloud Mane closed his eyes again. It was weird how the bird had adopted them. He flew off every day and Jack expected him to disappear, but he always came back.

I wish the Bard were here, Jack thought sadly. *I hope he's happy on the Islands of the Blessed. I wish I really was a witch. I'd turn every one of the Northmen into toads—except Rune. And I'd turn Thorgil into a slimy earthworm and feed her to Olaf.*

Chapter Eighteen

THE SEA OF TROLLS

The air turned cold and more clouds filled the sky as they went north. Fog showed up earlier and stayed longer. The shoreline became steeper. Olaf urged his men to row swiftly. "We're almost home!" he bellowed. "We carry great wealth! We're covered with honor! We're the Queen's Berserkers!" The men burst into the song that ended with *Fame never dies*.

"The Queen's Berserkers?" said Jack. "I thought you served the king."

"Yes, well, he hasn't quite been himself since he got married," admitted Olaf.

"That's why we call him Ivar the Boneless," said Sven.

"Only not to his face," said the giant. "I can hardly wait to hear the song you've written about me. You can perform it at the welcome-home party." Olaf looked radiant at the prospect of showing off his personal bard before the king and queen.

Jack tried to appear enthusiastic. He had a wonderful poem, courtesy of Rune, but it had so many complicated words, Jack was sure he was going to mess up. Which would be a very grave mistake, Rune told him, with the emphasis on *grave*.

Soon the mist closed in, and while it wasn't thick, it was damp and depressing. Jack understood why the Northmen couldn't dry their own salt. Now and then the mist parted to show a forbidding scene. Waves clashed against cliffs. Rifts in the shoreline led to gloomy and barren valleys. It looked like a place dragons would love.

"Those are fjords," said Olaf, who was all smiles now that he was about to be fêted and praised.

"Does anything live back there?" said Jack, peering into an especially grim inlet.

"Nothing good," said the giant, laughing. "Of course, *we* live at the end of a fjord. But we aren't good either."

You can say that again, thought Jack.

"I fought my first Jotun in one of those," Olaf said. "I was only a beardless youth, and the troll still had his baby fangs. Ah, where does the time go?"

"You won, I suppose."

"Of course. Warriors who don't defeat their trolls get eaten. I'll tell you about it sometime so you can write a poem." Olaf continued reminiscing about his youth. He knew every rock and tree along the coast. His memory was fantastic, and soon Jack was sorry he'd asked questions.

They came to a place where the land broke off. The sea became rougher, and a wind rose and blew the mist away. The view thus revealed was anything but cheerful. Great swells rolled from the north under a strange milky sky. The water was pale green, and the wind carried upon it the smell of ice. The ship tipped dangerously as they turned and followed the coastline to the east.

"We call that the Sea of Trolls," said Olaf.

"They live out there?" said Jack.

"They came from there. Now they live in the high mountains where the snow never melts."

"I didn't know Jotuns knew how to make boats." Jack thought of them as huge and clumsy. They were supposed to be—or perhaps were hoped to be—stupid.

"They walked," Olaf said.

"On the water?" Jack was appalled. Father said only very pure monks could do that. There had been one on the Holy Isle, though he'd given up the practice to avoid the sin of pride. It was shocking to think a dirty troll had the same power.

"Not on water. Ice. Long ago this sea was frozen," said Olaf. "No human ever saw it so, but the Jotuns have been here much longer. Their old home lay in the Utter North near a mountain that belched fire."

"You're joking," said Jack.

"Such things exist. Rune saw one in Italia. He said a dragon lived inside it. Anyhow, the trolls' mountain belched so much fire that it split in two, and their land sank beneath the sea. The Jotuns had to run away across the ice."

"Maybe they lied about the whole thing," said Jack, who couldn't believe the rolling, endless sea to the north had ever been frozen.

"Trolls don't lie," Olaf said simply.

"They kill people and eat them, but they're too virtuous to bend the truth?"

"What I mean is, they *can't* lie. They don't talk as we do, though some have learned our speech. They *think* at you."

And Jack remembered something the Bard had said long ago about trolls: *They can creep inside your mind and know what you're thinking. They know when and where you're going to strike before you do it. Only a very special kind of warrior can overcome them.* "They get inside your mind," Jack said.

"That's it!" said Olaf. "They're impossible to ambush because they know what you're up to. At the same time they can't trick *you*. They can't *think* lies at you."

Jack considered this as he clung to the railing. The ship rolled in the pale green sea, and poor Cloud Mane, who was tethered to the mast, kept slipping and sliding. The cliffs to their right were topped with massive trees. Clouds of seabirds wheeled above foaming rivers that tore down the mountainsides. "How can you fight an enemy who knows your every move?" Jack wondered.

"Ah! That's where berserkers come in," Olaf said. "*We* never know what we're going to do when the fit is on us. We can't even remember what we've done. Jotuns can't read our minds because we don't have any!"

So that's the special kind of warrior the Bard meant, Jack thought. He glanced at Olaf, who was standing tall and proud at the helm. The wind blew back the giant's white beard and ruffled his bushy eyebrow. Olaf looked as eager as a child at a Yuletide party. His face was rosy with cold, and his eyes were bright blue and excited.

It was hard to hate Olaf when he was like this. It was hard to remember how he killed monks and slaughtered entire villages down to the cows and horses. And perhaps that was because *he genuinely didn't remember what he'd done.* There was Good Olaf, who carved toys for Lucy, and Bad Olaf, who sat panting on the ridge overlooking Gizur's village.

What Jack had to keep in mind, though, was that both of them were supremely dangerous.

"Without berserkers, humans would never have survived here," said the giant. "Do you know what the trolls used to call us? 'Two-legged deer.' 'Jotun snacks' was another term. The first humans were hunted like livestock. The skinny ones were fattened up in pens."

Jack shivered. "Do trolls still, um, do that?"

"It's more of a sport now. They know we're people and not animals. A young troll can't have his browridge tattooed until he brings down his first human. He's still allowed to eat the trophy. Oh, look! There's one of the vessels from our battle group."

Olaf pointed at a raiding ship that had just darted out of a fjord. The three ships of Olaf's group had become separated during the long sea voyage. "I'll bet Egil Long-Spear thinks we're enemies and is coming out for battle," Olaf said, naming the captain of the other ship. "Is *his* face going to be red when he realizes his mistake!"

But Egil's face was more a chalky white when he recognized the berserkers. He bawled apologies across the water. "You'll pay for this with a skin of wine!" Olaf roared back. Good Olaf was in control at the moment, and Egil, fingering the charm around his neck, gratefully promised the giant a wineskin.

The two ships sailed on together. Of the third there was no trace. Egil shouted that he thought it had gone down in a storm. No one, at least among the berserkers, seemed depressed about that. Thorgil said the men had been lucky because now they were feasting in the halls of Aegir and Ran. "I'd rather go to Valhalla, though," she said. "It's much more glorious."

I wish you were there already, thought Jack. She was going to give Lucy to Frith, rider of Nightmares. Jack remembered the being who had passed over the Bard's house. *It had ridden a horse draped in shrouds of icicles that broke off and clattered into the room. The rider had been even darker than the sky, so black that it sucked the light out of the stars. Its thorny legs had clasped the belly of the horse, drawing white, oozing blood that was more like pus than anything.*

Jack felt dizzy with fear. He understood it wasn't actually the queen riding the Nightmare, but her spirit. If that spirit, weakened as it was then from being cast across the sea, was that terrifying, what would it be like up close? Jack felt the rune of protection about his neck. It radiated warmth like a small sun clasped to his chest.

Should he give the rune to Lucy? She'd need it more than he, if she fell into Frith's hands. Once given, it was gone forever. He could not take it back. Jack watched Lucy, who was playing peekaboo with Eric Pretty-Face. The grim warrior covered his ruined face with hands that resembled slabs of bacon. "Peekaboo!" shrieked Lucy when he uncovered his eyes. "HAW! HAW! HAW!" rumbled Eric Pretty-Face. It was far too babyish a game for her, but Jack realized it was perfect for the slow-witted Northman.

Lucy was simply too little to understand the importance of the rune. The only thing that would interest her was the bright gold, and that would only be visible while Jack transferred the rune to her neck.

"What do you keep clutching?" came Thorgil's voice.

Jack dropped his hand at once.

"You're hiding something there. Give it to me!" She snatched at his throat, and Jack kicked her. Thorgil immediately fell on him, screaming and pounding him with her fists.

Jack tried to defend himself, but he was no match for the shield maiden. Not only was she better trained, she threw herself into battle with complete abandon. Jack found himself on the deck, his ears ringing and blood pouring from his nose. She put her knee on his chest and snatched again at his throat.

"Aaaaiii!" Thorgil shrieked, falling back. "He burned me! He burned me!" By this time Olaf had arrived. He looked at Jack's bleeding nose and Thorgil's agonized face. She held up her hand, showing a raw square of charred flesh. "Throw him overboard!" she screamed.

"Seems to me you got as good as you gave," remarked Olaf.

"He used witchcraft! He's unnatural!"

"I've told you a dozen times not to fight with my thrall," said the giant. "For this *you* will be punished. You will not be allowed at the high table at our welcome-home feast. You will sit by the door with the better-class thralls."

"That's so unfair! I hate you! I'll kill you!" wept Thorgil.

"Keep that up and you can eat with the hogs," Olaf said. "If the lad used a little magic to defend himself, well, that's what skalds do. Now go to the stern and stay there until we've got into port."

Jack stuck his tongue out at her as she stumbled, weeping noisily, to the stern.

"You"—Olaf's big hand yanked him up—"can stop baiting her. I'll have order on this ship or you'll both be picking your teeth off the deck." He carried the boy to the mast and tied him by the neck next to Cloud Mane.

For the rest of that day Jack sat glumly with a rope around his neck. He wiped his bloody nose on his sleeve and felt his body for bruises. One of his teeth was loose. Lucy wasn't allowed to talk to him.

Being punished was nothing new in Jack's life. Being tethered like a horse was. He felt the shame of it deeply. "It's all right for you," Jack told Cloud Mane. "You aren't smart enough to feel insulted. You think everything's fine as long as you get your oats."

Cloud Mane gazed at Jack with dark eyes. He twitched his nostrils as though he smelled something bad.

"None of us have had baths, so don't take it out on me," grumbled Jack as the ship sailed east along the coast.

Chapter Nineteen

—⊸≡ʍ⌠ʍ≡⊸—

HOMECOMING

The next morning they met the first evidence that they were close to King Ivar's country. A fat, heavy-bodied ship hailed Olaf and Egil as it passed. Jack, who had been released from the mast, leaned over the side to watch. The ship was piled high with dried fish. The men who rowed it, while sturdy, did not have the lean, dangerous look of Olaf's crew.

"That's a *knorr*," explained Olaf. "We call it that because the timbers creak the whole time it's at sea—*knorr, knorr, knorr*. It takes getting used to, but the men who sail them say it's music. There's a *tolfaeringr*, or a twelve-oared craft. *Ptoo!*" Olaf spat over the side in the direction of a small but quite respectable ship. "Fit only for babies, in my opinion. That one's probably looking for herring. See the nets?"

Jack nodded. "What's our boat called?"

"A *karfi*," said Olaf, pleased. He patted Jack on the back and woke up all the bruises Thorgil had inflicted. "It's long, it's lean, it's fast. Best of all, it can go up a river and be pulled out on the sand. Perfect for raids."

"And *that*?" Jack pointed at a huge craft making its way along the coast ahead of them. Its sail was bloodred and its oars almost uncountable. They stroked the waves in unison, flashing a bright spray from the water. The sleek lines of the ship were almost unearthly in their perfection. Jack turned to see a look of hopeless longing on Olaf One-Brow's face. He seemed almost sick.

"That's a *drekar*, a dragon ship."

And Jack saw that the prow was raised in a graceful curve to form a dragon's head.

"It's called *Strider*. It belongs to King Ivar." All the smiles were gone from Olaf's face. Jack eased himself away, though he had little room to escape. He was confined to the prow of the ship as Thorgil was to the stern. "I'm *not* pulling into port behind that *drekar*!" Olaf shouted. "I will not be overshadowed by that joyriding weakling! *I'm* the one who's supposed to come home in glory! *I* braved the danger, not that—that—"

"Boneless one," finished Sven, and got a blow for his effort.

"When was the last time he did anything dangerous except run his fingers through Frith's hair!" The giant stormed down the ship, aiming blows in all directions. Everyone hunched down as far as possible. Finally—his rage somewhat eased—Olaf gave orders to pull into a small bay. Egil Long-Spear's boat followed.

The giant brooded by a campfire all afternoon. At nightfall Jack, at Rune's urging, sang the opening of his praise-song:

Listen, ring-bearers, while I speak
Of the glories of battle, of Olaf, most brave.
Generous is he, that striker of terror.

"Stop!" cried Olaf, blushing like a youth. "I don't want to open my presents before the party." He poked in the flames with his spear. "It's a lovely beginning, though."

Jack and Rune exchanged glances. Egil, who'd been tip-toeing around all afternoon, smiled at them.

"There's more, isn't there?" said the giant.

"Oh, yes," said Jack.

"Lots more," Rune wheezed.

"It wouldn't hurt to hear a different poem," Olaf said, so Jack sang the tale of Beowulf and his battle with Grendel. It was perhaps not the wisest choice, but it cheered up Olaf.

"I assume Dragon Tongue made that," he said. "I can tell it wasn't written in our language."

"I translated it," said Jack.

"And didn't do too bad a job," whispered Rune. "You used the wrong words for 'melancholy' and 'croaking toads.'"

"Poor Dragon Tongue," said Egil. "Frith would never have known who killed her sister if he hadn't bragged about it. He never knew when to keep his mouth shut."

"At least he had the courage to stand up to her," growled Olaf.

Jack was surprised. These men seemed to have liked the Bard. They certainly weren't fond of the queen. "If Frith—I mean, the queen—is a half-troll," he began, working out the idea, "can she tell when people don't like her?"

A chill seemed to descend over the campfire. "If you mean, can she read minds," said Olaf, "the answer is no. Half-trolls are very different from either of their parents. They are—what would you say?"

"An abomination," said Egil.

"Jotuns are honest folk. They're stupid, crude, and ugly—"

"*Very* ugly," said Egil.

"—but they're decent in their way. Why, I'd live next to a troll if the ground rules were worked out," said Olaf.

"A half-troll is a shape-shifter," whispered Rune. "It has no hold on reality. It hates everything."

"So . . . can Frith lie?" said Jack.

"Frith doesn't know the meaning of truth or any other virtue," Olaf said. "Now listen to me, boy, and listen well. We can speak of her here, but when we come to the palace, you must hold your tongue. And keep your pet crow out of sight. She hates crows. She thinks they carry tales about her to Odin."

"We honor Ivar for the man he was, but he's let the king-dom go to ruin," said Egil.

Jack was asked for another tale to round out the evening. He hadn't translated any more poems, so he gave them one of Father's bedtime stories. The martyrdom of Saint Lawrence was a huge hit with the Northmen. "Saint Lawrence was roasted over a slow fire," Jack told the ring of enthralled warriors. "The pagans stuck garlic cloves between his toes and basted him all over like a chicken."

"Sounds like troll work to me," said Olaf.

"What *are* pagans, anyhow?" said Sven the Vengeful.

When Jack got to the part where Saint Lawrence said, *I think I'm done. You may eat me when you will,* the listeners all cheered.

"Now *that's* a warrior," said Egil Long-Spear. "A man like that would go straight to Valhalla."

"I think he went to the Christian Heaven," said Jack.

"If there are people like that in Heaven, I might just become Christian," declared Olaf.

All in all it was a successful evening.

The next day was spent in camp. Everyone bathed in the sea and combed his hair for the big homecoming. Jack took Lucy to a private beach. Her original dress, sewn with such care by Mother, was in rags. Olaf had given her a new and beautifully embroidered frock.

Jack felt strange when he picked it up. It was as though the original maker had left something of herself behind. It hung like faint music in the air. "Ooh! That's nice!" cried Lucy, grabbing it. She discarded Mother's dress without a second glance. Well, she *was* very young, thought Jack. He buried Mother's dress high above the shore, where the tide would not reach it.

Thorgil bathed behind a rock, using a bar of soap she had looted from a Saxon village. She dried her hair in the sunlight, and Jack was surprised to see how golden it was. She was almost as pretty as Lucy. But then she yelled a string of curses at him and spoiled the effect.

Jack sat next to Cloud Mane and watched the preparations. Bold Heart perched on the horse's back. "You have to stay out of Frith's way," Jack told the crow. "I wish I could be sure you understood. You seem awfully intelligent, but you're only a bird. A kind of black chicken, really." Bold Heart ignored him and searched for ticks on Cloud Mane's back.

It was time. The awful moment when they would face Ivar the Boneless came nearer with every oar-stroke. Jack morosely watched the coast speed by as the warriors rowed with renewed energy. They'd decked themselves with finery— brooches, armbands, and finger rings, the more, the better— and exchanged their greasy leather caps for headbands worked in gold. Olaf wore a fine woolen cloak, pinned on the right shoulder to leave his sword arm free. Even Thorgil had a necklace of finely worked silver leaves over her faded tunic. With her bright hair streaming in the wind, she looked quite girlish.

Jack thought about telling her this, but he knew the penalty for baiting her.

They met boats of all sizes, though none as grand as King Ivar's *drekar* or even as large as Olaf's and Egil's ships. When they came to the mouth of the fjord, a swarm of little fishing boats scooted out of their way. The fishermen cheered, and Olaf stood tall and grand at the prow.

They followed the fjord deep into the land. The sound of

the sea died away. The waves disappeared. Soon the water was as calm as a lake. On either side were grim, forested mountains, with here and there a hawk coasting the upper air. And far away to the north lay high mountains covered in snow.

"Jotunheim," said Olaf.

Troll country, translated Jack with a sinking heart.

Presently, they saw farms high in the hills and steep meadows with herds of sheep and cattle. At a bend in the fjord, where the meadow came down to the water, was a large dock and many houses. A child saw them coming and ran back along a street, shouting. Immediately, the houses emptied out. Men, women, children, and dogs hurried to the dock, hollering and barking for all they were worth.

"Any sign of Ivar?" said Olaf.

"Not yet," said Sven the Vengeful.

The celebration on the shore went on. The people were working themselves into a frenzy, but there were some who were less joyful. They shaded their eyes and looked from one ship to the other. Jack guessed they were searching for the third ship, the one that presumably went down, or for kinfolk who might have been rescued.

"There's Ivar," said Sven.

Beyond the town was a shoulder of mountain leaning out over the fjord. It was an outcropping of dark blue stone, as bleak and lifeless as metal. On top was a long house Jack hadn't noticed before. A group of people—it was too far to see clearly—stood outside.

"He'll wait for you to come to him," said Sven.

"Troll-whipped weakling," muttered Olaf under his breath.

In spite of the absence of the king, the warriors' welcome was everything they could have wanted. The women hugged and kissed them. The men, who were mostly old, gave them friendly punches. Parents greeted sons; wives—sometimes two or three to a man—welcomed their husbands. Children ran around shrieking. Those whose family members had not returned wept quietly at the side. Perhaps their men were still on the way. Perhaps not.

Jack held Lucy's hand tightly. The crowd surged around them, pushing them this way and that. "What a pretty little thrall!" cried a woman, chucking Lucy under the chin.

"Go away!" shrilled Lucy.

"With a temper, too," the woman said approvingly.

Jack pulled his sister out of the crush until they were up among the houses. He didn't know what to do. He felt lonely and scared. No one in this town cared about them. They were livestock, to be sold or slaughtered. But he had to stay in control so he could protect Lucy. He looked around to find something to take his mind off his troubles and saw Thorgil walking slowly up the street. She, too, was alone. No one had come to greet her. She didn't even seem to have friends.

Something twisted inside Jack. How could anyone be that alone? No matter how desperate his and Lucy's situation was, they had each other. And they had parents who missed and mourned for them. They had a village where they would be greeted as enthusiastically as the returning Northmen. How could anyone come home to *nothing*?

Then, racing down the street, Jack saw a pack of dogs. They were unlike anything he'd ever seen and unlike the curly-tailed dogs frisking around the dock. These animals were *huge*, almost as tall as he. They had long, lean heads and small ears. Their coats were matted and gray.

Jack pushed Lucy behind him. The dogs galloped toward them like horses. But at the last minute they pulled up and danced around the children, baying and leaping.

"Slasher! Wolf Bane! Hel Hag! Shreddie!" yelled Thorgil. The dogs fell on her, yipping and licking. They rolled her in the dirt, and she pummeled them back. Then one of them— Jack thought it was Shreddie—left the tangle and came back to Lucy. He plumped his front legs down on the ground and waggled his rump in the air. His tail wagged furiously.

"Nice doggie," said Lucy.

"I don't think so," said Jack, his heart pumping.

"Stay away from them!" shouted Thorgil, fighting her way out of the tangle. "They're *my* friends. *Mine!* They're not for dirty thralls." She ran up the street. "Come, friends! Come to me!" she yelled back. The dogs took off like arrows.

Jack stared after her, glad the huge beasts had gone. "Nice doggies," said Lucy.

"Let's find Olaf," said Jack. It occurred to him that Thorgil, when she cried *Come, friends! Come to me,* had spoken in Saxon.

Chapter Twenty

THE WISE WOMAN

Olaf took them to his farm above the village. Several of his thralls—with slave rings around their necks—carried chests of booty. Jack wondered if he would be fitted with such a ring. It would be a terrible and unending humiliation. No one could look at him without knowing his status.

Any illusion Jack might have had about friendship between an owner and his slave was dispelled by the thralls' names: Pig Face, Dirty Pants, Thick Legs, and a man-and-wife couple called Lump and She-Lump. She-Lump led Cloud Mane to a stable. Even the horse had a better name.

The walls of Olaf's main house were curved inward. The ridge along the top formed an arc like the keel of an over-turned ship. At each end of the ridge was a carved dragon's head. Scattered about were other buildings—stables, storehouses, kitchens, and spare bedrooms.

Inside, as with Father's house, the floor was below the surface of the ground. Along the sides were benches and tables and, leaning against a far wall, a beautifully made loom. Everywhere were examples of Olaf's carving skills. Horses, birds, fish, and dragons decorated the roof beams and supporting timbers.

A fire burned in a long stone-lined trough down the middle of the hall. It made the air pleasantly warm, but smoky. Jack and Lucy started coughing the minute they got inside. "Good for the lungs!" cried Olaf, striking himself on the chest. "A hearty cough always tells me I've arrived home. Come on, ladies! Come and see what I've brought you!"

Olaf's three wives crowded around, along with his towheaded children. There were at least a dozen. They mobbed their father, demanding to see what he'd brought them. "A smack on the backside!" roared the giant. The children weren't a bit scared. They continued to climb on their father's legs and hang off his arms.

Finally, the wives unhooked them and the gift-giving began. There were shawls, tunics, bolts of cloth, and tools for the general running of the house. A heap of salt cakes brought cries of approval from the wives, who, Jack learned, were called Dotti, Lotti, and Heide. Olaf handed out embroidered headbands to the boys and scarves to the girls. Everyone got a new knife. He tossed necklaces, bracelets, and brooches to the wives, laughing to see them fight for the loot. "Who are the thralls for?" Dotti said. The women eagerly turned to look at Jack and his sister.

"He's my skald," said Olaf.

"Ooh! Your own personal skald!" cried Dotti.

"You deserve it, really you do," enthused Lotti. They were as alike as two apples from the same tree: blond and blue-eyed with fat, rosy cheeks and well-rounded arms.

The third wife was different. She had a broad, flat face and eyes that tilted up at the corners. Her skin was bronze, which made her light blue eyes all the more remarkable. But that was not the only difference. Jack felt the air tremble as she looked at him. A lazy, drowsy warmth crept over him, and Olaf's voice seemed to fade away. Nothing registered except this strange, dark woman staring at him. Then she laughed, and the drowsy feeling went away. "I like thiss boy," she announced in a heavily accented voice.

"Now, Heide, I'm not giving him to you," said Olaf.

"You haff not the giffing uff this boy," Heide said.

"And you have not the getting, woman. See, I brought you pots of herbs and medicines, as you asked."

Heide nodded, accepting the tribute. "How about the girlll?" Her voice was low and husky. Lucy hung on to Jack's hand, her thumb in her mouth. She stared at the smoldering fire in the middle of the room and appeared to be miles away in one of her fantasies.

"She belongs to Thorgil."

"*Thorgil?*" cried Dotti and Lotti together.

"It was her first capture," Olaf said. "She was pleased as anything about it."

"Thorgil," said Heide in her smoky voice, "iss not pleased about anything."

"Yes, well, I'm not going to break my rules and deprive her of her first capture."

Jack was fascinated to see how careful Olaf was with Heide. He might knock his crew around, and he probably smacked Dotti and Lotti as well, but this woman was in a different category. If anything, Olaf was afraid of her.

"What iss Thorgilll"—the name was drawn out—"going to do with the child?"

"Give her to Frith."

"No!" cried the other wives, and Olaf looked apologetic.

"She wants to be admitted to the Queen's Berserkers," he said. "It's her dearest wish. I can invite her along on trips, but I haven't the authority to admit her. The gift of Lucy—that's the little mite's name—will win her entry."

"It iss not well done," said Heide. "It iss supreme foolishnesss, my ox-witted Northman. It will end in disasterrr."

Now Jack did expect Olaf to strike her, but he only grimaced. "Don't try your witchy stuff on me, Heide. I'm tired, I'm dirty, and the only thing I want is a long sweat in the sauna and a nice bucket of mead."

"Bucket" was exactly what Olaf had in mind. Dotti filled one from a keg in one of the storehouses, and Olaf drank until his beard was dripping. "By Aegir's mighty shoulders, that's good!" he said. "Honey wine from your own fields. You can't beat it." Lotti hastily brought him bread and cheese.

"You know what would go with this?" said Olaf. "*Graffisk.* Fetch me some *graffisk!*" Lotti sped out the door. "You're in for a treat, boy," he told Jack. "Many's the time I dreamed of this dish while at sea. It truly means I've come home. Because I like you, I'll let you have some."

"Thank you," Jack said uncertainly. He wouldn't have minded the bread and cheese, but that hadn't been offered. Suddenly, an unbelievably foul odor wafted through the door. It was like toenails and rotten teeth and ancient bilge-water. Jack couldn't begin to describe it. He had all he could do to keep from bolting from the room.

Lotti danced in with a bowl. "I opened a fresh keg," she warbled.

Fresh? thought Jack. The bowl was full of purplish lumps floating in a slimy gray liquid. It looked every bit as horrible as it smelled.

"*Graffisk!*" said Olaf. He smeared some onto a chunk of bread and gobbled it down. A smile of contentment creased his beard. "Have some." He held out the bowl.

"I—I'm not hungry," Jack said.

"HAVE SOME."

So Jack took a morsel of bread and dipped the tiniest corner of it in the liquid. He put it into his mouth. He swallowed quickly, but not quickly enough. The taste coated the inside of his mouth like the mud coated his legs when he mucked out the barn. Jack ran for the door, bent down, and retched for all he was worth.

"Ha! Ha! Ha! Ha! *Brjóstabarn!*" Olaf said, guffawing. His wives and children joined in with merry peals of laughter. After a while Heide took pity on him and brought him a cup of water.

"That's hiss favorite joke with outsiders," she said. Jack stumbled after her, back into the room. He'd finally figured out what *graffisk* meant: "grave fish," as in dead, as in *rotten*.

"*Graffisk* is what we make when we have no salt," explained Olaf, who was mopping up the nauseous stuff with his bread. He really did like it! "Sometimes we find a herring run—thousands and thousands of herring!—so many, the sea is thick with them. You can lay an axe on the water and it will not sink. So! We bring the herring home. What then? We can only eat so many. If it's raining, we can't dry the rest.

"So we put the fish into barrels and bury them in the earth. For months we wait. The fish ripen like fine cheese. They turn purple. They get a delicious smell. The longer we wait, the better they taste."

"Why don't they poison you?" said Jack, thinking, *I wish they would poison you.*

Olaf grinned and slapped his stomach. "We Northmen are strong. Not like Saxons." All this while Lump and She-Lump had been stoking up the sauna. Lump came to the door. The giant stood up, brushed the crumbs from his beard, and followed the glum slave.

Jack went over to sit by Lucy. She was watching the fire in the middle of the room with rapt attention. "Lucy?"

No answer.

"Lucy?" He took her hand. She seemed strange, almost as if she wasn't there.

"It's so pretty," she said, staring at the fire. One of Olaf's girls came over and shoved her off the bench.

"Hey!" Jack yelled.

"Toad Face," said the girl. "I think that's what I'll call you. Toad Face. It's my turn to name a thrall."

"Leave him," said Heide, who had come up behind them as silently as a wolf. The girl fled. Jack put Lucy back on the bench. She stared at the fire as though nothing had happened.

"What's wrong with her? Is she sick?" Jack cried. Inside, he thought, *Is she insane?*

"Her spirit hass fled," said Heide. "It iss wandering in a strange place—a nice place, I think."

"Father used to tell her she was a lost princess," Jack said, somewhat reassured. "He said that someday knights would find her and take her back to the castle. I'm afraid Lucy believed him."

"I haff seen thiss before," said the dark woman. "In my land the winters are long and dark. People's spirits wander sso that they do not go mad. When spring comes, they return."

"I hope spring returns for Lucy."

"It may with your help. You are a special boy. I know. I haff looked inside."

"Are you a wise woman?" Jack asked.

Heide laughed, a sound as smoky as her voice. The other people in the house stopped what they were doing. It seemed everybody walked carefully around Heide. "Thank you for not

calling me a witch," she said. "That iss what *they* think." She
indicated the others in the room. "But yess, I practice *seiðer.*"

"Isn't that . . . witchcraft?" said Jack.

"It iss woman's magic. What skalds do iss man's magic. It
iss only witchcraft iff the two are mixed up."

Jack wasn't sure he understood, but it relieved his mind.
He was a skald, and so the magic he did was all right. Thorgil
wouldn't be able to accuse him. "Where are you from?" he
asked.

"Olaf won me in Finnmark. My father wass the headman
uff a village, and Olaf wass trading for furs."

So the giant doesn't always kill people and steal things, Jack
thought.

"I had many suitors. Many. A wise woman iss very valu-
able. But my spirit chose Olaf. I should haff married one uff
the others, but"—Heide shrugged—"he wass so big and
beautiful. I am not like them." She frowned at Dotti and
Lotti, who were examining their children for head lice. "I
only stay iff big ox-brain treats me right. Iff he insults me, I
will go."

Heide went back to her pots of medicine and herbs. Jack
stayed with Lucy. The little girl seemed happy enough, staring into the flames. When Jack brought her the wooden toys
Olaf had carved, she set about playing with them. Jack asked
Lotti for bread and cheese. He didn't really understand his
status—perhaps thralls got beaten if they asked for food—but
Lotti gave him what he wanted and a cup of buttermilk
besides. Jack fed the milk to Lucy.

One thing resulted from Heide's interest in him: Jack and Lucy were left alone. No one pushed her off the bench again, and no one threatened to name him Toad Face.

Late in the day Thorgil showed up, and Jack was horrified to learn that she lived with Olaf's family. She burst into the house, glowing and sweaty from her romp with the dogs. Heide ordered her to the sauna. Rune arrived for dinner, and Jack learned that he, too, was part of the household. "My wife died years ago, and none of our children lived past infancy," he whispered. "Olaf's hall is always as warm and friendly as a summer afternoon. It's like a great light in the midst of a wilderness."

Jack shivered. He'd heard those words before. "You mean it's like Hrothgar's hall before Grendel got to it."

"Did I quote that poem? Yes, I suppose I did. It was Dragon Tongue's finest work." Rune stretched his feet toward the fire pit in the middle of the room. "I have lived long enough to know that nothing lasts forever. Such joy as Olaf's will sooner or later attract its destruction. But I also know that to ignore joy while it lasts, in favor of lamenting one's fate, is a great crime."

Heide brought him a steaming cup of medicine to sooth his ravaged throat. They smiled at each other, and Jack felt the air tremble between the ancient warrior and the wise woman.

The evening meal was spectacular. Olaf's wives and servants had toiled all day to make it memorable. The giant's chair was dragged to the upper end of the fire pit. Tables set with wooden platters, spoons, and cups were lined up on either side. Each diner was expected to supply his or her own knife, but Jack was given one since his own was long gone.

Fine wheat bread, rounds of cheese, salmon baked in fennel, geese oozing delicious fat, stews wafting the seductive odors of cumin and garlic—all these and more were carted in by the servants. Buttermilk, cider, beer, and mead were there for the asking. Bowls of apples sat on every table. Jack had never seen so much food. It made up for the ghastly *graffisk* earlier.

Olaf sat in his great chair at the head of the fire pit. Rune and Jack were to one side of him, while his sons brawled for the best cuts of meat on the other. The wives and daughters, when they weren't fetching things from the outlying kitchens, dined in a more orderly way farther down the hall. Heide looked after Lucy. Even the thralls were given a place near the door. As far as Jack could tell, they got the same food as everyone else.

It was a joyous gathering with much impromptu singing. Only one person sat apart and did not join in the festivities. Thorgil was placed midway between the male and female family members. Olaf had relented on his threat of placing her with the thralls. Yet she was not in the place of honor and Jack was. She sat alone, a little patch of misery, in the noisy celebration. *Where is her family?* Jack wondered.

"You can help with the clearing up," said Heide to the sullen girl.

For answer, Thorgil dashed her wooden platter to the floor. "I do not do women's work!" she cried.

"There iss no shame in it. You are one of us, like it or not."

Everyone stopped talking. A breathless silence fell over the hall, broken only by the crackling of the fire.

"Pick up your things!" roared Olaf suddenly, sending a shock wave through the gathering.

"I'm not like them! I'm a shield maiden!" shouted Thorgil.

"You're an orphan living on my goodwill. If any of my men behaved as you did, I'd grind his face into that mess you've just created. NOW MOVE!"

Thorgil knocked over her stool and fled out the door. No one tried to stop her. Heide shook her head and bent down to clean up the scattered stew and bread.

Jack sat back, his heart pounding. He felt sick to his stomach. He'd been next to Olaf when the giant roared, and his ears still rang. Even worse, the rage and anguish coming from Thorgil had struck him like a blow. He couldn't understand it.

He was trained to serve the life force. When his mind was calm, he could feel its currents in the air, in the earth. He felt it between Rune and Heide, but that was no surprise. Heide was a wise woman and Rune was a skald. He liked them.

He absolutely hated Thorgil. She was crude and vicious. She gloried in death. There was nothing remotely attractive about her character, and yet . . . Jack remembered her walking up the street without a single person to greet her. Olaf had called her an orphan, so she had no family. He looked sideways at Rune calmly dipping his bread in his stew. "Where will she go?" Jack asked.

"Thorgil? She'll sleep in the sauna." The old warrior didn't seem worried about it. "If there's enough moonlight, she'll go up the hill and crawl in with the king's dogs."

"Her brothers and sisters," said one of Olaf's sons, a stocky lad with the beginnings of a beard. His eyes were slightly tilted, and Jack guessed his mother was Heide. "They're the only ones who'll put up with her."

"That's enough, Skakki," said Olaf. "She can't help her rages. She gets them from her father, and Odin knows, there was never a finer berserker."

Everyone murmured assent. "Are the king's dogs big and gray?" asked Jack.

"I see you've met them," said Olaf.

It was amazing how quickly the giant could switch from fury to cheerful good-naturedness. But Jack knew he could switch back just as fast. "They ran at Lucy and me this afternoon, but they didn't hurt us," he said.

"They'd never hurt a child," Skakki said. "You could put Hilda in their food dish"—he pointed at a somewhat overblown infant suckling noisily at Lotti's breast—"and they wouldn't even growl."

"Don't let them see a wolf, though," said Olaf. "Thor himself couldn't hold them back then."

"You might as well tell him the story," said Lotti, moving Hilda, who screamed at the interruption, to the other breast.

Olaf leaned back in his great chair, making it groan

dangerously. "Thorgil's father," he began, "was the greatest berserker who ever lived. His name was Thorgrim. He was always the first into battle and the last to leave. By the time he was sixteen, he had a necklace of troll teeth. His greatest bane, though, was his rage. When it came upon him, he neither saw nor heard what was around him."

"You couldn't stop him," said Skakki. "I remember."

"He had no proper wife—no one would marry him," Olaf said. "But he had a thrall. A Saxon. I forget her name."

"It was Allyson, dear ox-brain," said Heide. "Trust you to forget a woman's name."

"Anyhow, this Allyson gave him a son called Thorir. I told you what happened to him."

"Yes," said Jack, remembering the terrible murder.

"Afterward Allyson wasn't the same. She hardly seemed aware of anything around her. When she had a baby girl, the only word she said was 'Jill.' That was her name for the child."

"Only she had no right to name it, being a thrall," Skakki said.

"The midwife took it to Thorgrim, and he rejected it."

"*Rejected* it?" cried Jack. Such a thing was unheard of. No matter how ugly a baby was, it was sent by God. You *had* to love it.

"It is a father's right," said Olaf, looking sternly at his numerous offspring. It was obvious he'd never rejected one, and they didn't look at all worried about it.

"He wanted a boy," whispered Rune. Everyone fell silent

to let him be heard. "He wanted one to replace Thorir, and when the child was a girl, he ordered it thrown out into the forest."

Jack was so shocked, he couldn't speak.

"So the midwife took it far from the house and laid it under a tree," Olaf continued. "King Ivar had received a pair of Irish wolfhounds as a gift, and the bitch had given birth not long before. She went for a run in the forest and came upon the infant. I guess it was screaming."

"Like my Hilda," Lotti said fondly, unplugging her infant.

"She threw herself down and nursed it, just as though it were a puppy. When the keeper went to look for the bitch, he found her curled around the infant, keeping it warm."

"You keep saying 'it' when you talk of the baby," said Jack. "Wasn't it a girl?"

"It was nothing yet," said Rune. "It had not been accepted."

"But now Thorgrim had a problem," Olaf said. "Our law says that a child, once suckled, cannot be abandoned. Like it or not, the royal dog had suckled it. Thorgrim was forced to take it—now *her*—back. He named her Thorgil and handed her over to Allyson."

"Who never looked twice at her," said Heide. "She fed her and that was all. Thorgil's father ignored her too. The only one to give her any love was the bitch, and afterward her puppies."

So that was the story! It was as amazing as any tale the Bard had taught Jack. It would make a wonderful poem, except that it was so sad. It needed a happier ending, one Jack promised himself to work on.

The conversation turned to other things. After a while the warmth and good food made Jack extremely sleepy. Heide led him away to an outlying hut, where he was given a heap of straw and a rough blanket. Several young thralls were already snoring. Lucy had been put to bed in a corner of the great hall.

The blanket was full of fleas—Jack felt them hopping about—but he was too sleepy to care. He was vaguely aware when Pig Face, Dirty Pants, and Thick Legs came in later, smelling of sour beer and sweat, to burrow into the straw.

Chapter Twenty-one

GOLDEN BRISTLES

The next day Jack learned that no matter how well treated he'd been at the feast, he was a thrall, would always be a thrall, and would always look like a thrall to anyone he met. At daybreak he was pulled roughly from his bed by Dirty Pants and marched over to the farm's forge. There Dirty Pants hammered a slave collar into shape. The man forced the open ring around Jack's neck and wrenched it shut with a pair of tongs. "I made it big so you'd have room to grow," he commented. "You're to muck out the pig barn. It's that building near the apple trees."

Jack stumbled from the forge, numb with despair. His throat hurt where Dirty Pants had bruised it. The collar was cold against his skin and too large to hide beneath his tunic.

He walked in a dark dream toward the distant building

Dirty Pants had indicated. The life force seemed far away, and even the rune, nestled invisibly on his chest, took on a chill from the iron collar. A flock of crows rose from the pigsty. They circled, complaining loudly, before settling down. They had nothing to fear. It was only a thrall coming to muck out the barn.

One of the birds, finer and glossier than the rest, pranced along the edge of the roof. "Bold Heart!" called Jack. "Don't you remember me? It's Jack." But the bird gazed at him coldly and made no move to come nearer.

Surely it was the same crow. He was missing a claw on his left foot. "I know it's you, Bold Heart," said the boy. "I called you out of the sky and saved your life. I told Lucy you came from the Islands of the Blessed, and maybe you do. You're awfully clever."

Jack stood on a bucket and tried to reach the edge of the roof. His fingers brushed the bird's feathers. He flew away. Jack lost his balance and fell off. He saw the crow disappear into a tree, and though it was a small thing, the bird's desertion was the last in a long line of terrible events. Jack curled up on the ground, sobbing wildly. "It's true! It's true! I'm only a thrall. Even the birds know it. I'm like Dirty Pants and Pig Face! Oh, I wish I'd drowned in the sea! At least then I could have walked to the Islands of the Blessed and found the Bard." He was speaking in Saxon, which was unusual now. He used Northman all the time, except with Lucy.

Jack felt something pull his hair. He looked up and saw the crow bobbing and weaving. Bold Heart talked and talked in crow language, now keening, now warbling, dipping down to pull on Jack's hair or tunic. He ruffled his feathers. He swayed back and forth. If Bold Heart had been a dog, Jack thought, he'd be rolling on his back in abject apology.

"It's all right," said Jack, sitting up to smooth the crow's feathers. "I understand. You were off with your crow friends and forgot about me. It's natural you like them better."

The bird hopped onto Jack's lap and leaned against his chest. His warbling dropped down to a murmur. He shivered.

"I wasn't angry, you know. I was sad," said the boy. "There's a big difference. Who wouldn't be sad with a horrible slave collar? But I can put up with it as long as I have a friend." Bold Heart clacked his beak to show what he thought of slave collars. "Now I have to work," said Jack. "I don't know what they do to lazy thralls around here, but I'm sure it's nasty. You can watch me if you like." He found a rake leaning against the barn and went inside. Bold Heart followed, gliding to a roof beam. Three sows looked up expectantly.

As in Jack's village, most of the animals foraged outside during summer. Pigs roamed wild in the forest to be brought down as game, but a few piglets were captured and tamed every spring. They were intelligent beings. They'd follow you everywhere and oink contentedly when you scratched them behind the ears. This is what made things difficult when fall arrived, for in fall all the pigs were slaughtered, except for a pregnant sow that would provide piglets for the Yuletide feast.

The sows crowded up to the railing. They were pale,

athletic creatures with long legs, unlike the squat black-and-white pigs Jack was used to. Their ears stuck up alertly and their eyes sparkled with interest as they thrust their long snouts at him. They looked like they'd bowl him over in a second if he let his guard down.

"Look at all that muck." Jack sighed. The sows were knee-deep in it. The stench made his eyes water and must have bothered the animals, for Jack knew swine were basically tidy creatures. They kept themselves neat and clean if at all possible. He saw a small, clean pen at the side and understood this was where the animals should go while he worked on their sty.

Jack went outside to find something to tempt them. To his surprise, he saw Pig Face, Dirty Pants, and Lump sitting on a fence. No doubt they were delighted to have a newcomer to boss around. *They* certainly hadn't been doing their jobs lately. "Looking for fodder?" called Lump. Jack nodded. The man pointed at a stand of wild mustard.

"You'll have to close the door to keep them from running when you switch pens," said Pig Face. Jack gathered an armful of mustard and went back. The stench was enough to make a bird drop out of the sky. Jack saw that Bold Heart had sensibly positioned himself near a hole in the roof.

The only light came from that hole when the door was closed. The darkness made the barn somehow sinister. Indistinct shapes of farm equipment hung from the rafters and reminded Jack of the imps Father said lie in wait for wicked souls.

"I'm letting my imagination run away with me," he scolded himself. "That's a rope and that's a scythe—I think—anyhow, something sharp. That's a saw." Jack climbed into the clean pen and dropped the mustard on the floor. The sows whuffled eagerly.

He found the gate between the two pens and opened it. The sows raced through, knocking him over in their eagerness. This part of the job was certainly easy. "Enjoy yourselves, ladies," he said, laughing at their greed.

Bold Heart exploded off his perch, and Jack scrambled to his feet in alarm. He saw an enormous creature rise out of the muck in the farther pen. Filth streamed off its flanks as it sprang forward, mouth open, monster tusks aimed at his face. Jack tried to slam the gate, but the creature was too powerful. It barreled through, turned, and came for him.

Jack climbed the fence. He had only a second to make up his mind. He could leap into the muck on the other side—but the creature would only rush back—or he could jump for a roof beam. He jumped. Splinters pierced his hands as he struggled to pull himself up. He swung his leg over and balanced precariously with his arms and legs around the narrow beam.

What *was* that down below? Jack squinted into the gloom, and the creature raised its massive head and squealed. It was a giant boar! Even for a boar, he was bigger than any pig Jack had ever seen, and beneath the filth Jack saw a patch of golden hair. The animal would have been magnificent if he hadn't been covered in muck. The creature screamed again, and Jack almost fell off the beam. He couldn't hold this position for long. Slowly, carefully, he wriggled his body around until he was able to sit. He had to brace his hands against the roof to keep from tipping off. Now his backside hurt as well as his hands.

The boar squealed murderously as he paraded below. He reared up and gnashed his teeth. Where were the thralls? Jack thought. Didn't they know he was in danger? Jack opened his mouth to yell when he heard another sound from outside.

Laughter. The thralls were laughing! They'd known about the boar and hadn't warned him! In fact—Jack saw it now—there'd been no real reason to close the door. The two pens would have contained the pigs. But the *darkness* had been the point. The thralls knew the boar would be hiding in the muck and that he would be nearly invisible with the door closed.

"I'm such a fool," moaned Jack. Yet how could he have imagined such malice? He'd never done anything to those men. They were all thralls together, and their enemy should be the one who'd enslaved them.

"Is he getting chomped?" said Dirty Pants.

"I hope so, the little weasel, sitting up there at the high table with his lordship," said Pig Face.

"Maybe we should rescue him," said Lump. "Him being a kid and all."

"Naw, once Golden Bristles starts something, you have to let him finish," said Dirty Pants. "Besides, we don't want witnesses."

"Suppose you're right," said Lump.

Golden Bristles must be the name of the boar, thought Jack. It was a glorious name, but there was nothing glorious about the beast in his current condition. He was so covered with black filth, his body seemed cased in a suit of armor.

Bold Heart warbled from his position by the hole in the roof.

"I can't fit through there," said Jack. "And I can't fly to it like you can, old friend. I'll have to wait till someone comes looking for me." Even as he said it, Jack's heart sank. His arms ached from the effort of keeping his position. How could he endure it for hours? And would anyone think to look for him?

Bold Heart warbled again. It was an unusually sweet sound for a crow, and Jack had never heard the like of it. "What are you telling me? What are you telling *him?*" For Jack now saw that Golden Bristles had raised his muzzle and was watching the bird closely. "You *like* that," the boy said, wondering.

And then it came to him. Mother sang to calm the ewes and rams. She sang to the bees before taking their honey. She'd taught Jack this small magic, but it hadn't seemed important to him. It was trivial compared with the knowledge the Bard had to impart.

Jack began with a charm to calm angry bees:

Generous spirits of the air,
Rich and full your halls
When you return from the far fields,
The wind at your back.

He went on with a lullaby to soothe newborn lambs and then, from somewhere, came a new song full of joy and life. He sang of the deep forest, of drifts of acorns under oaks, of dappled sunlight and wild leeks to unearth and savor. When he was finished, he felt light and happy, as though he himself had been running through the woods.

He looked down to see Golden Bristles grunting softly and gazing up at him with adoring eyes. The change in the brute was astounding. The sows, meanwhile, had finished their mustard and were snuffling about for more. They were soulless creatures, Jack decided. Not so Golden Bristles, who whuffled seductively. Plain as plain, the giant pig was saying, *More.*

So Jack sang another song, and all the while he edged along the rafter (thereby getting splinters in his backside) until he'd gone as far as possible. He wasn't out of range yet, but he had a chance to run to the outer fence before Golden Bristles caught him.

Jack dropped to the floor. He fell wrong, and his feet slid out from under him. Instantly, he was back up, but Golden Bristles was faster. The boar bounded to the fence and stood between Jack and freedom.

The boy and the pig stared at each other. Then Golden Bristles came forward, panting and whuffling, his chin in the air, for all the world like a dog begging for attention. Carefully, Jack reached out and scratched the boar under the chin. Golden Bristles grunted.

"You're an old softie," Jack crooned as he did with the pigs back home. "You'd melt like butter if I did *this*." He rubbed behind Golden Bristles's ears. The boar's eyes closed in ecstasy. "Well, well," said Jack. "I think the thralls are in for a surprise." He penned the sows and the boar into the clean sty and climbed out to open the barn door.

Pig Face, Dirty Pants, and Lump leaped back.

"You were singing," said Dirty Pants. "What was that about?"

"You ain't chomped," said Pig Face disappointedly.

"No, I'm not." Jack stood before them proudly, his hands on his hips.

"But I heard Golden Bristles scream," muttered Pig Face.

Jack was seething with rage, but he didn't intend to show it. He had other plans.

The thralls galumphed inside. "Hoo! It's foul," commented Lump.

"Not my fault," said Pig Face. "The boar's too fond of human meat by half. He's a troll-boar. I'm not getting close to him."

"You will if Olaf tells you," said Dirty Pants.

"That's what the new boy's for. Hey, boy! Come in here. You haven't done your job."

Jack went in and deliberately leaned over the fence. Golden Bristles trotted to him and lifted his chin to be scratched. "Gooood piggy," Jack crooned. The thralls' eyes almost dropped out of their heads.

"*Seiðer,*" murmured Dirty Pants. "That's what the singing was about."

"So that's why Heide was interested in him," Lump whispered.

"This is skald's magic, not *seiðer*," announced Jack, who wasn't entirely sure about it. "I'm a skald. I do not clean out pigsties." He handed the rake to Lump, who took it automatically. "If you annoy me, I'll make you come up in boils. If you try to hurt me, I'll drive you insane—or worse!"

The thralls looked stunned. It was clear they were trying to figure out what "worse" could mean. "If I tell Olaf what you've just done, he'll chop you into little bits." The thralls' white faces told Jack that this threat, at least, was entirely believable. "Now I'm going to the great hall for breakfast. I expect you to have the barn cleaned out by nightfall. And throw a few buckets of water over Golden Bristles. He's not happy about being covered with muck."

Jack strode out as if he were the captain of a *drekar*. He didn't look back. He had little enough going for him in this horrible land. If he could bully the thralls into fearing him, so much the better. He owed them nothing.

Once out of sight, Jack collapsed under a hedge, and the terror of his near destruction came over him. He trembled and tears leaked down his face. Why were so many people out to get him? How could he possibly survive so many enemies? He looked up to see Bold Heart chuckling to himself nearby. "I have at least one true friend," Jack said, wiping his eyes on his sleeve. "And maybe I have two, if you can count Golden Bristles."

Jack dug the splinters out of his hands while he calmed his nerves. He heard curses and shouts from the pig barn, so perhaps Golden Bristles wasn't being such a good piggy

anymore. This cheered Jack up considerably, and he saun-
tered to the great hall in a happier mood. Bold Heart followed him the whole way, not going off with the other
crows as he had done before.

Chapter Twenty-two

—•◦•—

HEIDE'S PROPHECY

"This iss not well done," said Heide as she arranged and rearranged Olaf's magnificent scarlet cloak. It was late afternoon, and the household was preparing to attend King Ivar's welcome-home feast. If welcome it was. In spite of Olaf's gifts, Ivar had waited an insulting two weeks before acknowledging the triumphant hero.

"You are giffing Ivar the troll-boar, but iff the king sees that boy, he will want him, too," said Heide. She fussed with Olaf's beard, which had been decorated with ribbons, before presenting him with his party helmet. Jack felt cold when he saw it. It had the same weird, hawklike mask. But this one was covered in gold and engraved with designs—a line of warriors marched around the rim, and beautifully wrought vines covered the top.

"He's going to sing my praises, woman. What good is that without an audience?"

"And whhhat"—Heide drew out the word like a sigh of wind off the sea—"will the king think iff you haff a skald and he does not?"

"Ivar's all right," said Olaf uncomfortably. "I've served him all my life. He's an honorable man."

"He wasss," Heide said with a sigh, "before *she* arrived."

"Yes, well, you're not changing a thing. Get my sword, boy. I'll have to take it off at the door, but it looks good with the cloak."

And so it did in the new scabbard Skakki had decorated with jewels he'd pried from a looted cross. Jack could hardly lift it, but Olaf strapped it on easily. Skakki would attend as well in his own finery, bearing a sword he had won in battle. He would never be as large as his father, but there was no mistaking his bravery.

Jack liked him. He had his mother's intelligence. He was gentle with the younger children and unexpectedly kind to the thralls. Olaf said regretfully that Skakki had not inherited his berserker tendencies, but he was proud of his son in spite of this flaw.

Dotti and Lotti were covered in jewelry—rings on every finger, bracelets, necklaces, charms, and three large brooches, two fastening the straps of their jumpers and one in the middle. From these brooches hung further items on copper chains: keys, combs, scissors, knives, and a small silver scoop Dotti said was a nose-picker. They had learned about nose-pickers from Heide and found them most useful.

Rune looked every inch a skald in a white robe with his harp slung on his back. He was unable to sing, but the music had not left his fingers. Even Thorgil had unbent enough to wear a clean green tunic. The necklace of silver leaves she had fallen in love with shone at her neck. At Jack's neck was the iron collar of a thrall.

Jack was nervous about meeting the queen, but after he sang (*without* mistakes, Rune warned him repeatedly), he could melt into the background. The real problem was Lucy. She would be given to the queen, and Jack couldn't do a thing to stop it. Olaf said Frith liked pretty children, perhaps because she had none of her own. She treated them well when she wasn't in a snit. As to what happened to the children when she *was* in a snit, Olaf was silent.

"At last! At last! I'm going to my castle!" Lucy cried. "I'm going to see my real parents."

"Mother and Father are your real parents," Jack said.

"No, they aren't," declared Lucy, and Jack didn't have the heart to disillusion her.

"Aren't you going?" he asked Heide, who was still in her stained work dress.

"The queen doess not like my presence," she replied in her smoky voice. "It makes her nerrrvousss."

Jack was disappointed. It would have been nice to have someone around who could make the queen nervous.

"I haff thiss to say, dear ox-brain," Heide continued as Olaf made ready to leave. "Iff you take this boy and his sister to the court of King Ivar, it will be your doom. I haff spoken uff this often, but you haff not listened. Now for the last time I entreat you. Do not show them to the queen. I haff seen you lying in a dark forest with your lifeblood soaking into the earth."

Rune looked startled. "You didn't tell me this, Olaf."

"Women's ravings," said the giant.

"I don't think anyone has ever accused Heide of raving."

"Listen well, old friend. Those who spend sheltered lives are ever afraid of danger. But you know danger is what we warriors were born for. Our spirits drive us seaward to sail the salt wave. Our happiness lies in risking all in some adventure, and if we survive, so much sweeter is our homecoming. But to all men, eventually, comes doom. Our only choice is to meet it boldly. It will come to us whatever we do."

Rune's eyes were shining. "You deserve the finest poem a skald could ever write."

"I do, don't I?" said Olaf, brightening up.

"You deserve a kick in the backside," cried Heide. "Who ever stuffed men's heads full of such nonsense? Whhhy can't you avoid trouble and fight another day?"

But no one listened to her except Jack.

The afternoon was cloudless and warm. The fields were covered with a haze of bees, and the farm horses frisked along the fence. Even Cloud Mane, who was more reserved, whinnied as they passed. First came Olaf, carrying Lucy. Beside him was Skakki. Clustered behind were Dotti and Lotti, Rune, Thorgil, and Jack. And to the rear groaned the cart on which Golden Bristles was penned. It was pulled by oxen and flanked by Thick Legs, Dirty Pants, and Lump, who, if not well dressed, were at least clean. Pig Face was at home recovering from a bite taken out of his leg, courtesy of Golden Bristles.

They walked up the mountain through pine forests and meadows. Lemmings bounded through drifts of wild garlic, and elk withdrew behind stands of cloudberries and cranberries. Jack saw a falcon hover and then dive to pluck a small, squealing rodent from the grass. He went back to check on Golden Bristles.

"This looks good to you, doesn't it, piggy?" he whispered, and the boar oinked in reply.

"Don't get attached to him," said Lump. "He's to be sacrificed to Freya."

"Sacrificed?"

"You don't keep a brute like that around for his looks," said Dirty Pants. The thralls had become friendly to Jack, once they realized he wasn't going to make trouble for them.

"I thought he was for—you know—making baby pigs."

"He's done that, all right," Lump said, snickering.

"He's not a normal boar," explained Thick Legs. "They're vicious enough, but his kind came over the sea with the Jotuns. He's in a class by himself. He killed a man when he was taken, and he ate two pig boys."

That's why you put me in with him, thought Jack, but he didn't say it aloud. "I suppose it isn't any worse than killing him for meat."

"Oh, it is. *Much* worse," said Dirty Pants. "They'll throw him, cart and all, into Freya's Fen. He'll sink slowly. Sometimes it takes hours, and he'll know what's happening. Pigs are smart."

"That's—that's horrible!"

"It's what he deserves, the human-eating monster," said Lump. "Too bad Pig Face can't watch it."

Jack walked along with the boar, singing in a low voice. He didn't want to attract Thorgil's attention. He sang of the Islands of the Blessed, where snow never came and where the air was ever sweet and the water clear as sky. Golden Bristles seemed to understand, for he grunted softly.

They came out of the forest to bare ground. Thorgil ran off at once to find the king's wolfhounds. The promontory known as Fang Rock jutted out over the fjord, and Ivar's hall loomed at the very end. It dwarfed all the outlying buildings. It even dwarfed Olaf's hall. Its humpbacked roof extended at least twice as far and was supported by at least two dozen pillars on each side. For all that, it was ugly. It reminded Jack of a giant sow bug with pillars for legs. Smoke rose from a dozen fire pits outside.

Other guests shouted greetings—Sven the Vengeful, Egil Long-Spear, and a new man introduced as Tree Foot. Tree Foot was shaped like a beer keg. His broad chest was covered by a curly red beard, but his most distinctive feature was his left leg. The lower half had been replaced by a beautifully carved wooden stake. It was decorated with the same fanciful designs that covered the beams of Olaf's hall.

"HA! HA! HA!" bellowed Tree Foot, stumping along. "SO YOU CHEATED THE FISHES." He slapped Olaf on the back.

"How's the leg?" asked the giant.

"NEVER BETTER. YOU'RE A MASTER CARVER."

Tree Foot was evidently as deaf as Eric Pretty-Face, and when that warrior showed up, Jack had to cover his ears. "What happened to his leg?" he asked Rune when they'd got far enough away from the two bellowing men.

"A troll bit it off," said Rune. "The same one who tried to get Eric Pretty-Face's leg."

More and more people came. They hovered by the fire pits to savor the odor of roast pork, salmon, goose, and venison. Rune struck up his harp, and people gathered around to sing. It was a happy crowd, but Jack couldn't help noticing that no one went into Ivar's hall. The area Jack could see through the huge open door was curiously dark. Windows weren't a feature of Northman halls, but they were brightened by hearth fires. There was a long hearth fire inside Ivar's hall. It seemed muted, as though the surrounding darkness was so thick, even light had to struggle to escape.

Since it was high summer, the sun was slow to go down, and when it did at last disappear, the twilight lingered. The snowy mountains to the north glowed red. *Jotunheim,* thought Jack. *Home of people who bite off legs.* The redness seeped into the sky and turned the earth the color of dried blood.

"I suppose we'd better go in," said Olaf.

Chapter Twenty-three

OLAF'S TRIUMPH

With evening, the inside of Ivar's hall didn't look quite as threatening. A long fire burned down the middle, and stone lamps filled with fish oil were placed here and there. They didn't improve the air of the hall, which had a distinctly sour odor. A trench ran along the walls and formed a narrow, but protected, sleeping space. Fang Rock, being exposed, was no doubt cold. Jack thought sleeping in a trench would be very similar to lying down in a grave.

At the far end was a raised dais framed by ornamental pillars. Not for Ivar was a simple chair at the head of the hearth. He required a platform from which he and his queen could tower over their guests.

The pillars and walls were covered in carvings, but not the playful animals that decorated Olaf's house. Long, headless, twisted bodies writhed and grasped one another with claws. When a head did appear, it was bulbous and pale with gaping eyes and a woeful mouth.

Along the walls were tapestries. They were done with great skill, and yet they gave no delight. More weird creatures stared menacingly over the hall. Even the human figures had strange horned heads and danced with weapons in their hands. Jack couldn't tell what they were up to, but it was nothing good, that was clear. Here and there were the figures of eight-legged horses.

On the dais at the far end sat two figures. Jack remembered the Bard's description of King Ivar: *His eyes are pale blue, like sea ice. His skin is as white as the belly of a fish. He can break a man's leg with his bare hands, and he wears a cloak made from the beards of his defeated enemies.* Olaf and his party, as guests of honor, were led to a table just below the dais, so Jack had an excellent view of the cloak. It was brown and black and blond and white, and it seemed very dirty. Ivar didn't look as if he could break a man's leg. He draped over the chair as though he could barely sit upright. As though he were, in fact, *boneless.*

Jack put off looking at the other chair for the longest time. He could feel her presence like a door into a winter night. The hearth poured warmth into the hall, but it tempered her not a bit. He felt the cold sucking at the rune on his neck. He looked up.

She was beautiful.

She was more than beautiful. Jack, who didn't notice girls

much unless he had to, was struck dumb. How could he have thought she was evil? Such beauty could only come from the gods—or the angels, depending on your religion. Her skin was as pale as cream; her hair—her *hair*—swept down in red-gold waves. It lay about her in a shining fall, all the way to the floor. It made Lucy's hair look like old hay.

Queen Frith smiled, and Jack rose at once and bowed to her. He couldn't help it. He hardly noticed when Rune pulled him down and forcibly turned his face in another direction.

Then—it was so odd—the coldness returned. When he wasn't looking at her, he felt a chill from his toes to the top of his head. "Do not gaze at the queen, boy," Rune whispered. "She will pull you to where she is, between the worlds. Concentrate on the poem. Go over your lines."

So Jack went over and over his lines, but he wanted terribly to see Queen Frith smile at him again.

The feasting began, with entire roast pigs and deer being carried in on giant platters. Geese stuffed with hens stuffed with larks stuffed with coriander were put on every table. Mead, wine, and beer flowed freely, though Rune sternly refused to let Jack have any. He had to keep his wits for Olaf's praise-poem.

And finally, when Jack thought it couldn't get any better, the king's cooks brought in bowls of flummery. "Flummery," Lucy said softly, the first word she had spoken all evening. "The best kind, with nutmeg and cream."

Jack had to choke back a strong desire to cry.

King Ivar rose, and the hall fell silent. "We are here to celebrate the return of our good friend Olaf One-Brow."

"HEAR! HEAR!" shouted Tree Foot from the other end of the hall.

"He has ever been the first into battle and the last to leave. He saved me when the Mountain Queen shut me into her cave, and he single-handedly forced the Elf King to give up the cattle he had stolen." Jack looked at Olaf in surprise. These were stories he hadn't heard. "Since Thorgrim's death he has led my berserkers." King Ivar raised his drinking horn high. "I honor him with this feast and look forward to hearing his victory poem. To Olaf!"

The king drained his horn, and the hall exploded with cheers and shouts. "TO OLAF!" boomed Tree Foot and Eric Pretty-Face.

"I honor him too," came a voice as sweet as a summer breeze across a field of clover. In spite of the din, Jack heard her clearly and so, apparently, did everyone else. Once again the hall fell silent.

"Olaf has ever been generous as well as brave," came Frith's caressing voice. Jack tried to look up, but Rune forced his head down. "He has gifted us with gold rings and fine cloth. He has brought us a fine troll-boar for the midsummer sacrifice. And now he has brought us a real skald. Too long has this court been without music. Too long has King Ivar done without a poet."

Wait a minute, thought Jack. *I'm not being given to the king.*

Olaf stood. Jack noticed that he didn't look up either. His eyes were directed at the queen's feet—and lovely feet they were too. They peeped daintily from beneath her gown, and then something else peeped out from behind her—an enormous cat! It muscled its way to the front, rubbing itself against Frith's dress and purring loudly. More cats lounged in the shadows at the back of the dais. They all had long, red-gold fur, and they stared out at the hall with pale gold eyes.

"Great Queen, before my skald sings, I have something important to do," said Olaf. "Thorgil went on her first raid and made her first capture. Instead of keeping it for herself, she insists on giving it to you, knowing that you like pretty children. I have always found Thorgil to be generous and brave. I would welcome her into my berserkers, if you would graciously agree." Thorgil rose and bowed. Her face was flushed and happy. She was also somewhat rumpled from playing with the dogs. Olaf lifted Lucy from her seat.

No! thought Jack. Now that the moment had come, he felt he had to snatch his sister away no matter what happened after. But then he looked up and saw the queen.

She was as fair and innocent as a May morning. No harm could possibly come from her.

Thorgil took Lucy's hand and led her up the steps of the dais. The cats came forward to inspect them, and Jack thought he saw Thorgil flinch. Certainly the creatures didn't like her, or perhaps it was the smell of dog. They laid back their ears and hissed. Lucy leaned forward to pet one of the brutes; Jack tensed, fearing the worst, but it rubbed against her and purred.

"They like you," said the queen.

"A cat kept me warm after I was stolen from the castle," Lucy informed her.

"Ah! So you are a princess."

"I'm *your* princess, silly," said Lucy. "Don't you remember? The trolls stole me from you when I was only a baby."

A gasp went through the hall when Lucy said *silly*. Jack guessed that no one ever insulted Frith. But the queen only laughed. "Now that you mention it, perhaps I do remember I had a daughter. I'm surprised the trolls didn't eat you."

You're half troll. You ought to know, thought Jack, and yet he couldn't believe such foul ancestry when he looked at Frith.

"Oh, they wanted to!" cried Lucy. "They started fighting among themselves. 'Shall we roast her with an apple in her mouth?' they said. 'Or shall we make her into a pie?' 'Pie! Pie!' roared half the trolls. The other half shouted for roast baby. They began to fight, and soon they had knocked each other senseless. That's when Father came and found me—I mean, my other father. The one who isn't here."

Lucy hadn't talked so much for weeks. She slipped into her role as princess with amazing ease. Well, she'd been practicing it all her life, thought Jack. Lucy walked up to the queen and confidently hugged her knees.

"What an imagination!" marveled Frith. "I can see you're going to be entertaining. Thank you, Thorgil. It is a most generous gift."

Thorgil muttered something and waited awkwardly. Social graces were not her strength.

"Yes?" said the queen.

"Could I—I mean, would you—could you—let me join the berserkers?"

"A young child such as you!" warbled Frith in her lovely voice. "Surely you'd rather learn maidenly things like sewing and weaving and cooking."

It was as though the queen knew exactly what would upset Thorgil. The shield maiden turned red from her effort to control herself. Jack thought she probably wouldn't succeed.

"Great Queen," interrupted Olaf. "She's the child of Thorgrim. There was never a finer berserker, and she has inherited his spirit."

"Indeed," said Frith somewhat coldly. "I wouldn't have thought a shield maiden would wear such a *feminine* ornament as that necklace of leaves."

So that's her game, thought Jack, who had stopped looking at the queen. It made his mind clearer. *She wants Thorgil's necklace.*

Thorgil undid the necklace and handed it to Frith. Jack could see it hurt her. "I don't want it," the girl said ungraciously. "It's an ugly girl thing."

"I suppose it wouldn't hurt *me*," cooed Frith. "Why, thank you. Now you may return to your table. I'm anxious to hear Olaf's praise-song and don't want to wait another minute."

Thorgil stumbled off the dais and threw herself down on the bench. Her face was purple with rage, and Olaf put his hand on her shoulder. "Later, my Valkyrie," he whispered. Thorgil softened somewhat at his praise, but she still looked like a storm cloud full of lightning. She'd given up her first capture and the beautiful silver necklace, and she still wasn't a member of the Queen's Berserkers.

❖❖❖

Jack looked out over the hall. At least a hundred faces looked back at him, many of them Ivar's men. Olaf had moved Tree Foot and Eric Pretty-Face to his table and threatened them if they talked during the performance. They'd removed their party helmets to hear better. Rune smiled gently as he rested his chin on his harp. This would be his triumph too, though no one would know it. Thorgil had withdrawn into her rage, but Jack wasn't singing for her anyway.

He cleared his throat. He felt, rather than saw, the queen behind him. *I mustn't think of her,* Jack thought. Cold ran a finger down his spine. He began:

> *Listen, ring-bearers, while I speak*
> *Of the glories of battle, of Olaf, most brave.*
> *Generous is he, that striker of terror.*
> *Lucky are they who sit in Olaf's hall,*
> *Gifted with glory, treasure, and fame.*
> *The wolf-headed men call him leader.*
> *Odin's skull-pickers name him friend.*

Jack warmed to his task as he sang. He forgot about the audience. He forgot about the queen. The life force shimmered all around in spite of the gory theme of the song. It was drawn, Jack thought distantly, by the magnificence of Rune's poetry. It made each line more lovely and Jack's voice more resonant. He was dimly aware that one of Odin's skull-pickers—a crow—was sitting in the rafters high overhead. This disturbed him briefly, but he forgot about it.

When he finished—and it was a very long poem—not a sound was to be heard. Even the hearth fire had stopped crackling. Then the great hall burst into cheers. "WONDERFUL! WONDERFUL!" bellowed Tree Foot, dabbing his eyes with his beard.

"IT CHOKES YOU UP, DOESN'T IT?" agreed Eric Pretty-Face.

"I really liked the part about skull-splitting," said Egil Long-Spear.

"And wading in blood up to your ankles," said Sven the Vengeful.

"It's not fair!" Thorgil said loudly. "Jack gets all the glory for doing nothing. He never fought a battle or pillaged anything!"

Rune sat with a quiet smile on his face. The compliments flowed around him like warm honey. Jack wished he could give him credit, but that would be dangerous at the moment. Perhaps someday Jack could show his gratitude.

"What a charming tune," trilled the queen's voice from behind him. Somehow the way she said it made Rune's achievement seem trivial and silly. Jack whirled around, ready to defend the old warrior's art. He remembered his peril in time and turned the movement into a bow. "Don't you think that was a pretty tune, Lucy?" Lucy, who had dozed off on the queen's lap, sat up and nodded.

"Life has been rather dull of late," said Frith. "What treats we have in store for us, with our new skald."

"He's my brother," Lucy said proudly.

"All the more reason for him to live with us. Don't you think so, my lord?"

Olaf, do something, thought Jack.

Ivar rose to his feet. He looked deathly pale and exhausted, as though some disease ate at him. "Is this skald a gift, Olaf?"

"No, old friend," the giant said simply. "I have given you much of my wealth-hoard. I have done so freely and gladly. I captured the great troll-pig on the borders of Jotunheim and gave him to you for Freya's sacrifice. Is this not enough?"

Ivar bowed his head. "I am ashamed to appear greedy."

"I've never thought of *you* as greedy, old friend," said Olaf.

"I suppose that means I am," the queen said. She stood up, dumping Lucy to the floor. Her cats came out of the shadows and surrounded her skirt, walking round and round like a stream of living gold. Lucy cried briefly and fell silent with her thumb in her mouth.

Frith came up to Jack and touched his lips with the tip of her finger. Ice coursed through his body, warring with the heat of the rune. "*Such* a lovely voice. What a pity not to hear it raised in your praises, Ivar." The cats rustled around Jack's legs now. They came up to his waist, so large were they, and their incessant movement made him dizzy. "Very well, then! I *am* greedy—but only for the glory of your court, dear husband. I want this skald for my own."

"Great Queen," began Olaf, and Jack noted that he called

Ivar *old friend*, but there was no such warmth when he spoke to Frith. "Great Queen, do not ask this."

"But I *do* ask it."

"Take something else," said King Ivar. The look the queen gave him caused him to stagger back into his chair.

"I have a new warhorse," said Olaf, and Jack could see it hurt him to say this as much as it had hurt Thorgil to give up her necklace. "I think his sire came from Elfland, and I intended him for my son Skakki. You may have him, if you leave the skald."

"I do not bargain, noble Olaf," said the queen. "Dear me! I'm not some fishwife in the market. The horse is of course welcome, but that doesn't settle the question of the boy."

"Yes, it does," said Jack. He was horribly afraid. He had to fight against her will and the cats walking incessantly around his legs. Then, too, he had to fight her beauty, but it was easier with the life force still hovering in the air. Frith was not as alluring in its presence. He glimpsed a shadow behind her that was in no way like her human form.

"This land has laws," Jack struggled to say. "Ivar is king, and he's told you not to take me." His throat almost closed up with fear, but he heard a murmur of approval from the hall.

"Father *always* tells Mother what to do," chirped Lucy. A ripple of laughter, quickly stifled, went round the room.

"I'll sing your praises, Great Queen," said Jack. "But I must honor King Ivar's will."

Frith's form wavered ever so slightly. The fish-oil lamps sputtered and the hearth seemed to dim. Then all returned to normal. "I see you are as clever as you are musical," the queen said. "I accept this compromise—for the moment. Give me a praise-song, boy, and I'll tell you if I like it."

Jack felt ready to collapse. He had no song ready, and his mind was emptied out. The cats continued to weave around him, now buffeting him with their bodies, now treading on his feet. "Could you—call off your cats?" he said weakly.

"They're not *mine*," trilled Frith. "They belong to Freya. They pull her sacrificial cart and obey her will. *I* certainly can't tell a goddess what to do. Her beasts have chosen to like you, and that's that."

"Liking" was not what Jack thought the cats had in mind. They bumped into him roughly and their feet were heavy. He'd played with farm cats back home. Sometimes they got into a mood, and just when they seemed happy, they'd decide you were prey and attack.

However, he had no choice. *What can I say? What can I say?* he thought. All the praise-poems he knew were about brave deeds or accomplishments such as playing the harp or swimming. They could be applied to men or women. None of them were suitable for Frith. Could he lie? *No,* thought Jack. A bard's skill came from the life force, and you couldn't lie to it.

So what was left? Her beauty. In praise-poems a woman's beauty was mentioned in general terms. It was there. It was good. Far more important was her character, but Frith had no character except lust and greed. Beauty it would have to be, then.

Jack began awkwardly. He was having to make things up on the spot. He raised his head and saw the crow hidden in the rafters. Bold Heart! It had to be him. He must have followed them from Olaf's hall. Bold Heart bobbed up and down, seeming upset. He couldn't have been happy about the cats. They could have swallowed him with one gulp and yowled for more.

"Why have you stopped?" said the queen.

Jack turned and saw her with Lucy snuggled once more in her lap. Or rather, Lucy was doing all the snuggling. Frith would never do anything so lovable. His sister's life was in his hands. He *had* to please Frith or find out what happened to children when she got into a snit.

He looked directly at the queen. Her beauty stunned him as it had before. He began singing, first of her white arms and then her perfect face. Except that it wasn't perfect. The one thing poets always mentioned about women was their eyes, and Frith's eyes were like doors opening onto nothingness.

Her hair! He could sing about that. It indeed was worth praising, a red-gold river fanning out around her like a cloak fashioned by elves. It flowed down to the floor, fell like sunlight from her white brow. Even Freya's cats were no fairer.

At the mention of cats one of the beasts turned his head and sank his teeth into Jack's leg. He shouted in surprise. The spell was broken, for spell it had been. Jack had felt the life force strongly, as when he called up fog. Frith's hair had become more golden, had fallen ever more gracefully. Had fallen.

With the breaking of the spell, Frith's hair simply detached itself from her head and fell to the floor with a little sigh.

The party guests held their breath. Frith looked uncertain, as though she hadn't realized what had happened. "It's *seiðer!*" yelled Thorgil, breaking the silence. "See? There's his familiar in the rafters!"

Bold Heart croaked balefully and sailed out the door.

"A crow?" Frith said, wondering. She felt her head. Then she screamed, a terrible scream unlike anything human. Her body bulged in a dozen places. Her features rippled and twisted like the beasts carved on the walls. Her head turned pale and bulbous, with gaping eyes and a mournful mouth. She screamed again and again. The hall emptied out, with warriors scrambling over one another and whimpering in a most unheroic way.

Jack tried to reach Lucy, but he was snatched away by Olaf. The giant cleared a path for his wives and friends, while Skakki brought up the rear. Tree Foot and Eric Pretty-Face carried Rune between them. The old warrior was too frail to fight his way through the panic. When they got outside, Olaf marched them to the edge of the forest. He watched as the party guests gathered a respectful distance from the hall.

The screams had stopped. The night was full of stars and a full moon hung at zenith. A faint glow on the horizon showed that even at midnight, the midsummer sun was not far away. No one spoke, and Jack was afraid to ask questions. What would happen now? What would happen to Lucy?

Finally, Rune whispered, "That was the biggest snit I ever saw."

It broke the tension. Olaf laughed ruefully. "Heide was right. She always is. I shouldn't have taken the children to the party."

"It was fated," Rune said.

"I'm sorry," said Jack, bracing for a blow, but Olaf was too preoccupied to hit him. He watched the door of Ivar's hall.

"Should I fetch the thralls, Father?" said Skakki at last.

"Yes," the giant replied. "Take Jack with you. He can calm the troll-boar while you unhitch the oxen."

They made their way back to the party guests, and Jack asked people what had happened to Lucy. No one knew and no one wanted to go inside to look for her. Jack wiped tears away as he followed Skakki down a path to Golden Bristles's cart. Thick Legs, Dirty Pants, and Lump were hiding under it.

"What was that *sound*?" whimpered Lump.

"The queen got into a snit. You can come along now," Skakki said. "Unhitch the oxen. We're getting out of here." The men worked with the beasts while Jack sang softly to Golden Bristles inside. All the while he sawed with his knife at the leather straps holding the pen's door. Finally, Skakki called him away.

"Good-bye, piggy," Jack whispered. "Good luck."

They walked in silence through the forest. The full moon marked out the path, and shadows massed under the trees on either side. But it was a clean darkness and not the perverted gloom of King Ivar's hall. Jack saw a crow cross the face of the moon, keeping pace with Olaf's party.

Chapter Twenty-four

THE QUEST

The next morning Olaf sent Cloud Mane to the king. "It may cool his anger. We haven't a hope of cooling Frith's rage."

"We should take ship and escape to Finnmark," said Heide. "My brothersss will protect us."

"No offense, dear wife, but I don't want to live in a smelly tent with your brothers. Nor do I want to be called a coward."

"Escape is the only sensible thinggg," Heide said, drawing out the last word.

"It's shameful. I'm King Ivar's man, not an oath-breaker."

"So you'd rather let us get slaughtered than risk your precious reputation." Heide was capable of standing up to Olaf as no one else could.

"Reputation is all a man is. Anyhow, you won't die. I know

Ivar. He may punish me and certainly Jack, but it won't go farther."

Jack would have welcomed the chance to take ship and escape to Finnmark, wherever that was. He wouldn't have minded living in a smelly tent forever, but he didn't have a choice. He was confined to the main hall, his slave collar fastened by a leash to a heavy table. *As if I were a dog,* Jack thought.

Thorgil, too, was confined, but she was trusted to obey. Olaf had been angered by her outburst in Ivar's hall. "As if things couldn't get worse," he'd growled, "you had to accuse Jack of *seiðer!*"

"He talks to crows," she'd muttered under her breath.

Skakki burst through the door. "You'll never guess what happened! Golden Bristles smashed open his pen and escaped. The queen is furious about it."

"Worse and worse," groaned Olaf. "They say when a man's fate calls him to death, everything he does goes wrong."

"The king wants you in his hall," Skakki said. "He wants Jack and Rune, too."

"Rune?"

"As a lore-master and expert on skald's magic. And he wants Thorgil because of her accusation of *seiðer.*"

"*Me?*" shouted Thorgil, outraged.

"You haff never known when to keep quiet," said Heide.

Everyone dressed quickly, and Rune wore his white robe because he was being consulted on affairs of magic. They trudged through the forest, with Olaf holding Jack's leash. *Like a dog,* the boy thought again. He wondered how the queen would punish him. Perhaps she'd steal his wits, as she had the Bard's. Or throw him into Freya's Fen to sink slowly. Or roast him over a fire. Jack could come up with a dozen possible fates, all of them horrible.

At least Golden Bristles had escaped. True, he was a vicious hog, and true, he probably didn't deserve mercy, but Jack liked him. It was rather flattering to have even a swine appreciate one's poetry.

The king and queen were seated on the dais. Their warriors lined the hall, and at the front were the priests of Odin and Freya. "The priests have been unable to reverse the spell," said the king.

Jack was relieved to see Lucy at the queen's feet. But when the little girl looked up, he saw that her mind had fled. Her eyes were vacant and she didn't recognize him. Where was her spirit? Not in the castle, certainly, and not in a fantasy with Frith Half-Troll as her mother.

He glanced at the queen, and at once her eyes caught his and held. He was unable to look away. She'd regained her human shape, but she no longer had her luminous beauty. She looked coarse and lumpy, like dough that hadn't been kneaded properly. Her hair lay in a basket on the floor, and she wore a shawl over her head.

"I want him punished," the queen hissed. The air stirred behind her, and Jack saw she'd lost none of her fell power. "I want him to suffer as no one has ever suffered before. I want it to take days. I want him to despair, feel hope, and despair again."

"If you do that, you'll never regain your beauty," said Rune.

"And how could that be? When he's dead, the spell will undo itself."

"I'm afraid not," said Rune. "This isn't some flimsy conjurer's trick. Jack was trained by Dragon Tongue."

"Dragon Tongue!" shrieked Frith. The warriors ducked and covered their ears. King Ivar turned ashen. *"He's dead! He's dead! He's dead!"* screamed the queen.

"His lore lives on," said Rune. "He was the most powerful skald in Middle Earth, and Jack is his heir."

"Now I know I want the boy dead!"

"Great Queen," said the priest of Odin, "if this is Dragon Tongue's work, only the person who cast the spell can undo it."

"That's right," agreed the priest of Freya.

Frith paused, seeming to gather her forces. The shadows behind her stopped moving. "Well then, boy," she said in a voice that was almost sweet, "what are you waiting for?"

Olaf pushed Jack to the front. The boy felt waves of cold wash over him. "I—uh—I—," began Jack.

"Go on! Remove the spell."

"I don't know how," Jack muttered.

"What?"

Jack swallowed. "I don't know how."

Then the queen did scream, and everyone, even Olaf, dropped to his knees.

"Well, that's done it," said the priest of Odin.

"I'm sorry, boy," groaned Olaf. "I thought we had a chance there."

"We still do," Rune said. Thorgil helped him rise and dusted off his knees, for the straw on Ivar's floor was littered with bone and gristle, not to mention fleas. "Jack may not know the magic now, but he can get it from Mimir's Well."

"Mimir's Well?" The priest was flabbergasted. "That's in *Jotunheim!*"

"I didn't say it would be easy."

"It is perilous beyond belief to pass into Jotunheim," said King Ivar. "I know. I've been there."

"And I as well," said Olaf.

"But with safe passage, it might be done," Rune said.

All turned to Frith, who glowered back at them. "I have no love of Jotunheim. My own mother cast me out."

"She didn't cast you out," King Ivar said patiently. "She married you to me."

"Same thing," sneered Frith. "I wanted a fine ogre or a goblin, but *no*. Mother insisted I marry a puny human." King Ivar passed his hand across his eyes as though he'd had this argument many times.

"It looks like—" Jack cleared his throat as Frith's attention was drawn to him. Even in her diminished form, she made his mind go blank. "It looks like your only chance to be cured is for me to find this Mimir's Well and—and—what am I supposed to do with it, Rune?"

"Drink the song-mead it contains," the old warrior said softly. "It's the dream of every skald. I've wanted it all my life—

well, no point regretting what can never be. Song-mead waters the roots of Yggdrassil, the tree that rises through the nine worlds. It's pure life force, as Dragon Tongue would have said."

As Rune talked Jack felt a strange sensation. It was like wind over the sea and hawks diving with their wings furled and far-off hills covered in mist. He could see himself walking through a forest of giant fir trees. The air was filled with the smell of ice off a glacier. *Good heavens,* thought Jack. *I think I like this adventure.* The feeling was so unusual, he wondered if he was sick.

He opened his eyes and saw Thorgil looking quite sappy about it. "Finding Mimir's Well," she said. "What a quest!" Even Olaf had a distant expression.

"It does sound wonderful," King Ivar said with a sigh. "Alas, I can no longer do it. Well, my little troll-flower. Will you give Jack safe passage so your relatives know he's a guest and not, um, a two-legged deer?"

Frith scowled and made things difficult. They had to flatter her and plead with her. Ivar promised her many presents, and in the end Frith agreed. From her robe she produced a golden chess piece that she'd stolen from her mother. "It's the queen," she said. "I hope it spoiled her set. Anyhow, she'll recognize it. But I want to be sure you return and don't go sneaking off like a pack of oath-breakers."

"We're *not* oath-breakers," growled Olaf.

"The troll-pig broke free in the night," said Frith. "He's probably halfway to Jotunheim by now, and that means I have no sacrifice for Freya."

Tough luck, Jack thought.

"I thought about using Cloud Mane," the queen said, smiling to see Olaf's dismay. "Then I had a clever idea. This gift of yours, Thorgil, has turned sour. She won't talk or anything. She's boring. So I thought, 'Why not sacrifice Lucy to Freya?'"

"No!" shouted Jack.

"It's *years* since I gave the goddess a human. Lucy's a pretty mite, and Freya won't care if she's stupid."

"You can't do that! I won't let you!" Jack tried to run to the dais. He fell back as the full force of the queen's malevolence struck him. He gasped for air. He was surrounded by foul darkness and cold. Only the rune saved him from freezing.

"If you kill him, the quest fails," Rune said.

The dead darkness went away. Jack opened his eyes and saw that his body was covered with ice crystals that melted even as he looked at them.

"I'll wait until the harvest festival," said Frith. "That gives you time to reach Jotunheim, find Mimir's Well, and return. If you are late—or have slunk off with your tails between your legs—I'll put Lucy into the sacred cart and throw her into Freya's Fen myself."

It's my fault. It's all my fault, thought Jack as they returned through the forest. *The Bard lost his wits because he gave me the rune of protection. I let Lucy get carried off by Northmen, and I messed up the magic with Frith. If I hadn't freed Golden Bristles, Lucy wouldn't be headed for sacrifice. Now I've caused everyone to go on this stupid quest to a country where people bite off legs. I'll never find that well. Or I'll fall into it and drown.*

A shadow loomed overhead and settled on Jack's shoulder. Bold Heart's claws were sharp. "Ow! Stop it!" Jack cried. The crow transferred to a nearby bush. Olaf, Rune, and Thorgil halted.

"Maybe he does practice *seiðer*," said the giant.

"I *told* you," Thorgil said.

"Nonsense. He merely talks to animals," whispered Rune. He'd spoken at length in King Ivar's court, and now his voice was almost gone. He'd argued for rewards if they returned triumphant from Jotunheim. He had the law on his side and the backing of the priests of Odin and Freya. It was the king's duty to reward heroism.

If Jack was successful, Rune had argued, he and Lucy should be given their freedom. They should be taken home. "If you want Jack to return, he needs something more than life as a thrall before him." The queen hadn't liked this, but she also couldn't understand why anyone would risk his life for anyone else. The reward—or the "bribe," as she'd called it—made sense to her.

"I've heard dragon's blood gives you the ability to talk to birds," Rune whispered now.

"I've heard that too," said Olaf. "Dragon Tongue spoke of a man called Sigurd who killed a dragon. He was putting his sword away when he accidentally pricked his finger and stuck it into his mouth. The finger still had the dragon's blood on it. Sigurd immediately understood what a pair of larks were saying."

"I remember that story. Nobody ever accused Sigurd of *seiðer,*" said Rune.

"And no base thrall ever killed a dragon," muttered Thorgil as they continued on their way.

Dotti and Lotti were extremely relieved to see Olaf again. They fell on him, hugging and weeping. Even Heide gave him a kiss. "Dear ox-brain! You escaped the wolves!" The wives were not as pleased when they learned about the quest.

"You've just come back," wailed Lotti. "Why do you have to go off after trolls?"

"It's the king's orders," Olaf said, settling Lotti on one knee and Dotti on the other. "We have to find Mimir's Well so Jack can cure the queen."

"Who *wants* to cure her?" pouted Dotti.

"That's a verrry good question," said Heide.

"If we don't do it, little Lucy gets sacrificed to Freya." Olaf bounced his junior wives up and down as though they were children playing horsey. They squealed and begged for more.

"It will be a great quest," Thorgil said, her eyes shining. "We'll meet trolls and goblins and ogres. We'll raid the forges of the dwarves for gold. I might even fall gloriously in battle."

"You are sssooo stupid," said Heide.

"And Jack will drink song-mead from Mimir's Well," whispered Rune. "It's something I always dreamed of."

"I expected idiocy from the others, but not you." Heide threw up her hands and went off to work on her weaving. She had a large loom fastened at an angle to a wall. The warp threads were held taut by stones dangling from the ends, and the weft thread was passed through by hand and tamped into place with a long strip of whalebone. The cloth Heide was making was a beautiful red, yellow, and blue plaid, finer than anything Mother had ever attempted.

Mother, Jack thought sadly. He didn't know whether she or any of the others were alive. His pathway home lay through Jotunheim, where you met goblins and ogres as easily as you ran into sheep on Father's farm. He was never going to make it. Never.

Chapter Twenty-five

———⟨⟩———

JOTUNHEIM

Olaf had his long, lean *karfi* pulled out of the water. He caulked the seams with plugs of animal hair and wool. He chipped off barnacles and checked the ropes for signs of wear. Dotti and Lotti repaired holes in the sail. Skakki and Heide took care of provisions. Jack ran around and helped everybody with everything.

They would need only a small crew, for this was no war mission. Six men, including Sven the Vengeful, Eric Pretty-Face, and Eric the Rash, volunteered. At the end of a week they were ready. The dock was crowded with well-wishers, and fishermen aboard small boats cheered as they passed. Before they got out of sight of the village, Bold Heart landed on the deck, cawing loudly.

"I wasn't trying to leave you behind," Jack explained. "I

only thought the trip was too dangerous for you. We're going to see trolls and ogres and stuff. It's not the place for a bird." For answer, the crow turned his back and deposited a dropping on the deck.

"Stop talking to him. It makes me nervous," growled Sven the Vengeful.

Thorgil steered them back down the fjord to the open sea, for Jotunheim was not to be reached by land until the last part of the journey. A direct trip over the mountains was far too dangerous for humans, according to Olaf.

"The Sea of Trolls," murmured Jack as they came out into the gray-green vastness.

"It's ours now," said Olaf. "It was theirs when it was covered in ice. Jotuns don't like deep water, nor do they like sunlight. They were made for ice and winter. Some call them frost giants."

"So that's what frost giants are," said Jack. "The Bard told me they lie in wait for humans, stunning them with their misty breath. He said you could never lie down outside in the dark of winter, no matter how tempting it was. The frost giants would make you sleepy when in fact you'd be freezing to death."

"Sounds like a troll trick to me," said Olaf.

In spite of everything, Jack found the trip exhilarating. The endless sea and sky filled him with joy. He loved the cry of the gulls. Bold Heart wasn't as fond of gulls. He rose from the ship and drove them away, but the gulls always came back.

Jack learned to play the Wolves and Sheep game with the warriors. He joined them in their songs. *Fame never dies!* rang out again and again over the waves. Even Thorgil sang until Rune told her she had a sweet voice, causing her to withdraw in a fit of sulks.

They saw fewer villages as they went north along the coast and met fewer ships. After a while they saw nothing at all. The trees towered up and up, and their trunks were so thick, six men could hide behind one of them. You could believe it was a forest made for Jotuns and not men. Giant elk with horns wider than Olaf's outstretched arms stared out at them from the shadows. Once Jack thought he saw a bear.

One afternoon they met a herring run, and Jack saw what Olaf had meant when he said you could lay an axe on the water and it wouldn't sink. Thousands upon thousands of the thrashing fish crowded the sea and absolutely stalled the boat. Eric the Rash dipped them out with a net and Bold Heart made off with one in his claws, but you could have taken them out with your hands.

"A shame to waste all this bounty," said Olaf. "By Thor's bottomless belly, I wish I could send these home."

"Thor would be a good companion now," Sven the Vengeful said. "He knew how to sort out trolls."

"The Jotuns stole his hammer once, did you know?" Rune said to Jack.

The boy shook his head.

"Thyrm, the king of the trolls, took it while the god was

sleeping," said Olaf. "As you know, Thor's strength is in his hammer. Thyrm said he'd give it back if Freya would marry him."

"As if anyone would hand over the goddess of love to a dirty Jotun!" said Sven.

Olaf continued: "Thor put on a dress and veil and went to Jotunheim. 'Ooh, let me in, you big, strong Jotuns,' he said in a squeaky voice. 'I'm Freya, and I think you're all so cute!' You can bet they opened the gate fast.

"'Ooh, I'd like a bite to eat,' said Thor. They brought him eight salmon, a roast ox, ten chickens, a pig, and a sheep. Thor ate the lot and washed it down with a keg of beer.

"'Thunder and lightning, this goddess eats a lot,' said the Jotuns. Thyrm lifted her veil, saw Thor's burning eyes, and jumped back as though he'd put his hand on a stove. 'She's hot!' he cried. 'I can tell she's in love with me.' The trolls brought out Thor's hammer to trade for Freya. Thor threw off his veil and grabbed it." Olaf paused, watching Jack expectantly. The other warriors wriggled in anticipation.

"What happened next?" Jack said at last.

"He bashed out everyone's brains and went home!" crowed Olaf. The warriors laughed and punched one another with glee.

"That was the end of Thyrm, all right!" Sven cried.

"Bang! Crash! Crunch! Smash!" Thorgil swung an imaginary hammer.

I'll never understand Northmen, Jack thought.

"THE FISH ARE LEAVING," said Eric Pretty-Face. Jack

saw the seething, shimmering mass move away to the south. The ship trembled and broke free.

"Let's pull in and eat before we get to Jotun Fjord," said Rune. "I don't think we'll have much time to relax once we're there."

Jotun Fjord. The water was dark and deep as they went in. In the distance, towering over the far end of the water, was a mountain covered with ice. The cliffs on either side of the fjord were seething with kittiwakes, auks, puffins, cormorants, and gulls. Thousands of nests clung to the rocks, and the air was full of the crying of birds. Sea eagles soared lazily as they surveyed their prey. The water, too, was teeming with cod, haddock, halibut, and salmon.

"It's like this at the border between worlds," Rune said.

"I don't understand," said Jack.

"We're leaving Middle Earth and entering Jotunheim. The life force is strongest here. Yggdrassil encircles the border with one of its branches."

"I don't see anything."

"Try harder," said Rune. So Jack went to the prow and cast his mind out. At first he saw nothing. The noise of the birds distracted him, and Eric Pretty-Face's humming didn't help. Jack was afraid he might call up fog by accident or, worse, a downpour. He didn't really know what he was doing.

Reveal yourselves, living presences of the earth and sky. Show me your pathways in the sea. Uncurl in the leaf, flash in the sun, fill the air with your music. Jack didn't know where the words came from. They were simply there, shimmering all around. The air thickened like honey; the water began to stir.

It was full of roots. They snaked everywhere, drawing the sun to their green depths. Fish glided in and out of their coils. The roots grew upward and became branches when they reached the air. They unfurled leaves such as were never seen in Middle Earth. Green and gold they shone, and the birds hid their nests among them.

It was too much. The vision was too intense to bear. Jack felt his head swim and then he fell. He woke with Rune holding a skin of water to his lips. Olaf knelt at his side. "What did you just do?"

"I—uh—" Jack choked on the water.

"He called to Yggdrassil," said Rune.

Jack sat up to see Eric Pretty-Face, Sven the Vengeful, and the others clustered at the other end of the ship. They looked utterly spooked. Bold Heart perched on the mast and warbled joyfully. He, apparently, hadn't found the presence of Yggdrassil upsetting at all.

"Rune said the life force was strong here and that I should try to see it," Jack said.

"Don't do that again," said Olaf. "We heard you chanting a poem. The air filled with the sound of wings. I thought a dragon had discovered us. Then the sea churned, and Sven thought we were being attacked by a sea serpent. I know you're used to such things, but the rest of us don't like them."

"I'm sorry," Jack said.

"It's my fault," said Rune. "He's untrained and likely to overdo things."

"Like turning the queen bald. That was a good trick, though." Olaf smiled. "You're a fine skald, and if we survive, I expect many poems out of you."

"I could write poetry too," said Thorgil. "If I tried."

"You? Don't make me laugh," said Olaf. "Everyone knows women can't write verses. It's only for men."

"I can do anything a man can!" cried Thorgil. Her face turned red.

"You're a good shield maiden, and you'll be a great berserker someday. Don't ask for the moon."

"I can do it! Don't laugh at me!"

"Better I laugh than throw you overboard," said Olaf. His voice had become quiet and dangerous. Thorgil stopped arguing, but she cast poisonous looks at Jack as she plied the rudder.

As they went deeper into Jotun Fjord, the teeming bird- and fish-life disappeared. Jack saw only one salmon rising to snap at a fly. But that salmon was enormous. Jack's skin tingled, and he heard something—wind in the trees, perhaps—that was too faint to identify. "It feels strange here," he said.

"That's because we're in Jotunheim." Rune's voice, always quiet, was even quieter now.

"Already?"

"We've crossed the border from our world into theirs.

They"—the old warrior indicated the forest, the mountains, the fjord—"belong. We don't. What you feel is the *watching*."

Jack wished Rune hadn't said that. Now he could feel the attention directed toward the ship. The trees seemed more alert. The mountains loomed closer, and yet they couldn't have moved—could they? Eyes watched from beneath the spruce and junipers. Jack couldn't see them, but he knew they were there.

"They don't like us, do they?" he said.

"We don't like them either, when they invade our world," said Rune. "Fortunately, a troll is far weaker in our world than in his. If it weren't so, Eric Pretty-Face's teeth would be decorating a Jotun's chest instead of the other way around. We'd never have captured Golden Bristles on his home ground."

"Does that mean *we're* weaker here?"

"Yes," said Rune.

The ship glided deeper into the fjord. The snowy mountain Jack had noticed when they entered seemed higher now. The air over it shone with a kind of shimmering, shifting light.

"That's where the Mountain Queen lives," said Olaf, who had joined them. "Frith's mother."

"Who's Frith's father?"

"Some poor wretch," said Olaf. "He may have been a great hero. I don't know. He died long ago."

"Jotuns are long-lived," said Rune.

"Why would any human marry a troll?" asked Jack.

Olaf and Rune looked at each other. "It isn't a matter of choice," Olaf said. "Troll-maidens get their husbands by capture. They're bigger, you see. They usually find themselves a nice lout."

"'Lout' is what they call a male troll," explained Rune.

"But now and then they'll go for an ogre or even a largish human."

"Like . . . you?" Jack said, looking at Olaf.

The giant winced. "I escaped that fate, though only by the greatest good fortune. Ivar wasn't so lucky. We'd been poking around, trying to find a dwarf forge and perhaps some gold. The Jotuns ambushed us. I fell down a cliff trying to get away and landed in a lake. The trolls thought I'd drowned, but they got Ivar. The Mountain Queen shut him up in her cave."

"So Frith didn't capture him. Her mother did," said Jack.

"The Mountain Queen was getting a little desperate. None of the louts would have Frith. None of the ogres or goblins, either. The Mountain Queen could have tortured them into agreeing, but it's a poor way to start a marriage."

"Was . . . Ivar tortured?"

"Oh, no! He was delighted. He couldn't see Frith's true nature, as the others did. He thought he was getting the most beautiful princess in the world."

"He was always somewhat shallow," commented Rune. "*I* could have seen through her in a second."

"By the time I arrived, they were already married," said Olaf. "I *did* knock a few Jotuns around to free Ivar, but they didn't resist much. The Mountain Queen was anxious to move her daughter out of the house."

They had come now to the end of the fjord, where it

widened out into a lake. On the far side Jack saw a meadow covered with swaths of blue, pink, yellow, purple, and white flowers. The perfume reached them from across the water. "That's nice," said Jack, wishing they could stay in the meadow and not get closer to the mountain.

"Hellebore, wolfsbane, nightshade, and troll's breath," said Rune. "In our world they're poisonous if you eat them. In this one the perfume alone knocks you out."

"You're joking!"

"This is Jotunheim. Everything's nastier."

Jack eyed the approaching shore with dismay. The flowers were larger than the ones he was used to and swayed slightly in the breeze (*was* there a breeze?). The ground beneath them looked boggy. "Once you're on the other side, there's a reasonably safe stretch of forest. You can camp there," said the old warrior.

"*I* can camp there? What about you?"

"Once I would have welcomed such a quest, but now . . ." Rune sighed. "Speed and concealment are important for your success. Thus, only two men will go with you. Olaf will, of course, be one of them. The rest of us will wait back in the fjord. This lake, peaceful as it seems, isn't a good place to stay."

Jack was stunned. He hadn't welcomed the trip to Jotunheim, but the presence of six Northmen plus Olaf, Rune, and Thorgil offered some safety. Now he was down to two! "How will we ever find you?"

"We'll return here every day," said Rune. "I'd suggest waiting in the forest until you can see us."

They stopped some distance from shore, where the perfume wasn't too intense. Still, when the breeze shifted, the Northmen moved more slowly and Bold Heart fell off his perch a couple of times.

They packed food and some water, though water would be plentiful until they got to the ice. Rune gave Jack a small bottle of poppy juice to dull pain, "in case you need it." *That probably means I* will *need it,* thought Jack. The bottle was of blown glass, not the dull flasks the Bard stored his best elixirs in, but clear as ice with a poppy molded on its side. "Sometimes pain can kill as surely as a knife blade," said Rune.

He gave Olaf a flask molded in the form of a wolf's head. The odor sent a chill along Jack's nerves. It was bog myrtle, already brewed and ready to go. Somewhere along the way Olaf intended to go berserk.

"I've selected Thorgil to go with us," the giant announced.

"Thorgil!" cried Jack. "She's impossible! We need a full-size warrior, not this—this—runt!" Thorgil threw herself at him, and Jack stepped aside and yanked her leg out from under her. He'd learned a thing or two about fighting in the past weeks. She twisted around and grabbed him. They both fell to the bottom of the ship. Olaf pulled them apart. He held one in each hand, shaking them the way a dog shakes a rat.

"Save your anger for the trolls! I'm letting Thorgil come because I think she's earned a quest. Besides, she wants to fall in battle, and this adventure is a perfect opportunity. By the way, you're *both* runts." Olaf dropped them to the deck. Jack and Thorgil glared at each other, breathing hard.

Bold Heart fluttered over to land on Jack's shoulder. "Not *you*," he cried, trying to brush him off. "This trip isn't for birds."

"And I don't want a witch's familiar along!" screamed Thorgil.

Bold Heart dug his claws into Jack's tunic and refused to leave. The boy stopped hitting at him and slumped dejectedly in the bilge. "I can't take you along, so get used to it."

"I wonder," Rune said, kneeling with some difficulty to look at the crow. "I wonder why this creature came to us in the middle of the sea. And why he stays with us." He extended a gnarled finger, and Bold Heart gently nibbled at it. The old warrior smiled.

"He stays because he's a witch's *curse*," snarled Thorgil.

Rune smoothed the feathers on Bold Heart's head. The bird warbled and cooed. "I think . . . even if we keep him here, he'll escape and follow you, Jack. He's part of your fate."

"Are you telling us to take him?" Olaf said.

"Oh, no!" cried Thorgil.

"I don't think we have a choice. He'll go whether we like it or not. You'll have to carry him through the meadow, Jack. Birds faint more easily than people in poisonous fumes."

"You got your way," muttered Jack as Rune slung a bag, containing Bold Heart, around his neck. "But you're not going to like it."

Chapter Twenty-six

~⊂═══⊃~

THE DRAGON

The last part of the trip was made at top speed. The warriors rowed for all they were worth and rammed the boat onto the shore. Eric Pretty-Face and Eric the Rash jumped out to steady it. Olaf, Thorgil, and Jack started running the second they hit the ground.

Jack had been right. The ground was boggy. The mud sucked at his feet and made it difficult to move fast. Bees as large as walnuts drifted over the meadow, and Jack saw one struggling in the grip of a particularly large and sticky-looking leaf. The leaf appeared to be *folding* itself over the unlucky bee. Then Jack brushed against one of the leaves and found, to his horror, that it stuck to *him*. He tore himself loose and immediately blundered into more. They were everywhere!

He was tiring rapidly, or perhaps it was the smell of the

flowers. His foot came down on a slug as long as his arm. It reared up, pale yellow with liver-colored spots, and waved its eyestalks at him. Bold Heart poked his head out of the bag and cawed. "Get back inside," panted Jack, shoving the bird down.

The perfume was so strong, he wanted to throw up. His vision blurred and his senses swam. *No! No! No! I won't stop!* He had the distinct impression the slug was no innocent visitor to the meadow. It was looking for food, and what better meal than a stunned human boy? Jack staggered and stumbled. He kept his eyes on the forest, but he knew he couldn't reach it. He sank to his knees.

"No time for a nap," grunted Olaf, plucking him from the rustling leaves. The giant ran through the meadow and on through the trees until he reached a hill. He bounded up the side and deposited Jack on a sunny field. But it was normal grass, not the eerie leaves of the meadow. Thorgil lay not far away. Olaf removed Bold Heart from the bag and put him next to Jack.

The boy stretched out in the sunlight, letting the fresh air clear his senses. He felt for Bold Heart and was encouraged when the bird flapped his wings. "Get up if you want to see the ship," Olaf called.

Jack, woozy and sick, got to his feet and dragged himself to the top of the hill. He saw the ship moving across the lake. Olaf waved, and someone—it was too far away to see who—waved back. The warriors were rowing vigorously. Jack saw—or thought he saw—the ripple of something long and dark following them.

"Whew! I don't want to do that again," said Olaf, leaning

back against a rock. "I didn't know the poison would be that strong. I went another way last time."

"Why didn't we go that way this time?" said Jack. He was still dizzy, and Thorgil was too weak to sit up. She kept trying to rise and failing. It made her furious to see that Jack had recovered faster than she. She'd do better, Jack thought, if she didn't waste her breath on all those curses. Bold Heart had managed to get to his feet, but he kept tipping over. He grumbled to himself. It may have been crow curses, for all Jack knew. It certainly didn't sound nice.

"I ran across a nest of baby dragons on the other route. I figure they've grown up by now." Olaf drank some water and handed the skin to Jack. "I had to carry Thorgil out of the meadow and then go back for you. It was almost too much for me. Whew! I'm not as young as I was."

Jack wanted to lie down, but it was much more rewarding to sit up and irritate Thorgil. He moved his head from side to side, to see if the dizziness was still there. It was. "What were those leaves in the meadow?"

"Sundews. They trap and eat bugs," said Olaf.

"Plants eat things?"

"Sundews do. Hey, that sounded like poetry. Maybe I'll turn into a skald yet. In our world sundews are tiny, but in Jotunheim . . ."

"I know. Everything's nastier," said Jack.

"I think we should spend a day here. Give us time to recover. I saw a place in the rocks that should be easy to defend." Olaf got up and began to gather firewood.

"The thrall should do the menial chores," Thorgil called. Olaf ignored her. Jack studied the trees surrounding the field. They were enormous firs towering up and up, with deep green needles and trunks so dark that they were almost black. It went without saying that the shade beneath them was equally gloomy. *I wonder what lives in there,* Jack thought. He heard the same odd murmuring—almost whispering—he'd noticed on the ship. He strained his ears to make out the sound. Or was it voices?

Jack got up and moved closer to Olaf.

"Don't leave Thorgil alone," said the giant. "She's more helpless than you."

"I am *not!*" shouted Thorgil.

After a while Olaf carried her to a campsite he'd selected in the rocks. It was a shallow cave the giant had explored carefully, and once inside you were hidden from the outside world. The entrance was concealed by a fallen tree. Olaf struck sparks with a piece of quartz and his knife and started a small fire. They ate dried fish and bread you had to gnaw at like a rat. Jack's jaw ached by the time he was finished.

Thorgil revived considerably with the food. She was back to her old habit of ordering Jack around until Olaf told her to stop. "We're on a quest. All of us are equal."

"Including that witch's familiar?" she sneered, pointing at Bold Heart.

"I don't know what role the crow is to play, but Rune thought he was important. That's enough for me." The giant stretched out his legs and tried to get comfortable. The roof of the cave was so low, he couldn't stand up, though it was more than high enough for Jack and Thorgil. Because it was midsummer, darkness was late in coming and would not last long.

Perhaps that's good, thought Jack. *Who knows what comes out in the middle of the night?* He thought of wolves and bears, then of stranger creatures he'd heard about in Father's tales: cockatrices, manticores, and dragons. How big was a baby dragon? How big was its mother? "We've started badly, haven't we?" he said to Olaf.

"Quests always have their ups and downs," rumbled the giant. "The point is never to give up, even if you're falling off a cliff. You never know what might happen on the way to the bottom."

"Or you could die heroically and go to Valhalla," added Thorgil.

"You're always talking about dying," said Jack. "What's wrong with living? Anyhow, from what Rune says, shield maidens don't have a great time in Valhalla. They just wait on tables for the men."

"You take that back!" shouted Thorgil. "That's not true! Valkyries are beloved of Odin!"

"Seems to me they're just glorified servants."

Thorgil screamed and launched herself at him. She was weak and so was Jack. They ended up panting for breath and draped over each other on the ground. "That's the most pathetic fight I've ever seen," commented Olaf.

They went to bed before sunset. All three of them had

knives at the ready, and Olaf stretched a rope across the entrance to the cave, to trip unexpected visitors. Jack woke up once in the brief darkness. *Whisper . . . whisper . . . whisper* went the trees outside, though there was no wind.

"Ahhh! It's a fine day for adventure!" said Olaf, stepping out of the cave. "I smell ice." Jack crawled out and sniffed the air. It was clean and fresh and invigorating. Bold Heart chased a black squirrel out of a tree. It fled round and round the trunk with the crow nipping at its tail until it disappeared into a hole. Bold Heart fluffed out his feathers and warbled.

"You're right. It's that kind of morning," agreed Jack. "Where's Thorgil?"

The shield maiden was still curled up by the fire. She glared at both Olaf and Jack and took her time about rising. "We'll look for food," suggested Olaf. "You can build up the fire." He shouldered his bow and arrows and strode off with Jack in his wake. Jack was glad to get away from the sullen girl. If she called him a thrall one more time, there was going to be serious violence.

The forest looked cheerful in the early sunlight. Beams of light fell through the trees and picked out golden-flowered moss, purple violets, and spotted pink orchids. There were many other plants Jack couldn't identify and large butterflies— *really* large butterflies—fluttering from blossom to blossom. "Are any of these, um, dangerous?" Jack asked.

"You can never relax here, but I've found this forest fairly safe," replied Olaf. "This is a protected valley and warmer than most places in Jotunheim. Beyond we'll have rock and ice, so we should enjoy ourselves while we can."

They came to a tangle of fallen logs with thick undergrowth filling the gaps. Suddenly, something gave a shrill whining cry followed by *puk-puk-puk* and a scurrying noise. Jack almost ran into a tree, he was so startled. "You hear that?" whispered Olaf. "That's a grouse. These woods are full of them."

A grouse, thought Jack, trying to calm his pounding heart. Only a bird. No bigger than a chicken. Of course, that was a Jotunheim chicken, he realized a moment later. The grouse flew up with a loud whirring sound. It was three feet long and had a wingspan like a bad dream. Olaf brought it down with an arrow.

The giant slung it over Jack's shoulder and tramped on to find more. The grouse weighed as much as a lamb. Its claws got hooked under the slave collar and dug into Jack's neck, but he didn't dare stop. Olaf was going ahead at a great rate, and the boy decided a few scratches were better than being left behind.

He saw giant mushrooms growing up the side of a tree. They were so white, they glowed, and he saw one of the liver-spotted slugs feeding on them. Another grouse exploded from the undergrowth, and Olaf brought it down. "That's probably enough," he grunted, heaving the bird to his own shoulder. "I'll eat one, and you and Thorgil can have the other. Come on. I'll show you something interesting."

They went uphill to a high cliff where the trees broke off

and bare rock lay below. Jack saw a huge U-shaped valley with a river meandering along the bottom. At one point, just below the cliff, a deadfall of trees had formed a kind of dam and the water spread out into smaller rivulets before breaking through on the other side. An elk—one of the magnificent animals with giant horns—came out of the deadfall and trotted upstream.

"There's a hollow inside," explained Olaf. "The elk use it to hide when they come down to browse on moss. We'll use it tomorrow before we follow the river north." The rocks in the valley were dark blue and dotted with white patches of snow. At the far end was the great ice mountain.

Hide from what? Jack thought. The land was so barren and forbidding, it seemed they could see an enemy for miles before there would be any danger.

"Let's rest awhile," said Olaf, and Jack was glad to lay down the grouse. "I'm unusually tired," the giant admitted. "Jotunheim is always hostile to humans, and perhaps that's what I feel. But it's a little worrying."

Olaf tired? Jack thought. Maybe that meant the giant could rip up only one tree by its roots instead of two. Jack hoped so. The idea of confronting trolls without Olaf's strength was indeed worrying.

After awhile the boy saw something detach itself from a distant cliff and sail lazily down the river valley. It had brilliant golden wings and a long, whiplike tail that sawed back and forth as the creature balanced itself on the air currents. "Is that what I think it is?" whispered Jack.

"A dragon," said Olaf softly. "She's the one I used as the model for the prow of Ivar's ship."

"You made that?"

"It was an honor. Ivar was a great king before Frith trapped him."

The elk looked up, realized its danger, and started galloping for shelter. The dragon folded her wings and dropped, rocking from side to side as she gathered speed. She grasped the elk, opened her wings in a flash of gold, and swept upward in a great arc that brought her close to Olaf and Jack's perch. Jack tried to flee, but the giant held him firmly. "Look into her eyes!"

Jack saw the huge, scaly head of the dragon turn and regard them as she passed. Her eyes opened wide, and in their depths the boy saw a flame kindle. Then she was gone. She sailed off to the distant cliff with the bellowing elk in her claws.

Olaf sighed. "That's a sight few men have seen, and lived!"

Jack was trembling all over. He'd heard about dragons from Father and the Bard, but nothing had prepared him for their awful grandeur.

"It's good, too, that she's eaten," Olaf pointed out. "They hunt every week or so and spend the rest of the time napping. They're a lot like cats."

"W-Will th-there be m-more dragons?" Jack said.

"Not on our path," Olaf said cheerfully. "When the young ones grow up, the mother drives them away. This is her valley. She probably has a nest up there now. Most of the dragonlets don't survive. They kill one another off by fighting."

The giant smiled as he gazed out over the scene. Good Olaf was in charge today. He looked so mellow, Jack decided to risk a question. "Why does Thorgil hate me so much?" he asked.

"She hates you because that's her nature," replied the warrior, "and because she was once a thrall."

"*Thorgil* was a thrall?"

"I'm not giving you a stick to beat her with, boy. If you mention one word about this, I'll break your neck."

Olaf's threats were never idle. Jack nodded most respectfully.

"The child of a female slave is a slave. Thorgrim never freed her."

"Then how—?" Jack said.

"King Ivar waged a war against King Sigurd Serpent-Eye. Thorgrim and I, as berserkers, were in the front line. What a fine man he was! He put me in the shade as far as courage went. You're not to say that in my poems, though."

"Of course not," said Jack.

"Thorgrim outran everyone in his eagerness to fight. He chopped right and left with his battle-axe and went through the enemy's shields—bang, bang, bang—one after the other. I can still see him, though I was cleaving a skull or two myself at the time. But Thorgrim got surrounded. He'd received his deathblow by the time King Ivar and I reached him.

"He asked for a hero's funeral, and Ivar agreed at once. He

asked for the proper sacrifices to be made. That meant Allyson would accompany him on his journey to the afterworld, and Thorgrim also asked for a horse and a noble dog."

"I see," said Jack, who was sickened by the whole idea. What bloated sense of self-importance demanded that an innocent woman and faithful animals be slaughtered? It was monstrous. All Jack's initial loathing of the Northmen came back.

"'What about Thorgil?' I asked," said Olaf.

"'Who?' he said. Thorgrim had forgotten he had a daughter.

"'Allyson's child,' I said. 'I'd like her, to remember you by.' I was afraid he'd ask for her death, you see.

"'Oh, the thrall,' he said. 'You can have her, and also my second-best sword.'

"We carried his body home and had a grand funeral." Olaf's eyes were misty at the memory. "We pulled his ship to the graveyard and filled it with the things he liked—wine, weapons, furs—and laid Allyson's body next to his and the horse and dog at his feet. King Ivar gave him the wolfhound bitch who'd rescued Thorgil, which I thought quite fine. Then we set fire to it all and sent his spirit to Valhalla."

What a totally, thoroughly sickening story, thought Jack. It wasn't enough for Thorgrim to take Thorgil's mother. He had to demand the one creature who'd shown her love as well. Then he cast his daughter away like an old shoe. Jack couldn't trust himself to speak for a while. He was afraid he'd say something nasty and bring Bad Olaf out of hiding.

More elk were browsing by the river below. They were safe, though they didn't know it. They kept looking up and acting spooked. Maybe they could smell blood.

"I gave Thorgil her freedom immediately," said Olaf, breaking in on the silence. "That was three years ago, so she remembers well how it was to be a thrall."

Jack fingered the slave ring on his neck and the scratches the grouse's claws had inflicted.

"I should have had that removed before we left," said Olaf, noticing. "I had Dirty Pants put it on to protect you."

Jack looked at him, surprised.

"A free skald could be commanded by Ivar. To take a thrall, he'd have to go through me. I never intended you to clean out the pig barn, by the way. That was Pig Face's idea."

"I didn't know you'd found out about it," Jack said.

"Oh, Heide has ways of learning things she wants to know. If you'd complained to me, I would have killed the thralls involved. As you didn't, I left them alone. It was honorable of you not to take revenge on lesser men." Olaf rose, helped Jack lift his grouse, and shouldered his own. He walked off, not looking back to see if the boy was following.

Jack felt ridiculously happy with Olaf's praise. *Lesser men.* That meant he, Jack, was *greater.* The giant didn't think of him as a slave. For the first time the boy approached the quest with enthusiasm. They were three warriors on a perilous adventure full of glory and honor. They were equals. And their fame would never die.

Chapter Twenty-seven

THE DEADFALL

On the way back Olaf flushed out another grouse, so they had more meat than they knew what to do with. He built a second fire in the grassy field to roast them. "You don't want the smell of meat close to where you're sleeping," he said, without saying why.

Jack plucked the three giant birds while Olaf whittled spits and Y-shaped stands to hold them. Thorgil did nothing. When Jack had removed the feathers from one bird, Olaf heaved it to Thorgil. "Clean it," he said.

"I don't do thrall's work," the girl sneered. Olaf swept her upside down by the ankles.

"You've not been on a quest before, so you don't know the rules," he explained as she struggled to free herself. "All members do all tasks, no matter how lowly. Even Thor cooks when his companions are busy. Understand?"

Thorgil's face was red from the blood rushing to her head. "Yes," she gasped. The giant put her down. She furiously cleaned the grouse, splashing blood and guts over her clothes.

"Something Thor would *not* do," Olaf remarked, "is attract wolves by smelling like a grouse." The girl continued to work furiously.

Eventually, all three birds were roasting over the fire. Jack went off to wash himself in a stream, and later Olaf did the same. Thorgil didn't. She was determined to be difficult, and as the day wore on she began to smell gamy. Still, dinner was superb. Olaf had stuffed the interior of the birds with wild garlic. There was more than enough for everyone, including Bold Heart, who pecked the remnants from the bones.

When they were done, Olaf put the uneaten food in a bag. Jack climbed a tree and cached the bag high above the ground. Then they retired to the cave, and Olaf marked out a game of Wolves and Sheep in the dirt. They used juniper berries for playing pieces. Thorgil won several times. She cheered loudly and said it was easy to beat such simpleminded opponents. Thorgil was a bad winner as well as a sore loser.

They woke to cracking and crunching. Something big was tearing branches off a tree in the distance. Olaf eased out his sword. "What is it?" whispered Thorgil. The giant signaled for quiet. The forest outside was pitch-black.

Jack thought about how their fire, now glowing coals, could still make a beacon in such darkness. The fallen tree blocking the entrance might protect them, though. Jack had his own knife at the ready, and he grasped a handful of sand from the cave's floor to throw into the eyes of whatever it was.

The snapping and crunching went on for a while and then ceased. They heard nothing more. The forest began to lighten with early dawn, and when it was possible to see, they covered the fire and departed. They hurried along a blue-shadowed trail through the trees. It wound here and there, following natural openings in the brush, and gradually went downward until it came into the U-shaped valley Jack had seen the day before.

The sky opened out. Grim, bare rock lay before them, and a cold wind blew from the ice mountain. Still, the presence of sunlight was cheering. Jack was glad not to be enclosed by trees, where anything could hide. Bold Heart, who was perched on his shoulder, murmured softly as though he, too, was relieved to be out in the open.

"What made that noise?" Thorgil repeated her question.

"Something that likes roast grouse," Olaf said.

Jack realized they hadn't gone back to their food cache. He felt queasy. The bag with the grouse had been stashed as high in the tree as he could manage. Whatever found it had been too large to merely slip through the branches. It had ripped them out of its way, and they'd been large branches, too.

Olaf led them across the valley floor. The wind burrowed under their clothes, and a fine grit blew off the land and made Jack's eyes water. The change in temperature was amazing. The forest had been warm and summery. This was a place winter never, apparently, left. Ice sparkled in places the sun hadn't reached, and fields of snow made stark patterns on dark blue stone. As Jack looked toward the mountain he saw less rock and more snow until there was a continuous white sweep up to the heart of Jotunheim.

They came to the deadfall. Jack looked behind him to see the vast cliff where he and Olaf had observed the dragon. The forest massed at the top, and no doubt through the years, hundreds of trees had fallen from its edge and wound up here. They made a small mountain of logs, branches, dry moss, and twigs. He could hear water rushing ahead.

"This is the last shelter before we reach the mountain," Olaf said. "We should rest awhile, and you, Thorgil, should bathe and sponge off your clothes."

"It's freezing!" she cried.

"If you'd washed in the forest, you wouldn't have found it so bad," the giant said. "Last night's disturbance was a warning. Something up there is hungry, and thanks to you, it won't find it hard to track us."

You could have smelled Thorgil all the way to the Mountain Queen's front door, Jack thought. The grouse blood and guts had ripened gloriously overnight. He didn't know how Thorgil stood it, but in her perverse way she probably thought it made her seem tough. He looked forward to hearing her yelps when she got into the river.

Olaf led them into the tangle of trees, though Bold Heart refused to enter. They went down a twisting passage to a cave-like hollow. The black river swept through the middle under a roof of trunks and branches. Jack looked up uneasily. He could see patches of sky, and it seemed little would be needed to bring the logs crashing down. But Olaf said the hollow had been there many years. Its floor was deep in pine needles, and Jack saw places where animals had lain. A faint barnyard smell hung over the place.

The air was slightly warmer. But not too warm, Jack thought happily as he and Olaf turned their backs so Thorgil could take a bath. Jack heard her gasp and then curse richly as she splashed. He heard her wiping off her clothes with damp clumps of moss.

"You can turn around now," she called. She still didn't smell good, but she was passable.

"Do you know what's following us?" Jack asked.

"Maybe nothing," said Olaf. "With any luck, it's too afraid of the dragon to come out."

"Dragon!" cried Thorgil.

"Keep your voice down. Jack and I saw one yesterday."

"Why didn't you tell me?"

"You weren't in a talkative mood," Olaf said. "Anyhow, the dragon's digesting an elk right now. She won't be hunting for at least a week, but whatever it was in the forest doesn't know that."

"Whatever *what* was?" insisted Jack.

"If I knew, I'd tell you," Olaf said crossly. "We'll rest here awhile and then push on. It'll take three days to reach the hall of the Mountain Queen. It looks near, but the last part's steep and slippery."

Olaf cleared away pine needles and drew a picture in the dirt of the route they would follow. It was straightforward enough: Follow the river to its source at the foot of the mountain. If they hadn't encountered trolls by then, they would climb until they did. "Jotuns patrol their territory regularly," said Olaf. "You can tell they're near—I don't know how to describe it exactly—by a tickling in your mind. Kind of like whispering."

"Whispering?" Jack said. "I've been hearing that ever since we arrived."

"That's interesting. I haven't," said the giant. "Maybe you pick things up more easily because you're a skald."

"Or maybe because he's a witch," said Thorgil.

"I've been meaning to ask this," Jack said. "What's to keep the trolls from attacking the minute we *do* run into them?"

"First of all, because we're not trying to hide, they'll be curious. They'll ask our business before trying to beat our brains out. That gives us time to produce the chess piece." Olaf beamed as he laid out this strategy.

"Are you sure that's how they'll react?" Jack said.

"Pretty sure."

"I've written a poem," Thorgil announced suddenly.

They turned to look at her. She stood and bowed as though they were in a fine hall rather than a drafty burrow.

> *Listen, everyone, while I tell you*
> *About Olaf, who can fight, sing, sail,*
> *Carve wood, and play Wolves and Sheep*
> *(Though he doesn't usually win).*
> *(I'm better.)*
> *Still, Olaf's good at most things,*
> *And we all think he's great.*

"Maybe we'd better get going," said Olaf. "We've got a lot of ground to cover before nightfall."

"Don't you like my poem?" Thorgil said.

Olaf sighed. "Give it a rest, Thorgil. You'll never be seven feet tall no matter how much you stretch, and you'll never fly no matter how fast you flap your arms. Some things aren't meant to be. Girls can't write poetry."

"*I can! I can do anything better than Jack!*" she yelled.

"Keep your voice down. You're a better warrior, but you'll never outdo him as a skald."

"*I hate you!*" she screamed.

A sudden cry from Bold Heart made them all freeze. The crow flew shrieking round and round the top of the deadfall— Jack could see him through gaps. The quality of his cries made them all draw their weapons. The roof overhead quivered as something heavy climbed on top.

Chapter Twenty-eight

GLORY

"What is it?" whispered Thorgil.

"I don't know," Olaf whispered back. His head reached the roof of the hollow, and he held his sword ready to stab whatever it was through the gaps. The timbers groaned and shifted slightly.

"Shouldn't we go outside?" said Jack.

"Maybe our chances are better here. We can hold it off in the passageway."

They saw a huge, hairy foot plunge through a gap. Olaf chopped at it. The creature screamed and black claws tore out strips of wood as it regained its footing. Jack's face was sprayed with blood.

Bold Heart sailed past another opening. The monster growled and swayed back and forth. Branches and pine needles rained down. Thorgil gazed up at the logs with a wild and joyful expression on her face.

"We have no chance at all if the roof comes down," urged Jack.

The creature roared as Bold Heart made another pass. "I think that bird is *attacking* it," Olaf said in wonder.

"He's giving us a chance to escape," said Jack. Both Olaf and Thorgil turned to him.

"Escape is for cowardly thralls," Thorgil sneered.

"And getting killed is for idiots," said Jack. "That thing is too big for all of us put together."

"I have never, ever, fled from battle," rumbled the giant. "I am a berserker from a great line of berserkers. I would not shame my sons."

"Your sons won't know anything if we all die!" cried Jack.

"*You* will tell them. I give you permission to flee. You will return and write a poem saying how I met my fate gladly."

"You can write one for me, too," Thorgil shrilled. Her voice tended to get squeaky when she was excited.

"What about the quest? What about finding Mimir's Well? What about saving Lucy?" Jack despaired of making any dent in Olaf's stupidity. All the while the creature bounded back and forth over the deadfall, probably chasing Bold Heart, who was still shrieking and attacking. The logs groaned and debris showered down.

Olaf took out the flask with the wolf's head on its side. "Oh no!" cried Jack. "You can't go mad now! You've got to escape and save Lucy!" But the giant ignored him. He drank most of the liquid and handed the rest to Thorgil. The strong smell of wolf-brew made Jack's nerves tighten with alarm. He felt like running—but whether from or toward danger he couldn't tell. Olaf started to breathe heavily. Thorgil began to pant. The pupils of her eyes opened wide. They both whined.

"I think that foot belonged to a troll-bear," Olaf said, his voice almost a growl as the bog myrtle took effect. "Besides dragons, there's no more dangerous beast. I doubt we shall survive this battle."

"Ours will be a magnificent death to be sung about until the end of time," said Thorgil.

"Fame never dies," said the giant.

"Fame never dies," she agreed. She sounded drugged.

"Why does everyone want to die?" cried Jack. "What's wrong with living?"

Olaf and Thorgil panted like dogs, tongues protruding from their mouths. Suddenly, they howled and rushed into the passage, banging against the sides as they followed its twists and turns. Branches scraped Thorgil's arms and face. They tore holes in her tunic. She never paused. Olaf roared. Saliva streamed from his mouth, flying off in long tendrils.

Jack ran after them, but more carefully. By the time he got outside, the two were already climbing the deadfall, bounding from log to log. Olaf's foot came down hard and collapsed a small section.

"Come back!" Jack yelled. He might as well have tried to stop a landslide. The two warriors screamed their challenges— Olaf booming like thunder, Thorgil shrieking like a scalded cat. And now Jack saw their opponent rear up from the far side of the deadfall.

It was a bear all right, but huger than Jack had dreamed possible. It was more than twice the size of the dancing bear that came to the village fair. And it was a fantastic pale gold color. The creature rose up on its hind legs and swayed from side to side, snuffing the air. Its long, black claws were at the ready. If ever a berserker bear existed, this was it!

It absolutely dwarfed Bold Heart, who continued to circle. One of the beast's feet was soaked in blood, and one of its eyes was destroyed, apparently by the crow. Jack's hopes rose.

Then three things happened almost at once. The troll-bear caught Bold Heart's wing during one of its lunges. It threw the bird clear over the deadfall to land in mud. Thorgil, in her rush up the logs, came down wrong and fell with her leg trapped in a hole. She screamed. The sword fell from her hand. She tried to pull herself out and failed. Jack started up to rescue her.

The troll-bear dropped to all fours and hurled itself at Olaf. The two met with a jarring crash. Olaf slashed and stabbed. The bear clawed and bit. But from the very beginning the man had no chance. Even half blinded with a wounded foot, the beast was twice his size. It grappled with its arms around his body and tore at his back and shoulders.

They rolled over and over on the top of the deadfall. Then, with a tremendous crack, the mountain of logs caved in. The center crashed down into the hollow. Logs farther out rolled free and bounced down the sides. One barely missed Jack's head. He ducked and kept scrambling. The whole pattern of the deadfall was rearranging, with gaps opening and closing as the whole structure shifted. The hole confining Thorgil's leg gaped and slammed shut as a huge tree trunk rolled into place.

But not before Jack had pulled her free. He hadn't known he had such strength. He hauled her up, skittered down the still-shifting deadfall, and dashed across the valley floor without thinking. He dumped her down and fell to his knees, gasping from the effort.

Her face was white with pain, but she didn't utter a sound. She stared up, shocked. Jack was shocked too. It had happened so quickly. He'd lost Bold Heart, Olaf, and perhaps Thorgil as well. He didn't know how badly she was hurt.

After a long while he recovered enough to examine her leg. Her foot was twisted. He could see no other injury. "Can you hear me?" he asked Thorgil.

She nodded.

"I'm going to leave you for a few minutes. I've got to look for Olaf. Is that all right?"

She nodded, tears welling in her eyes.

Jack ran back to the deadfall. The tunnel to the hollow had collapsed. He climbed up, freezing when the structure threatened to move. He got to the top and looked down.

The center was a welter of splintered wood. To one side sprawled the troll-bear, its head crushed by a log. To the other was Olaf. He was bleeding in a dozen places. His legs were broken, and he had terrible gashes in his arms and chest. But he was alive. He raised his hand in greeting.

Jack climbed down. This part of the deadfall at least seemed stable. The hollow was filled in, and the logs had nowhere else to fall. "Can you hear me?" he asked.

"I hear," said Olaf. The wheezing in his voice told Jack there might be more injuries than he could see. "Thorgil?" wheezed the giant.

"She has a broken ankle. That's all, as far as I can tell."

"The bear?"

"It's dead."

"Good," said Olaf.

"I have the pain medicine Rune gave me," Jack said. "I'll leave it with you and go back to the ship."

"Waste of time," said the giant.

"No, it isn't. Rune's a healer. Eric Pretty-Face and Eric the Rash can carry you."

"I'm dying," whispered Olaf, and Jack knew it was true. There were simply too many wounds. By the time he found the ship—assuming he survived the poisonous meadow—it would be too late.

"At least let me give you poppy juice."

"I'll take a little," said Olaf. "It will help me wait . . . until Thorgil can come." Jack, weeping, handed him the flask. The man swallowed a few drops and waved the boy away.

Jack hurried back to Thorgil, but on the way he saw Bold Heart lying in the mud. The bird was flapping his good wing and trying to rise. "Bold Heart!" Jack cried. He gently lifted the crow and saw that although the right wing was damaged, no serious injury had occurred. The mud had broken the bird's fall.

"I won't leave you behind," Jack promised. He went on to find Thorgil also attempting to rise, but her injury was worse. "I know how Father's leg was treated by the monks," he told her. "I can tie your ankle straight with sticks. It will hurt, but the bone will grow straight. The trouble with Father's leg was that they left it till too late."

He kept talking, more to calm himself than anything, as he gathered sticks and tore strips of cloth from his cloak. "I'll do a quick job now and a better one later. Olaf wants to see you. We've got to hurry."

At the mention of Olaf, Thorgil showed interest for the first time. "He's dying," the boy said, choking on the words, "but he killed the bear."

Jack's hands shook as he bound her ankle tightly and hauled her to her feet. She gasped and clung to him, hopping along on her good foot. With each hop, she caught her breath. Jack found the trip especially grueling because he had Bold Heart slung in a bag around his neck as well. They slowly worked their way back. Then it became easier because she could use her arms to crawl up the deadfall. Jack wondered at her silence. If it were him, he'd be groaning by now. The broken ankle had to hurt like fire.

They got to the crater in the middle and went down. Olaf smiled weakly. "Thorgil Olaf's Daughter," he said.

"W-What did you say?" said Thorgil.

"I've named you my daughter," he said. The pain medicine seemed to make it easier for him to speak. "I told Skakki and Heide this before I left."

"B-But I d-don't want to live w-without you," she wept.

"Is that any way to show gratitude? I am being called by Odin. I can see the Valkyries standing on the hills."

"I'll die with you! I'll be sacrificed as Mother was!"

"No!" roared Olaf, and subsided into coughing. He spat blood over his beard. "No," he said more softly. "I didn't save you from Thorgrim for this. You have survived the battle honorably. You must go on. Your quest is not over."

"B-But I want to d-die."

"Well, you can't. Nobody dies of a broken ankle."

Thorgil burst into sobs. She tore at her face with her fingernails until Jack pulled her hands away.

"You must take the Mountain Queen's chess piece, Jack," said Olaf. "It's in my travel pouch. The sun stone is for Skakki. Thor's hammer is for you, Thorgil, daughter of my heart." Jack found all three. The latter was a silver talisman many of the Northmen carried.

For a while Olaf was silent, breathing with difficulty. Jack offered him pain medicine, and he refused. "She will need it more." The giant nodded at Thorgil.

As the day wore on the sun circled the horizon. It would sink into darkness for only four short hours. Olaf talked with Thorgil, growing ever weaker. Jack watched miserably. Now that the emergency had passed, he was able to assess their situation. Most of their supplies lay in the collapsed hollow below. He hadn't a hope of reaching them. They had to travel three days to the Mountain Queen's hall—though with Thorgil's injury, it might take a week or more.

In a week the dragon would have digested her elk.

Meanwhile, what would *they* eat? The valley farther on was bare of plants. They'd have to fast. Once they got to the ice mountain—if they weren't slaughtered by trolls first—they had to ask for the Mountain Queen's help in finding Mimir's Well. Did she even know where it was?

Afterward, they would have to retrace their steps, including the meadow full of poisonous flowers, and return in time for the harvest festival to prevent Frith from sacrificing Lucy.

It was too much. Jack bowed his head in complete dejection.

He distracted himself with rebinding Thorgil's ankle. She turned whiter still as he eased her foot into place, but she uttered no sound. He unpacked what few supplies Olaf had to offer. He felt bad about taking things from a man still living. The giant assured him this was only sensible.

"I only wish I could have had a hero's funeral." Olaf sighed.

Jack straightened up. "You can, sir," he cried. "You have your sword and your bow and arrows. Thorgil and I can't use them. We can't even lift them. And you have the troll-bear at your feet. Not even Thorgrim had such a sacrifice. Even better, I learned to raise fire from the Bard. When it's—when it's time, I'll burn this entire deadfall. No one has *ever* had such a funeral pyre. They'll see it all the way to Valhalla. And when I return, I'll make you a poem no one will ever forget!"

The giant's eyes shone with joy. "My fame will never die," he whispered.

"It never will," Jack assured him. "Would you like me to repeat the song I performed in King Ivar's hall?"

"Oh, yes," murmured Olaf, who was fading even as the sun lowered toward the horizon. So Jack stood and repeated Rune's poem, and it was even more glorious than it had been before.

> Listen, ring-bearers, while I speak
> Of the glories of battle, of Olaf, most brave.
> Generous is he, that striker of terror.
> Lucky are they who sit in Olaf's hall,
> Gifted with glory, treasure, and fame.
> The wolf-headed men call him leader.
> Odin's skull-pickers name him friend.

When Jack mentioned Odin's skull-pickers, Bold Heart stuck his head out of the bag and warbled. As Jack chanted he saw the sky turn a deeper blue. A wind came up and sang with the voices of women over the broken timbers of the deadfall.

When it was over, he looked down and saw that Olaf's soul had fled. Jack took Thorgil's hand and helped her up the side of the crater and down to the valley floor. The light was fading, and they had to move while he could still see.

Jack helped Thorgil hobble to a space between two boulders, and he settled Bold Heart, still in his bag, into a small crevice. It wasn't much shelter from the icy wind, but it would have to do. "I'm going back to raise fire," he told them.

I hope, he added as he settled himself on the ground. He knew how to light kindling. He did it on the sly when no one was watching, just to feel he hadn't lost the skill. This would be much harder. The logs were thick and many were damp, but the moss was dry. He'd have to concentrate on that.

Jack shivered in the wind and drew his cloak tight around him. The sky was deep blue with a thousand stars winking and twinkling overhead. He looked across at the distant cliffs and saw a fire burning at the top. Where had *that* come from? Were Jotuns making camp? Were they watching the valley? Then Jack remembered the dragon.

I wish I could get her to light this fire, he thought. *No, I don't. She'd take Thorgil and me off to feed her dragonlets. Nothing in this place is any good. Well,* he thought, *here goes.* Jack concentrated on the hot sun pouring into the earth like summer rain. It was stored deep down, waiting for him to call it forth.

It was hard for the boy to keep his mind clear. His body was freezing. The wind pulled at the cloak and tried to tear his hood back. His ears were numb. *Concentrate. Concentrate,* he thought.

What an awful fix they were in. They'd probably die before the Jotuns had a chance to bite off their legs. This world belonged to the frost giants, and they'd snuff out any fire before it got going. Jack felt overpoweringly sleepy. It would be so nice to give himself up to drowsiness. *Lie down, boy,* the frost giants whispered. *It's a fine old bed, ice is.*

"I'm freezing," said Jack aloud.

It's only freezing if you think it is, the Bard said.

"That's all right for you," Jack said resentfully. "You're sitting under an apple tree on the Islands of the Blessed. Winter never comes there. Here it never leaves."

Are you sure? said the Bard.

"It's supposed to be summer," Jack agreed. "It's only cold because of the nasty trolls and their nasty ice mountain. They aren't happy unless everything's half dead. But they're wrong. It *is* summer. The sun's just waiting to rise on the other side of those mountains." He searched for it, felt its midday heat. Light was always there if you knew how to look for it.

Jack felt more confident. Magic seemed a lot closer to the surface here. Just look how easy it had been to see Yggdrassil. And he felt the *whisper, whisper, whisper* of the lives around him. Olaf had said it was the thoughts of the Jotuns, but Jack knew better. It was them all right, but also the hawks, the trees, the fish—everything that lived in Jotunheim. What Jack heard was the breath of life itself moving throughout this strange land.

Jack reached down for the buried sunlight of summers past. He traveled through cold and darkness until he found it burning furiously at the heart of the frost giants' world. It was at war with the ice. At his call it roared forth, eating its way out. It boiled up, sweeping all in its path—

Thorgil screamed a warning. Jack opened his eyes. Here, there, everywhere puffs of light appeared in the deadfall as the moss kindled. Flames spread rapidly, hissing and crackling in the dry pine needles. The twigs caught, the branches flared, and then the tree trunks exploded in a sheet of flame that rose and twisted up into a massive pillar.

Jack was so alarmed, he ran for the shelter of the rocks. He and Thorgil clung to each other, enmity forgotten, as the pillar rose higher. It put out flaming branches like a tree, spangling the night with whirling sparks. The heat was so intense, they had to hide behind the boulders. Bold Heart clawed his way out of the bag, and Jack swept him to safety.

"I should be with Olaf!" Thorgil cried suddenly. She began to crawl toward the flames. Jack hauled her back by her good ankle.

"You idiot! He wanted you to live!"

"I don't care! I want to go to Valhalla!"

"Then why don't I just knock you on the head with a rock?" he yelled, beside himself with fury.

"No! No!" she screamed, her voice full of real panic now. "If a warrior dies by the hand of a thrall, he doesn't go to Valhalla. He goes straight to Hel. It's a shameful death."

"Then stay here," Jack snarled. "Live, damn you, or I *will* knock you on the head with a rock!"

"You wouldn't be so cruel!" she wailed.

"Try me!"

A shrill cry made them stop in the middle of their fight. It came again, growing louder. Jack looked up and saw the dragon sweeping toward them. She flew over the pillar of fire with a harsh scream, swerved, and came back again. The light reflected on her belly and the undersides of her wings. Back and forth she went, like a sheet of living gold, screaming her challenge at the fire.

For challenge it was, Jack realized. "She thinks another dragon has invaded her valley," he murmured.

"No. She's honoring Olaf," said Thorgil. Her face was shiny with tears, and Jack didn't contradict her. Perhaps the dragon *was* honoring Olaf. They were both creatures larger and grander than normal beings. Perhaps even now Olaf was watching this tribute from the gate of Valhalla and thinking he had a finer funeral than had ever been seen in Middle Earth.

Chapter Twenty-nine

THE FROZEN PLAIN

Dawn reddened the ice mountain, and a cold wind rose and swirled the ashes of Olaf's funeral pyre into a gray cloud. They turned white when they reached the sunlit upper air and streamed away to the south. A few charred logs marked out the edge of the deadfall, but all the rest had vanished. The river flowed through the middle as though nothing had ever been there.

Jack went through their meager stores. They had a bag of dried fish, a skin for water, the flask of poppy juice. For weapons Thorgil and Jack had their knives—Thorgil's sword had disappeared in the deadfall—and she had a battle-axe.

"You should leave me behind," said Thorgil.

"Why? Your ankle will heal," Jack said.

"Not soon enough. I'll wait here for the dragon and make my stand."

"Nobody's waiting for the dragon. You're coming with me or I'll knock you on the head." Now that Jack had discovered how terrified Thorgil was of dying by the hand of a thrall, he knew he had a weapon against her. He'd never have killed her, but she didn't know that. She judged him by her own behavior.

"That only means we'll *both* be eaten somewhere else," she said with a melancholy smile.

Jack took Thorgil's axe and hiked into the forest to look for a stick she could use for a crutch. He found an ash tree— unusual in such cold woods—and chopped off two branches. One had a fork at one end for Thorgil to lean on. The other was a staff for himself. He hadn't planned to make one, but the gnarled wood reminded Jack of the blackened staff the Bard had used. It gave him a strange feeling to hold it, as though he were following a trail the old man had made long ago.

On the way back Jack gathered a patch of early cloudberries for Thorgil. "*You* eat them," she said with a sigh, pushing them away. "They're wasted on me, for I shall soon die."

Jack was tired of arguing with her. He shared the cloudberries with Bold Heart, and they all had a long drink of water. He pulled Thorgil to her feet. She immediately slumped to the ground. He pulled her up again. "Come on! You have to try!" he cried as she collapsed.

"It's pointless. I'll fight the dragon here."

Jack hauled Thorgil up, none too gently, and tried to plant the crutch under her arm. She hurled it away.

"You will . . . *use* . . . this crutch," Jack said between gritted teeth. "You will . . . *walk* . . . with me, or I will . . . *knock you on the head with a rock and send you straight to Hel!*" He retrieved the crutch, and Thorgil, her mouth twisted with rage and pain, obeyed him. She refused any help and Jack didn't care. He had enough trouble carrying Bold Heart and the supplies.

Slowly, they crept along the valley floor. Jack led the way with the crow on his shoulder. Bold Heart couldn't fly and might never do so again. He seemed lively enough, though, and muttered to himself as he dug his claws into Jack's tunic.

The boy looked up to see a puff of smoke from a cliff. He knew the dragon was up there, brooding, perhaps on a nest full of dragonlets. She'd be hungry long before they got to the ice mountain.

At night they camped in the open. Jack made a small fire of lichen and moss, but it burned quickly and soon left them as cold as ever. They huddled together under their two cloaks with Bold Heart between. Sleep was fitful. Thorgil woke up weeping. Jack dreamed of dragons. When he couldn't sleep, he thought of trolls and how to catch their attention with the gold chess piece before he got his leg bitten off.

When day came, they crept on. There were no trees now and no bushes. The patches of snow were larger and the ground was treacherous with ice, which slowed them even more. Jack noticed that as Thorgil weakened, she became a lot easier to live with. She stopped calling him a thrall, and she thanked him once when he handed her the water bag. Perhaps she didn't have the energy to be evil.

She isn't half bad in this condition, Jack thought. She listened to his tales and asked questions about his life. She was particularly interested in Jack's parents. It amazed her that Father devoted himself to making Lucy happy. "It's why she's weak," Thorgil decided. "He should have beaten her and made her sleep outside without a blanket to toughen her."

"Is that what your father did?" Jack asked, appalled that anyone could be that cruel to a small child. But then, Thorgrim had ordered his newborn daughter thrown out for wolves to devour.

"Of course," Thorgil said proudly. "It made me what I am today."

You've got that *right,* thought Jack.

"Maeve kept me warm, though," the girl said. "She always found me when I had to sleep outside."

"Maeve?"

"She was an Irish wolfhound. She belonged to King Ivar."

"Ah," said Jack, understanding. This was the dog who had saved Thorgil when she was an infant. "Did you know Maeve was named for a famous warrior queen?"

"No! Really?"

"Dragon Tongue told me about her. She ruled Ireland long ago. He said she still lives on the Islands of the Blessed with all the great heroes."

"I've never heard of the Islands of the Blessed."

"They're in the Utter West, where the sun goes down. The

sea around them is as clear as sky and winter never comes."

"Do they allow dogs on the islands?" Thorgil said softly.

"I'm sure they do." Jack had a big lump in his throat and couldn't trust himself to speak. They crept on through the barren valley with the ice mountain seeming as far away as it had been when they started. Jack thought of the Bard sitting under an apple tree with the great hound Maeve at his side.

In the morning Thorgil refused to stand. Her ankle was swollen, and her eyes had deep shadows under them. She hadn't eaten in days. "I will die here," she announced.

"You're worn out from pain," Jack said. "Olaf told me to save the poppy juice for you. He said you'd need it before this trip was done."

"I want to suffer. Odin loves warriors who can endure pain."

"You Northmen are crazy," Jack said.

"We're *brave*," Thorgil corrected. "My uncle, when he was dying of an arrow wound, tore the arrow from his chest with a pair of tongs. He laughed as the blood gushed out and said, 'See how well nourished this heart is!' Then he died standing up like a true berserker!"

"It would have made more sense to let a wise woman treat him," Jack said.

"I wouldn't expect a Saxon thrall to understand."

"*You're* half Saxon. Or have you forgotten?"

"My mother was of no account. I am all berserker," Thorgil said.

Jack was about to remind her that she'd been born a thrall when he remembered his promise to Olaf. "You know . . . I think I'll call you Jill."

"What?"

"It's what your mother named you. Thorgil is a boy's name, and it doesn't suit you," he said.

She sat up. She looked a lot more alert, which was Jack's intent. You couldn't reason with Thorgil, but you could count on rage to get her moving.

"Jill's a fine old Saxon name," Jack said.

"I hate it!"

"Oh, but it suits you. Such a pretty name for a pretty girl. Jill! Jill! Jill!" By now Jack was dancing around and Thorgil was hauling herself up in a perfect fury. She panted with the effort, but it didn't stop her. She hobbled after Jack with murder in her eyes. Bold Heart squawked and scrambled out of her path.

"Oh, Jill! Sweet Jill! Give us a kiss, Jill! How nice you'll look with ribbons and flowers in your hair!"

"My name isn't Jill!" Thorgil raised the crutch to hit Jack and fell over with a jarring thud. Her eyes rolled up in her head. She passed out on the icy stones.

Oh, heavens, what have I done? thought Jack. He knelt at once by the fallen shield maiden and tried to see whether she was still breathing. "I didn't mean to hurt you, Thorgil," he cried. "Please, please, please wake up. I won't do that again."

Thorgil sank her teeth into his hand. Jack yelled and pulled back. He was bleeding! "You pile of sheep droppings! You *kindaskitur*!" he shouted.

"Hurts, doesn't it?" She grinned.

Jack trembled with rage, wanting and yet not wanting to hit her. "Yes, it hurts," he said.

"So we're even."

"We'll *never* be even," Jack said, "but we can call a truce. I know"—he held up his hand as Thorgil tried to interrupt—"berserkers never sign truces. But we're on a quest, and Olaf said we should work together."

At the mention of Olaf, Thorgil's face became solemn. She looked at him for a long moment, and her eyes became suspiciously damp. "You're right," she said at last. "I've behaved dishonorably. You have my oath I will not try to hurt you again."

Thorgil's apology was so unexpected, Jack stared at her. Was she joking? Was this another trick? "I hope you aren't an oath-breaker," he muttered, expecting her to fly at him again.

"Thorgil Olaf's Daughter is not an oath-breaker," she replied gravely. She didn't even try to hit him.

Jack forced the wound on his hand to bleed and washed it in the icy river. He kept watching Thorgil and wondering at her sudden change of mood. "You know, it's the duty of all members of this quest to keep up his or her strength."

"That's true," she admitted.

"You should eat. And if you took some of the poppy juice—as Olaf commanded—you'd be able to keep walking."

"I will eat one dried fish and take one drop of poppy juice," she said. "When the dragon comes, I'll at least have the strength to stand and fight."

Jack glanced up at the cliffs. He didn't see any smoke, but he knew their time had run out. If the dragon didn't find herself another elk, she had a dandy snack sitting just below her nest.

Jack got Thorgil to eat two dried fish and take two drops of poppy juice. He retied her splint, frowning at the puffiness of the flesh over her ankle. "Why is pain so important to you?" he asked.

"I told you. Odin loves those who can endure it." Thorgil clenched her teeth as Jack eased the splint into a firmer position. "Pain gives you knowledge."

"Joy gives you knowledge too."

"Only about foolish, trivial things. When Odin wanted the lore that would make him leader of the gods, he had to pay for it with suffering. He was stabbed with a spear and hanged for nine days and nights on the tree Yggdrassil."

"That's just plain stupid," Jack said.

"*Your* god was nailed to a cross. It's the same thing."

"No, it's not."

"Anyhow," Thorgil went on, "Odin needed even more knowledge to gain power over the nine worlds, so he had to drink from Mimir's Well."

"Mimir's Well? That's where we're going."

"If we survive and if we can find it."

"Aren't you the cheerful one," said Jack.

"I'm only being realistic. Odin wasn't allowed to drink

until he sacrificed something of great importance. He tore out one of his eyes and threw it into the well," Thorgil said. "They say it's still there."

"Tore out an *eye?*" Jack felt sick. He couldn't imagine doing such a thing, but the Northmen probably thought it was normal, like trimming your toenails.

What are you doing today, Odin old boy?

Oh, I thought I'd rip out an eye after lunch.

Jolly good.

"Wait a minute," Jack said. "Can't you, you know, just dip a cup into Mimir's Well?"

"You have to sacrifice something of overwhelming importance before you're allowed to drink," Thorgil explained patiently. "It could be your right hand or your tongue. You can agree to die horribly later or see your firstborn devoured by a wolf."

Jack bowed his head, appalled. Rune hadn't mentioned this feature. It wasn't Jack's idea of a quest at all. You expected to walk a long way and to endure cold and hunger. You might have to fight trolls (to be exact, he'd expected Olaf to take care of the trolls). Nobody said you had to tear out an eye.

"Don't worry," Thorgil said. "We probably won't find the well. Rune and Dragon Tongue didn't."

"I didn't know Dragon Tongue came here," said Jack. "If he couldn't find it, we don't stand a chance." *And Lucy doesn't stand a chance either,* he thought with a pain over his heart.

"It isn't a matter of cleverness," Thorgil said. "Rune says the path is guarded by Norns. They choose who finds it."

"Norns? Wonderful. Something else in this wretched place that wants to stomp on you or bite off your leg."

"Oh, no!" Thorgil was shocked. "Norns keep the tree Yggdrassil alive. Without them, nothing would exist."

"So what are they? Huge, horrible trolls?"

"They're women," Thorgil said. "Well, they *look* like women. That's what Rune says, though he hasn't seen them. They show up when you're born and decide what kind of life you're going to have."

"I guess they were in a rotten mood when I came along," Jack said. He loaded up the water bag and supplies.

"Me too," Thorgil said gravely.

As they neared the ice mountain the air grew steadily colder. When the wind came from that direction, it actually hurt to breathe. Jack wrapped his cloak over his nose. Only his body heat kept the water bag from freezing solid.

Bold Heart shivered and his feet sparkled with ice crystals as he tried to hook his claws on to Jack's shoulder. "Poor old fellow," Jack said. "I'll bet you're sorry you ever met us. I'll carry you for a while." The crow sank gratefully into the bag, and the boy slung it around his neck.

I feel like a donkey in a lead mine, Jack thought as he trudged along. *I'm loaded up with stuff. I'm hungry and cold. All I've got to look forward to is more work and a nasty death. The Norns certainly don't love* me. *Oh, I'm really in luck now! Thorgil wants to lean on me.*

Perhaps two drops of poppy juice had been too much, or perhaps Thorgil, in her starved, weakened state, couldn't handle it. She staggered and clung to Jack. Her eyes kept closing, and he feared she would fall over right there. He couldn't possibly carry her. He could hardly stand himself. *I am the most miserable, Norn-cursed boy alive,* he thought as Thorgil reeled into him again. *Things couldn't possibly be worse.*

But he was wrong.

Chapter Thirty

DEATH FROM THE SKY

For such a large creature, the dragon was able to float along with scarcely a sound, or at least nothing Jack could hear over the wind and his own labored breathing. She came up behind them like a leaf coasting on a breeze. Her claws swooped them up before he could even scream.

She did not kill them at once. That would have been too kind. She merely picked them up from the ground and sped off with her talons locked around them like a cage. For a moment Jack couldn't understand what had happened. He was surrounded by black bars—bars that were *hot*. He saw the ground disappear. He felt the wind whistle past his ears.

He heard a terrible, deafening, heart-stopping shriek and recognized it at once. It was the same challenge that had been hurled at Olaf's funeral pyre. "It's the—it's the—" Jack couldn't get the words out. The dizzying ride and his own fear made him sick.

"It's the dragon," Thorgil finished for him. He saw her trying to chip away at the talons with her knife. She was woozy and weak but still attempting to fight.

"It's hot," Jack said. And it was, uncomfortably so. The talons radiated heat, and he had to shift to keep from getting burned. By now they were high above the ground. The dragon flew along, level with the cliffs. Each wing-beat blew a blast of heat past Jack's face, and the dragon's bones creaked mournfully, like a ship under full sail. *It's a* knorr, Jack thought foolishly, echoing Olaf's words from weeks ago: *They call it that because the timbers creak the whole time*—knorr, knorr, knorr. *It takes getting used to.*

The dragon rose and hovered in the air. She opened her talons, and Jack and Thorgil tumbled out into a ring of stone. Around them beady eyes watched intently. Jack realized, with a sick rush of terror, that they had been brought—as a cat might bring mice for her kittens—to teach the dragonlets how to hunt.

"Strike between the chest plates below their necks," Thorgil said in a low voice. "That's what Olaf told me."

Jack could hardly believe his ears. She was up and ready for battle. He was anything but ready. He found himself hypnotized by the dragonlets. They hissed and swayed back and forth, craning their necks. Their eyes were lit with evil intent. How could Thorgil think of fighting now? It was all over. They were doomed.

Four of the monsters—each twice Jack's size—were working up the courage to follow their mother's bidding. The dragon crouched at the side of the nest, making a bubbling noise like a pot of boiling water. Her great, golden eyes were half closed.

Bold Heart stuck his head out of the bag and cawed sharply. The dragon reared back as though stung. Bold Heart climbed out and hopped to the ground. He cawed again and mumbled something in crow talk. The dragon burbled.

"Are they *talking*?" Jack whispered.

"I don't know. Keep your eyes on the green one. He's bolder than the rest." All Thorgil's attention was given to the dragonlets. She was correct: The green one was curling a long, snakelike tongue over his scaly lips as he gazed at the tidbits his mother had brought home. Saliva—or something like it—fell to the ground with a hiss. The other three creatures eyed their brother nervously. They were smaller and golden, like their mother. Jack guessed they were females.

Bold Heart had worked himself into a perfect frenzy of cawing and warbling. He seemed to be trying to convince the dragon of something. She hissed and lashed her tail. Then, abruptly, she rose and soared off down the valley. Bold Heart turned his attention to the dragonlets.

They, too, seemed to understand him, but they were too young to pay attention for long. One of the golden females scratched her potbelly with long fingernails. She seemed to be dozing off. "Thorgil, lie down," Jack whispered.

"I'm not a coward," she said.

"This is strategy. I think they don't know about hunting. If we lie still and don't move, they'll ignore us."

"Thorgil Olaf's Daughter does not retreat."

The green dragonlet arched his neck to study her. His snaky tongue flicked out. Jack despaired of getting through to the shield maiden. If she kept moving, she'd get them both killed. "Lie still and get him to lower his guard. Then you can stab him," said Jack.

This must have made sense, because Thorgil immediately obeyed. The dragonlet considered her for a long moment before being distracted by a passing hawk.

Bold Heart hopped in front of the creature. Jack waited breathlessly for a fatal strike, but the crow seemed to be discussing something with the young dragon. The bird cawed and hopped, flicking his head at the smaller siblings. Jack couldn't understand what was being said, but the meaning was clear: *Hey, look! Mother's away from home. It's a perfect time to get rid of rivals.*

The longer Bold Heart cawed, the more agitated the green dragonlet became and the more nervous were the golden ones. Suddenly, with shocking speed, the green dragonlet hurled himself across the nest, barely missing Jack and Thorgil with his talons. He seized his sisters by the neck—bang, bang, bang, one after the other—and threw them off the cliff!

Jack heard them wail all the way down. They were only chicks. They couldn't fly. The green dragonlet threw back his head with an ear-piercing shriek of victory . . . and Thorgil raised herself up and stabbed him between the chest plates below his neck. The victory scream stopped in midshriek. The dragonlet thrashed and beat at the knife, but the blow was mortal. He collapsed onto the shield maiden.

Jack immediately grabbed his stubby wings and pulled him off—fortunately, the creature was far lighter than he looked—but, to his horror, he saw Thorgil clawing at her face. Some of the dragonlet's blood had splattered onto her and was raising blisters. He washed her frantically with the bag of drinking water and wiped her with his cloak. It seemed to help. She had blisters on one cheek and on her lips, but her eyes, thank goodness, had been spared.

Thorgil looked stunned. Her eyes were wild, and she seemed hardly aware of things around her. But after a moment she rallied and, clinging to Jack, hobbled out of the nest. He took her behind a boulder and ran back to retrieve what supplies he could find.

Her crutch had snapped in two in the dragon's talons on the trip up. His staff was still intact, and he still had the gold chess piece, sun stone, and poppy juice in a pouch around his neck. The food was ruined. The water bag was empty. His cloak had gaping holes from where he'd dropped it in the dragonlet's blood. So did the bag he'd used to carry Bold Heart. Jack decided to abandon them. He wanted to pull Thorgil's knife free, but it was covered in gore and he was afraid to touch it.

Bold Heart, meanwhile, had hopped onto one of the stones encircling the nest. "You were wonderful!" Jack cried. "I had no idea you could talk Dragon." The crow burbled, and

Jack flinched and looked behind him. "All right, all right. You really *can* talk Dragon."

Bold Heart strutted up and down as if to say, *I am the greatest! I am the greatest! I'm the toughest crow in Middle Earth, and in Jotunheim, too!*

"Yes, you are," agreed Jack, "but you'd better hop aboard. We've got to find a hiding place before the dragon returns." He lifted the crow to his shoulder and hurried back to Thorgil.

They squeezed between boulders, working their way back from the cliffs. Jack searched anxiously for a cave or a hole—anything that could conceal them from the dragon. He found nothing but a confusing jumble of rocks. Thorgil was tiring rapidly. It was amazing that she'd had the energy to kill the dragonlet. Now her strength flagged, and she leaned more and more on Jack.

Jack, too, was exhausted. Thorgil was hanging on to one shoulder and Bold Heart clutched the other. The wind on the high cliff was fierce, freezing, and continuous. It hurt to breathe. It hurt to walk.

Odin must really love me, Jack thought. *I'm suffering enough for six Northmen.* They staggered into a narrow ravine and concealed themselves as best they could in the shadows. The shadows, of course, were especially icy.

"We have to rest," Jack whispered. "*I* have to rest. You were magnificent, Thorgil. I never dreamed anyone could be that brave."

She said nothing.

"It's all right to enjoy praise," he said. "Olaf loved it. I can tell you, if we survive, I'll make you the best poem a warrior ever had—you and Olaf, of course."

Thorgil made a choking sound. Jack bent down, squinting in the shadows. Her lips were badly blistered, and he had a horrid thought. "Thorgil, open your mouth." She did, and he saw, to his dismay, that her tongue was blistered too. She didn't talk because she couldn't.

"Oh, no, no, no," Jack whispered, holding her. It was a sign of her utter weakness that she didn't push him away. "I don't have water, but I'll look for ice." He searched along the rocks until he found a pocket of snow. He brought it to her. She ate it, little by little, and it seemed to reduce the swelling of her tongue. At least she wasn't choking anymore.

Jack leaned back and gazed at the strip of sky over their hiding place. He had no idea what to do. Out of habit, as he did whenever he was upset, Jack clutched the rune of protection around his neck. It was barely warm. Even it had little encouragement to add to their desperate situation.

Bold Heart crouched and moaned. It was unlike any sound he'd made before. Jack looked up and saw a blob of snow at the top of the ravine. Where had that come from? A second later it was joined by *another* blob, and another and another. *Hooo-uh, hooo-uh, hooo-uh, wuh-wuh-wuh,* said the first blob.

The other blobs responded with doglike barks, cackles, shrieks, and hisses. *Hooo-uh! Hooo-uh!* the first blob said emphatically. It was hard to see against the bright strip of sky, but Jack made out a huge, round head with yellow eyes. It was an enormous owl, big enough to carry off a lamb—or attack a pair of desperately weak humans. Bold Heart hid behind Jack.

Hooo-uh wuh-wuh-wuh! yelled the first owl. The others replied with a variety of indignant cries, working themselves into a frenzy. They fluffed their feathers, hunched their shoulders, and spread their wings. *Krufff-guh-guh-guh!* they shouted. They danced back and forth on fat, feathery legs.

Jack looked down to see Thorgil staring at them with a look of utter terror on her face. *Thorgil* scared? She'd stood up to dragons!

A terrible, wailing scream echoed over the cliffs. The owls exploded from their perch in a flurry of wings. Jack heard an ominous creaking. The dragon had discovered the destruction of her nest.

"I don't think she can see us," Jack whispered to Thorgil. "Stay still. We should wait until she gets tired of hunting." But the dragon didn't get tired for a long time. Back and forth she went, searching the cliffs. Her shadow passed overhead several times as the sun slowly worked its way across the sky. The shadow in the ravine became deeper.

When it seemed the dragon was far away, Jack crept out and filled the water skin with snow. He trickled it into Thorgil's mouth and a little into Bold Heart's beak. He himself sucked on fragments of ice he found on the rocks. It was all they had and all they would have.

At last the dragon appeared to settle down. They heard occasional outbursts of grief, but the position of the creature didn't move. "Mm," said Thorgil, grasping Jack's hand.

"What is it? Do you want water?"

"Mm!" the girl insisted. She still couldn't talk. She pulled at Jack and pointed down the ravine.

"That's not the way to the ice mountain," he said, "but I suppose it doesn't matter. We can't get down the cliff, and we'll freeze to death here." With afternoon, the wind had picked up and was whistling through the ravine. Jack lifted Bold Heart, who seemed noticeably weaker. None of them had eaten much for days. The bird's injured wing drooped and his feet were clumsy. He didn't have a covering of feathers on his legs like the owls.

Jack's body ached with tiredness, but he put one arm around Thorgil and used the staff to steady them both. Bold Heart clung to his shoulder. The ravine was full of loose rocks, and their progress was slow. They went down and down as the cliffs towered up and up until it was almost dark at the bottom. They came to a place where the trail—if it was a trail—divided. Jack stopped. He was so exhausted, he couldn't make up his mind.

Thorgil, however, had no problem. She firmly steered him to the left. They came to more divides. Each time, Thorgil chose a direction, almost as if she knew where they were going. Jack didn't care. At least someone was making decisions.

To his very great surprise, they came out into a little valley full of trees. A stream chuckled down the middle, and on either side were bushes full of raspberries and blueberries. The ground was covered with tiny mountain strawberries. The air was warm and sweet.

"Oh, Thorgil," murmured Jack. He sat her down on a bed of clover and hurried to gather fruit. All three of them feasted, though he had to squash the berries and drip the juice into Thorgil's mouth. Bold Heart gorged himself.

Jack hid two more drops of poppy juice in the berries he fed the shield maiden. He wasn't sure if this was wise, but it seemed she would never survive if she didn't rest. Soon she was stretched out on the clover, snoring. Her face was more peaceful than it had been since . . . well, since forever, Jack thought.

The light turned blue with evening, and a mist rose from the stream. Jack walked along the edge. It was hard to feel that anything could go wrong in this place. Everything was so peaceful. Flowers—ordinary flowers, not troll-blossoms that wanted to kill you—grew on the mossy banks. Mushrooms of all shapes and colors dotted fallen logs.

Jack bent down to fill the water bag. The stream was *warm*—not hot, just warm enough to feel nice. He bathed his face and hands. Then he stretched out beside Thorgil and Bold Heart. They had only one cloak, but it was enough in the soft, sweet air of the little valley. Jack went to sleep watching the bright chips of stars in the dark sky overhead.

Chapter Thirty-one

THE CAPERCAILLIE

Nothing horrible came out of the woods that night. Nothing ripped branches or belched fire or tried to bite off anyone's leg. Jack opened his eyes on a forest full of birds. They sang and chattered in all the trees. The air was full of trills and warbles and chirrs as the birds greeted the dawn. Crossbills flew out of pine trees. Woodpeckers drilled at bark. Thrushes and finches darted through aspen, oak, and birch, for this warm, hidden pocket was like a forest in England.

"Isn't it lovely?" Jack said with a sigh, smoothing Bold Heart's feathers. Thorgil looked terrified. "It's all right," Jack assured her. "It's only different from what we expected. I don't know how you found this place, but I'm awfully glad you did. The stream is warm, by the way. If you want to bathe, I'll help you to the edge."

Thorgil looked at him as though he were completely crazy.

"Oh, I know. You Northmen like to stink to High Heaven, but the water feels nice. I wish we didn't have to leave. At least we'll be able to rest."

"Ahnt to go," said Thorgil with difficulty.

"You can talk! Open your mouth so I can see how much the swelling's gone down." Thorgil obeyed. Jack was pleased with her progress. Her face and lips looked better too. The blisters had almost vanished, leaving only a slight puffiness.

"Ahnt to go *now*," said Thorgil.

"Oh! I'll go beyond those trees and give you privacy."

"Not *att*. Go out valley. Soopid thrall."

Jack stared at her. He might have known. If something was good, she'd be sure to reject it. "It's a mistake, you know, to call someone a 'stupid thrall' when he has the only knife."

"Ate birds. Huh-huh-*hate* birds," Thorgil said, and burst into tears.

Jack was confounded. In spite of himself, he felt sorry for her. She'd saved him from the dragon, after all, and she'd found the valley. What was wrong with her? "Is this place dangerous?" he asked. "Is there something I should know?"

"No. Hate birds, is all."

"Well, that's not enough," Jack said. "I like them. I even talk to them, or at least smart ones like Bold Heart. We absolutely have to rest. If you don't like the singing, stuff moss into your ears. I'm going off to find food—another of our little problems, in case you've forgotten."

She did as he suggested: stuffed moss into her ears. Then

she sat staring at the stream with tears rolling down her cheeks.

He left Bold Heart to keep her company. There was no reasoning with the shield maiden. She was determined to suffer no matter how nice things were. His mood lifted as he walked along the stream. The life force seemed to be everywhere, in the leafy trees, the ecstatic birds, the lemmings and voles that rustled through the strawberries, in the butterflies, midges, and beetles. The place was simmering with activity.

Jack found berries, but he wanted something more sustaining. He considered the mushrooms—or were they toadstools? He found and dug up wild leeks.

He froze as he heard something crackling in the underbrush. Slowly, carefully, a magnificent bird stepped from the shadows. Her majestic brown tail fanned out behind her, and around her feet flocked ten speckled chicks. Jack's mouth watered. It was a capercaillie, big as four hens put together. Heide had served one in Olaf's hall. Jack remembered clearly its rich flesh flavored with lingonberries from Dotti's garden.

The capercaillie gazed at him haughtily. Her eyes, topped by patches of red that resembled eyebrows, seemed mildly surprised. She wasn't even afraid. Jack felt for his knife.

The creature moved toward him. The speckled chicks pecked at the ground and glanced up for approval from their mother. The capercaillie lowered her head and clucked softly. Jack knew she could feed them for days. He could roast her with the leeks he'd gathered earlier and serve her with the wild strawberries her chicks were so busy eating.

The bird walked past him with a dignified tread. She wasn't afraid of him. It would take only a second to cut her throat, but Jack couldn't do it. The Bard had told him it was evil to use the life force to lure game. This valley was brimming with it, and the capercaillie felt secure in its presence. To kill her was—somehow—wrong.

I must be stupid beyond belief, he thought as he watched the bird disappear into the forest. Soon, however, he came into a different sort of woodland. He saw apple, walnut, hazelnut, and pear trees among the more familiar pines and aspens. They were covered with both flowers and ripe fruit, as though spring and autumn had run together. Jack took off his tunic and used it as a carrying bag.

And then he heard a buzzing in the distance that sent a thrill along his nerves. It was an uncountable number of bees, so many that there must have been hundreds of hives up ahead. Jack, who was well used to the insects from Mother's work, understood the quality of their hum. You could tell their mood by the sounds they made.

He'd heard angry bees and cheerful ones, worried bees and some so despairing that the whole hive was sinking into death. But these were possessed by mad joy. Jack could imagine them rising and falling in their thousands over the trees. It filled him with alarm, though he'd never been afraid of the creatures before. Their emotions were simply too strong to bear. Jack turned away.

Thorgil was still staring at the stream when he returned. He sliced up ripe pears for her. He found a flat rock and pounded nut meats into powder. She ate and went back to watching the stream.

You're welcome, Jack thought. But after awhile he got up and changed the binding on her ankle. She couldn't help being an infuriating berserker. He saw that the puffiness over her ankle had vanished, as had the blisters on her cheek. In spite of herself, Thorgil was recovering.

The rest of the day was spent dozing or playing a game of rolling a walnut back and forth with Bold Heart. Jack knew he should make plans to leave, but he was far too contented. It had been a long time since he'd felt so good.

Toward nightfall he took another stroll and saw the snowy owls sitting in a small clearing. They were feeding on cloudberries and *hoo-hoo*ing among themselves. Jack noticed a vole working earnestly on a sprig of wild pea in their midst. The owls Jack was used to would have pounced on the little creature at once.

Jack decided to stay longer, although Thorgil argued against it. She could talk now and did so at great length. "We're on a quest," she said. "I don't expect a thrall to understand, but it means we mustn't get too comfortable. It's our duty to see the Mountain Queen as soon as possible. Olaf would have wanted it that way. I've had enough of lying around."

"That's all you've been doing," Jack retorted. "I went out and found food."

"I found the valley."

"How *did* you manage that?" Jack asked.

Thorgil flushed red. "It was a lucky guess."

"Anyhow, your ankle needs to heal. I can't carry you around like a pet cat."

"I'm not a pet cat! I'm Thorgil Olaf's Daughter. I'll crawl on bloody hands and knees if I have to!"

Jack was pleased to see her old spirit back. It meant she was returning to normal. For a broken bone, her ankle was healing with amazing speed. In a day or two she'd be able to walk, and he intended to wait until she could move easily. He felt no urgency.

The lush valley with its warm air grew more attractive with each passing day. Jack fell into a schedule of strolling out each morning for food. He bathed in the stream at midday and explored in the afternoons. Between times he talked to Thorgil (who had turned increasingly sullen as she recovered) and Bold Heart, who seemed not quite happy with the situation either.

The air hummed with joy. At moments Jack felt a feverish desire to roll in moss or to cram raspberries into his mouth and let the juice drip down his chin. At moments he did just that. Sometimes he laughed and laughed for no reason until he couldn't catch his breath. *This place has to be pure life force,* he thought.

Jack sat up abruptly.

He remembered the Bard talking about his training with his best friend in Ireland. *Day after day we sat, struggling to open our minds to the power of the life force. And just as quickly retreating when it got too close. But my friend liked the feeling of power. He refused to stop while it was still safe. One day some-thing went* snap. *He gave a mighty howl and ran off as fast as he could go until he got to the Valley of Lunatics.*

I could hear the lunatics cackling before I could see them, the Bard had gone on. *It was a terrible sound, so like laughter and yet so completely joyless. All the failed bards in Ireland had found their way to this one place, where the life force was stronger than anywhere else. And there they stayed.*

"Maybe it isn't a good idea to laugh until I can't breathe," murmured Jack. His eyes had been closed as he let the power of this place flow through him. Now he opened them on a most unwelcome sight.

Before him stood the first dangerous creature he'd seen in this enchanted valley: a great, hulking troll-boar with his mouth hanging open. Jack could see razor-sharp tusks.

The boy was stupefied. All he could think to do was chant Mother's charm for calming angry bees. He sang it again and again, feeling it echo in the life force. That power was too close, too strong. It was like a wave of flame sweeping toward him.

Jack felt himself knocked onto his back into a strawberry patch. His mind cleared and the flames vanished. The boar was whuffling him all over, placing little kisses on his arms, chest, and face.

"Golden Bristles?" the boy cried. He hugged the monster's head and scratched him behind his leathery ears. "You found your way home. Goooood piggy!" Jack pulled himself up and petted the brute all over his bristly back. "I'm so happy. Isn't this a lovely place?" Golden Bristles oinked in agreement.

Jack led him back to the camp Thorgil had made. The instant she saw him, she stood up and aimed a rock at the boar's head. "No, no, no! He's a friend," Jack cried. "See?" He climbed onto the pig's back, half expecting the creature to toss him off. But Golden Bristles was perfectly happy to be ridden like a donkey.

The pig grunted, and Bold Heart warbled back. "He says you freed him," Thorgil said with a scowl like a thundercloud.

"I did. Wait a minute. How do you know what he said?"

"None of your business. Olaf almost got killed capturing him!"

"So what? He was only going to drown him. Unlike pea-brained berserkers, I don't like suffering."

"You stupid thrall! Now Lucy will take his place," cried Thorgil.

"That's not my doing!" Jack shouted, jumping down from Golden Bristles's back.

"It is so, you Saxon fool!"

"*Brjóstabarn! You're* the one who gave her to Frith!" yelled Jack. They stood toe-to-toe, panting with rage. Jack's mind was clearer than it had been for days. Fury swept away the dream-like enchantment of the valley. He suddenly remembered Lucy. By Heaven, she was why he was here, and he'd forgotten! He couldn't even remember how much time had passed.

"That's right," Thorgil said, correctly reading his face. "While you've been drooling into the raspberries, time has passed."

"Oh, Lucy," he whispered. Then another thought struck

him. "You *did* know what Golden Bristles said. You've been practicing *seiðer* all along. You lied to me!"

Thorgil bowed her head. "I never lie. This accursed power came upon me suddenly. I'm so ashamed," she murmured.

"You? Ashamed? I'd sooner expect that of Freya's cats."

The shield maiden squared her shoulders. She was not one to turn away from pain. "I can't understand the troll-boar, but I do know what Bold Heart says. And all those wretched little birds!" She shook her fist at the trees. "It's like being in a hall full of drunk warriors. Yak, yak, yak all the time. They say things like 'Get out of my tree' or 'Did you ever see such beautiful chicks?' Or they say, 'Excuse me, I've got to poop.' And they never shut up from the minute they wake until they fall asleep! The owls keep it up all night."

"That's how you found this place," Jack said. "The owls."

"Yes! That was the first time I realized I could understand birds. They were upset about the dragon and what she'd do when she found her children dead. One of the owls told the others how to find this valley. Apparently, the dragon's forbidden to come here."

"You're like Sigurd. You got dragon's blood in your mouth."

"I wish I never had! It's turned me into a horrible witch!"

"It's a wonderful skill, Thorgil," Jack said.

"*I hate it!*" She was determined to despise her good fortune. Jack would have loved to understand birds, but the dragon's blood would probably have killed him. It had almost killed Thorgil.

"I guess we'd better leave," he said. "The sooner we get to the Mountain Queen, the better."

"About time," grumbled Thorgil.

Packing was no problem. They had almost nothing. Jack gathered a supply of nuts and fruit for the journey. He used Thorgil's cloak to carry it. She would be cold when they left, but so would he and they needed the food. On the way back he saw the owls lying in the meadow. They were so weak, they couldn't fly.

They had fled the dragon only to encounter an even greater peril here. The peacefulness of the valley had lured them, as it had Jack. They hadn't realized they wouldn't be able to hunt. Owls could not survive on fruits and berries alone.

Jack put down the food and carried each owl out of the meadow and up into the barren rocks of the nearby hills. He left them on a trail leading up to the cliffs. They were out of sight of the valley and seemed more alert when he left them.

"What took you so long?" Thorgil complained when he returned.

"Owls," Jack said shortly, and didn't explain.

He carried the food over one shoulder and grasped his staff for a weapon. Thorgil took the one remaining knife on the grounds that she was better at using it. Bold Heart perched on Golden Bristles's back, for the boar had already been on his way to the Mountain Queen's cave when they met. He was good friends with her, he said, and always dropped in when he was in the neighborhood.

Jack learned this in a roundabout way. Golden Bristles spoke to Bold Heart, who translated from Pig to Crow so Thorgil could understand. Then she passed on the information. Or some of it. She kept most things to herself, either because Golden Bristles asked her to or because she wanted to irritate Jack.

Chapter Thirty-two

THE ICE BOW

At the end of the valley, where the stream plunged under-ground, Golden Bristles found an opening hidden by vines. It was invisible until you were actually in it, and when you got to the other side, all you saw was a crack in the hillside. The air turned cold at once.

This trail was at the bottom of another deep ravine. It twisted and turned with occasional forks as it went down. Golden Bristles selected their path. When darkness fell, they were still in the ravine with only rocks to lie on.

It was a cold, miserable night. Jack and Thorgil slept sitting up with the troll-boar's massive body for a back-rest. The pig was infested with troll-lice. They crept through his hair and through Jack's and Thorgil's hair as well, though they didn't bite. They didn't seem to like human blood. Jack still woke every time he felt their stealthy claws.

Not that he slept much between times. The wind found its way into the ravine, and toward dawn an icy frost came down. Jack sheltered Bold Heart under his tunic, which helped them both a little.

Only Golden Bristles spent a comfortable night under his layers of fat. He snored atrociously, slobbering and whining through his long snout, and his trotters jerked when he dreamed.

"How much more of this is there?" Jack moaned as they slipped and clattered over the stones after dawn. He could hardly keep his footing, even with the staff he'd cut from the ash tree.

"I'll ask," Thorgil said. She was noticeably cheerful now that they were all suffering. She put the question to Bold Heart, who put it to Golden Bristles. The boar replied at length. The crow translated, taking a long time about it. Then Thorgil answered: "Not long."

"That was a lot of talk to end up with 'not long,'" Jack said.

"Yes, it was," Thorgil said happily.

"You're hiding something."

"You'll never know."

Brjóstabarn, thought Jack. They stopped to eat, though little was left. A cloak full of fruit and nuts didn't last long when you had to share it with a troll-boar. Thorgil and Jack took turns riding on the pig's back. He was so wide, they could barely hold on with their legs, and he snarled when they tried to grasp his ears.

On and on they went until Jack despaired of ever getting anywhere. Then, just as he thought he'd collapse with weariness, they came out onto a dazzling sheet of ice. The sunlight was blinding after the shadowy ravine. The ice itself was as clear and blue as a river, and he could see the bodies of animals and humans and far stranger things suspended in its depths. It made him queasy to look down.

Even worse was the shiny surface. Thorgil tried to hurry, and her feet slid out from under her. She scooted along, coming to rest at the edge of a crevasse. After that she was more careful. Jack held on to Golden Bristles's fur in spite of the pig's complaints. The boar seemed to have no trouble, but of course he was made for such things. His massive trotters dug in like knives, and he left a trail of deep scratches behind him.

"Look!" cried Thorgil as they came around a bend. Ahead rose the ice mountain, higher than Jack had dreamed possible and more complicated and magnificent than it had appeared from a distance. It resembled an enormous castle with turrets and airy walkways and courtyards. It was like something from one of Father's stories, and Jack wished Lucy could have seen it.

"How are we ever going to cross *that*?" he murmured. For reaching out from the shelf where they stood to the home of the Mountain Queen was a soaring bridge. It arced above unimaginable depths, going up and up and then down and down in a shining bow of ice—brilliant, breathtaking, and slippery.

Bold Heart croaked urgently. "He says Golden Bristles will have to carry us," Thorgil translated.

"Can he ask whether the boar will let us hold on to his ears?" Jack said, looking into the chasm under the bridge. He couldn't even see the bottom. A cold mist shifted and flowed around the base of the mountain. Bold Heart put the question to Golden Bristles, who growled.

"I take it that means no," said Jack.

"He says his ears are sensitive. He'll let us hold on to his hair, if we don't pull too hard," Thorgil translated. She looked doubtfully at the chasm. "I wonder if people who fall off bridges go to Valhalla."

"I'm sure they do," said Jack. "It's dumb enough to qualify."

At the last minute he had a clever idea. He tore Thorgil's cloak into strips and made a long cord. He looped one end around Golden Bristles's neck for a collar and looped the other end around his and Thorgil's waists. They sat, legs spread wide on the giant hog's back, with their hands clutching his hair. Jack had tucked the staff under the pig's massive chin. It made no sense to take it, but it reminded him of the Bard, and Heaven knew he needed the Bard's help now. Bold Heart was nestled inside Jack's tunic.

"Let's go," the boy said with a sigh, thinking, *I hope I'm allowed to visit the Islands of the Blessed when we fall off.*

Jack sat in front and Thorgil was behind as the troll-boar began to climb the bridge. His trotters bit into the ice. Jack could see fragments break off and disappear into the gorge. His stomach lurched, and he forced himself to look straight ahead.

Scritch, scratch, scritch, scratch went Golden Bristles's trotters on the bridge. The ice shivered under his weight. An eagle—a Jotunheim eagle, so it was enormous—coasted by. It turned when it saw the humans and flew close enough for Jack to look into its yellow eyes. "Go away!" Thorgil shrilled, brandishing her knife. The bridge shuddered.

"Don't move!" Jack cried.

The wind, which had calmed during the trip across the ice sheet, picked up again. It whistled past Jack's ears and blew down the neck of his tunic. Bold Heart moaned. Jack's hands were turning blue.

The eagle streaked by a second time and struck Jack on the shoulder with its talons. He felt the blow but no pain. He was too numb with cold. "I'll kill you!" roared Thorgil from behind him. She lunged at the eagle and almost fell off. The bridge shuddered again. Jack was too sick with shock to yell at her. He didn't hurt, but his body knew something grievous had happened. He began to tremble uncontrollably.

"Hang on!" screamed Thorgil. "If it comes by again, I'll get it."

Jack wanted to tell her to stop moving. If she unbalanced the boar, they'd all fall into the chasm.

Scritch, scratch, scritch, scratch went Golden Bristles's trotters on the ice. They'd reached the top of the arc. The hog grunted and started down. The eagle streaked by a third time, and Thorgil leaned out and stabbed it. Shrieking, it tumbled away, but her lunge sent her over the side. Jack tried to hang on. His hands were too numb, and he followed her down.

The only thing that saved them was the cord tied around their waists. Both Jack and Thorgil hung over the abyss from Golden Bristles's neck. The wind twirled them round and round, and the cord tightened around Jack's waist and drove the breath out of him. *Hurry, hurry, hurry,* he begged the pig silently.

But Golden Bristles moved slowly and carefully. He was not made for climbing down things, especially with a rope around his neck. He wheezed.

The staff had slipped partly out of the pig's collar during Jack and Thorgil's fall. Only the last few inches were still jammed under Golden Bristle's throat, but it was enough to cut off the animal's breath. Jack reached up and grasped the end of the wood. It pulled free, but he almost dropped it. *Warmth. I need warmth,* he thought. He saw spots in front of his eyes. The staff began to slide from his numb fingers.

It's only cold if you think it is, said the Bard from somewhere.

It's supposed to be warm. It is warm, Jack thought as he reached for the life force burning at the heart of the frost giants' world. Heat radiated from his hands and flowed out the end of the staff. A jet of flame shot up and struck the ice bridge. Water dripped off. Golden Bristles's trotters lost their purchase, and he began to slide.

Grooooooink! roared the giant troll-boar as he slid down the bridge, going faster and faster until he shot off the end and rolled over and over in the snow beyond. Jack and Thorgil were yanked after him into a deep drift. Thorgil was up at once, digging Jack's face out of the snow. She untied the cord and pulled Bold Heart out so he could breathe too. Her eyes were wild with joy.

"What—a—*wonderful*—adventure!" she gasped. The cord had almost strangled her, too, but she was too elated to care. "I fought a giant eagle! I hung over the edge like Odin on Yggdrassil! I'm—so—*happy*!"

Groooooink! Golden Bristles said resentfully. Jack, whose senses were reeling, looked back to see a hole melted right in the middle of the bridge. Only two little bars of ice remained at each side. His staff had melted into the snowdrift—he could see the blackened end poking up.

"I didn't know you could do such magic," Thorgil cried. She danced around in a kind of mad glee.

"Neither did I," Jack said. Now that they were safe, he could feel the deep wound the eagle had left in his shoulder. A shadow fell over him. A foul, sulfurous smell belched from somewhere.

"Maybe you'd better do more magic," Thorgil said, feeling for her knife. But it was gone. It had plummeted into the abyss with the eagle.

Jack looked up to see a creature from his very deepest and worst nightmares. It was eight feet tall with a shock of bristly orange hair sprouting from its head and shoulders. Eyes the color of rotten walnuts brooded under a browridge that resembled a fungus growing out of tree bark. It had long, greenish fingernails crusted with dirt, and its teeth—for the creature's mouth was hanging open—were like jumbled blocks of wood. Two fangs the size of a billy goat's horns lifted the sides of the creature's upper lip in a permanent snarl. It belched, and the sulfurous smell drifted over Jack again.

He couldn't help it. He fainted. He had just met his first troll.

Chapter Thirty-three

FONN AND FORATH

He was lying on an incredibly soft bed. The room he was in was so beautiful, Jack thought he must have died and gone to Heaven. The walls were painted like the ones in the Bard's Roman house, except that these pictures were new. Jack saw trees covered in flowers, a house with a man and woman sitting outside, and children playing with a dog.

The floor was made of different kinds of wood, inlaid to make a pattern of autumn leaves. A metal bowl filled with glowing coals stood on an ornately worked metal stand. Jack felt its warmth on his face, which was the only part of him sticking out of the covers.

The coverlet, too, was a marvel of color and design, and it was padded with feathers. Jack sank down under it, as snug as an acorn in its cup.

Bits of memory began to come back. Carefully, he felt his shoulder. It was swathed in a bandage and didn't hurt as much as he'd expected. *He's waking up,* someone said. No, not *said.* Something else. The words just appeared in Jack's mind.

He's kind of cute for a two-legged deer.

You give him breakfast and I'll tell Mother. Jack heard heavy feet and a door open and shut.

I'm not in Heaven after all, he thought miserably. *I've been taken prisoner by Jotuns. Maybe if I keep my eyes closed they'll think I've gone back to sleep.*

"It won't work," said a harsh voice. "We can tell when humans are lying."

Jack opened his eyes and just as quickly closed them.

"I know. Trolls take getting used to. Personally, I think humans look like boiled frogs, but I've learned to overlook it."

Jack opened his eyes again. The troll—female he guessed from the bulges under her blouse—was even larger than the male he'd encountered at the ice bridge. She, too, had orange hair sprouting from her head. Her shoulders were covered, so he couldn't tell whether she had hair there, too. Her ears stuck out like jug handles, and she wore heavy gold earrings that dragged the lobes down until they dangled below her chin. Her upper lip rounded over two dainty fangs—dainty in comparison with the male troll.

For all that, she was much better groomed. Her nails were clean and polished. Her teeth, though alarmingly large, were orderly. Her expression was cheerful. If she'd been standing farther away, Jack thought she wouldn't be completely horrible.

The Jotun barked, a sound that made Jack burrow deeper into the bed. "Not completely horrible! I like that! Well, you're not completely horrible either, though your manners need work."

"I'm sorry," Jack said.

"It's all right. My name's Fonn. My sister Forath and I have been watching over you."

"Thank you," Jack said, not sure exactly what "watching over you" meant. Perhaps they were only making sure he didn't run away before they ate him.

Fonn barked again. It seemed to be a kind of laugh. "We don't eat two-legged deer anymore—unless we bag one in a fair fight. Especially, we don't eat humans who arrive with the queen's missing chess piece."

"I'm glad I still had it. I was afraid I'd dropped it when I fell off the bridge."

"Frith gave it to you, eh?"

Jack nodded.

"She'll want something in return. Frith never does anything unless it's for a selfish reason. Mother's been upset that she couldn't host a chess game for the Norns. She had a new piece made, but of course it didn't have magic and they rejected it."

A dozen questions popped into Jack's head at once. What kind of magic? Where were the Norns? How did Fonn know Frith? And who was "Mother"?

"Slow down," said Fonn with her barking laugh. "You aren't ready for so much activity. I can tell you it was touch and go for a while with that wound on your shoulder. I thought you'd never use your arm again, but Mother sang the poison out."

"Who's Mother?" Jack asked.

"The Mountain Queen. Forath and I are her daughters. As is Frith, unfortunately."

"You don't look like Frith."

"Thank you. She had a different father. Poor man. He languished in this room for years, ever wanting to return to Middle Earth and his family. That's them on the wall."

The paintings of the man and woman and the children playing with the dog took on new meaning. "Why didn't the queen let him go home?"

"His family was dead. They died in an avalanche and Mother rescued him, but he never believed her. I've always thought his unhappiness may have affected Frith. But, of course"—Fonn sighed, a sound like a small gale—"her real problem is that she belongs nowhere. Humans can marry other humans no matter where they come from. But troll/human or elf/human marriages almost never work, and their children are always torn between two worlds."

Forath burst into the room, and Jack, in spite of himself, dived under the covers. *Two* nine-foot Jotuns with bristly orange hair and fangs were a lot to take.

"Come out, you coward," said Thorgil. Jack reappeared. He was never so glad to see another human. She was dressed in new clothes and sported a new knife at her belt and another strapped to her leg.

"You've done all right," he observed.

"Why wouldn't I? This is the most exciting place I've ever been. I *love* trolls!"

Jack sat up. Dizziness made him lie down again. "Bold Heart! I forgot about him. Is he all right?"

"He's in the main hall with Golden Bristles. Did you know the queen healed his wing? She sang it back into shape. He's flying all over the place. I'm a special guest because I'm Olaf's daughter. Queen Glamdis was in love with him and wanted him in her harem, but she'd given her word he could go."

"That was lucky for Heide, Dotti, and Lotti," said Jack. He could imagine Olaf trapped in this room.

"They'd have survived," Thorgil said carelessly. "The louts—those are male trolls—are champion fighters. They've been teaching me dirty tricks."

"Wonderful," Jack said, sinking back into the soft mattress. The pain in his shoulder seemed sharper, and his whole body was drained of energy. He felt for the rune. Something was missing. "The thrall collar—," he said.

"Oh, that old thing. As Olaf's daughter, I inherited you," Thorgil said. "He said he was going to free you when we returned, so I did it here. Don't think that gets you out of the quest. You owe me eternal gratitude, and I expect you to die cheerfully if it becomes necessary."

"Or live cheerfully," murmured Jack. Forath herded Thorgil out of the room, for which the boy was thankful. Much had happened, and he needed quiet to take it all in. The Jotuns, whom he'd been taught to fear and hate, had turned out to be not so bad. Olaf always said he wouldn't mind living next to them as long as the ground rules were worked out. It seemed he knew more about them than anyone realized. And Thorgil—evil-tempered Thorgil, who called him a thrall on every possible occasion and had shown him nothing but contempt—had freed him.

It was all extremely puzzling.

One of the hardest things for Jack to get used to was the constant *whisper, whisper, whisper* of thoughts around him. They were jumbled up because everyone was thinking all the time, but he picked up words if someone was close by.

He let Fonn spoon soup into his mouth. She broke up chunks of soft, white bread and spread them with butter and honey. She placed a bowl of fruit within his reach.

"What's that?" said Jack, pointing at a cluster of purple berries.

"Grapes," Fonn said proudly. "I grow them in the greenhouse. Olaf brought us the seedlings from Italia on one of his trips."

One *of his trips?* Jack thought. "How long have I been sick?"

"A week. You were in bad shape when you arrived, so Mother thought it best to make you sleep."

A week! Jack had lost complete track of the days. He didn't know how long he'd been in the hidden valley, and now he'd wasted another week. How much time was left for him to rescue Lucy?

"Don't worry," Fonn said in her harsh, yet oddly gentle,

voice. "Worry makes it difficult to recover. Everything is decided by the Norns, and nothing any of us can do will change it." She drew a thick curtain over a window Jack had noticed but had not looked at closely. He wondered what lay outside. He fell asleep thinking of Olaf trapped in this little room, carving toys for children he would never see again.

Another week passed before Jack was strong enough to walk around. The eagle's talons had been tainted and had poisoned his blood. Only the queen's magic had saved him. He grew used to Fonn and Forath, though the latter found it difficult to speak aloud. Jotuns communicated from mind to mind. They had no use for speech, but a few had made the effort to learn it for strategic reasons. Humans sometimes invaded Jotunheim, and trolls—especially teenagers—liked to go on raids to Middle Earth.

The view outside the window was of a seemingly bottom-less cliff of ice. It was both beautiful and cruel-looking. No human could possibly escape that way. There might have been land far below. Jack could see nothing through the swirling ice crystals.

The Jotuns loved cold. They complained of heat when the temperature rose above freezing. They had managed to keep a pocket of eternal winter in their own world, but Fonn said summer made inroads every year. Once, she said, the earth had been a sheet of ice. The sea had been frozen as well. You could walk all the way from Utgard to Jotunheim.

"Utgard?" Jack asked.

"The Land Beyond the Sea. Our ancient home."

"Olaf mentioned something about that," Jack said. "He said it was destroyed by a volcano."

"Yes," Fonn said sadly. "My great-great-great-grandmother walked from there over the breaking ice. It was that which sundered us from the heart of our world. We can never return, and with each age, the forces of summer move deeper into our realm. Someday it will be entirely gone."

"I—I'm sorry," Jack said. "Isn't anything left of Utgard?"

"Forath speaks to whales. That's her special skill. They say a small island remains. At the center is the volcano, and all around lie empty windswept fields of ice. It sounds lovely." Fonn sighed.

"Can't you build a boat and go back?"

"We're not made for ships. We're too heavy, and all of us have a terror of deep water. A few of us, like Forath, go on whale-back, but only near the coast."

Bold Heart visited every day, and Thorgil burst in from time to time with horrid stories about how to kill things. The Jotuns weren't cruel about slaying their enemies, but they were very efficient. They appeared to have taken a shine to the enthusiastic little berserker. Once, Golden Bristles came in, and Fonn translated for him. He thanked Jack for freeing him from Freya's cart, and Jack remembered, with a sick rush of guilt, that Lucy would soon be trapped in it.

How much time had passed since he'd arrived in Jotunheim? He wasn't sure. From the position of the moon he guessed three weeks, but that meant he'd spent *no time at all* in the little valley near the dragon's lair. How could that be? All Jack really understood was that time was passing, slowly perhaps, but still moving. And that the day of Lucy's sacrifice was drawing ever closer.

—◁◁◁∭ʃ∭▷▷—

THE HALL OF
THE MOUNTAIN QUEEN

The hall of the Mountain Queen was very different from the little room where Jack had recovered, but it was also beautiful—in a huge, Jotun-like way. The walls were of ice, and tall windows let in the blue light surrounding the top of the mountain. Frost-laden air swirled great, white curtains on either side.

Most of the Jotuns were dressed in furs, though a few louts wore only loincloths to show off their bodies. Jack decided long fur cloaks were an excellent fashion. Those lumpy shoulders sprouting orange hair, those wrinkled pot-bellies and yards and yards of flaky troll flesh were greatly improved by being covered. Even that wouldn't have concealed the browridges on the males. These were proudly displayed, the bigger the better, and those who had a human kill to their record were tattooed.

Queen Glamdis sat on a golden throne sparkling with dia-monds. It had been made by dwarves, Fonn whispered as they waited by the side to be summoned. The queen wore a glit-tering crown in her orange hair and a long blue dress embroi-dered with gold. Over this was a bearskin cloak. Her face was much older than Fonn's, and her features were sharp and hawklike. Jack thought she looked quite noble. He was getting used to trolls.

To one side of the throne was Golden Bristles with Bold Heart on his back. Thorgil sat proudly at the Mountain Queen's feet. On the other side was arrayed the harem.

Sixteen louts of varying ages were dressed in finery. The oldest sat on a throne only slightly less imposing than that of Queen Glamdis. He was so aged, his browridge had collapsed over his eyes and he propped it up with a Y-shaped stick.

"That's my father, Bolthorn," Fonn whispered.

Jack himself was dressed for the occasion in three sets of woolen clothes, one on top of the other, beneath a cloak of marten fur. He was still cold. His boots were made of cow skin with the hair still on to help his feet grip the floor. It was made of polished silver, very bright and beautiful, but as slippery as ice.

"Come forth," said Queen Glamdis in a harsh voice like Fonn's. Jack knew it took effort for the Jotuns to speak at all, and they were not capable of making themselves sound sweet. He came forward, as he'd been instructed, and bowed deeply.

"So you're the one who melted my ice bridge," said the queen.

Uh-oh, thought Jack.

"You're a fire wizard," she declared.

"I'm a bard, Great Queen. I serve the life force."

"I met another of your kind. He was called Dragon Tongue, and he melted a hole through that wall." She pointed at a patch of darker ice near a window. "I had it mended, of course, but the scar's still there."

"He was trained by Dragon Tongue," Thorgil piped up.

Be quiet, Jack thought.

"I'll decide who will or won't be quiet," said the queen, and Jack cursed himself for stupidity. He'd forgotten Jotuns could see into his mind. "However, I detect no malice in you," Glamdis went on. "Thorgil Olaf's Daughter has told me of your quest, and I've agreed to help. I should warn you that the Norns obey no one, not even the gods. I can ask that you be present when they visit. That's all."

"Thank you, Great Queen."

"You don't have to use that 'Great Queen' nonsense with me," Glamdis snapped. "That's the sort of thing Frith lives for. I *am* a great queen, and everyone knows it. You're still a cub, so you can call me Mother."

"All right, M-Mother," said Jack. It sounded strange to use the word for anyone who wasn't his real mother. "I'm truly grateful that you cured my shoulder and healed Bold Heart."

"Ah, Bold Heart," said Glamdis with a gleam in her dark eyes. "There's a cheeky rascal." But she didn't explain what she meant. "And now I bid you all to a celebration of Olaf One-Brow's life. It shall be as he wished, a feast with music, dancing, and good food. I'm sorry he's gone to Valhalla, but I know Odin will be glad to see him. He was the finest two-legged deer I ever met."

Jack's eyes filled with tears, and even the queen—or Mother, Jack reminded himself—wiped her eyes with the edge of her cloak. Thorgil wept aloud.

Finally they left the throne room and proceeded down long hallways until they got to an inner courtyard. It was huge and round, more like a frozen lake than anything else. It was open to the sky, and booths were set around the edge. Jack smelled roast grouse. He was seated at a small table with Thorgil—the Jotun tables were far too large for them to use. Fonn and Forath kept them company at the side.

For the first time Jack saw troll-children—or cubs, as they were called. They darted in and out among the tables and stole treats when no one was looking. They slid across the ice, collided with one another, and roared challenges that often ended in play fights. There weren't many of them. Fonn said they grew slowly—ones that appeared to be Jack's age were actually fifty years old. Fonn herself was not considered old enough to start a harem.

No one seemed to mind that the cubs brought chaos wherever they went. The adults smiled indulgently as the young climbed curtains, overturned chairs, and threw snowballs. At home Jack would have been thrashed for doing far less.

Jack and Thorgil were offered grouse with lingonberry preserves, rabbit stuffed with onions, bear paws (Jack passed on the bear paws), and slices of elk. The Mountain Queen gnawed on an elk haunch all to herself, and both Fonn and Forath tore chunks out of giant salmon. Table manners were no more part of a troll feast than they had been at King Ivar's party.

"One foot on the floor!" roared a young lout who kept ogling Fonn. "That's the only rule around here. You have to keep one foot on the floor while you're eating."

"He's trying to impress me by learning human speech," said Fonn.

There was also bread with fresh butter and honey, spiced apple pudding, grapes from Fonn's greenhouse, and cheeses that Thorgil said came from a creature called a yak. She said the queen kept a herd of yaks in her barn. Buckets of cider, mead, and beer were passed around. The louts kept trying to lure Thorgil into a drinking contest, but she firmly said no.

"They'll win. They know it. I'm not going to humiliate myself," she declared.

When all was eaten and cleared away, the singing and dancing began. The louts shuffled to one end of the lake while the troll-maidens gathered at the other. The louts preened and displayed their browridges because the maidens would decide whom they danced with. Forath and several others provided the music. It was a strange kind of singing without any words Jack could understand. It echoed around the walls and seemed to vibrate in his rib cage. It was so melancholy, Jack felt tears come to his eyes again.

"Is that a dirge?" he asked Fonn.

"Oh, no! That's a whale-song. Quite cheerful, really. They're singing about Utgard, our beloved home lost to us forever beyond the sea."

If that was a happy song, Jack knew he didn't want to hear a sad one. He had all he could do to keep from bursting into sobs.

"Do you mind if I join the dancers?" Fonn said shyly.

"Of course not," both Jack and Thorgil cried.

So Fonn trotted over to the line of troll-maidens. First they fanned out over the lake. They approached the louts, who had worked themselves up into a frenzy of display. One by one the maidens selected a partner by clomping him on the shoulder with one heavy hand. The couples spread out onto the ice.

Whump! Slide, slide, slide. Whump! Slide, slide, slide. The troll-maidens led their partners around the lake as Forath and the others wailed and moaned an accompaniment.

"I'm sure Olaf is honored," Thorgil said, sighing over her cup of cider.

"I had no idea he was so loved," said Jack.

"Yes, well, neither did Heide, Dotti, and Lotti," said Thorgil with a trace of a smile.

At the end of the evening, Jack found his way to the queen's table. He bowed politely and asked, "Are the Norns coming tomorrow?"

"Perhaps. They'll arrive when it suits them," said the queen.

"Couldn't you—you know—hurry them up?" The day of Lucy's sacrifice loomed in Jack's mind.

"Nobody hurries Norns."

"But if they knew how important—"

"Listen, little cub," Glamdis said kindly. "If they mean you to succeed, their coming early or late will make no difference. All will happen as it was intended."

"I can't just sit here and wait!" Jack didn't mean to be rude—especially to a nine-foot troll-queen—but he was so desperately worried.

"I'm afraid you'll have to. Fonn can show you around the palace."

"She doesn't have to baby-sit me," Jack muttered.

"One thing I do know," the queen went on. "To ignore joy while it lasts, in favor of lamenting one's fate, is a great crime."

"That's what Rune told me," cried Jack.

Glamdis smiled, showing her dainty fangs. "He learned it from me. Now run along, little two-legged deer. Enjoy these hours before the chess game." And she turned away to munch on the remains of an elk leg—her third, Jack guessed, from the pile of bones around her feet.

Jack spent the next day touring the vast palace of Queen Glamdis. He visited the kitchen, the armory, the harem, and the greenhouse. Fonn's greenhouse was made of sheets of clear ice. The intense mountain sunlight shone through, and its heat was trapped. The walls inside were slick and wet as water trickled down into the soil, but the outer part stayed frozen. A lout threw water over the outside to ensure that the walls stayed thick.

Jack had never seen grapevines, although he'd seen them painted on the walls of the Roman house. He found other trees that had existed only in his imagination: peaches, apricots, and almonds. All these had been supplied by Olaf from his raids into Italia.

"He said they couldn't grow on his own farm," Fonn explained. "He didn't have a greenhouse. Dragon Tongue taught me how to build one, to make up for melting a hole in the palace wall."

"Just why did he do that?" Jack asked.

"Oh, there was some argument about Frothi. Frith was still living with us, and Frothi was her full sister. Now, *there* was a troublemaker if I ever saw one. She caused no end of mayhem at Hrothgar's hall, and Dragon Tongue had been responsible for her death. Well, if it hadn't been him, it would have been someone else." Fonn didn't seem grieved by the loss of her half sister.

"It seems Olaf visited here a lot," Jack said delicately. He didn't want to upset Fonn, but he was consumed with curiosity about the relationship between the Northman and the Mountain Queen.

"Mother was head over heels in love with him," Fonn said, not the least embarrassed. "She almost never fell for humans, and the behavior of Frith and Frothi taught her how unwise it was to marry one. But Olaf . . ." The troll-maiden's eyes became misty. "Olaf was so big and beautiful."

Jack remembered Heide saying the exact same thing.

"Of course, he didn't want to live here. He had a family

in Middle Earth. He came every other year with presents. He brought me seedlings, and he gave Forath a flute and a carving of a whale. He always knew exactly what would please us."

"Did he ever give anything to Frith?"

Fonn gave her barking laugh. "No human in his right mind would go near Frith."

"Do you know how she lost her hair?"

Fonn didn't. When Jack told her about the sorry events that led up to his trip to Jotunheim, she laughed and laughed until the tears rolled down her cheeks. "Oh! Oh! I wish I'd been there to see it! Frith is obsessed with hair. She nagged Mother until she got a full head of it."

"The queen *gave* her that hair?"

"Through magic. Frith is a shape-shifter, but when she took human form, her hair was exactly like mine. Mother gave her human hair, which also made it possible for her to keep her human shape more easily. When she lost it, she reverted to being halfway between the worlds. Did she go into a snit?"

"I'll say," said Jack. "Northmen were climbing the walls."

"What a treat! Frith's snits were famous even here."

All in all it was a pleasant day. Jack had grown to like the gentle troll-maiden and her silent and melancholy sister. He visited the harem and was made welcome by Bolthorn, Fonn and Forath's father. He had been Glamdis's first love, and she still treated him with respect.

Jack couldn't imagine being part of a harem, but Bolthorn clearly thought himself honored. "She dragged me right off the ice and threw me into her cave," the ancient Jotun rumbled, fondly remembering their courtship. "I had scratches all over my browridge!" Jack looked away, embarrassed, without exactly knowing why.

He found the louts good company, but their personal hygiene left a lot to be desired. They considered it manly—or whatever the troll equivalent was—to be filthy and to never clean their nails or teeth. Perhaps that's what attracted Thorgil, and they certainly admired her.

She had turned from a sullen, miserable brat into someone quite likeable. Maybe, Jack thought as he saw her playing Dodge the Spear with a pair of young louts, this was the first time she'd ever been the center of attention. She was tolerated, but not liked, by Olaf's wives and children. No one was glad to see her except Slasher, Wolf Bane, Hel Hag, and Shreddie, the dogs with whom she'd been raised. This was the first time she'd ever made friends.

Chapter Thirty-five

⸺⊶⊷⸺

YGGDRASSIL

"You are not to speak," said Fonn, settling Jack and Thorgil in a corner. A long table sat in the middle of the hall. Torches burned on metal stands around the walls, and their light flickered on a set of golden chess pieces. Jack recognized the queen piece as the safe-conduct Frith had given him.

"Is the queen—I mean Mother—going to play chess with the Norns?"

"She *hosts* a game," Fonn said with emphasis. "No one plays chess with the Norns. They play each other."

"Doesn't sound like fun, just watching someone else," said Thorgil.

"This is deadly serious," the troll-maiden said. "You're here so the Norns can see you, but you're not to speak unless they ask you something. I've left you snacks. If you think you're going to be afraid, now is the time to leave."

"We're not afraid," Thorgil said stoutly. "I am Thorgil Olaf's Daughter and this is my thrall."

"Ex-thrall," said Jack.

"Everyone's afraid of the Norns," Fonn said. "You can't help it. Just don't knock anything over or bolt from the room."

What could possibly be so terrible about something that looked like a woman? Jack wondered. He and Thorgil had already faced a troll-bear and a dragon. He watched nervously as Fonn left. They were alone in the hall. Bowls of fruit and bread sat on the table, so the Norns presumably ate.

Thorgil selected a honey cake from their own little table. She appeared calm, but her hand trembled. "I think we can talk until they come," she said.

"What have you heard about Norns?" said Jack.

"Rune says they decide when Ragnarok happens."

"What's that?"

"The final battle between the gods and the frost giants. It's when everyone dies and everything is destroyed."

"That's a bleak view of the future," murmured Jack.

"Odin selects the bravest warriors for this final war. They train each day until it's time to die."

"But they come back to life," said Jack, remembering something Olaf had said about warriors getting killed and rising to feast all night in Valhalla.

"Not after Ragnarok. Darkness falls over everything."

"Even the *gods* die?"

"When the Norns say so, yes." Thorgil watched the door at the far end of the room. Her hand kept straying to the knife on her leg, but that was merely habit.

"What could be more powerful than a god?" Jack asked. He, too, watched the door. The torches blazed and wind beat uselessly against the heavy white curtains covering the windows.

"Time," said Thorgil. "Rune says the Norns are Time itself. He doesn't quite understand it and neither do I. Shh!"

Jack saw the door move and froze. But it was only the Mountain Queen coming to take her seat on the throne. She didn't look at them, and they knew better than to speak to her. Then all three of them sat and waited.

Gradually—Jack couldn't tell exactly when—a presence gathered at the far end of the hall. It was a crowd of people, or perhaps it was only a few. It was hard to tell. The curtains stirred and the torches dimmed. Voices came from a great distance, voices that sent alarm through Jack's body. They were like something he'd heard in a terrible dream. They murmured of every fear he'd ever experienced—of falling down a cliff or of losing his parents or of being in a dark place where he could weep forever and never be found.

Thorgil put her hand on his arm. Jack realized he'd been about to do the very thing he'd been warned against: flee the room. Thorgil looked pale. No doubt her own private terrors were being revealed.

It was a world of loss far more terrible than the songs of vanished Utgard. It was more devastating than the destruction of Gizur Thumb-Crusher's village. It was Everything Gone. The voices of the Norns whispered about the passing of all that was bright and brave and beautiful. You could only watch it die. You could only go down to defeat and darkness.

Jack heard a slight noise. He turned and saw Thorgil holding her knife before her. Her message was clear. She would go down bravely, and if fame truly did die, she would still run to meet her fate.

Jack clutched the rune. A Norn looked up. She was young and fair. She stood at the beginning of the vast procession that shuffled through the hall. Round the table they went. One put her hand out over a bowl of fruit, and it withered. They sat down, and now Jack saw there were only three, though the air shifted and whispered behind them. They arranged the chess set.

One watched and the other two played. The game went on for a long time. Jack blinked. It seemed as though the chess pieces moved by themselves. They were no longer on a table in a darkened room, but standing in front of houses or tilling fields or shearing sheep. They went about their lives, unaware of the silent Norns watching them, and now and then a hand reached down and took them away.

The game went on until only a few pieces were left on either side. A Norn with a cavernous mouth and hollow eyes made the final move. *Checkmate,* she soundlessly murmured.

The other player, the young and beautiful Norn, bowed her acceptance. The third Norn was far more difficult to see.

She kept flickering and shifting, like a shadow under a wind-swept tree.

Then all three looked up and beckoned to Jack.

He couldn't move. His legs had lost their strength, and his mouth had turned bone-dry. Thorgil nudged him. He couldn't obey. She stood, took his hand, and drew him forth. In her other hand she held the knife. Her face was almost white in the dim light. Merciful heavens, was she going to try to stab a Norn?

Jack clutched the rune. To his surprise, it responded with a rush of warmth. He squeezed Thorgil's hand and willed the warmth into her as well.

It came to him that they were not pawns in a game that only led to destruction. The Norn's way was not the only one. There was the Bard sitting under a tree in the Islands of the Blessed. There was the sad-eyed woman Olaf had slain during the storm. She surely was on her way to Heaven with her lost daughter. And Mother believed, though she hid this from Father, that souls returned with the sun to be born anew into the world.

I serve the life force, Jack thought. *I do not believe in Ragnarok.*

They walked forward together, and as they went the ice walls fell away and the rustling white curtains vanished. The air was soft on Jack's face, and a stream flowed along the floor of a little valley with a chuckling sound. On either side were bushes full of raspberries and blueberries. The ground was covered with sweet mountain strawberries.

"We're here again!" cried Thorgil. "*This* is where Mimir's Well was hiding?"

The capercaillie stepped out of a thicket with her ten speckled chicks behind her. She lowered her head and clucked softly, deep in her throat. "It seems so," Jack said uncertainly. "I felt something before, but I was afraid to look for it." The two of them watched the capercaillie sweep majestically on into a leafy glade.

"One thing's the same," Thorgil said. "Those stupid birds are still going on about their utterly boring lives."

Jack led the way. He took them past the field where the snowy owls had collapsed. He found the woodland of apple, walnut, hazelnut, and pear trees. "So this is where you got that food," the shield maiden said.

"Listen." Jack held up his hand. The hum of thousands and thousands of bees rose and fell ahead. It sounded as though you'd have to push them out of the way just to squeeze through.

"I don't like bees," Thorgil said. "I was stung by a lot of them once, when I tried to rob a hive."

"They're all right if you don't upset them," Jack said. "My mother taught me a charm to calm angry bees."

"I'm not sure . . . I don't understand their language as I do Bird, but it seems they're not angry. And they're too wild to be merely happy. I'd say they were frenzied."

"Berserk?" Jack guessed.

"Something like that."

You'd know, Jack thought. He remembered the kind of

mad joy that had possessed Olaf and his men before they slaughtered Gizur's village. Jack and Thorgil stood for a long time, listening to the incessant hum.

"Would your charm work on berserk bees?" she asked.

"I have no idea," he replied.

"Well, it's better than nothing." Thorgil drew both her knives.

"What are you going to do? Stab all the bees?" Jack said. "We've been allowed to come here by the Norns. They'll either let us get to the well or they won't. Nothing either of us does is going to change that."

Thorgil reluctantly sheathed her knives. She took Jack's hand, and they went on through the grove. The land gradually inclined upward until it led to a large hill. *"Look!"* Thorgil cried. At the top rose an enormous ash tree—*the* Ash Tree, Yggdrassil itself rising up and up and up until you could hardly believe human eyes could see that far.

Branches swept everywhere, teeming with life. All the birds in the world roosted on its arms, and all the insects, too. Some bored into the bark and destroyed it. Some nibbled the leaves. Wherever the Tree went, creatures fed on it, but they also bent it into bowers for their young. Jack saw deer with their fawns, wolves with their cubs, and men and women—for the branches reached into Middle Earth as well—sitting with their children in the leaves.

The roots plunged down on either side of the hill, some to the World of Fire and others to the icy halls of Hel. A giant serpent coiled in the depths and sank its fangs into the blood of the Tree. But in the high branches a giant eagle fanned its wings and drove the breath of life back into the leaves.

Up and down the mighty trunk scampered a bedraggled squirrel, shrieking insults. "That's Ratatosk," whispered Thorgil. "He carries gossip throughout the nine worlds."

At the very top, so far up it seemed to be higher than the moon and yet so clear you were tempted to reach for it, was a golden fence with silver fence posts. Inside lay a heavenly green field and a grove of trees. Many fine palaces and towers rose over this field, but the finest of all had a gate so wide a thousand men could march through it at once.

"That's Asgard where the gods live and that's the gate of Valhalla," gasped Thorgil. "Oh, tell me if you see Olaf. Oh, I want to go there now."

"You can't," Jack whispered, holding her. She trembled like a wounded bird. "It looks close, but you could climb a hundred years and get no nearer. I know what this Tree is. It's pure life force. It's being chewed on and nibbled at and cut with axes, but it never dies because it's the earth itself."

"Never dies? What about Ragnarok?" cried Thorgil.

"That's what the Norns want you to believe in, a future where all that exists is war followed by destruction. But their vision is only one leaf on the Tree. There's the Islands of the Blessed, where the great queens and heroes go."

"Where Maeve went," Thorgil said softly.

"Yes, and there's High Heaven for Christians like me and a lot of other places I don't know about. Yggdrassil contains all of them."

A constant rain fell out of the Tree like a shower of silver arrows, but the rain never reached the ground. Bees—and here at last were the bees—gathered the honeydew up in midair. Great golden honeycombs hung off the branches like heavenly fruit. No winter came here, and so the bees had no need of hives. They rose and fell in their thousands, and the sound of their humming was pure joy.

Chapter Thirty-six

MIMIR'S WELL

At foot of the tree, where Yggdrassil touched the valley, was a well. It was an unassuming little well at the top of a hill, with a bucket on a rope like the one beside Mother and Father's house.

"It looks so ordinary," Jack said.

"'Always look behind the door before entering a house,'" said Thorgil, quoting a favorite Northman proverb. "Also: 'Never set foot outside without weapons.' Would you like one of my knives?"

"This is a *spiritual* quest," Jack said with some annoyance. "Why do you always assume there's an enemy lurking somewhere?"

"Because there always has been," the shield maiden replied simply. "Anyhow, you have to sacrifice something of overwhelming importance before you can drink."

"I don't know . . . it looks too peaceful for that. Maybe all you have to do is walk up there."

"Nothing is gained without suffering," said Thorgil.

"I think that's a Northman trick to squeeze pain out of a perfectly decent situation."

"It's *so* like a thrall to avoid heroism," sneered Thorgil.

"All heroism means to you is a chance to get beaten up," Jack snarled back. They were toe-to-toe again, and his hand itched to strike her. He could tell she was itching to strike him. The hum of the bees became almost deafening, and one bumped into Jack's face. He stepped back. All around them swarmed an eager tornado of bees. Thorgil's eyes were wide with alarm.

"Sit down," Jack ordered. She obeyed. "Breathe deeply. Think of peaceful things."

"I don't know any peaceful things," Thorgil said.

"Well, think of playing Dodge the Spear with the louts. Something happy."

The shield maiden closed her eyes, and by the smile on her face Jack knew she was in a pleasant memory. He himself thought of sitting under a rowan tree with the Bard so long ago. The bees wandered back into the branches of Yggdrassil and continued their incessant gathering of honeydew.

"Why did they attack us?" said Thorgil, opening her eyes.

"They haven't attacked us—yet. Bees are sensitive to whether someone's angry or afraid," Jack said. "My mother never gathered honey when she was upset. We were fighting, and that doesn't seem to be allowed here."

Thorgil started to reply when she glanced up at the bees and thought better of it.

All I have to do is walk up that hill, thought Jack, suddenly reluctant to move. *That's easy. I've drawn water hundreds of times at home.*

"Want me to do it?" Thorgil said sarcastically.

"I'm just thinking." Jack stood and forced himself to begin. The hill was steeper than it looked. By the time he was half-way up, he had to stop and catch his breath. He went on and on, edging closer to the mighty Tree and the innocent-looking well. He heard Ratatosk the squirrel shrieking vile insults overhead. He heard the myriad worms and beetles chewing on bark. He got to the well.

What if I look over the edge and see Odin's eye lying at the bottom? he thought. *What if it looks up at me?* His hands shook, but he forced himself to reach for the bucket. The instant he touched the wood it was as though a great hand reached out and swatted him away like a pesky gnat. Over and over he tumbled down the hill, rolling faster until his fall was broken by his head banging against a rock.

"Told you you'd have to sacrifice something of over-whelming importance," said Thorgil.

"Stop gloating and help me!" cried Jack. He saw blood drip onto the grass from his scalp. Thorgil pressed her hand on the wound until the bleeding stopped. She cut a strip from her new tunic to bind it. "You certainly know how to treat injuries," Jack said grudgingly.

"Done it hundreds of times. Now, what are you going to sacrifice?"

"I don't *have* anything," Jack said.

"Of course you do. You could cut off an ear—I'd help you, of course—or smash the fingers of one hand so you'd never play the harp again. That's a good one for a skald."

"Chopping yourself to bits is for *Northmen,* not sane, sensible Saxons!" shouted Jack. "I can't believe the life force demands such a thing."

"You have to show you really care!" Thorgil shouted back, ready as always for an argument. "This isn't some village fair where you win prizes by pitching walnuts at a target. This is Yggdrassil. Not even Odin approached it without sacrifice."

"Well then, Odin was an idiot."

"He was not! You take that back!"

"I won't! Odin is a vicious bully, and so is everyone who believes in him. He makes shield maidens wait on tables in Valhalla."

"That's not true!" shrieked Thorgil. The bees had come down again and were swirling around in a loud, maddening swarm. "Odin stands for courage and honor, something a *thrall* would never understand!"

"How can you understand it, then? *You* were a thrall until three years ago!" Jack regretted it the instant he said it. Thorgil reeled back as though he'd struck her with an axe. He could see the light of true madness in her eyes. She was a berserker from a line of berserkers, and the fit came upon her whether she willed it or not. "I'm sorry!" Jack cried.

"You're not a thrall! You're a shield maiden! Odin loves you, and he'd never make you wait on tables!" But he was too late.

"I vow," said Thorgil, quivering with rage, "that I will kill myself after drawing water from Mimir's Well. I offer my life up to bring it to Jack so that he may heal Queen Frith and save his sister. I swear this by Yggdrassil, Odin, and the Norns!"

"Don't do this!" shouted Jack, but Thorgil was already racing up the hill. She pushed ahead, heedless of the wall of bees between her and the top. They roared around her in their thousands, but they didn't sting. They seemed beside themselves with wild joy.

Jack watched the shield maiden struggle up the steep hill, but she never stopped to rest. She got to the well and reached for the bucket.

The same invisible hand knocked her back. Thorgil rolled over and over down the hill with the bees fleeing from her path. She bumped against the same rock. This time Jack treated the head wound. Thorgil seemed stunned, more than he. She stared blindly at him.

"They wouldn't accept my sacrifice," she managed to say at last. "The Norns . . . Odin . . . Yggdrassil. They wouldn't accept my life. Is that . . . because I was born . . . a thrall?"

"No, no, of course not," said Jack, holding her closely as he had once held Lucy after they'd escaped drowning. "Olaf freed you and named you daughter. The Jotuns honor you. No one thinks you're a thrall because you're so much, much more.

Don't cry. Please don't cry." He stroked her hair and felt her sobs echo in his own body. "I think they rejected your sacrifice because you have to offer something of overwhelming importance. Your life means nothing to you."

"It's truly meaningless now," said Thorgil. "I will kill myself anyway. I have nothing to live for now that Olaf's gone."

"You mustn't do that! He wanted you to live. *I* want you to live."

"Too late," Thorgil said. She drew a knife, and Jack did the only thing he could think of. He was no match for her fighting skills or her determination, though he'd become as strong as she was in his time with the Northmen. He pulled the rune of protection from around his neck. At once it became visible.

It was a pendant of heavy gold. On it was a pattern that might have been a sunburst, except that each ray had branches like a budding tree. The tree, Jack realized now, was Yggdrassil.

"So that was what you hid around your neck," Thorgil said, pausing with the knife in the air. "It burned me like fire."

"That was because you tried to take it by force. The rune can only be given." Jack felt empty and sad. It was his only link with the Bard. It had faithfully guarded him through danger and despair, and now it would be gone. He hung it around Thorgil's neck.

"I suppose it will burn me anyway," she said. "I'll suffer greatly, but it's only what I deserve."

As Jack watched, the pendant vanished. He felt devastated.

"Mother," whispered Thorgil. "I can see her in my mind." She put down the knife.

"Queen Glamdis?"

"No . . . my real mother. Allyson. I was so cruel to her. I called her names and I never treated her kindly, even when she was crying. Father used to beat her. He called her useless because she bore him no son."

"She did bear him a son. You had an older brother, and your father killed him."

"I was to be his replacement, but I failed." Tears rolled down Thorgil's face.

"How could you possibly fail by being born a girl?"

"Mother cooked me special meals when Father wasn't looking. She combed my hair and made me beautiful jackets and boots. I never thanked her."

"Olaf said she never spoke."

"She did to me, in Saxon," said Thorgil. "I made fun of her for using a slave's speech. That's when she stopped talking. And then—and then they sacrificed her so she could accompany Father to Valhalla."

"You know what? I don't think she went to Valhalla at all. Dragon Tongue said you get to choose your afterlife. I think she went to the Islands of the Blessed with Maeve."

"I hope so," said Thorgil. "Oh! I just remembered. One of the last things I said to Olaf was 'I hate you.' How could I have done that?" She burst into fresh tears.

"I imagine people told Olaf they hated him at least once a day," Jack said dryly.

"That's true," said Thorgil, brightening up again. But then she remembered other crimes from her past. She seemed to have an endless fund of them. She had smashed Heide's loom after the wise woman made her a dress. She had jeered at Rune's voice when he tried to sing a praise-song for her. She had tied together the tails of Slasher, Wolf Bane, Hel Hag, and Shreddie to make them fight. And these were dogs who loved her, practically the only creatures who did.

Jack couldn't imagine harboring that much malice. The stories poured out like pus from a wound. It seemed to be the first time Thorgil even realized she'd done anything wrong.

"I feel so strange. Like something's missing." She picked up the knife again, and Jack was afraid she'd try to stab herself. "You know . . . I don't feel like killing myself."

"That's good."

"No, it's not. It's not like me. I don't want to fall in battle, either." She sat up suddenly, staring wildly.

"*Now* what?" said Jack.

"I've lost the desire to slash and burn! I don't want to kill people! I don't remember how to run berserk! *I'm not a shield maiden anymore!*" She completely lost control then, rolling on the ground, pulling up handfuls of grass, keening and groaning and sobbing for all she was worth. Jack could only watch her. He didn't know how to deal with such extreme grief.

After awhile Thorgil tired herself out. She lay, pale and exhausted, on the ruined grass. She'd managed to gouge a few holes out of the earth with her knife as well.

"I think I know what's happened," Jack said when she was calm enough to listen. "The one thing I valued most in this world was the rune of protection. Now I've given it to you. The one thing you valued most was being a berserker. The rune made you value life rather than death, so you can't go berserk anymore. You're still a shield maiden—hear me out," he said as Thorgil attempted to argue. "You're like Skakki now. He's no berserker and never will be. Heide's good sense runs in his veins. He's a brave, intelligent warrior, and he'll live long to protect his family and village."

"We're both losers. So what?" said Thorgil.

"We can both drink from Mimir's Well, that's what." Jack pulled her to her feet.

"If I drink, I might become a greater skald than you," Thorgil said with a hint of her earlier malice.

"Don't count on it. The well, as far as I can tell, gives you the knowledge you need. Odin asked for mastery and got it. I need poetry to undo the charm I cast on Frith. What you need is anybody's guess."

Hand in hand they walked up the hill. This time it didn't seem steep at all, and when they arrived at the top, they both laid their hands on the bucket—quickly, before they could get swatted away. Nothing happened. Jack sighed in relief. "See? I was correct."

"The bees are gone," Thorgil observed. They could still see

them dancing in the upper air, gathering the honeydew that fell from Yggdrassil.

"Here goes," said Jack. He heard the bucket splash far below and pulled it dripping from the depths. A marvelous smell rose from it, of flowers and green fields and pine forests and honey. "It's the smell of life," said Jack, smiling.

He drank first. It was sweet, but not the heavy sweetness of mead that drugged you with sleep. Rather, it woke you up. Jack thought it tasted like light captured in water. A dozen memories ran through his mind. He was a young boy watching his father build their house. He was sitting in front of the beehives listening to his mother sing. He was under the rowan tree with the Bard. Every green smell and warm flavor came back to him. Every bright cloud floating over a mountaintop, every fish rising to snap at a fly, every swallow turning in the air appeared before him. It was all wonderful. It was all full of life.

"Did it work?" whispered Thorgil. "Can you heal Queen Frith?"

"I don't know how yet," Jack said, "but I will when the time comes."

Thorgil drank then. The deadly pallor that had come over her in the field below lifted. Her cheeks became rosy. Her eyes, so sad and hopeless, filled with lively interest.

"The birds!" cried Thorgil as she put the bucket down. "They're actually interesting, in a featherbrained way. And the flowers—*look* at the flowers!—they're red and blue and yellow and pink. I never saw such colors. And the light under the

Tree. It's moving all the time, like the waves of the sea."
Thorgil wandered off down the hill, exclaiming at each new
discovery. She was lost in the wonder and beauty of the little
valley.

Jack took out the bottle with the poppy on the side. Its
contents had been used up, and Fonn had washed it for him.
Jack dipped it into the bucket.

No, said a voice full of shadows.

Jack saw the young Norn standing next to the Tree. She
held out her hand for the bottle. *It's for Rune,* Jack said in his
mind. *He's too old to come here, but he's earned the right to
drink. He sacrificed his voice in the service of his people. And he
gave his greatest poem to me.*

The Norn was silent. She moved closer to the Tree, and
presently, Jack couldn't see her at all in the deep shadows and
fissures in the bark.

"What are you looking at?" called Thorgil.

"The capercaillie," said Jack, laughing, for the ridiculous
bird had marched out of the same shadows with her speckled
chicks crowding and hopping behind. She raised her eyebrows
at him and strode on. Jack poured the rest of the contents of
the bucket onto Yggdrassil's roots. "All trees need water, even
this One," he said.

He and Thorgil walked through the forest. A golden light
hovered over the trees, for sunset was near, and blue shade
flowed out of the surrounding hills. They walked until dark,
with Thorgil translating the evening chorus of birds. She was
right, Jack decided. The birds *were* awfully featherbrained.

As the boy and girl passed between two beech trees, they came out into a darkened hall surrounded by walls of ice. The braziers of coals were almost out, and the vast white curtains over the windows trembled under the blast of mountain winds. The Mountain Queen herself was snoring on her throne with her mouth open, so you could see her fangs. The fruit and bread in every one of the bowls on the table had turned to slime and dust.

Chapter Thirty-seven

THE QUEEN'S GIFTS

"Skkkrrrnnk—wha? What was that?" said Queen Glamdis as she came awake.

"Great Queen, we have returned," said Jack.

"I've told you not to use that 'Great Queen' stuff on me," Glamdis said crossly. "Call me Mother."

"Yes, Mother," said both Jack and Thorgil.

"Well? Was it successful? Did you find Mimir's Well?"

"Yes, Great—er, Mother," said Jack.

"Good. I never know what the Norns are going to do. Sometimes they send people into a dark wood to wander."

"Why do you entertain the Norns?" Thorgil asked. "It can't be interesting, watching them play chess."

"You'd be surprised," the Mountain Queen said. "I learn all sorts of things about what's going to happen. Most of it's sad, of course. People die. Whole islands disappear under the sea. I feel it gives me a certain control over the future. I saw Olaf's death long before it happened."

"You did?" Thorgil's eyes were wide.

"Such as he could never live to old age." The Mountain Queen sighed. "He was too grand and too impossibly pigheaded. Well! I see I can't offer you any food here. Why don't we go to the harem, and I'll ask the louts to fix us some snacks."

They walked down the long room, Queen Glamdis leading and Jack and Thorgil following behind. The golden chess pieces were strewn across the playing board. "Why do you serve the Norns food when they don't seem to eat?" Jack asked, eyeing the bowls full of dust.

"They like to wither things," Glamdis replied. "Turning bread to mold and fruit to slime is as good as a feast to them. I gave up trying to understand Norns years ago."

The meal in the harem was one of the best memories Jack took away from Jotunheim. Bolthorn presided over the festivities, and Golden Bristles and Bold Heart joined in. Two louts sang a wandering, tuneless kind of song while others danced the Jotunheim Reel. It was loud and cheerful, with much stamping. Fonn directed a play about the retreat from Utgard across the breaking ice.

They ate surprisingly good pastries, meat pies, and flummery—the best kind, with nutmeg and cream. Thorgil went into raptures over each new dish. "I had no idea things could taste so good!" she exclaimed. "This is all so delicious!"

"Is she all right?" whispered Queen Glamdis to Jack.

"Just crazy in a new way," Jack whispered back.

They left early in the morning, as dawn reddened the hall of the Mountain Queen. Glamdis and her family accompanied them down the long tunnels to the bottom of the mountain. For a people who had haunted Jack's nightmares so long, he was surprisingly sad to leave them. "I can't believe one of you bit off Tree Foot's leg," he said as they came out to the cold, windswept courtyard at the beginning of the U-shaped valley.

"Believe it," said Fonn. "Humans and trolls have been at war for a long time. We have a truce for the moment, to honor Olaf One-Brow, but we battle for the same lands. When winter ruled the earth, so did we. Now summer comes on and we are weakened. But we will never give up."

"And neither will we," Thorgil cried. She was dressed in wolverine fur with smart little boots and a new sword at her belt. "To refuse battle would do neither of us honor."

"We will meet at Ragnarok," said Fonn gravely.

"At Ragnarok!" shrilled Thorgil.

Bold Heart, who was perched on Jack's shoulder, cawed and shook his head.

"I give you these parting gifts," said the Mountain Queen, signaling to a young lout. He brought out cloaks of a material Jack couldn't identify. They shimmered like the light off a glacier, and they smelled sharp and sweet at the same time. "They're made of silk we harvest from the spiders that live in our forests," the queen said.

How do you get silk from a spider? thought Jack, who only understood how to shear sheep.

"You may have noticed the curtains in our halls. They're of the same substance, strong enough to withstand the heaviest storm and light enough to wear comfortably. This silk has the property of taking on the colors around it. These cloaks will hide you from the dragon." Glamdis held up the garments. They were long and roomy. The hoods would easily conceal a face. Jack saw their color shift from ice white to the dark blue of the Mountain Queen's dress.

"Thank you, Great Queen—I mean, Mother," said Jack, bowing. "This is indeed generous."

"I'm deeply honored," said Thorgil, bowing as well.

"Don't go near the rocks on either side of the valley. Walk next to the river. Travel by dark. Hide by day. When you reach the forest, go north around the field of flowers. The elk have made trails. You should come out on the fjord and meet your friends."

Jack was dressed in his marten-fur coat and the cow-skin boots that gripped the ice. He carried Olaf's sun stone for Skakki and the bottle of song-mead from Mimir's Well for Rune in a bag around his neck. Thorgil wore the little silver hammer she'd been given by Olaf. Both of them had sacks of provisions and various weapons.

Last of all, the queen gestured to Bolthorn, who came out with Jack's staff wrapped in cloth. "You take it," Bolthorn said, holding it out as though it were a poisonous snake.

"I thought about casting it into the chasm beneath my

window," said the queen. "Then I thought about keeping it from you. It's the staff of a fire wizard. I last saw one when Dragon Tongue visited, and I can't tell you how much trouble *he* caused. Still, it would be unworthy to steal from a guest. You may take it home with you, but be warned. If you ever return with *that* in your possession, you'll find out right away whether we trolls bite off legs." She grinned, showing her dainty—but businesslike—fangs.

"I promise," said Jack, bowing again. He hefted the staff. It had turned black, but it wasn't burned. It had called out flame from the heart of Jotunheim and, in the process, had gone beyond fire to something harder and stronger. Jack felt a faint thrumming in the wood when he put his hand on it.

They said farewell then, thanking the Jotuns again for their generosity. Jack hugged Golden Bristles as best he could, given his short arms and the boar's huge neck. "Good-bye, piggy," he said. "I wish you could come along, but you wouldn't find much welcome in Middle Earth." The troll-boar whuffled and nuzzled Jack's hair.

Then Jack, Thorgil, and Bold Heart set off down the U-shaped valley to the distant forest. For a while they could hear Forath singing a farewell whale-song. *I wish she wouldn't do that,* Jack thought. *It makes me feel so dreadfully sad.* They turned after a mile and looked back. The ice mountain seemed unmarked. They couldn't make out any windows, turrets, walkways, or doors. It was as though the Jotuns had folded themselves inside and all the glaciers and ice crags were deserted.

❖ ❖ ❖

"This cloak smells weird," said Thorgil. They were tucked into a deep side channel of the river. They had to lie on a sandbar crusted with ice. The wind scoured the ground just above their heads, but they were hidden from the dragon. Jack had shared out meat pies and cider.

"It's made of spider silk. Maybe spiders smell weird. I've never been close enough to tell," he said. Bold Heart was huddled against him, pecking meat shreds from Jack's hand.

"I keep expecting the cloth to be sticky."

"Just don't walk through a swarm of flies."

"This is so boring," Thorgil fumed. "Why can't we go out in daylight if the cloaks can hide us?"

"The queen had some reason for telling us to lie low."

"The dragon can't see us. There's nothing else out here. You can see for miles." Thorgil balled up her cloak and jammed it into the sand.

The dragon had been visible for some time as a puff of smoke by day and a red fire at night. Occasionally, she spread her wings and floated over the valley, looking for prey. So far she hadn't got anything.

I wonder if she's laid more eggs, Jack thought. He felt vaguely guilty about killing her brood, but they hadn't had a choice.

"I'm *bored,*" said Thorgil. The new Thorgil was almost as annoying as the old one. She no longer fell into mindless rages—though she was perfectly capable of getting angry—

but she was filled with a thirst for new experiences. She had missed so much in her former life that every rock and clump of moss enthralled her. She wanted more and more and more entertainment, to make up for lost time. Sitting with her for hours was sheer torture.

"Why can't we find out whether the dragon can see us?" she complained. "We could always run back here."

"Because," Jack said for the tenth time that day, "once the dragon notices us, she isn't going to give up. She'll check every nook and cranny."

"Bold Heart could talk to her. Tell her we taste bad or something."

"She's not going to believe *him*," Jack said. Bold Heart had revealed—and Thorgil had translated—that he'd told the dragon she had a rival at the other end of the valley. He'd worked her into such a rage, she'd sailed off to do battle. Then he'd incited the green dragonlet to kill his sisters.

"I suppose not," grumbled Thorgil. She felt for the rune at her neck.

Jack watched her with a sick feeling of loss. "You can't take it off, you know," he said. "Once removed it can never be returned."

"You've told me that about a thousand times. I'm never going to take it off. It makes me feel safe."

I know, thought Jack sadly. He smoothed the feathers on Bold Heart's head. The crow nibbled his fingers. The wind whistled and howled, and from a great distance they heard the dragon scream. She did this regularly, whether from rage or merely for exercise Jack didn't know. It was when she was silent that they had to worry.

"I'm bored. Tell me a story," said Thorgil.

Jack had gone through his entire collection in the days they'd spent crossing the valley. He'd told her all of Father's gory martyrdom tales and all of the Bard's sagas and even all of Lucy's bedtime stories. He'd described every inch of the farm and every rock on the beach back home. He was almost reduced to introducing her to the black-faced sheep. He stood up and looked over the edge of the embankment.

The forest wasn't that far away. The dragon had sounded as though she was flying away from them, perhaps back to her nest. He shaded his eyes. He thought he saw a puff of smoke from the distant cliff.

"We might make it," he said.

"What! Really?" cried Thorgil, popping up to look around the valley.

"That's where Olaf's funeral pyre was, and there's the trail into the forest," Jack said. "It should take only a couple of hours. I don't know. Maybe we should wait for dusk."

But Thorgil had already shouldered her bags and wrapped herself up in the cloak. She was out before he could stop her.

"Stop! Don't you ever think anything through?" Jack hurried after her while struggling with his own carrying bags and cloak. Bold Heart sailed overhead.

Jack had to admit it was a lot nicer traveling by day. They kept bumping into things in the dark or falling on patches of ice. The sunlight was exhilarating, and even the wind wasn't bad in their warm clothes. The Jotuns had certainly been generous. Jack wondered for the first time why they had clothes that fit human children. *No,* he thought. *They couldn't have.* But he didn't really know. There was a war between Jotunheim and Middle Earth. Children might not be safer here than they'd been in Gizur's village.

"Isn't this fine?" Thorgil chirruped. Jack could hardly see her under the silk cloak. She looked as clear as a soap bubble. He supposed he was equally hidden, except for his hand gripping the ash wood staff. Jack was of two minds about the staff. He could keep it at the ready. Or he could sling it on his back and depend on stealth. He slung it onto his back under the cloak. He wasn't sure he could raise fire in a hurry, and anyhow, what difference did fire make to a dragon?

Jack looked back occasionally to see whether the dragon had moved. A thin column of smoke put his fears to rest.

"Those boulders are such interesting colors," Thorgil said. "I used to think they were all gray, but they aren't. Some are like oyster shells and others are like fog and still others are speckled like a robin's egg. And the shadows! You'd think they were the same, but some are dark and others are bright and—oh, look at that one!—it's purple."

Save me from Thorgil's enthusiasm, Jack silently prayed. He thought he'd never miss her rages and sulks. At least when she was sulking she was quiet.

The forest drew ever nearer. The dragon seemed content to roost. *Things might actually work out,* Jack thought. They were still walking along the river, and to their right, at the edge of the valley where it went up into the surrounding hills, was a huge cream-colored boulder. Around it was a cluster of cream-colored rocks.

"Isn't that sweet?" Thorgil warbled. "It's like a mother rock with her babies."

Wonderful, thought Jack. *Now we're going to stop and pet the baby rocks.* A long scream echoed over the valley. "Run, Thorgil! The dragon's up!" yelled Jack. She reacted instantly. She might sound featherbrained, but the shield maiden of old was still underneath.

"Hide in the rocks," Thorgil cried. "We're not going to make the trees."

"Wait!" Jack shouted, trying to keep up with her. "The queen told us to stay away from them."

"No time!" She reached the rocks first and crouched down. The cloak instantly took on a cream color. Thorgil was even the right size, though a little lumpier than the others. Jack threw himself down beside her. They both fought to regain their breath as the dragon—to go by her cries—zigzagged back and forth over the valley.

"She can't see us. I *told* you she couldn't see us," whispered Thorgil.

"I hope she leaves soon. This is uncomfortable," said Jack.

"Lean against the rocks. . . . I say!"

"What?"

"This one's soft," said Thorgil.

Jack felt the surface by his side. It *was* soft. The dragon's cries retreated up the valley toward the ice mountain. He opened the cloak slightly to look. The rocks were all the same size, which was odd in itself, and the odor they gave off was so intense, it made him queasy. "This place smells like—"

The giant boulder suddenly stood up on eight giant legs and began frantically gathering the little rocks into a silk bag.

Chapter Thirty-eight

SPIDER MUSIC

Jack desperately tried to reach his staff. He couldn't undo it without throwing off his cloak. The spider moved like lightning, collecting her eggs. She whisked each one up with whatever those things were on either side of her fangs and tucked them away.

When she got to Thorgil, she puzzled over the shape. She reached back with two of her legs and whipped out a long line of silk. This she coiled around Thorgil until the girl looked just like one of the eggs. Thorgil, cursing richly, disappeared into the sack.

Satisfied, the spider reached for Jack. He felt the creature's fang probe gently, and then he felt himself twirled round and round as the silk rope belted him in. He was lifted, handled in those awful things beside the fangs, and settled onto a soft bed of spider eggs.

The spider took off running. Jack could feel each footfall as the egg sack jounced and swayed. He could hardly breathe, and what air he did get was drenched in that sharp-sweet, nauseating smell. He struggled to reach the knife on his belt. The ash wood staff dug into his back.

The mother spider ran for a long time. Presently, she seemed to swing through the air and land with a jarring thump. She moved more slowly then, picking her way carefully until at last she stopped and dropped the egg sack. Jack heard wind whistling outside. He tried to saw a hole with the knife, but spider silk, for something that looked delicate, was as tough as leather. Jack sawed and stabbed until he saw spots before his eyes. His heart pounded and he was slippery with sweat.

He saw the tip of a fang penetrate the silk.

"You could at least help me," complained Thorgil. "I can't do *all* the work while you lounge around."

"You're wonderful," Jack murmured. It wasn't a fang. It was Thorgil's sword. He immediately set about widening the hole. When he was able to wriggle out, he was astounded at the sight before him.

They were high in a canopy of giant trees. Wind whipped the branches, bringing a welcome freedom from the spider-stink. The whole of whatever they were sitting on billowed and swayed so that they had to hang on to the sack to keep from falling. "What *is* that?" said Thorgil.

Jack squinted. The colors shifted as the structure moved, but eventually, he was able to make out the shape. "I think it's a huge spiderweb," he said. Because the silk took on the colors around it, parts looked as transparent as air, while others were dark green or brown from the trees below. The sack was anchored to a particularly tall fir that jutted above the web.

In one direction there was only trees. In the other Jack saw round webs covering the forest as far as he could see. Here and there huge cream-colored spiders sat with their legs outspread. Some had egg sacks to the side like the one next to Jack and Thorgil. Others had dismal lumps where some creature had been captured. A few of these lumps were being fed upon.

"Now what?" said Thorgil. Jack had to hand it to her. Where most people would have screamed and fainted, the shield maiden was ready for battle.

Jack looked down. They were so high, the forest floor was lost in darkness. To reach it, they would have to pass through the web. If it was sticky—and it probably was—they wouldn't get far. "Maybe we should go up," he suggested.

They retrieved their food and water bags from the sack. Climbing would have been easy if the wind hadn't been blowing, but of course it was. Jack wasn't thrilled about the height either. They struggled through the branches to a perch near the top where they could sit.

The spider was brooding at the center of her web. Jack could see the bulge of her enormous belly and her spinnerets. At least she was facing away. "Why didn't she eat us?" said Thorgil, ever practical.

"We smelled right," said Jack. "Our cloaks made us seem like baby spiders."

"I'm trying to look on the bright side," the shield maiden said, clutching the rune. "Our situation, as far as I can tell, is this: We're so high, we'd never survive if we fell. But sooner or later we'll get too tired to hold on. Or the spider will find us first and eat us. If we wait long enough, the eggs will hatch, and a hundred or so babies will climb up and eat us."

"That's the bright side?" said Jack.

"I'm only trying to work things out," Thorgil said. "Maybe you should use that staff to call up fire."

Jack untied the staff. His back was sore from where it had pressed against him. He pointed it at the mother spider and felt it thrum in response. All around, the trees went *whisper, whisper, whisper.*

"I don't have much control over this," he said. "What if I set the whole forest on fire?"

"You'll just have to be careful," Thorgil said crossly.

Jack pointed the staff again. "This doesn't feel right."

"Would it feel better to have the juice sucked out of you?"

"I think there's another way."

"Oh, Freya!" swore Thorgil. Jack saw a huge eagle, like the one that had attacked him on the ice bridge, sail overhead. It turned and circled the tree. Thorgil drew her sword. The eagle veered away with a harsh scream, but it came back with its claws out—and ran into a strand of spiderweb. The bird squawked and tried to free itself, but it only fell onto the main web, miring itself completely.

The spider dashed out and sank her fangs into it. The eagle tore at her with its beak and claws, but it was greatly outmatched. Soon it was wrapped in silk while the spider sat back, waiting for her poison to work. After awhile the bird stopped moving. Jack and Thorgil clung to each other as they listened to the monotonous sucking sound of the spider's feast. When she was finished, she dropped the husk to the forest floor far below.

"*Now* will you call up fire?" said Thorgil.

"Wait," said Jack. The giant spider approached the egg sack. Jack tensed, his staff at the ready in case she made a rush up the tree, but she merely set about mending the hole the eagle had torn in her web. She moved back and forth, pulling long ropes of silk from her spinnerets. When she had laid one line, she squatted down and deposited a glob of goo. Delicately, she plucked the rope with one claw-tipped leg. The goo immediately vibrated out into droplets along the line.

Jack watched intently. This was extremely interesting. Not all of the web was sticky. If you could step between the droplets, you wouldn't stick at all. The spider occasionally leaned back and looked up at the tree where Thorgil and Jack were. At the top of her body was a turret with eight shiny black eyes, but she didn't seem to see the two humans cowering in the branches.

Now the spider did another interesting thing: She walked up to the egg sack and rested her fangs on it, apparently lost in an ecstasy of motherhood. Jack was convinced that was exactly what she was doing. He could feel the whisper of her thoughts and the tiny responses from the hundred or so eggs inside. She plucked rhythmically at a thread holding the sack. The whispering intensified, becoming more joyous.

"You know . . . I think that's a lullaby," said Jack.

"That's a huge, ugly, people-eating spider," Thorgil said. "Don't go soft on me."

"You're the one who cooed over the baby rocks."

"I didn't know what they were. Burn all of them up. They're our enemies." Thorgil looked fierce enough to attack a hundred spiders.

"I've been studying the mother. She seems almost blind. She didn't see us when she looked straight at us. I suppose the dragon had to get close before she realized the danger to her young. The spider can't hear, either, or she would have gotten you when you were cursing so loudly in the egg sack."

"So she has weaknesses. It makes it easier to kill her."

But Jack couldn't bring himself to do it. When he drank from Mimir's Well, he'd remembered those moments when everything felt exactly *right*. When Mother sang to the bees or Father built the house, they were doing it so lovingly and well, the simplest activities were lit up from inside. They were filled with the life force. What the mother spider was doing now was the same.

It was necessary to kill to feed or protect one's family and self. That was what the spider had done with the eagle. If she attacked Jack or Thorgil, he would have to slay her. But Jack also understood that if he killed the spider without need, he would lose his power and his music would go from him. He put the staff away.

"You are so *stupid,*" fumed Thorgil. She cursed him roundly as they clung to the tree trunk in the tossing wind. "I should go down there and stab her—and stab all those eggs, too."

Jack knew she wouldn't. The reckless frenzy that had driven Thorgil was gone. She was capable of great courage and daring, but she wouldn't throw her life away.

In the early afternoon the spider returned to her vigil in the middle of the web. The wind dropped, and Jack felt safe enough to pass out the last of the meat pies and cider. "Our last meal," Thorgil said sarcastically.

"Look," said Jack, pointing. In the distance they saw a tiny speck. It grew larger until they could see it was a single crow flying back and forth. Jack stood up and waved.

Bold Heart sped straight to the top of the tree. He balanced there, cooing and warbling. "I'm glad to see you, too," said Jack. "As you can tell, we're in a mess. You mustn't get close to the web."

"Tell Jack to kill that spider," ordered Thorgil. Bold Heart cawed back. "He says—idiot bird—he says you don't have to kill her. You can send her to sleep. I think it should be a *permanent* sleep, but who listens to me?"

"All right," said Jack, wondering how this could be done. "What then? Do we climb down?" Bold Heart clacked and burbled and cawed, going on at great length.

"He says, 'Wait here. Help is on the way,'" said Thorgil.

"That was a lot of conversation for such a short translation. I'm sure he said more."

"You'll never know," Thorgil said smugly.

Bold Heart sped off, and Jack climbed down to the egg sack. The spider loomed at the middle of her web. One eagle probably wouldn't satisfy her for long. She might be ready for dessert. He drew the staff from the sling on his back, just in case, and cleared his throat. He began singing. The words came out awkwardly. He couldn't seem to get the right music. How did you serenade a deaf spider?

After awhile Jack stopped. It was a waste of time. The spider ignored him, and he'd run out of poetry. Far away a large bird blundered into one of the other webs and was pounced on. *Birds must be what these things live on,* Jack thought. Bugs wouldn't even whet their appetites.

How did you serenade a deaf spider?

The same way a spider sings lullabies to her young. Of course. Jack had studied the harp with the Bard, but he hadn't made much headway. His voice was his best talent. Voice wouldn't do him any good here, though. He put the staff away. He needed both hands for what he was about to do.

Spiders are nearly blind and deaf, but their sense of touch makes up for it. They can feel every quiver on their webs, thought Jack. Wonderful. He'd have to come up with something that felt like music and not dinner. He remembered the rhythm the mother spider had plucked when she was soothing her eggs. It was a thing Jack noticed automatically, being musical. *I think I can repeat it,* he thought. *If I'm wrong, I'll find out soon enough. And I thought the Northmen were a tough audience.*

Jack leaned over the edge of the egg sack. He could see—barely—the long strands of the web. If you thought about it right, you could imagine they were harp strings. He lay on his stomach and studied them. He'd have to pluck the strands between the globs of goo, which also were hard to see. The whole web was hard to see. That, of course, was how it worked.

Jack found two dark green lines stretching over a cluster of fir trees. He thought he could just make out a safe area. He reached out.

Sproinnnng! The spider reared up on all eight legs. It was like she was on tiptoe. Jack froze. He certainly had her attention.

"I'll come down and defend you!" called Thorgil.

"Stay where you are! I know what I'm doing," cried Jack. *I hope,* he thought. At least the spider didn't react to his voice. She really was deaf. *I'll have to do this fast,* he thought. *No stopping, no matter what she does. My only chance of success is to play the lullaby back to her. It has to be perfect. No stopping.*

Jack then began the most important music recital of his life. He emptied his mind of everything but the rhythm. He plucked and picked, he chanted and caroled, he yowled and yodeled and twanged. He needed the sound to keep his fingers true.

The spider crept so close, she was almost on top of him. She cast a dire shadow that almost made him faint, but he didn't stop. He could see her fangs glint and her mouthparts working. He didn't stop. Jack felt her quiver—the motion came to him through the web. He felt an answering quiver from the eggs below. All the little spiderlings were dancing in their shells.

The spider suddenly keeled over. Her body flattened sideways in an untidy tangle of legs. She was still alive, he knew, because he could see the tips of her claws move. She was dreaming!

Jack climbed the tree as fast as he could go. "Where's Bold Heart?" he cried. "Where's the help he promised? I don't know how long she's going to be out. Merciful heavens, I don't *ever* want to do that again." He burst into sobs.

"Over there," said Thorgil, pointing.

Jack saw four enormous white birds and one small black one gliding above the forest. He was shaking so much, he thought he'd fall out of the tree. His teeth were chattering.

"It's all right. You did it," said Thorgil, putting her arm around him. "The owls said they wouldn't come until the spider was asleep. I have to say that was the worst music I ever heard."

"H-How do you know? Y-You aren't a s-spider," said Jack.

"Thank Freya for that!" swore Thorgil.

The owls came in a cluster. *Hooo-uh, hooo-uh, hooo-uh, wuh-wuh-wuh,* they cried. They barked and cackled and shrieked and hissed.

"They say we have to leave at once. They'll take you first," said Thorgil.

Jack didn't understand what she meant until the owls

clamped on to his arms and legs and flew off. *I can't take much more of this,* he thought as the forest sped by below. After a short time the owls deposited him in a meadow and took off. They returned with Thorgil.

"By Thor! That's a wonderful way to travel!" she exclaimed. "If only we could train birds to carry us! We could attack our enemies from the air."

Hooo-uh wuh-wuh-wuh, said one of the owls.

"He's thanking you for saving their lives. I didn't know about that," said Thorgil.

"It happened in the little valley after we escaped the dragon. They were starving to death, and I took them outside so they could hunt again," Jack said. "You're very welcome." He bowed to the birds. Bold Heart sat on a nearby bush and warbled.

"Bold Heart says they've told him a safe way to the fjord," said Thorgil.

Hooo-uh! Hooo-uh! Krufff-guh-guh-guh! screamed the owls.

"What was that?" asked Jack.

"They're giving their opinion of spiders. I don't think I'll translate it," said Thorgil.

Jack and Thorgil waved good-bye to the snowy owls, and then, with Bold Heart leading the way, they found an elk trail at the edge of the meadow. On the way they gathered blueberries, each one as big as a plum, and cracked giant hazelnuts for lunch. In late afternoon they reached the fjord.

Jack built a fire—a normal one using quartz and steel because he couldn't trust the ash wood staff to make anything small. Soon they saw the ship approaching over the water. Something large was hanging on the prow. It was a scaly green head with a crest of spikes and long whiskers. Eric Pretty-Face roared greetings, and the other Northmen all cheered.

Imagine, thought Jack. *I'm actually glad to see Northmen.*

The longboat came in close, and the warriors jumped out to make it steady.

"WELCOME BACK!" bellowed Eric Pretty-Face. "WAS IT A SUCCESS? DID YOU KICK THE TROLLS' BUTTS? LOOK AT THE SEA SERPENT I CAUGHT."

And Rune said, "Where's Olaf?"

Chapter Thirty-nine

FAREWELL TO JOTUNHEIM

"It was fated," said Rune that night as they lay at anchor in the fjord. They had started too late to reach the open sea. "I always knew Odin would call Olaf in the prime of his life. Warriors like him are too great for Middle Earth."

"We saw his funeral pyre," Sven the Vengeful said. "We didn't know what it was then."

"It went straight up to Valhalla. I thought it was a pair of dragons fighting," said Eric the Rash.

"There was a dragon." Jack was mortally tired, but he felt he owed Olaf's friends at least part of the story tonight. "She flew back and forth over the flames, shrieking."

"I think I heard that," said Sven.

"She was honoring Olaf," Thorgil said heavily. She had been crying off and on all evening. Now that there was no danger to occupy her, she could give herself up to grief.

"Wasn't that wonderful?" said Sven with an envious sigh. "And you say there was a troll-bear at his feet."

"Yes," said Jack.

"A FIRST-RATE FUNERAL," Eric Pretty-Face declared.

"I've warned you about talking after dark, Eric my friend," said Rune. "We won't be safe until we leave Jotunheim, so silence is important."

"OH. ALL RIGHT."

The Northmen sat quietly under the stars. Even the stars seemed larger in Jotunheim. The water was as still as a sheet of black ice. One by one the warriors lay down to sleep, except for Rune, who was on watch and never slept much anyway. Bold Heart kept him company but soon nodded off like the others. Jack, for all his exhaustion, found it hard to relax. So much had happened. So much had changed. He had never dreamed, in his little village on the English coast, that he would ever meet such things as dragons and trolls. They were something that lived far away. Well, here he was: far away.

Jack resettled the grain bag he was using as a pillow. The deck was hard, and the bilge was as fragrant as ever. *Whisper, whisper, whisper* went the trees, birds, and animals of Jotunheim in his mind. Jack covered his ears, knowing it would do no good.

He didn't know how he was going to cure Frith yet. But Mimir's Well had taught him not to try to force the order of things. Leaves uncurled and flowers opened when it was their time. Knowledge would be given to him when the moment came.

Toward dawn he awoke and saw Rune sitting by the sea serpent's head at the prow. A silvery light shone on the water. Jack got up and picked his way through the sleeping bodies.

"That's going to stink in a couple of days," said Rune, running his fingers over the scales. "I wouldn't dream of asking Eric Pretty-Face to leave it behind, though. He was so proud of killing it. It followed us around from the day we left you, working up its nerve to attack. It's only half grown, you see."

"I see," said Jack, noting that the head alone weighed twice what Eric Pretty-Face did.

"It came at us yesterday, tried to wrap itself around the boat and sink us. Bad mistake."

"Rune," said Jack.

"Yes?"

"We found Mimir's Well."

"What great good fortune! I hoped you had, but we were speaking of Olaf earlier, and I didn't want to change the subject." The old warrior's voice was sad.

"I don't want to talk about it with the others. Not yet. I don't think it would be right."

"I'll shut them up," Rune said decisively. "I'll tell them it has to do with the magic. Did you drink?"

"Yes, and so did Thorgil."

"She *did*? I thought she seemed different. She didn't once try to hurt anybody. Tell me, how did it taste?" The longing in the old man's voice was almost unbearable.

"You tell me," said Jack, handing him the bottle with the poppy on the side.

"Ohhhh," Rune said with a deep sigh.

"It's all right. I told the Norns you had sacrificed your voice to defend your friends and had given me your best poem. That seemed to satisfy them."

"You've seen Norns too? How wonderful!"

"I didn't like them," said Jack.

"Shh. It's never good to offend the forces that govern our lives. I can really drink this?"

Jack nodded. Rune opened the bottle and drank. A light came into his eyes, and he stood straighter than Jack had ever seen him do. "So, what does it taste like?" Jack said.

"Like the sun coming up after winter. Like rain after drought. Like joy after sorrow."

"Your *voice*!" Jack cried. For the old man no longer whispered. His words were strong and new. Rune didn't have a young man's voice. He would never again be the magnificent singer of his youth, but he sounded deeper and more moving.

"Why is everyone making a racket?" grumbled Sven the Vengeful. "I haven't had nearly the rest I wanted. Are you talking in your sleep again, Eric Pretty-Face?"

"NOT ME," said Eric Pretty-Face.

That morning they came to the mouth of the fjord. The cliffs on either side were seething with birds, and thousands of nests clung to the rocks. The water was silver with haddock and salmon. Bold Heart chased off a few seagulls when they tried to land on the sea serpent's head. "We're leaving Jotunheim," Jack said somewhat regretfully.

"And entering Middle Earth," said Rune.

The birds swirled and screamed. Thorgil crouched in the bilge with her hands over her ears. "She understands what they say," Jack whispered. They came to open water and turned south on a bright gray-green sea with a brisk wind. Eric the Rash and Eric Pretty-Face put up the sail.

Jack felt as though something had lifted that had weighed on him ever since they'd entered Jotunheim. "This place welcomes us," he said in wonder as he gazed at the coastline slipping by to their left.

"This is where we belong," said Rune. "Jotunheim ever hated our presence."

Jack turned and looked out over the vast ocean toward the place where Utgard had lain. Fonn's great-great-great-grandmother had walked from there when it was a sea of ice. But each year summer moved closer to the heart of the frost giants' world.

"I can't understand the seagulls anymore," Thorgil said. "Well, I can, but I can't pick up every single word."

"Don't you like that? You hated listening to them," said Jack.

"I did . . . but it was still kind of nice."

"Magic is closer to the surface in Jotunheim," said Rune. "I'm sure you haven't lost the ability. You'll just have to work harder at it."

And Jack, too, felt the life force had moved deeper. It was there, but it would not come easily to his bidding. Which wasn't a bad thing, he decided, grasping the blackened ash wood staff. He'd become afraid to summon its power in Jotunheim. The fire was too wild and unpredictable.

They traveled south, camping at night on little beaches. Jack and Thorgil told the warriors most of what happened, keeping only the Norns and Mimir's Well to themselves. The Northmen were mightily impressed with Thorgil's slaying of the dragonlet as well as Jack's triumph over the spider. They hadn't been idle either. Besides the fight with the sea serpent (which now stank to the heavens), they'd battled with a giant, evil-tempered pike.

"Tried to get me every time I drew up water," said Sven the Vengeful. "I finally showed it what was what."

"TASTED GREAT WITH CRANBERRIES," commented Eric Pretty-Face.

Then there had been a battle with a pair of huge wolverines when the warriors went foraging on shore, and an encounter with a giant lynx, and one afternoon, when Eric the Rash took a nap under a tree, he woke to find that a slug had devoured most of his shirt and part of the skin underneath.

They met more ships as they approached the entrance to King Ivar's fjord. The fishermen cheered as they passed and begged to be allowed to visit and take a close look at the sea serpent. Eric Pretty-Face threw his chest out proudly. *But he'll never equal Olaf One-Brow,* Jack thought with a pain over his heart. *None of them will.*

The sound of the sea died away as they went inland. The water became placid, and here and there on the shore Jack saw deer and rabbits—normal-size deer and ordinary rabbits. Far away to the north lay high mountains covered in snow. *Jotunheim,* thought Jack. It looked unreal. Perhaps it *was* unreal.

Presently, they saw the farms high in the hills and the steep meadows dotted with sheep. They saw the dock, which was filling up with people, and beyond, on a shoulder of dark blue stone as bleak and lifeless as metal, Ivar's palace. Heide, Dotti, and Lotti scanned the ship anxiously.

Oh, heavens. How can I tell them? thought Jack. In the end, no one had to tell them. If Olaf wasn't visible, he wasn't there. You couldn't hide him. Dotti and Lotti screamed and tore their clothes. Heide wept silently, after the manner of her people. Skakki led them all back to Olaf's house.

"I told him," said Heide, standing before the long fire in the middle of the hall, "'Iff you take the boy and his sister to the court, it will be your doom.' I sssaw him lying in a dark forest with his life blood soaking into the earth. Poor Ox-brain."

"It wasn't quite like that," said Jack.

"The visions are neverrrr exact. The meaning wasss clear."

Dotti, Lotti, and the children sat solemnly around the sides of the fire trough, with Olaf's friends and companions. Skakki occupied Olaf's great chair. It was too large for him and always would be. Skakki, at age sixteen, was now head of the household.

"He died as he wished, in battle," said Rune in his new, strong voice.

"And had a funeral worthy of a king!" cried Thorgil. Then she sang:

Half a forest was felled to hold him.
At his feet lay the troll-bear, direful and deadly,
Yet no match for Odin's beloved.
The Valkyries called to him from the hills,
The gates of Valhalla swung wide,
And even the Mountain Queen wept at his passing.

A hush fell over the hall. For a moment no one moved. Then Rune said, "That was *poetry*."

"Women can't make poetry," said Sven the Vengeful.

Everyone turned to Thorgil, expecting her to fall into one of her rages. She only sat down, looking stunned. Bold Heart sailed from the rafters to her shoulder and warbled into her ear. "I don't know how I did it either," Thorgil said, "but thanks for the compliment."

"She's talking to birds," whispered one of the smaller children. "Does that mean she's a witch?" Dotti shushed him.

"It means she's a wise woman," Jack said.

"But she's making poetry. Surely that's unnatural," insisted Sven. Again everyone turned to Thorgil, waiting for her to have a tantrum. Nothing happened.

"Thorgilll," said Heide, drawing out the name, "do you feel all right?"

"There's nothing wrong with her!" Jack cried. "Thorgil Olaf's Daughter can do whatever she likes. He accepted her. Why can't you? She fought the troll-bear by his side. She killed a young dragon. She tasted its blood by accident, just as Sigurd did. That's why she understands birds now. She drank from Mimir's Well. That's why she can make poetry now. Why can't you accept that?"

The long fire crackled and danced in a wind that came in under the eaves. The animals Olaf had carved on the rafters seemed to stir. "You shame us," murmured Skakki.

"I—I didn't mean to," stammered Jack. "It's just that—"

"No, you're right," said the boy, standing, and now he did resemble Olaf. "I name you sister, Thorgil Olaf's Daughter. I welcome you to the family."

"And I name you daughter," said Heide. "And so do Dotti and Lotti." She glared at the two junior wives.

It was too much for Thorgil. She was used to being the outcast. So much friendliness overwhelmed her, and she burst into tears and fled the hall.

"Where will she go?" said Jack. No one else seemed disturbed by the shield maiden's departure.

"Up the hill to find the king's dogs," Rune said calmly. "Slasher, Wolf Bane, Hel Hag, and Shreddie will be delighted. They haven't seen her yet."

"Nowwww," said Heide in her smoky voice, "tell me about the Mountain Queen weeping over Olaf."

It seemed Heide wasn't completely ignorant of Olaf's activities. She had noted her husband's trips, loaded with presents, and had concluded he had an extra wife. "But a *troll?*" she exclaimed. "Had the man no taste at all?"

"The queen is rather nice—oof!" gasped Jack as Rune elbowed him in the stomach. "But ugly. Very ugly," he finished. At Heide's insistence, Jack described Glamdis.

"Orange hair sprouting from her head? Nine feet tall? *Fangs?* Wasss Ox-brain insane?" seethed the wise woman. Dotti and Lotti looked considerably cheered up by Heide's annoyance.

Then Jack explained how the troll-maidens practiced marriage by capture and how the Mountain Queen had a harem of sixteen louts. He told the fascinated assembly about the miserable human who had fathered Frothi and Frith. "He painted pictures of his human family on the walls," Jack said. "At least Olaf escaped that fate. He was able to go and come as he pleased."

"Yesss, well, Ox-brain wass impossible for anyone to control," said Heide, somewhat mollified.

"He couldn't help being captured," Lotti pointed out.

"No, no, of course not." Heide shook her head. "And he wasss so big and beautiful." All three of the wives sighed.

As for Olaf's friends and companions, they were delighted with the story. "HE MADE A TROLL-QUEEN FALL IN LOVE WITH HIM! WHAT A FEAT!" said Tree Foot, completely wowed.

"What a man!" said Egil Long-Spear.

Chapter Forty

FREYA'S FEN

"If you're going to be a skald, you must look the part," said Rune, stepping back to observe Jack's white robe. It was Rune's own, shortened to fit the boy. A message had been sent to King Ivar the week before, but no welcome had been issued until today. Tonight was the full moon, and tomorrow was the day set forth for Freya's sacrifice.

Jack was deeply worried by the delay, but he could do nothing about it. No one, apparently, entered Frith's presence without permission. *You'd think she'd be anxious to get her hair back,* he thought. *But she probably enjoys making me suffer.*

"This doesn't feel right," he said, belting the robe to keep it on. It was still too large. He knew real bards were old, fierce, and scary. Jack didn't feel scary. *Scared* was more like it.

"Shh. You have to start somewhere. Frith is going to be

difficult, and you'll need to impress her. Do you know what you're going to do?"

"No," Jack said miserably.

"It will come to you," Rune said.

Thorgil sat by the door, tapping her foot with impatience. She was dressed in her wolverine coat from Jotunheim. Her boots had been brushed and her sword polished. She was even clean, having been dragged to the sauna that afternoon.

"I'm going with you," said Heide.

"Is that a good idea?" said Rune.

"Perhaps not, but it will be interesting," said the woman. "I make Frith nervousss, which may be worth a great deal." Heide was dressed in a dark blue robe embroidered with birds and fish. Her hair was braided in two loops on either side of her head. They looked like the horns of some fantastic animal. She wore a necklace of silver charms—eyes, legs, and other body parts. She made Jack nervous too.

"Come *on*," said Thorgil. Bold Heart had chosen to ride on her shoulder. Jack felt slightly jealous, but he had bigger worries than a faithless bird. He grasped his staff and followed Rune out the door.

Night wasn't far off. The evening chorus of birds had begun, and long shafts of golden light crossed their path. The harvest moon had already risen. It was almost as large as a Jotunheim moon, Jack thought, as he glimpsed it between the trees. An owl hooted—*wuh-huh-huh*—but it was a small, brown bird, not something that could carry you off.

Skakki led the way as head of the house. Thorgil and

Heide followed, chatting like the best of friends. Thorgil had calmed down since leaving Jotunheim, but she still exclaimed over marvels she had surely seen many times. Heide listened patiently. Now and then the wise woman explained how a flower could be used or what had made that form in the grass.

Jack was having trouble walking because he wasn't used to robes. "Wait," said Rune when they passed an oak tree.

The old warrior cut off a long, thin branch. This he twisted into a kind of crown and set it on Jack's head. "Dragon Tongue used to wear oak leaves when he was about to work magic. I don't know why."

I don't either, thought Jack. Work magic? Half of what he did was an accident. The other half went out of control. *I'm not a bard. I'm a twelve-year-old farm brat. The most important job I ever had at home was mucking out the barn.*

"You're quite remarkable," said Rune quietly, as though he could see into Jack's mind. They'd fallen behind the others. Jack could hear Thorgil warbling about a speckled toadstool and Heide's low voice explaining how poisonous it was. "First you impressed Dragon Tongue, then Olaf—and Olaf wasn't the most perceptive of men," Rune said. "You went on a quest through Jotunheim and came out the other end alive. You survived a troll-bear and a dragon. You made friends with the Mountain Queen. You drank from Mimir's Well, and you outwitted a giant spider. Many warriors would give their sword arm for such a record."

"Please," said Jack, blushing. "I'm nothing special. I'm just a farm brat dressed up in fancy clothes."

"Listen to me and listen well: One of the first things you learn when you become a skald is that you *must not lie.*"

"But I'm not lying." Jack was startled by Rune's sudden anger.

"Your power depends on knowing what you are, both bad and good. Now, everything I've said about you is true. Deny it and—well, you might as well *spit* into Mimir's Well." The old warrior strode ahead and joined the others.

Jack followed, bewildered by what had just happened. He *was* a farm brat. But he was also everything Rune had said. To deny his achievements did seem to be a form of lying. *I guess . . . I guess I'm kind of heroic.* Jack walked along, deep in thought.

The sun had set by the time they emerged from the forest. King Ivar's hall was lit from within and without, for they were expected. A crowd of curious people had gathered to see how Jack would restore Frith's hair to her. They moved aside, respectfully, and Jack heard a woman say, "Doesn't he look impressive? He's a real skald from across the sea. Trained by Dragon Tongue. I wish we could get our Egil to pay attention to music."

"Egil's about as tuneful as Freya's cats," said her husband resignedly.

Jack straightened up. He was a skald from across the sea. He was Dragon Tongue's heir. Giant spiders swooned when he played.

The inside of King Ivar's hall was a shock. Filthy straw covered the floor. Bones from old feasts lay everywhere, and someone had vomited in a corner. No one had bothered to clean it up. Fleas pattered against Jack's legs as he walked, and over all hung a dank, sour smell. Bold Heart gripped Thorgil's shoulder a little tighter.

At the far end the king sat on his throne, looking bloated and sick. His beard was matted, and his clothes were speckled with grease. Next to him Queen Frith glowered at the visitors. She looked worse than last time—lumpier and less wholesome. She didn't even have the honest ugliness of a troll.

Good heavens. Have they been sitting here the whole time? Jack thought. It seemed they'd been perched there for weeks, waiting for his return. The priests of Freya and Odin stood at their side. They looked as though they couldn't wait to flee the room.

"The quest has been fulfilled," said Rune.

Ivar looked up. His eyes were almost buried in puffy flesh. "Really? That's nice. Did you hear that, my troll-flower? The boy has returned. Now you can have your pretty hair back."

"About time," said the queen in a nasty, whining voice. "Get up here and fix me!"

"Remember the conditions we agreed on," said Rune.

"Yes, yes. The bribe. The boy and his sister go free."

"And must be returned home," said Rune.

"I *know* what we agreed on. You took your sweet time in Jotunheim. Now get off your backside and work magic."

Jack stepped forward, staff in hand. He felt a faint warmth in the blackened wood. "Where's Lucy?" he said.

"Who? I don't know any Lucy." The queen sagged over her chair like a steamed pudding in its bag.

"The thrall I gave you," said Thorgil, moving to stand by Jack. She had her hand on her sword. Jack hoped she wouldn't draw it, or at least not yet.

"Oh, that. She was such a disappointment. Wouldn't talk or look at me. All she did was moan."

"Where is she?" cried Jack. He felt the staff thrum with power. He knew he could draw fire from the earth without any effort now. Rage drew it forth.

Thorgil put her hand on his arm. "Great Queen, the child was part of the conditions. Without her, there will be no healing." That was an exceedingly brave thing for Thorgil to do. You didn't say no to a half-troll shape-shifter if you wanted to stay healthy. Frith loomed out of her chair with the shadows boiling up behind her.

"She's in Freya's cart," Freya's priest said quickly. "She's been there a long time, waiting for the sacrifice."

"Then I must go to her," said Heide. For the first time Frith noticed the wise woman's presence.

"You! Hel hag!" she spat out. "What are you doing in my fine hall with your nasty spells and witchcraft?"

"Trying to keep my skirts clean," said Heide. The birds and fish on her robe glowed, and her eyes were dark and dangerous.

"Get out! And take that croaking spy of Odin's with you!"

"Gladly," said Heide, holding out her arm for Bold Heart. "You should pray the girl is well," she added in her smoky voice. "I would not wishhh to be youuu if she isn't."

"Get out! Get out!" shrieked Frith. She began throwing things around—a goblet, plates, a footstool.

"Now, now, my little troll-flower," said King Ivar.

"Where's your old hair?" said Jack, feeling he should take charge of the situation. "I'll need it if I'm going to undo the charm."

"There!" screamed Frith. She kicked a basket at him. It rolled, and a disgusting sludge dribbled out the side.

"That doesn't look like hair," Thorgil said.

"It isn't! It went bad after you left! My mother made it, and it's turned to slime. Typical of her stupid enchantments!" Frith was so beside herself, she could hardly breathe.

"Then I'll—I'll have to find a substitute," Jack said. He'd had some idea of singing her old hair back, but that was clearly impossible now. *What to do? What to do?* he thought. Panic threatened to swamp his mind. Tonight was the harvest moon and tomorrow was the sacrifice to Freya.

Lucy would be drawn to Freya's Meadow, the site of the sacrificial ceremony, by the cats. There she would be garlanded and presented with a little image of the goddess. Then her hands would be tied to the cart. The priest would push it into the mist-shrouded fen to float, but ultimately to sink beneath its dark waters.

Jack took a deep breath. In his mind's eye he saw the sacred meadow with the full moon overhead. And then he knew what to say.

"*This* is how your beauty will be restored," he cried. Rune, Skakki, and Thorgil flinched. They turned to him in amazement. Jack knew he sounded different. His voice filled the hall, and he could see fear in the eyes of his friends and King

Ivar. He was no longer a mere boy, but an agent of the Norns. *They* spoke through him from their haunt by Mimir's Well.

"You will cut hair from Freya's cats—not too much. Take a third and leave the rest for the cats to keep themselves warm. Go to Freya's Meadow and lay out a white cloth to catch the moonlight. Over this you must place the hair and lie down upon it. When the moon is at zenith, your beauty will be restored."

Jack gazed at Frith in the smoky light of the fish-oil lamps. He felt no fear. He felt no hate, only a calm assurance of the truth of what he had said. Frith had turned pale.

"You look like—" She stopped, seeming to gather her thoughts. "My mother used to host a chess game with some-one like you." She shook her head. "Well, it doesn't matter. I'll try your little trick. If it doesn't work, I can still sacrifice your sister." She strode over to King Ivar, who was watching Jack with his mouth open. "Wake up, you weakling!" Frith screamed. "Call your warriors! Tell them to *bring me my cats!*"

Moments later Ivar's warriors dragged in the cats on leashes. They had bound their feet and mouths, but the cats managed to get free. They bit and scratched and yowled and hissed. The men yelled and swore and *shaved*. Under Frith's orders, they shaved off every bit of the beautiful red-gold hair from the beasts until they had a bag bulging with fur and nine absolutely maddened and naked cats.

"Now I know where those things come from," Jack remarked to Thorgil, who was relishing every minute of the animals' humiliation. "Jotunheim. They're troll-cats."

"Troll-*rats,* from the look of them," said Thorgil.

"Oh, my, my, my," groaned Freya's priest. "She's taken all their fur. They'll never forgive me."

"I want him and her with me at the meadow," commanded Frith, pointing at Jack and Thorgil. "And bring Freya's cart. If anything goes wrong, I want the boy to see his sister die!"

"No wonder the Mountain Queen threw her out," muttered Thorgil as she and Jack were herded through the forest by Ivar's warriors. Skakki and Rune had been forced to stay behind.

"I wish she'd married Frith to an ogre," Jack said.

"Even ogres are picky."

Behind them the cart rumbled along the forest road. Jack badly wanted to see how Lucy was, but the warriors stopped him. He caught only a glimpse of her in Heide's arms. The cats pulling the cart were pale in the moonlight. They were in a towering rage and raked their claws at anyone who got near.

Behind them came Frith with a group of house-thralls and King Ivar. He was so infirm, he could barely walk and had to lean on two of his men.

Wuh-huh-huh went the little brown owls in the trees. A lynx screamed in the distance. The cool, green smells of the forest filled the night, and the road was brilliant with the full moon.

They came to a clearing covered in white flowers—Freya's Meadow. It was like a mass of stars fallen to earth, and beyond, where the meadow ended, stunted trees rose over peat bog and black water. That was Freya's Fen.

The cart was pulled to the edge of the meadow. Four of Frith's house-thralls laid a white cloth over the flowers. Two more scattered the red-gold fur on top, but it looked black in the moonlight. The cats hissed and spat when they saw it.

"They'll never forgive me," mourned the priest of Freya.

"Shut up or I'll have your tongue!" shouted Frith.

A murmur rose from among the warriors. "She'd attack a priest?" one of them whispered.

"Shut up or I'll have all your tongues! All of you get back into the trees—not too far. The boy and Thorgil are to stay here." The Northmen withdrew, half carrying King Ivar, whose feet were swollen from the walk.

The house-thralls then disrobed Frith. Jack closed his eyes, but Thorgil nudged him. "You want to see this. It's interesting," she said.

And it was. Horrible, but interesting. Frith's body was white under the harvest moon, and her skin looked soft, like a fungus growing on spoiled meat. It kept reshaping itself with bulges and puckers and seams, never quite human and never quite troll. Scales formed on her arms and flaked off. Her toes splayed out, six or seven on each foot, before shrinking to normal human size. Altogether it was disturbing to watch.

The house-thralls folded her clothes at the edge of the meadow. On top glinted the necklace of silver leaves that Thorgil had so coveted and that she had been forced to give up. Jack saw Thorgil's hand tighten on her sword.

"Don't even think of attacking me, shield maiden," came Frith's cold voice. "You're ringed with warriors. One move and I'll have your sword hand cut off. How would you like that? Forever disabled and never to fight in battle again."

Jack heard the girl's teeth grind. In the old days she would have attacked and to Hel with the consequences. Mimir's Well had taught her patience.

Frith sent her thralls away, and now there was only her, Jack, and Thorgil in the center of the meadow. The moon was almost at zenith. Frith lay down on the fur, and it rustled softly under her weight. There was so much of it from nine, huge, long-haired troll-cats. Frith would surely have hair that would be the wonder of Middle Earth.

Slowly, the moon crept up until it was overhead. A loon called from the fen, and something splashed. Wavelets lapped against the far edge of the meadow. "Look," whispered Thorgil.

Here, there, all over the white cloth the fur began to move. Strands joined together, making long tresses. They writhed and rustled up to Frith's head and attached themselves. Soon she was lying in a bed of long, beautiful hair, and now she herself began to change. Her body lengthened and thinned. Her face became heart-shaped, the kind of face that made kings throw away their crowns. Jack understood why Ivar had fallen in love with her. Even Freya could not be more fair.

But the fur kept on rustling. Frith had been told to take a third, and she had taken all. The rest crept over her body and then her face. Frith seemed hypnotized or else unaware of what was happening. She stared up at the moon as more and more and more fur covered her until she was as hairy as a wild beast. Her body changed again to something large and shaggy that had never been seen before.

She put her hand to her face and screamed. It was a savage cry with nothing human in it, and nothing troll, either. Frith sprang to her feet and tore the white cloth as easily as you might tear a gossamer web in early-morning dew. She ripped it to shreds, all the while screaming and shrieking. There were no words in her speech. Perhaps she was incapable of them in her new form. Then she reared up and bellowed her rage at the moon.

Jack dashed to the cart to free Lucy and Heide. The warriors had come back, but seeing Frith's new shape, they halted under the trees. The cats had gone berserk. They bared their teeth and yowled ferociously. The hair would have stood straight up on their backs, if they'd had any. Thorgil drew her sword and slashed their leashes.

They sprang into the meadow. Frith immediately saw her danger and fled. She bounded into the fen, still screaming, with the nine cats in pursuit. Jack heard their feet splashing and their cries disappearing in the distance.

There were safe places to walk through the fen, Rune said, if you knew where. Perhaps Frith and her pursuers knew. Perhaps not.

"Oh, Jack," Thorgil said, collapsing against the cart with a sigh. "That was the most satisfying thing I've *ever* done!"

And the priest of Freya walked up and down the edge of the fen, calling, "Here, kitty, kitty, kitty. Here, kitty, kitty, kitty."

Chapter Forty-one

LUCY'S RETURN

Jack lifted Lucy from the cart. She was smaller and lighter than he remembered. She sagged in his arms. "Lucy, it's me," whispered the boy. "You're safe now. We can go home." But she didn't respond.

"Her mind iss far away," said Heide, climbing down. "It may be a good thing. She wass not made to endure such as Frith."

One of Ivar's warriors offered to carry the little girl, and Jack walked at his side, holding her hand. King Ivar was loaded onto the cart—he was much too heavy to carry. A pair of Northmen pulled it along. The king seemed bewildered by what had happened, even when it was explained to him several times.

"My little troll-flower should be here," he complained as

the cart creaked along. "She doesn't like being out so late. She needs her beauty sleep, does Frith."

"There iss someone else whose mind iss traveling," said Heide.

Skakki and Rune shouted for joy when they returned, and as the news of Frith's disappearance spread, Jack heard cheering from the crowd gathered outside Ivar's hall. He was too wrung out to feel much joy. He was glad when they left the hall and turned toward Olaf's home.

Dotti and Lotti took Lucy from the warrior's arms and immediately set about cleaning her up. Her dress was so filthy that they had to burn it, and her hair was in such a wretched state that they had to cut it off. She looked even more woeful then, like a little drowned mouse.

"Will she ever come back?" Jack said as Heide wrapped her in a blanket and placed her near the fire.

"She may iff you call her," the wise woman replied. "I could try, but my voice would not reach as far. It iss you she wants to hear." Heide placed a tray of food and drink by them. Then she and the others left them alone.

Jack watched his sister's face in the flickering light. He talked to her for what seemed like hours. Now and then he felt her face to be certain it was still warm. She was so still, he sometimes feared she had died. "We're going home," he said again and again. "Mother and Father are waiting for us. They'll be so happy! Do you remember the footstool Father carved? You used to sit on it by the fire, and Mother heated cider for your breakfast." He brought out memory after memory, trying to reach the place where Lucy had hidden herself, but nothing worked.

Jack got up and walked around the hall. His body was stiff, and in spite of the fire, he was cold. Bold Heart stirred in the rafters, where he'd been sleeping, so it must have been nearly dawn. Jack stumbled over a litter of toys Olaf's children had left behind and saw four little wooden figures in a heap: a cow, a horse, a man, a woman. They were the toys Olaf had made for Lucy so long ago. Jack gathered them up and knelt by the little girl. He folded Lucy's fingers around the horse and put the other three in her arms. "Do you remember playing with these on the beach, dearest? You made a fence out of sticks and you drew a house in the sand. You used shells for chickens because Olaf hadn't made you any."

Bold Heart swooped down and landed on the floor. He watched the toys intently. "Yes, you stole them, didn't you?" Jack said to the crow. "I could never figure out whether you were really playing a game. It seemed too clever for a bird." The crow darted forward and plucked the horse from Lucy's hand. "Stop that!" Jack yelled. Bold Heart dropped the horse and chuckled, deep in his throat.

"How could you take something from a helpless child?" Jack cried. He put the horse back in Lucy's hand. Bold Heart made off with the cow.

"Come back, you thief!" shrieked Lucy. She sat up in her blanket and clutched the other three toys. Jack could only stare. His heart was too full to speak. Bold Heart hopped back and insolently dropped the cow out of Lucy's reach. She lunged forward and grabbed it. The crow bobbed up and down, warbling and chuckling.

"Oh, Lucy," said Jack.

"He thinks he can get away with it, but I'm watching," the little girl said.

"Do you know who I am?"

"Of course!" Lucy said scornfully. "You're Jack and that's Bold Heart. He came to us from the Islands of the Blessed. When *are* we going home? I'm getting tired of this adventure."

"Soon," Jack said, his throat threatening to close. He drew Lucy's attention to the tray of food. She immediately grabbed a bowl of cold stew and began eating, scooping it out with her fingers. Jack tore bread into bits for her and cut up an apple. Lucy ate and ate and ate. She finished with a cup of buttermilk.

"I was so hungry!" she cried. "Oh, my! My stomach hurts, but it feels so good!" Then she keeled over and went back to sleep. Jack looked up in alarm at Heide, who had just entered.

"She iss only sleeping it off," the wise woman assured him. She wrapped the little girl in the blanket again and placed her in a corner behind the loom. "No one will step on her here," she said as Dotti, Lotti, and a dozen children streamed in to get warm by the fire.

The year was growing old, and Jack and Lucy had to be returned to their village before the winter storms set in. Skakki checked over his father's ship. It would be his first voyage as captain, but as he was only sixteen, he enlisted the help of such experienced sailors as Rune, Sven the Vengeful, and Eric Pretty-Face. For the most part, he asked ordinary warriors to join his expedition, not berserkers. This was a trading voyage, not a raid.

Jack didn't have to return to Ivar's hall, for which he was grateful. Skakki said it was being scrubbed from top to bottom, though it would take many months to remove all trace of Frith's presence. She'd had a habit of stashing bones in little crevices to gnaw on later. It accounted for the rank smell in the hall.

Skakki proudly brought home Cloud Mane. King Ivar said he rightfully belonged to Olaf's heir, and the horse certainly liked the boy. He trotted up to him willingly and nuzzled his hand. "His sire came from Elfland," said Heide after she studied the animal's fine lines. "Elf-horses are small, swift, and loyal, and they do not throw their masters."

"Have you seen elves?" Jack asked.

Heide only smiled and did not answer.

King Ivar also returned the wealth-hoard Olaf had gifted him with, and Skakki gave some of it to Jack. "It's little enough for what we owe you," he said. "Ridding us of Frith has brought life back into this kingdom." Jack accepted the silver coins gravely. There was no telling where they had come from. Silver flowed back and forth like water in the lands of the Northmen.

They sailed on a sunny morning with a breeze behind them and a cheering crowd on the docks. Jack watched Heide,

Dotti, and Lotti grow smaller and smaller until they faded into the shimmer over the water. The warriors plied the oars with Thorgil at the rudder, and Bold Heart sat on the prow cawing his defiance at the seagulls. The smelly sea serpent's head had been removed to Eric Pretty-Face's house.

We're really going home, thought Jack, and he worried that they would meet storms and be blown away. But the weather was perfect. They didn't follow the same route—the Northmen weren't as good sailors as they led everyone to believe. They simply aimed themselves in the right direction and went on until they bumped into land. Most of the time it worked.

So Jack didn't see again the coastlines of Magnus the Mauler's and Einar the Ear-Hoarder's lands, nor the ashes of Gizur Thumb-Crusher's village. He and Thorgil played Wolves and Sheep, and they tried to teach Lucy, but she was too young. She kept trying to change the rules to save the sheep. When she was told this was impossible, she flew into a snit and knocked all the pieces into the bilge.

At night Jack sang to the little girl and told her tales he'd learned from Rune and some he made up about the Jotuns. Gradually, very gradually, Jack drew out the story of what had happened to her while he'd been gone.

It was a terrible tale of hiding behind curtains and under benches, of stealing morsels of food from Freya's cats. When the cats caught her, they dragged her in front of Frith. The queen screamed and pulled her hair. But because Lucy never responded, Frith lost interest and left her alone.

Lucy crept around in the background for weeks. She watched Frith and Ivar sink into madness while the filth in the hall piled up. At night the little girl slept in a heap of flea-infested straw, and during the day she amused herself by pulling strings from the tapestries on the walls. When the cats were asleep, she tied these around their tails. If you did it right, the cats went wild, trying to claw them off.

Finally, Frith caught her at it and ordered her penned in Freya's cart. There things became slightly better. At least the priest of Freya fed her regularly. But long days went by without anything happening at all, and so Lucy slipped away.

"Where did you go?" Jack asked, holding her in the darkness.

"To the *real* queen. She was good to me because she loved me. She gave me a beautiful room. There was a tree covered with honey cakes, and a little dog, too. It had a green collar with silver bells. I could hear it running through the castle." On and on Lucy went, spinning out the tale Father had told her over and over ever since she was born.

Jack didn't try to argue with her. In Heide's land the winters were long and dark. People's spirits wandered so that they did not go mad, but when spring came, their spirits returned. As had Lucy's.

—⟨⟩—

Chapter Forty-two

JACK AND JILL

"I can't *believe* I never noticed all these colors," Thorgil enthused, watching the waves slide by. "Those clouds! They're like fresh milk. And the wind smells so good!"

"Didn't she say that yesterday?" Skakki muttered. He was taking his duties as captain very seriously, checking the sail, inspecting the oars, and turning the sun stone back and forth to study how it worked.

Sven the Vengeful watched the horizon for signs of land. "Yes, she did," he said, squinting at the line between earth and sky.

"And she'll say it tomorrow," Rune added. "Get used to it."

"Look at the brightness over the water," said Jack, holding his sister up. "That's where the Islands of the Blessed lie."

"Where Bold Heart came from," Lucy said.

"What? You're right!" cried Sven. "That brightness does mean land." The warriors shipped the oars and made for it. Presently, Jack saw a barren, windswept shore loom up out of the gray-green water, but the gentle light moved on beyond it as though something else lay shining beyond the margin of the sea.

"There's your Islands of the Blessed," said Sven, laughing and pointing at the crude turf houses among the rocks.

"He's wrong," whispered Lucy.

"Yes, he is," Jack whispered back.

Wild-eyed cattle stood in the surf and munched seaweed. The inhabitants of the village came out with axes and hoes, but when they recognized Sven, they laid them down. Skakki had brought trade goods—furs, sea ivory, and amber—but he didn't waste much time on this forsaken island. It was simply a place to get freshwater and stretch your legs.

But to Jack it was the farthest reach of his native soil. He was Here and not There. He treasured every pebble and stunted blade of grass. As they sailed on, his excitement grew until he was almost as giddy as Thorgil. Both of them exclaimed over each new island until Skakki begged them to stop.

Now the land was continuous, broken only by streams and inlets. The air smelled of heather, and a few crows came out to inspect the ship. Bold Heart talked to them for a long time. "He's not saying anything important," Thorgil said. "Just 'How are you?' and 'Nice weather we're having.'"

"He's taking a very long time for something that simple,"

Jack said, as he had before. "Aren't you leaving something out?"

"You'll never know," Thorgil said happily.

They came to the wide bay and the town where Jack had almost been traded to Picts. He looked with dislike at the fine wharf and prosperous houses. These were people who dealt in slaves. They asked no questions about how the Northmen obtained their captives. They merely bought them as you might buy apples.

Here, too, Skakki spent little time. He and Sven went into town to see merchants while the rest of the warriors made camp. They would sail at dawn. "Why aren't we waiting for market day?" Jack asked Rune as they sat around a fire roasting gobbets of meat on sticks.

"The goods we carry can be traded privately and quickly," the old warrior said. "We have no time to waste. I can feel the storms brewing in my bones."

"We'll make up for it next time," one of the men volunteered.

Jack stared at him. "What does that mean? 'Next time'?"

"Oh, um . . ." The Northman seemed to have trouble thinking of an answer.

"It means they'll come raiding," Rune said.

Jack was flabbergasted. The thought had simply not crossed his mind. "*No!*" he cried.

"They're warriors," Rune said.

"They don't have to be! They can farm."

"We have barely enough decent land to feed ourselves in

a good year. Most of our years are bad. We live by trade and plunder."

"You're worse than trolls!" Jack shouted. There was a murmur of anger among the assembled Northmen, but Jack didn't care. He'd been lulled into thinking of these people as friends. They were still foul, evil destroyers!

"Listen well, young skald," said Rune, and he looked dangerous in spite of his age and many scars. "When you visited Jotunheim, you were protected by the Mountain Queen. You may have a rosy picture of Jotuns, but let me assure you that they're capable of slaughtering whole villages down to the youngest child. They're enemies, though they have honor."

"Yes, well, you don't have to imitate them," said Jack.

"Need drives us. Nothing you or I say is going to change that. Skakki has taken an oath not to harm your village, but no such oath stands between him and others of your kind."

Jack couldn't believe his ears. Kind, likeable Rune, who'd saved him from Olaf's wrath and given him his best poem, had turned into a monster. Jack felt betrayed.

"For a long time you felt safe on your little island," Rune went on. "The ocean protected you. Your lives were as warm and friendly as a summer afternoon. But your land was too beautiful, and so, like all bright things, it attracted destruction."

"Like Hrothgar's hall," Jack murmured.

"Frothi destroyed Hrothgar's joy, and her sister Frith

brought desolation to you. Now that such attention has been drawn here, it will not turn away. Tales of the Holy Isle's wealth have echoed throughout our lands," said Rune. "Even now Magnus the Mauler and Einar the Ear-Hoarder are building ships and planning war."

"It's so unfair," whispered Jack. He looked across the beach to where evening shadows were gathering. In the blue dark between the houses he thought he saw a Pict.

"Life and death are in constant battle. There's no way in this world for happiness to exist alone," said the old warrior.

"But what are we to do?"

"Wake up," Rune said simply.

When night came, Jack stayed on the ship with Lucy. He didn't want her to meet any Picts, and he didn't want to talk to the Northmen. Skakki and Sven returned, clanking with many new weapons. They'd had a successful day. Late into the night Jack heard them singing and playing their silly games. Thorgil got into a belching contest with Eric Pretty-Face and won.

They sailed past the lonely towers of the Picts. There was never anyone around them, and Jack never saw friendly trails of smoke to show anyone was warming himself or cooking a meal. The few villages appeared deserted as well. Bold Heart went off with a flock of crows.

"He's leaving us!" Lucy cried in alarm.

It wouldn't surprise me, Jack thought. *Everyone here is evil and faithless.* But Bold Heart returned at evening. After that he took many trips to the mainland, to Thorgil's annoyance.

"He has such interesting things to say," she complained. "Not like the other birds."

"Too bad," Jack said, turning his back on her.

"Those are really nice trees on the shore," she said. "What are they called?"

Jack ignored her. He thought about calling up fire and burning the ship when they camped at night. That would fix the Northmen, but it wouldn't do anything about Magnus the Mauler or Einar the Ear-Hoarder.

The ship sped south, far from shore to avoid attention. This was the coast Olaf had raided, and Skakki wanted to avoid complications. And at last they came to Jack's land. They drew up on a deserted beach in late afternoon. The Northmen brought down several geese and roasted them over a fire.

"It's our last night together," said Rune. "Let us spend it with good stories and good food."

"Ooh! I love stories," cried Lucy.

"We have two skalds here, so we should have no end of tales. I'll go first." Rune told them of Loki, whom Odin had met in Jotunheim.

"I thought he was a god," Jack said, intrigued in spite of his determination to snub the old warrior.

"He was a shape-shifter like Frith. His father was a troll and his mother a goddess. If you think a Jotun/human cross is bad, you should see what happens when you mix gods and trolls. Loki *appeared* to be handsome and clever, and Odin was besotted with him."

"BIG MISTAKE," said Eric Pretty-Face.

"Odin named Loki brother. They cut their wrists and mingled blood to seal it. God blood flowed into Loki's veins and shape-shifter blood into Odin's. It didn't do either of them any good. Ever after, Loki had the run of Asgard. No one dared throw him out. Odin gave him the goddess Sigunn for his wife."

"A great waste," said Skakki.

"Sigunn was gentle and sweet, so of course Loki was bored with her. He went straight back to Jotunheim and married an ogress. She was nasty enough to entertain him. They had foul, monstrous children—a giant serpent, a giant wolf, and Hel, whose icy hall waits for cowards and oath-breakers."

Jack was trying to remain uninterested in Rune's story. He wanted to hate the Northmen, but they kept being nice to him. If they noticed Jack's silence, they didn't show it. They were probably used to people who got angry and sulked.

"Fenris, the giant wolf, was so fierce, the gods imprisoned him on an island covered by iron trees. But Fenris grew. Soon he was beyond the power of the gods to control, and Odin decided he would have to be chained. The problem was, of course, how to get the chain around his neck.

"They made a game of it. 'Here, wolfie, wolfie, wolfie,' called Thor. 'Wouldn't you like to play with this string? A big, strong beast like you could snap it in an instant.' Fenris was flattered. He let the gods put the heavy chain around his neck, and then he snapped it in two."

"It was the biggest one they had," added Skakki.

"So they had to ask the dwarves for help," Thorgil burst in for the first time. She looked truly beautiful in the firelight, Jack thought. Her eyes shone, and her hair—vigorously washed that evening—framed her face like a dandelion puff. She had always been beautiful, the boy realized, but her blighted spirit had hidden it. Now she was happy. Jack felt an ache over his heart. She would be leaving in the morning. He'd never see her again, not even in Heaven.

"The gods knew they had to have a magic cord made of the secret things of the world—the roots of a mountain, the footfall of a cat, the breath of a fish," said Rune. "Only the dwarves had the knowledge to make such things. When they were finished, they presented Odin with a cord that looked like a silk ribbon, but it was stronger than death.

"'Here, wolfie, wolfie, wolfie,' called Thor, trying to lure Fenris. 'This one's going to be even more fun.' But the wolf was no fool. He knew what the gods were up to, though he had complete confidence in his strength.

"'I'll wear that thing if someone puts his hand in my mouth,' he growled. Odin's son Tyr, bravest of the brave, stepped forth and put his hand between the wolf's slavering jaws. The others bound Fenris with the ribbon." Rune paused, and the Northmen turned to Jack.

Here we go again, thought Jack. Whenever the Northmen paused in a story, it meant something horrible was about to happen. They loved making Jack ask for the ending because he was so satisfyingly disgusted. Sven the

Vengeful was practically bouncing up and down with excitement.

"Oh, very well." Jack sighed. "What happened?"

"Fenris struggled and howled and fought, but he could not break that fetter, and so he was trapped on the island," said Rune.

"But first he bit off Tyr's hand!" Sven cried.

"*I* was supposed to finish the story," Rune said.

"And he chewed it up and swallowed it!" Sven was too carried away to stop.

"Crunch! Mangle! Chew!" yelled Thorgil.

I'll never understand Northmen, Jack thought.

"What did it taste like?" asked Lucy, not at all bothered by the tale's gory ending, and a lively discussion of what Tyr's hand tasted like followed. Then Jack told them the story of the Jotuns' escape from Utgard and how the whales carried them the last few miles when the ice disappeared.

In between tales, they feasted on roast goose and drank the cider Skakki had saved for this occasion. The stars moved toward morning, and Lucy went to sleep. Finally, when the first trace of dawn showed over the sea, Thorgil said, "I have written a poem."

"Girls can't write poetry," said Sven, but no one paid attention to him.

"Let's hear it. Your eulogy for Olaf was fine indeed," said Rune. "I'd say the song-mead was not wasted on you."

"It's about Mimir's Well," she replied, and Jack was surprised. They'd agreed not to discuss it. She stood and bowed.

Jack and Jill went up the hill
To fetch a pail of water.
Jack fell down and broke his crown,
And Jill came tumbling after.

Thorgil waited.

"That's it?" Skakki said, puzzled.

"My mother named me Jill," Thorgil explained. "And Jack and I climbed a hill, and we fell down."

"DOESN'T SEEM LIKE MUCH OF A STORY," Eric Pretty-Face said.

"Well, it really happened, and a poem doesn't *have* to tell a story," Thorgil cried.

"Yes, it does," said Sven.

"It's nice. Really it is," said Rune as Thorgil looked ready to lose control. "It's not the kind of thing that lasts, but it's sweet."

"It is not sweet!" shrieked Thorgil. *"And it's going to last! People will be saying my poem long after your moldy old verses disappear!"* She ran off down the beach and hid herself behind some rocks.

The Northmen, as usual, paid no attention to her flight. They began to pack up. Jack followed her. The light was growing swiftly, and the boat would soon leave. He found her behind a rock, sobbing as though her heart would break.

"Jill," he said softly, kneeling by her.

"Have you come to make fun of me?" she said.

"Oh, no! I thought it was a wonderful poem, and I think it will endure."

"Its fame will never die?" She looked up at him through her tears.

"That's right. Sven doesn't know anything about verse, and Eric Pretty-Face hears only half of what's said. Rune, well, he's set in his ways."

"You think it's good?"

"I'm a skald trained by Dragon Tongue," Jack said sternly. "Of course I think it's good."

"Oh, thank you!" Thorgil flung her arms around him. They held each other for a long moment in the pearly light. The birds of the forest had awakened and were greeting the new day. Thorgil sat back and unclasped the necklace of silver leaves she'd retrieved from Frith. "I want to give this to Lucy."

"Are you sure?" Jack said. "I thought you really liked it."

"I'm allowed to be as generous as anyone else," she snapped. "Are you calling me a miser?"

"No, no," Jack said.

"Well then. I *do* like it. That's why it's a great sacrifice to give it up. Besides, I have Thor's hammer and—this." She closed her hand over the invisible rune.

Jack looked longingly at her hand. "Someday you'll have to pass that on."

"Someday *everything* has to be passed on. But I will do it gladly and without regret," the shield maiden said proudly.

They returned to the others. Lucy was sitting up, half dazed, with Bold Heart on her lap. The ship was already in the water, and all the Northmen were aboard except for Rune. "Here," he said, handing Jack the glass bottle with the poppy on the side.

Jack held it up. At the bottom were a few drops of liquid. "Song-mead!" he cried.

"When I went to store the bottle, I saw that it wasn't quite empty," said Rune. "I don't know how much good so little can do, but I think you'll find it useful."

"Thank you," the boy said. Now that the actual moment of parting had come, his anger at the old warrior had vanished.

"Thank *you*. You saved us from Frith and gave me back my voice. You're a brave lad. If you were a little more vicious, you'd make a fine warrior."

"I don't think so," said Jack.

Then it really was time to go. Thorgil and Rune climbed into the ship, and Skakki gave orders for them to row. "Goodbye, Jack. Good-bye, Lucy. Bold Heart, you can come with me if you like," called Thorgil. But the crow ruffled his feathers and stayed put.

The long, beautifully made craft slipped through the water with scarcely a splash and made its way to the open sea. It disappeared into the mist as though it had never been.

"Come on, Lucy," Jack said, lifting his little sister to her feet. "We have a long walk ahead, and Mother and Father are waiting."

Chapter Forty-three

WELCOME HOME

Mist drifted through the trees and water dripped off the leaves. Jack followed a path he knew led to the Roman road. He had his blackened staff from Jotunheim in one hand and Bold Heart on his shoulder. With his other hand, he led Lucy.

"Can't I lie down?" she complained. "I'm sooo tired."

"We'll rest when we get to the road. And *you* should stop getting a free ride," Jack told Bold Heart. The crow only gripped harder.

The boy trudged on. Sorrow fought with joy in his mind. He was going home, but he had lost Thorgil and Rune forever. For the past months all he'd thought about was returning here. Now he felt let down. There'd be no more sailing, no more adventures. But he missed his family dreadfully. If only they didn't live in a tiny village where the most exciting thing was a ewe having twins. How could he go back to hauling water, stacking firewood, and chasing black-faced sheep?

"I want to sit down *now*," said Lucy.

Jack could see the Roman road looming through the bracken. He led her to its moss-covered stones, and they both rested for a while. Jack shooed Bold Heart away. The crow landed nearby with loud caws of complaint. "If you don't like it, go back to Thorgil," the boy said. He rubbed his shoulder where the bird's claws had dug in.

He took out food the Northmen had given him: roast goose and dry bread they had traded for farther north. Lucy nibbled the bread, and Bold Heart pecked at a shred of meat. Water dripped all around. They were getting soaked.

"How much farther is it?" said the little girl.

"An hour's walk. Maybe more."

"I'm tired," she said.

To divert her, Jack took out the necklace of silver leaves. "Thorgil wanted you to have this."

"Ooh!" Lucy grabbed the necklace and put it around her neck. "It's from the queen," she said, running her fingers over the bright metal.

"It's from Thorgil," he corrected.

"No! I saw the queen wearing it. She took me away to her palace. She gave me honey cakes and flummery."

"That's not true," Jack said, losing patience. "You were sleeping on filthy straw and starving."

"I was not! The queen sent me this necklace!"

Jack yanked it from Lucy's neck. "You can have this back

when you're grateful to the person who really gave it to you."

"You *kindaskitur!*"

"Call me 'sheep droppings' all you want, but—" Bold Heart cawed and flew into a tree. Jack was instantly alert. "Hide in the bracken, dear," he whispered. Lucy, without a word, tumbled off the edge of the Roman road and scurried under a bush. She had certainly learned about avoiding danger.

Jack stood in the middle of the road. He heard footsteps and a tuneless whistling. He saw a figure emerge from the mist. At the same time the figure saw him.

"Don't hurt me!" the boy yelled, turning and fleeing back down the road.

"Colin!" cried Jack, but the blacksmith's son pounded away as fast as he could go. Jack looked down at himself. He was wearing the clothes the Mountain Queen had given him. Beneath his marten-fur coat he wore a fine green tunic and brown pants stuffed into his cowskin boots. He had a leather scabbard on his belt, and the knife from that scabbard was in his hand.

"Oh, my," said Jack. "I look like a Northman. Come on, Lucy. We'd better get home before someone shoots me with an arrow."

She climbed up and took his hand. "If I'm with you, they won't shoot," she said, which was so brave and perceptive, Jack leaned over and kissed her on the top of her head. They walked on. Bold Heart immediately fastened himself to Jack's shoulder.

After awhile they heard many voices in the distance. The mist was thinning and sunlight broke through, turning the autumn forest red and gold.

"There he is! Wait! Don't shoot yet! There's a girl with him!" said several voices.

Yet? thought Jack. They came out to a clearing. Several men crouched with the kind of weapons you found around farms. John the Fletcher had an arrow nocked to his bow.

"Father!" shrieked Lucy, running forward.

"Lucy?" said Father, dropping his scythe. *"Jack?"* He swept the little girl into his arms. John the Fletcher lowered his bow.

"It's a berserker!" yelled Colin. "He came at me with an axe!"

"Don't be silly," said the chief of the village. "That's Giles Crookleg's lad, but he's so big."

Jack stood forth with his ash wood staff. Bold Heart sat on his shoulder. He knew he couldn't have grown much in the time he'd been gone, but he must look entirely different. He certainly felt different from the boy who'd been dragged away by Northmen.

"He saved me from a horrible monster. And he fought trolls and dragons!" Lucy told Father.

Father looked completely bewildered. "You're alive," he said. "My son, you're alive." Giles Crookleg began to cry, and Jack began to cry too, which spoiled some of the grand effect he was trying to make.

"I know what's different," the chief declared. "See that crow? Ow!" he said as Bold Heart snapped at him. "That's what bards carry on their shoulders. Jack went off an apprentice and has come back a full-fledged bard—about time, too. The old one hasn't been making any sense."

Everyone congratulated Jack then, and Father hugged him. They set off for the village with John the Fletcher running ahead to spread the good news. In a low voice Jack told Colin, "If I *had* been a berserker, your head would have rolled on the ground before you'd gone three steps," and he was gratified to see the boy turn pale.

An eager crowd waited outside Giles Crookleg's farm. They cheered when they saw Jack and Lucy. The little girl danced before them, basking in the attention. Her dress was a wonder never seen in the village. Heide had made it after the style of her people. It was bright blue, with green embroidery at the neck and hem and white flowers scattered over the rest. Lucy looked like a real princess.

Everyone laughed and clapped. The little girl didn't even notice Mother standing far back, at the door of the house. But Jack went to her immediately, fending off the hearty congratulations of well-wishers. Father had begun to recount the brief story Jack had given him of their captivity. "He saw trolls and dragons and giant spiders!" Father cried.

"Go on, Giles, that's just one of your fantasies," someone yelled.

Jack and Mother slipped to the back of the house. "I should fetch Lucy," the boy said.

"Let her have her moment," Mother said softly. "What happened to her hair?"

"It's a long story. You won't believe what happened."

"I might. We suspected you'd been taken by berserkers. Father thought you were dead, but I never believed it. I looked into the water and saw you standing in a swarm of bees."

Jack shivered. Mother was a wise woman, though she was careful to hide it. He wasn't sure what "looking into the water" meant, but he'd seen Heide staring into a bowl, and everyone else tiptoed around when she did it. "How's the Bard?" he asked.

She sighed. "He eats and sleeps, but his behavior is that of an infant. He screams at odd times, and he keeps waving his arms."

"Is he at the Roman house?"

"He can't take care of himself," Mother said sadly, "and he's so difficult that Father had to build him a shed near the back fence. People take turns caring for him. I don't know what we'll do when winter comes."

They went down a path to the fields. Giles Crookleg's farm was in magnificent shape. Stands of wheat were heavy with grain. Black beans and broad beans, turnips and radishes, parsnips and carrots grew in orderly rows. It had been a wonderful year, aside from getting raided by blood-thirsty berserkers from across the sea.

"You look very bardlike with that staff and that crow on your shoulder," Mother said. "Is he tame?"

"Sometimes he snaps at people," Jack said. But Mother fearlessly stroked the bird's feathers, and Bold Heart warbled deep in his throat.

"You'd almost think he was talking."

"Actually, he is. A girl I knew could understand what he said."

"My! You *have* had adventures. I can't wait to hear about them." Jack heard screams in the distance. His hand went automatically to his knife. "It's only the Bard," said Mother. "Sometimes he keeps it up for hours. We don't know what he wants, and he can't tell us."

Jack approached the shed with a feeling of dread. Those cries! They were scarcely human. "Is he violent?"

"No, only very frightened. Everything we do frightens him."

The door was secured with an iron bolt. Jack pulled it back. The inside of the shed smelled bad. The Bard scuttled to the far wall. His hair was wild and his fingernails as long as claws. His clothes—a rough tunic belted with a rope—were smeared with excrement.

"We try to keep him clean, but he gets so agitated when we attempt to bathe him that we're afraid he'll die of fright," Mother said.

"Sir, it's me, Jack. I've returned. Your enemy Frith is gone. You don't have to be afraid." But the old man only cowered in the deep straw that covered the floor. "I've brought you something that might heal you," said Jack. "It's song-mead from Mimir's Well. There's only a few drops, so you can't waste them."

"Wud-*duh*. Gaaw," said the Bard. He raised his clawlike fingers to defend himself.

How am I ever going to get anything into his mouth? thought Jack. He took a step forward, and Bold Heart suddenly swooped from his shoulder and flew straight at the old man.

"Wud-*duh!*" shrieked the Bard.

Caw, caw, caw! screamed Bold Heart. The two collided and fell to the floor as though struck by lightning.

"No!" cried Jack. He rushed to the old man and lifted him up. The Bard's eyes were staring, and he wasn't breathing! "Mother! What should I do?"

She knelt on the other side and felt the old man's pulse. "His heart has stopped!"

"No, no, no," moaned Jack. He'd been so close.

"Pour that song-mead or whatever it is down his throat!" said Mother. She pulled open the Bard's jaws, and Jack upended the bottle. A spoonful of bright liquid fell into the old man's mouth. Jack shook the bottle, and one more drop formed.

"That's all there is," he whispered.

Suddenly, as though he were waking from a deep sleep, the Bard quivered and opened his eyes. "Jack, my lad," he said in a hoarse voice.

"You're back! You're back!" Behind him Jack heard a fluttering. Bold Heart was struggling to rise. "Frith's power is broken, sir. You're safe."

"I know," said the Bard. "My stars, I'm a mess! Hasn't anyone given me a bath?"

"We tried," said Mother, laughing and crying at the same time.

Bold Heart staggered through the straw. His wings hung

down as though he'd forgotten how to use them. "What's wrong?" Jack said, alarmed. He reached for the bird, and it slashed at him viciously.

Bold Heart shrieked, backing against the wall.

"Has he gone mad?" Jack said.

"No, he's only a poor, frightened bird," said the Bard, rising with Mother's help. "These past few months have not been kind to him."

"But—but he was my *friend*."

"*I* was your friend, Jack," the Bard said. "Don't you remember the story of Beowulf? How I threw myself into the body of a pike? When Frith hunted me down, the only way I could escape was into the body of a crow. I traded places with him. It was touch and go getting back, though. If you hadn't roused me with that song-mead, both of us would have died."

"*You* fought the troll-bear? *You* talked the dragon out of eating me? *You* brought back Lucy's spirit?"

"I have some skills, even in the body of a bird," the Bard said with understandable pride. "Brains, you know. But don't discount your own contributions. You've shown remarkable ability. Remarkable."

Jack glowed under the praise.

"All this time I've been trying to reason with a bird," said Mother.

"You can't reason with a bird. It isn't bright enough," said the Bard. The old man stretched his fingers and toes as though getting used to them again.

"Bold Heart," murmured Jack. In spite of what the Bard

said, he missed the cheeky crow. Surely something of its character had remained when the man had taken over its body.

"He'll have to learn to fly again," said the Bard. "I'll keep him with me until it's safe for him to be on his own."

"And I'll heat water for a bath," said Mother.

"Another thing you can't do with birds," the Bard said, wrinkling his nose, "is house-train them."

They were sitting under the rowan tree in the little valley. Bold Heart was in a cage some distance away. The Bard had opened the door, but the crow was too frightened to go out.

"He can fly and he's healthy enough," said the old man. "He just lacks confidence."

Nearby a bubbling spring fed a small pool. Some of Mother's bees still explored the smooth gray branches of the tree, though the time of rowan flowers was gone. Perhaps they liked to be where the life force was strong.

"How did you find me, sir?" said Jack. "After I was taken."

"I asked crows on the way. They're great gossips. Know everything that's going on. They didn't know you personally, of course, but something like a Northman ship heading up the coast caught their attention. The storm forced me to take shelter, and I didn't reach your boat until it turned eastward for the last long stretch of the journey."

"Yet you followed me over the sea." Jack was deeply moved.

"It was foolish. If you hadn't called me down, I would have drowned."

The wind at the top of the valley had been cool, but something about this place held on to the warmth of summer. Dandelions and clover still dotted the grass, and frogs peeped in the marsh grass around the pond.

"Why didn't you come back here?" said Jack.

"Too dangerous. Frith could find me as long as I was in this body. And she would have made sure that everyone in the village was killed. Besides, I rather liked being a crow. Sometimes I liked it too much."

"What do you mean, sir?"

"There's a danger in taking another form. Sometimes you forget who you are."

"Like when we first got to Olaf's house?" Jack guessed.

"I was so glad to get to the end of that beastly voyage—what with storms and fog and the burning of Gizur's village—I took a vacation. Went off with a flock and clean forgot I was human." The Bard shivered at the memory. "When I realized what I'd done, I was careful never to leave you again."

A crow soared overhead, circled, and came down to the cage. "Look," whispered Jack. The crow warbled deep in its throat, going on and on as though trying to reason with someone. Bold Heart stuck his beak out the door. *Warble, coo, warble,* said the strange bird. Then it flew off. Bold Heart tumbled out of the cage and took off after it, cawing wildly. He disappeared over the rim of the valley, still calling.

"You see all sorts of things other people miss when you serve the life force," said the Bard.

"Even when you tell them, they don't believe you." Jack had described his adventures to the villagers, and they'd listened politely. But when he was finished, they said, *Tell us what really happened. We're used to Giles Crookleg's lies.* No amount of protesting shifted them.

"Don't be angry," the Bard said. "Most people live inside a cage of their own expectations. It makes them feel safe. The world's a frightening place full of glory and wonder and, as we've both discovered, danger. Flying isn't for everyone."

Jack had worked up the courage to ask the one question he thought might upset the old man. "Sir . . . was I right to give Thorgil the rune of protection? She's still a shield maiden and she's still our enemy."

The Bard smiled gently, gazing at the empty cage. "No kindness is ever wasted, nor can we ever tell how much good may come of it. The rune was meant to go to Thorgil. The life force demanded it, and she, like it or not, has been enlisted in its service. I'm sure she'll be peeved when she finds out."

"Why didn't you tell her who you were?"

"Oh, I did. The tiresome child refused to believe me. The Mountain Queen saw through my disguise at once. Very little is hidden from her."

"I'd love to hear the story of how you melted a hole through her wall," said Jack.

"Not today," the Bard said firmly. "I've hardly got my

voice back after all the screaming my body did while I was gone. Let's just sit here and watch the last of summer."

And so they did. The bees hummed over the remaining flowers, the spring bubbled, and the rowan tree rustled in a warm breeze. The magic was deep and harder to reach here than it had been in Jotunheim, but it was more humane. There was no other place on earth, Jack decided, that he'd rather be.

Appendix

—⫘⟊⫘—

THE HOLY ISLE

The destruction of the Holy Island of Lindisfarne on June 8, 793, shocked the Anglo-Saxons in the same way 9/11 shocked Americans. It was a completely unexpected blow from a completely unexpected direction. The Saxons believed the sea protected them. They also believed that no one would attack a peaceful, trusting group of monks. They were wrong.

The abbey of Lindisfarne was founded in A.D. 635, and by 793 it was a center of great learning and art. When the raiders arrived, the monks ran to greet them and to invite them to dinner. The description of what happened next is in *The Sea of Trolls* and is taken from *The Anglo-Saxon Chronicle*. Amazingly, one beautifully illuminated manuscript survived the fire: the Lindisfarne Bible.

This attack was the beginning of two hundred years of Viking raids on the British Isles.

NORTHMEN

Viking is a term that means "pirate" or "raider." Vikings could come from Denmark, Norway, or Sweden, and I have chosen to use the word *Northmen* for them in the book. They would have spoken Old Danish or Old Norse. Jack would have spoken Anglo-Saxon.

Languages change over time. Anglo-Saxon morphed into Old English and then into the English we speak today. Old Norse changed into Icelandic, which is what the Northmen in the book use. Kristin Johannsdottir, an Icelander teaching in Canada, very kindly provided the correct translations.

ICELANDIC PRONUNCIATION

The accent, in Icelandic words, is usually on the first syllable, as in *music* or *wonderful*. Most letters are pronounced as they would be in English, with a few differences:

r is trilled, as in Spanish.
þ is like *th* in *think*.
ð is like *th* in *that*.
æ is like *i* in *English*.
J is like *y* in *yes*.
t, d, l, and n are pronounced with the tongue on the

back of your front teeth, not at the top of your mouth. The differences between *o* and *ó* and *a* and *á* are too difficult to explain here. Use *o* as in *sofa* and *a* as in *father*.

TROLLS, JOTUNS, AND FROST GIANTS

In the legends of northern Europe these three names seem to refer to the same creatures. They were large, they loved ice and snow, and they were the enemies of mankind as well as the gods. Most of the time they are described as ugly, but there are stories of some who were very beautiful.

According to the sagas, the Jotuns occupied the north-land of Europe first. The worshippers of Odin fought them for centuries to get control of Norway and Sweden. An eleventh-century manuscript describes the Jotuns as wild people who attacked from the mountains in sledges. They wore animal skins, and their language sounded like the growling of animals.

Even more interesting, the sagas say humans were not allowed to settle in Norway until they intermarried with Jotuns. There are frequent references to historical figures who were part troll. So it's possible that trolls really existed. There are (or were) many unusual tribes living in the far north from Norway to Siberia. It's even possible that Jotuns are a distant memory of the Neanderthals.

Their original home was said to have been Utgard, which was in the Utter North. I have placed it on Jan Mayen Island, a lonely volcano not far from the North Pole.

IVAR THE BONELESS

Ivar was a half-legendary king. He probably lived around 880, though I've placed him earlier. I invented his wife Frith. Ivar's father was called Ragnar Hairy-Britches, and he was a thoroughly nasty swine. He was eventually thrown into a pit of poisonous snakes by a Saxon king, a good trick since there are almost no poisonous snakes in England.

BERSERKERS

Most of the Viking warriors were ordinary men. A few were berserkers, who were sent in first to demoralize the enemy. Berserkers weren't afraid to die. Their aim was to kill as many people as possible before they fell in battle and went to Valhalla. Some berserkers may have taken a drug to go mad, but for others it just ran in the family. You could call them an early form of terrorists. Thorgil is patterned after a shield maiden in *The Saga of King Heidrek the Wise*.

BARDS AND SKALDS

At the time the novel takes place, the worship of Odin, the old Celtic nature worship, and Christianity existed side by side. The traditional Celtic priests (or druids) had been replaced by wise women and bards. They were said to have the same magic powers.

Skalds were the Viking form of bards. They weren't as well known for magic, but they had a lot of power. In a time before written records, only they could ensure a man's fame with their poetry and songs. The Vikings also had wise women.

JACK AND JILL

The nursery rhyme comes from a Norse legend of two children who were sent by their father to collect song-mead from Mimir's Well. On their way back, with a full bucket of mead, they were carried off by the moon god.

Sources

Dasent, George Webbe, *Popular Tales from the Norse and North German* (London: Norrœna Society, 1907).

D'Aulaire, Ingri, and Edgar Darin, *Norse Gods and Giants* (Garden City, NY: Doubleday & Co., 1967).

Davidson, H. R. Ellis, *Gods and Myths of Northern Europe* (Middlesex, England: Penguin Books, 1964).

———.*The Viking Road to Byzantium* (London: George Allen & Unwin, 1976).

Fee, Christopher R., *Gods, Heroes, and Kings: The Battle for Mythic Britain* (New York: Oxford University Press, 2001).

Foote, Peter G., and David M. Wilson, *The Viking Achievement* (New York: Praeger Publishers, 1970).

Glob, P. V., *The Bog People* (New York: Ballantine Books, 1965).

Griffith, Paddy, *The Viking Art of War* (London: Greenhill Books, 1995).

Hartley, Dorothy, *Lost Country Life: How the English Country Folk Lived* (New York: Pantheon Books, 1979).

Jesch, Judith, *Women in the Viking Age* (Woodbridge, UK: Boydell & Brewer, 1991).

Kennedy, Charles W., trans., *An Anthology of Old English Poetry* (New York: Oxford University Press, 1960).

Kurlansky, Mark, *Salt: A World History* (New York: Walker & Co., 2002).

MacKenzie, Donald A., *Teutonic Myth and Legend* (London: Gresham Publishing, 1890).

Markale, Jean, *The Druids: Celtic Priests of Nature,* trans. Jon Graham (Rochester, VT: Inner Traditions, 1999).

Matthews, John, *The Druid Source Book* (London: Blandford Press, 1996).

Motz, Lotte, *The Beauty and the Hag* (Vienna: Fassbendaender, 1993).

Page, R. I., *Chronicles of the Vikings* (London: British Museum Press, 1995).

Poertner, Rudolf, *The Vikings: Rise and Fall of the Norse Sea Kings,* trans. Sophie Wilkins (New York: St. Martin's Press, 1975).

Ross, Margaret Clunies, *Prolonged Echoes: Old Norse Myths in Medieval Northern Society* (Odense, Denmark: Odense University Press, 1994).

Serraillier, Ian, trans., *Beowulf the Warrior* (New York: Scholastic Book Services, 1968).

Simpson, Jacqueline, *Everyday Life in the Viking Age* (New York: G. P. Putnam's Sons, 1967).

Squire, Charles, *Celtic Myth and Legend* (London: Gresham Publishing, 1890).

Sturluson, Snorri, *Heimskringla: History of the Kings of Norway,* trans. Lee M. Hollander (Austin: University of Texas Press, 1991).

Taylor, Paul B., and W. H. Auden, trans., *The Elder Edda* (New York: Random House, 1970).

Thorpe, Benjamin, *Northern Mythology,* vol. 2, *Scandinavian Popular Traditions and Superstitions* (London: Edward Lumley, 1851).

Tolkein, Christopher, trans., *The Saga of King Heidrek the Wise* (London: Thomas Nelson & Sons, 1960).

Trevelyan, G. M., *History of England,* vol. 1, (Garden City, NY: Doubleday Anchor Books, 1953).